Praise for the Enchanting Novels of

BETINA KRAHN

"Betina Krahn writes with flare. Her plots and characters
are humorous, witty and original. Talented and gifted,
Betina Krahn is a joy to read." —*Literary Times*

"One of our most creative writers . . . Krahn's ingenious
romances always entertain and leave readers with a
warm glow." —*Romantic Times*

"Krahn is the kind of writer that makes you smile at the
end of her novels and wish her next book were already in
your hands." —*Contra Costa Times*

"Krahn uses a light touch to address serious social issues
(i.e., the vulnerability of women in Victorian society),
combining wit and whimsy with a high degree of sensuality
in gracefully written, well-plotted, and unpredictable
stories." —*Library Journal*

"Genuinely funny Elizabethan sexual puns, a strong,
believable heroine, and an absorbing story of forbidden
love make *The Husband Test* an enjoyable read."
—*Booklist*

"Following Krahn's delightful *The Husband Test*, this
laughter-laced historical perfectly packages witty dialogue
and engaging characters into a captivating romance."
—*Booklist* on *The Wife Test*

Bantam Books by Betina Krahn

THE UNLIKELY ANGEL
THE PERFECT MISTRESS
THE LAST BACHELOR
THE MERMAID
THE SOFT TOUCH
SWEET TALKING MAN
THE HUSBAND TEST
NOT QUITE MARRIED

NOT QUITE, MARRIED

Previously published as *Rapture's Ransom*

BETINA KRAHN

BANTAM BOOKS

NOT QUITE MARRIED
A Bantam Book / July 2004

Published by
Bantam Dell
A Division of Random House, Inc.
New York, New York

ISBN 0-553-57518-X

Manufactured in the United States of America
Published simultaneously in Canada

OPM 10 9 8 7 6 5 4 3 2 1

For the southern gentleman
who brought love back into my life

NOT QUITE, MARRIED

One

The South of England, 1787

E'S AT IT AGAIN, my lady." The groom jerked his head toward the stable as he steadied Brien Weston's stirrup and helped her dismount.

Shouts and wails burst from the stable door as she rushed toward it. Inside, down the brick-paved alley, she found a shirtless boy cringing against a mound of straw in an empty stall, begging for mercy from Seaton, the estate's raw-fisted stablemaster.

She froze for a moment at the sight of a dozen bloody streaks across the boy's naked chest and arms. Another blow fell, and the child cried out as the jagged shards of metal on the broken bridle bit into his flesh. Suddenly the bloody stripes on the boy's pale skin were all she could see.

"Stop!"

There was a hitch in the stablemaster's movement. After a glance at her from the corner of his eye, he brushed aside the command and drew back for another stroke. She lunged for his arm and managed to stay it.

"Cease this! *Now!*" Anger poured strength into her limbs and made a biting rasp of her voice. "Or as God is my witness, Mr. Seaton, I'll see you receive ten blows for every one you deal this boy."

"Outta th' way, lady. Th' wretch needs a taste of th' lash to teach 'im to 'eel to 'is master."

Seaton tried to shake her off, but she threw the force of her weight against his arm and succeeded in immobilizing it. Their glares met as they stood locked in a shockingly physical contest of wills. It apparently took a moment for him to realize that to continue dispensing this punishment, he would have to remove his wealthy employer's daughter from his arm by force. Was he angry enough or brazen enough to set hands to a lady? He lowered his arm and wrenched it free with a growl, then jolted back a step.

"Your cruelty may know no limits, Mr. Seaton, but my sufferance of it does." She rubbed her hands down her skirts as if contact with him had contaminated them. "Your abuse of this boy has been your last act on Weston land. Pack your belongings, draw your wages, and be gone by sunset. Never set foot on Weston land again."

"I'll just wait an' see what 'is lordship 'as to say about that." His mouth twisted into a defiant sneer.

"No, you won't." Deep inside, a fierce calm settled through her, solidifying her resolve. "My father will not return for some time. And if you are found on these lands after sunset, any who find you will have free rein to mete out whatever punishment they see fit." She edged closer, eyes narrowing, her fury focusing, driving home her point. "Your manner has so endeared you to the people who live and work on these lands that you will do well to see the dawn."

A searing moment passed as the stablemaster searched the lady's resolve, sounding the depths of her determination. Abruptly he hurled the blood-flecked bridle against the stall, shoved past the grooms who stood gaping in the alley, and stormed out the doors. The sound of his furious oaths and the pounding of his boots on the packed earth of the stable yard wafted back through the stunned silence.

Brien slowly expelled the breath she had been holding and felt the surge of strength that had flooded her beginning to drain from her limbs. A moan from the nearby stall brought her attention back to the injured boy. She knelt in the straw and gathered his thin form against her, cradling his head, rocking him as she inspected his wounds and made soothing, shushing sounds. The small, thin shoulders quaked with sobs against her. Moments later she looked up and ordered the grooms who now stood at the opening of the stall to carry him into the house.

"His stripes are bloody, but with proper tending will heal well. Tell cook to salve and bind them up and then to put him in one of the empty maids' rooms while he mends. I'll come shortly to check on him." She gave the boy's hair one last stroke and his dark eyes filled with tears of both misery and gratitude as they lifted him from her.

"Thank 'e, my lady," he whispered, watching her as the grooms carried him out.

She sat for a time in the red-stained straw, alone, trembling. Then she closed her eyes against the blood on her hands and clothes, and let the tears come.

SEVERAL DAYS LATER, just at dusk, the earl of Southwold reined up in front of his country house and Brien arrived at an upstairs window overlooking the entry court just in time to see him hand his mount over to a waiting groom. He had barely settled into a chair by the blazing hearth of his study when she saw the housekeeper, Mrs. Herriot, knock on the open door, pause to await permission, then enter and close the door behind her.

At dinner that night, Brien's suspicions were confirmed.

Down the long, linen-draped table, between the well-polished silver candlesticks, she could read annoyance in every aspect of her father's posture and expression. Each scrape of silver, each clink of crystal against china caused her to start in expectation. She knew Mrs. Herriot had delivered the news about Seaton that afternoon, and she could tell from the way her father scrutinized her that he was deciding what to do about it.

"Brien." His tone was a command for attention. "Mrs. Herriot says you fired Seaton. I will have an accounting for that, my girl."

Her head snapped up. "I-I was returning from a morning ride when I came across Seaton beating a stableboy with a broken bridle. I ordered him to stop, and when he refused, I fired him."

"It is not your place to fire stablemasters," he said sharply, picking up his wine and rising. "Decent horse masters are hard to come by. Your meddling will cost me dearly."

Meddling? She reddened. As wealthy as he was, there was nothing her father hated more than being "cost." But she reckoned "cost" quite differently. Her heart thudded faster as the sickening image of the boy's wounds flooded back to her. Five days later, the child was only now able to move about without a great deal of pain.

"How can you call the man decent?" She shoved up from her chair so quickly that she had to steady herself against the table edge. "He took a cat's equivalent to a boy of nine. And he was no better with horses. He used cruel bits and whipped some of the carriage horses until they trusted no one."

Weston was clearly taken aback by her response. "Seaton's flaws are not at issue here. You had no right to take such act—"

"No right?" She stepped around the end of the table and moved quickly toward him, halting after only a few steps. "I had every right. I am lady here in your frequent absence, and it has been my lot numerous times to guard the well-being of Byron Place's people. Seaton was a brute. Cruel and callous. Frederick, at just sixteen, knows more about horses than he did."

"Enough!" Weston slammed his goblet down on the table, spilling ruby liquid over the pristine linen and upsetting a nearby water glass. "The man was placed in authority and would have been held accountable. *By me.* It was not your place to meddle in the affairs given in to his charge."

"The boy is *my* charge." She moved toward him, her chin up and her hands clenched at her sides. "He was entrusted into my care from the orphanage at St. Anne's. He needs a place to live and grow, not an overseer with a lash." She edged closer, her expression nothing short of defiant. "Will you declare me wrong and call Seaton back? Will you hand him the bloodied strap to finish the beating?"

After a long, acrid moment Weston stalked to where she stood and glared down into her upturned face. "You will never"—his voice came low and fierce—"*ever* presume upon my authority again. You will keep to your place and never again interfere with the running of this estate. Is that clear?"

It gave the earl little satisfaction to realize his daughter was trembling. Nothing else about her indicated the slightest fear or failure of will. He jerked his waistcoat down and stalked off to prop an arm on the room's great marble mantel, frustration visible in his every movement. Clearly the chastisement meant to subdue and humble her had missed its mark.

After a moment, he turned to stare at his daughter, searching her erect posture and regal bearing. That was what bothered him most, he realized: this display of unwomanly pride and assumption. Why wouldn't she weep and yield to his authority, or appeal to his fatherly mercy like any other young woman would have done?

"If you cannot learn to be a real woman," he muttered,

jerking his gaze from her, "at least learn to bow to the God-given authority of men like a real woman does." Staring into the glowing coals on the hearth before him, he missed the way she steadied herself against the table and the color drained from her face. When he heard the soft click of the latch, he looked up just in time to see the door close behind her.

His taunt rumbled about in his own head. She deserved it, he told himself. She had overstepped her bounds and had to be taught a lesson. But even as he thought it, he sensed that it was he who had somehow stepped out of place . . . trespassed on ground he had long since abandoned.

He grabbed a decanter of claret off the dining table and made straight for the comfort and quiet of his study. Dropping into a chair before the fire, he drank with determination and brooded over his confrontation with his headstrong daughter.

He was loath to admit it, but she had been right about Seaton. He had seen evidence of the man's cruelty himself, but had brushed it off with one excuse or another. He was too busy to be bothered with such stuff. His conscience prickled. If he were too busy, why did it bother him so, that she had set the matter to rights?

Because she was his daughter, not his son. It wasn't right for a woman to mix in such things. As he thought of her standing there, meeting his anger, brazenly—*confidently*—defending her actions, uneasiness gripped him. He had not known exactly what to expect from her, but an apology or a spate of tears would have been more to his liking. Instead, she defended her action and glared at him as if *he* were to blame.

She had changed. He reexamined his impressions, noting each nuance of her appearance. She seemed more womanly than he remembered, more . . . ripened. Her hair was still that unusual combination of honey colors, but a bit more dramatic. Her features were finely sculptured and her mouth was full and her lips well-defined. Her dove-gray eyes seemed larger . . . striking, as they flashed at him. Despite her rounded form, she had a presence about her that spoke of strength and pride of bearing. He didn't remember her exhibiting such decisiveness, such composure.

Not that he had looked too closely of late.

He had spent most of his time at his London house since the death of his elder daughter, when not traveling and tending the far-flung interests of his trading company. How many years had he lived this way? Shuffling between cities, dining and sleeping alone, marking time by mergers and acquisitions? Ever since Denise was thrown from a horse. Four years? Five? Too soon after his beloved wife Alice's passing. The loss of both wife and daughter, coming barely a year apart, had overwhelmed him. In a fog of grief, he had moved Brien to his late wife's dower house, Byron Place, and then fled to London to immerse himself in his business interests.

He picked up an andiron and poked at the embers in the hearth before him. He had left her alone for too long; that much was clear. She'd grown independent and uncommonly self-possessed for a girl of—eighteen? Twenty? Twenty-two? Just how old was she?

That uncertainty skewered his last untouched bit of conscience. He didn't even know his daughter's age! A flood of guilt rose to overwhelm him.

What did he really know about her or her life here at Byron? Did she have friends? Did she go out? He was fairly certain she hadn't been to London in the last four or five years; she would have had to stay in their London town house and he had been there himself, alone, much of the time.

He ran his hands down his face with a groan, but forced himself to continue this painful inventory. Clearly, she was of marriageable age. When had she last been to a dance, a party, or even to a neighboring hall for a holiday dinner? She didn't have a chaperone other than the housekeeper,

Mrs. Herriot. His eyes widened. Good God—the realization struck him dead center—she had never even been introduced into society!

Lawrence Weston, wealthy and powerful earl of Southwold, propped his graying head in his hands.

What had he done?

Two

IN THE SIX WEEKS since the sacking of the stablemaster, the incident had almost been forgotten. The earl had stayed at Byron Place only long enough to see another stablemaster hired and then had left for Paris, citing urgent business. Now he returned in the dead of night, alone and riding hard, and summoned her to his study first thing the next morning.

Brien dressed carefully, choosing her best blue silk with a voile bodice insert gathered to a cameo, and pristine white cuffs. Her maid took pains with her hair and produced a simple but dignified chignon. She knew her father felt she was headstrong and unwomanly, and was determined to give him no grounds for criticism.

Pausing just outside the huge double doors to take a deep breath, she smoothed the folds of her skirt, squared her shoulders, and entered. The earl sat behind his ornate teak desk, seeming immersed in a document in his hand. He looked up as the click of the door latch and the rustle of her skirts announced her presence.

"You sent for me?"

"I have a matter of some importance to discuss with you." He waved her into a chair facing his desk.

"What matter is that, Father?" She sank onto the edge of the seat. He had made it painfully clear on his last visit that he wanted no interference or even help from her. What could be so important now, that he would actually consult her?

"I've recently returned from Paris and have decided—" He halted, tossed the document onto the desktop and rose, deciding to start again. "We will have visitors a fortnight from now. Two members of the Trechaud family of Paris—" He halted again, clasped his hands behind his back, and paced away.

Guests? The thought surprised her. His French associates were paying him a visit? Did he expect her to entertain them? She glanced around at the worn comfort of the study and thought of the age and wear apparent all through the house. Surely he didn't intend to bring them here. Then she realized that he was wrestling with something more and a knot of anxiety formed in the pit of her stomach. Anything that caused the earl of Southwold such consternation must be a difficult problem indeed.

"You will be twenty-two years old in three weeks, Brien," he began in an emphatic tone, looking up from his boots. "It has recently come to my attention that I have been remiss in planning for your future." He straightened, assuming his most lordly manner, and she braced instinctively. "While in Paris I called upon the marquis de Saunier, a man respected in French financial circles. He and I agreed that a marriage between our children would be most desirable."

"Marriage?" Her chest contracted around her lungs, reducing the word to a whisper.

"Seeing you wedded and settled into such a prosperous family will set my mind at ease." But there was little ease or pleasure in the smile he produced. "Your husband-to-be, Raoul Trechaud, will join us in a fortnight. The nuptials will take place a month after that. I have already made arrangements." His announcement delivered, he returned to his desk and sat down as if relieved of a burden.

She was to be wedded? To a Frenchman? In little more than a month?

"But, I didn't think I would be required to . . . you never said anything about . . ." The full impact of his edict finally broke through the shock that had immobilized her. She pushed to her feet, reeling. Was this her punishment, long delayed, for sacking Seaton? For presuming upon her father's precious authority? "You have promised me in marriage to a man I have never seen? Without the slightest regard for my wishes?"

"With full regard for your *interests*. A far more important consideration." He swept her with an appraising gaze, which caught momentarily on her waistline. "There are few families about with sons who might make a suitable match."

A suitable match. She saw the direction of his gaze and sensed his underlying thought. Despite her wealth, a plump, bookish female who had no knowledge of society would scarcely be considered a matrimonial prize. Her outrage was abruptly undercut by a hot surge of shame.

"You've waited this long to demand— You might have at least given me a chance to meet some gentlemen and—"

"You were unlikely to find candidates in local society," the earl said flatly, once again a baron of commerce, ordering and dispatching. "I have saved you the trouble of a season in London and secured a far better match than you might have managed there." He watched color flooding her face and his tone grew firmer. "You have been too long with your books and charities. Too much learning impedes a young woman's sense of balance and propriety. It's time you took your place in society and set about giving me some grandchildren."

"But what if the man . . . what if he is not . . ."

"Agreeable?" he offered.

"Acceptable!" She found the word she searched for. "What if the man is not *acceptable?*" she repeated angrily.

"Brien—" Something caused him to rein what would have surely been a furious outburst. "I would never force my only daughter to wed a man she found distasteful. I have seen him. He will be acceptable in every way."

Was that his opinion of the man or a command that she agree no matter what her true feelings? She bit her lip to hold back words that would only worsen her situation. A pitched battle here would only confirm his conviction that she had been allowed to run her own life too long already. In a wave of insight, she saw that his charge against her was all too true; she *had* run her life without interference for too long to bend easily to society's expectations or to her father's dictates.

Taking her silence for surrender, he nodded and his voice softened. "I've engaged a dressmaker—the best in London—who will arrive this afternoon. We have much to do and just over a month to prepare. The wedding invitations have already been sent."

Invitations? Already sent? A London engraver had been given more notice of her wedding than she had? Choked with outrage, she headed for the door.

"Brien." His voice halted her, but she refused to turn back. "This was sudden, I know. In time you will see that it is best."

As the door closed behind her, she gathered up her skirts and ran through the great hall and up the stairs. Standing in the middle of her bedchamber, trembling, scalding tears searing paths down her cheeks, she felt betrayed by her own good sense as much as her father's manipulation. She should have known there would be retribution for Seaton, should have prepared herself for it. But how could she have imagined that it would take so drastic a form? And what could she possibly have done to prevent it?

Seizing the bolsters from the bed, she flung them with all her might across the room, smashing a vase on her dressing table and sending a lacquered box crashing to the floor. The noise brought a young woman in servant gray rushing to the doorway.

"What's happened, my lady?" the maid whispered, hurrying to her side.

"He means to marry me off. 'It's time you took your place in society,' he said. What does he know of my place? He's barely spoken to me for five years!

"I've seen to the tenants, the planting and harvests, and the accounts. I've sat with Byron Place's people as they birthed and died and mourned and prayed . . . purchased them plows and looms and tools . . . found them work when necessary . . . provided medicines and shoes and schooling for their children. This is my home as it has never been his. This is my place. These are my people."

In the silence that followed, Brien sank into the cushions of the window seat and then wilted against the window frame, wiping at a stream of tears. She stared through the window, unblinking, unseeing at first. But gradually her vision began to focus. The gardens below were alive with color and vibrant with the warmth of the new summer. And yet, from this distance, it was clear that every shoot and blossom was constrained in a symmetry ordained by unnatural standards . . . staked and culled and pruned to please the human eye. Until that moment, she had never thought of gardens as the victims of human desire.

"Everything so neatly arranged. Everything in its place. And me in m-mine." Her voice broke.

With a familiarity beyond her servant status, the maid sank onto the edge of the window seat and put her arm around her lady's shoulders.

"Oh, Ella, I'm just a commodity—daughter—to be dispatched to its proper place," Brien whispered. As the energy of her anger dissipated, the sobs she had held at bay slipped through the cracks in her self-control. "I shall go from obeying my father to obeying a husband, never having known the world as myself."

Ella pulled a dry handkerchief from her apron and shoved it into her mistress's hands. After a few moments, the maid drew back a bit and studied her mistress.

"Well, ye didn't think ye'd get t' sit 'ere molderin' away forever, did ye? Th' surprise is, 'e ain't thought of marryin' ye off before now." The maid's dark eyes flashed and she ducked her head to engage Brien's gaze, producing a tart little smile. "An' as for seein' th' world . . . it's a bit overrated, if ye ask me. I grew up in Cheapside and ever bloke in my family run off t' sea an' adventure as soon as 'e got breeched. I seen folk comin' off ships from all over th' world, an' they didn't look no 'appier than folk 'ere on Byron Place. Yer not missin' much, my lady, I promise ye." When Brien sat back with a deep, shuddering breath, Ella gave her a smile that very near coaxed one from Brien.

"And 'usbands can prove useful, you know. Moreso than fathers." Her eyes twinkled with mischief. "They 'ave t' 'elp ye in and out of carriages . . . keep ye company at dinner . . . deal wi' disgustin' old squires that poach yer woods . . . fire stablemasters what need sackin' . . . buy ye jewels an' pretty dresses. Oh, yeah." She grinned. " 'Usbands 'ave their uses. So, what's this one yer gettin' like?"

"I have no earthly idea."

"Well, then . . . there's room t' 'ope. Maybe 'e'll be a prize bedwarmer."

"Ella."

"If you got no choice, then ye might as well look for th' good in what befalls ye. Who knows? 'E may turn out t' be a regular prince!"

IF SHE WERE a commodity, Brien realized later that afternoon as she witnessed the arrival of the dressmaker, she was at least being dispatched in style. The renowned French *couturier* arrived as promised with a huge retinue of drapers, cutters, and seamstresses, and an entire shop's worth of woven goods and ladies' accessories.

The slight, dapper Monsieur Lamont had a rapier-sharp wit and a tongue like a lash, but from the moment Brien presented herself before him with puffy eyes, a red nose, and a declaration that he was probably undertaking the greatest dressmaking challenge of his life, he seemed to like her.

Then, late on that first day, when he caught one of his beleaguered assistants sneaking a bit of food and was about to launch into a scalding rebuke, Brien interceded.

"Monsieur, does not Holy Scripture prohibit muzzling the ox as it treads the grain?"

Lamont hooted an irreverent laugh and declared he would create for her his very finest . . . which, it soon became clear, was very fine indeed. The next morning, he began to rework and modify the designs she had chosen, to enhance what he called her "assets."

"My 'assets'?" she muttered. "That shouldn't take long."

Embarrassment flooded her cheeks as he stared at her, then seized her by the wrist and dragged her before the large pier glass in the chamber set aside for the fittings.

"First," he declared, untying her corset and wrenching it tighter, "you must be willing to suffer for your beauty. See how this enhances the waist and bosom?"

She groaned. "And how it restricts breathing."

"There will be time for breathing when you are old and withered." He yanked her petticoat from her and she squealed.

"Really, Monsieur . . ."

"Ahhh." He seemed pleasantly surprised. "Such lovely

limbs. And trim ankles. We must see that you have lots of dainty slippers to show them off."

"Show off my ankles?" She was scandalized.

"Such an innocent." The monsieur patted her forgivingly on the head. "You must take care when you go out in the world, eh? There are wolves out there." His eyes twinkled. "And they adore fine ankles."

She almost said that her ankles were the only part of her that was in any way "fine," but she sensed in his genteel exasperation a true compliment and absorbed it.

Relentlessly, he analyzed her form . . . approving the color of her hair, the clarity of her eyes, and the smoothness of her skin. Slowly she began to see herself through his exacting but not unsympathetic eyes. Nicely tapered limbs. Strikingly light eyes. Her deficits, she realized, were actually problems of overabundance. Too much hip and waist . . . a bosom that was too bountiful to restrain neatly in the usual straight corset . . .

By the end of the second day, Brien was filled with conflicting feelings of insecurity and stubborn self-worth, and overwhelmed by the continual scrutiny and the endless choices required of her.

It was all happening so fast. There were so many changes around her and—she forced herself to admit—within her. She was surprised by how much pleasure the prospect of new garments gave her. But it was unnerving, having every aspect of her form and movement analyzed and discussed at length . . . in her presence.

She might as well resign herself to such scrutiny, she told herself, thinking of the social ordeal yet to come. A schedule of engagements and entertainments had already been planned. She would be paraded and inspected and assessed and compared. . . . And part of the assessing and comparing would be done by her husband-to-be. Her heart skipped a beat. What if he found her homely and rustic in manner and appallingly unsophisticated?

She refused to be daunted by the thought. After all, as the little monsieur said, she had assets. She peered at herself in the glass over her dressing table. She had no idea what her future husband's standards might be for a desirable wife, but she always strove to be honest and dutiful . . . was charitable to a fault . . . had a nimble wit . . . and was educated beyond the norm.

Her heart sank.

If Ella were to be believed, men cared little for such qualities in a woman. They wanted demure smiles, not wit; reverent attention, not conversation; and physical charms, not inner beauty. She sighed and sat down on the bench before her dressing table, staring at the big eyes searching her from the looking glass.

Ella's summary of men depressed her. Surely, somewhere, there were men of intellect and wisdom and honesty—men that would appreciate a capable, educated wife.

But what if there were? A stab of realism pierced her. Her future contained only *one* man. Raoul Trechaud. How likely was it that he would be the "prince" that Ella had hoped for?

Three

*E*NCHANTÉ, MADEMOISELLE."

Brien was speechless as Raoul Trechaud brushed her hand with his lips.

He was taller than she by several inches, with black hair gathered into a pale ribbon at the nape of his neck. His broad shoulders flexed as he presented a knee and bowed, emphasizing the narrow taper of his waist above long, slender legs. His gaze engaged hers boldly as he continued to hold her hand.

"*Monsieur,*" she managed, dismayed that her fluent French had deserted her completely. "I hope your journey was not too taxing." Her voice sounded oddly honeyed in her own ears. She stood straighter in her pale blue silk gown, feeling utterly exposed by her low neckline and up-swept coiffure of ringlets, and longing for a second chance at the looking glass she had shunned minutes before.

"In your presence the discomforts of the journey are forgotten." His deep, lightly accented voice had a strange, lulling quality.

Brien had tried not to think about her future husband until word came that he and his brother would not arrive until the very evening of the Hunt Ball. Feeling only a guilty sense of relief at the delay, she had promised herself that when the time came, she would welcome him cordially and try to make the best of the situation . . . no matter how many heads sprouted from his shoulders.

Now that Raoul Trechaud was standing before her, her pride reeled from this unexpected vindication of her father's judgment. By any standard he was a handsome man. She had to drag her gaze from him to avoid embarrassing herself. The sight of his features came with it: noble brow, slightly arched nose that complimented perfectly his square jaw and broad, elegantly curved lips. But it was his eyes that intrigued her . . . bold and dark, mesmerizing as he gazed at her with undisguised interest. She scarcely noticed his pallid, lean-featured brother, Louis, who was introduced next.

As they entered the coach, she felt her father's gaze on her and looked up to find him watching her intently, assessing her reaction to her intended husband. She flushed in spite of herself, knowing that as she did so she answered his unspoken question. She did indeed find the Frenchman acceptable.

THE HUNT BALL initiated the fall hunting season and signaled the beginning of the fall social season in the county. The neighboring Lord Pendrake, with six less-than-handsome daughters to marry off, thought it prudent to be generous with his hospitality and always hosted the event. Adding to the usual flurry of interest in this year's event was the emergence of the earl of Southwold from his self-imposed exile. Throughout the county there was eager speculation about the earl and his reclusive daughter.

Brien sat beside her father in the stuffy, overwarmed carriage, feeling Raoul's gaze on her and self-consciously refusing to meet it. What did he see when he looked at her? Did she meet his expectations? What was the man behind that handsome face like?

A thousand questions, banned from her consciousness in these last three weeks, now clamored for answers. Despite the lingering warmth of the late summer evening, she shivered under his oddly tactile gaze and fanned herself to mask her unsettlement. She caught a glimpse of his hand lying on his thigh and experienced a strange burst of warmth against the underside of her skin. What would it be like to take a turn around the dance floor with him? To feel that muscular hand at her waist?

Banishing those shocking thoughts, she flushed visibly and heard Raoul chuckle. She glanced up in spite of herself and had the fleeting thought that the smile he aimed at her somehow did not quite reach his eyes.

They were received just as she had suspected they would be, with polite face-to-face smiles and curious sidelong glances. Her father escorted her through the drawing room, salon, and upstairs ballroom, exchanging pleasantries and introducing both her and their guests to old acquaintances. It was clear from the pointed questions and comments that the doyennes of local society had already guessed his motives for reemerging into society. And they quickly turned their curiosity on her and Raoul.

After a time she managed to escape her neighbors' intense scrutiny by retiring to one of the upstairs bedchambers where servants awaited the lady guests. But the chamber was soon invaded by a drove of fashionably dressed girls and matrons who straightened coiffures, loosened lacings, and shed tight slippers for a few blessed moments of relief. The chatter rose to a din as the rooms filled with wails about lost ribbons or misplaced combs. She watched with fascination until two voices loudly whispering behind a nearby screen stole every bit of pleasure from the experience.

". . . two of them! Imported from France, no less. It must be costing her father a fortune."

"And that gown," a second girl responded. "The cost of the yardage alone must have been staggering!" Both girls tittered.

Brien felt something inside her go cold. She knew jealousy when she heard it, but her own awareness of her shortcomings prevented her from simply dismissing their spiteful words. She waited until everyone else had gone and she heard the music begin again downstairs before she emerged from behind the screen and headed for the door. On the way she caught a glimpse of herself in a pier glass and stopped.

Staring back at her was the image of an attractive young woman in a stunning silk gown that blued the pale gray of her eyes. Even to her critical gaze her lush moiré trimmed in silk brocade shot with strands of gold surpassed the gowns worn by every other woman at the ball, married or unmarried. Taking a deep breath, she set aside her embarrassment and determined not to let a few cruel words mar her evening.

Raoul spotted her the moment she reentered the ballroom. He watched his brother Louis claim her for a dance and watched her smile and slowly begin to relax and find the rhythm of the music and movement. He strolled around the room, drawing admiring glances and returning polite nods to those ladies bold enough to smile at him from behind their fans.

When the music ended, he appeared at Brien's elbow.

"Monsieur Trechaud, you startled me." Her cheeks were pink from the exertion of dancing and hid her blushing as she plied her fan.

Her first impression of him—handsome—now seemed a paltry description. The man was nothing short of devastating.

He knew how to use the color of his raiment to advantage
and had chosen a rich, blue-gray velvet coat and dark blue
breeches for the evening's festivities. There wasn't a woman
in the ballroom who wouldn't trade places with her at that
moment.

"The party is lovely." His accent poured over her like
cream. "The next dance is mine, yes?" He stood so close
that she inhaled the masculine warmth of him on her next
breath. Their eyes met and held for a moment. His intrigu-
ing brown-black eyes that she found difficult to read, she
also found impossible to refuse.

"Yes, I believe this one is yours."

When the music began, she absorbed the warmth of his
hand as it brushed her waist and marveled at the ease with
which he led her through the movements. From the corner
of her eye she could see the other ladies and unmarried girls
staring enviously and whispering behind their fans, and felt
a vengeful twinge of pride at having him for a partner. She
nearly stumbled in the midst of a promenade when she realized that he was intended to partner her not only in this
dance, but in life as well.

When he claimed the next dance also, sending the clear
message that his attentions were already claimed, the sound
of hearts breaking about the room was nearly audible.

The second set ended and they made their way downstairs toward the refreshments laid out in the dining room.
Brien pressed the back of her hand against her hot cheek
and said she was thirsty. When he brought her a cup of
punch, she drank deeply and felt grateful for the cool sweetness. But the wine in the punch soon conspired with the
heat of the room to make her dizzy. He noticed.

"Perhaps the air of the terrace would refresh you?" He
steered her through the overheated rooms to the terrace
doors. As they made their way into the cool September
evening, Brien was acutely aware of his hard, muscular arm
beneath her hand and of the faint masculine musk of him.

This delicious bit of anticipation was not at all what she had imagined when her father sentenced her to an arranged marriage.

In the darkness of the terrace she glimpsed several couples strolling, laughing flirtatiously, and whispering with their heads close together. A flattering light played off their faces and forms, courtesy of a silver moon drifting in and out of thin, scattered clouds. Her eyes, too, caught the light and Raoul noticed her relaxed mood and smiled.

"You are very quiet, *monsieur*," she said. "Do you miss Paris already?"

"Raoul, please." He gave her a smile. "I make my home wherever I am, Brien."

The sound of her given name on his lips caused a sudden tightness in her throat. She started to walk again, searching for a subject that might distract them both.

"This is the start of the hunting season. I've never been able to fathom just what pleasure grown men can find in chasing a small fox with heavy-footed stallions and snarling packs of dogs."

He had stopped a pace from her and when she looked up she found him watching her closely. "Some creatures were made for hunting, others to be hunted." His dark, probing eyes made her wonder briefly into which class he would put her.

When he reached for her shoulders, she brought her hands up instinctively. The hardness of his body against her palms was something of a shock. Then he slid his arms fully around her and whispered her name, drawing her eyes to his. It was an irresistible silk-and-steel sort of sound that penetrated her skin and flowed unhindered along every nerve and sinew of her body.

She felt helpless, mesmerized. His mouth came down softly on hers and then pressed harder, reshaping her lips to accommodate his desire. Her attempt to pull away only brought her closer to his chest until she rested fully against him. His tongue traced the outline of her lips, seeking passage inward and at last finding it. It was a startling sensation. Pleasure warred with surprise at the heat and wetness of his mouth on hers, and she remained tense against him.

His hands slid down her back and relaxed, allowing her to break away. She clasped her trembling hands and felt their quaking begin to spread through her. Her first kiss was not at all what she expected. It produced curious melting sensations in her lips and sent alarming spirals of warmth winding through her skin.

"Raoul," she breathed, "we should go back."

"Not yet, *ma chérie*." His voice was husky and in the moonlight she could see his lips were parted in what seemed to be a smile. "We must settle something between us." In spite of her resolve to see this through, she turned and fled up the steps of a nearby gazebo. He followed, pausing at the bottom of the steps.

Did he think her silly and unsophisticated? Her body hummed with expectation and the heat of his kiss still burned her lips. Well, she *was* unsophisticated. And ignorant of the sort of intimacies men expected of women they intended to wed.

"What is it we must settle? Have I done something to offend you? I assure you—"

"*Au contraire*, Brien. You are a lovely and charming young woman." His voice deepened. "You know the banns for our marriage are to be read tomorrow, yes?"

Her heart pounded as he mounted the steps and closed the distance between them. She found her back against a post and froze. He dragged his fingertips over her lips, across her cheek, through her tawny curls, and then down the smooth skin of her bare shoulders to her breasts. Then his eyes returned to hers, and he smiled while probing the fear and excitement that burned within her.

"I must know . . ." He put his hands on her waist and drew her toward him.

She felt splintered, unable to collect herself enough to respond properly. It was not in her power to resist; the lure of the unknown and the promise of pleasure were too strong. He crushed her to his chest and he deepened the kiss. One hand stole up her side and over her breast, toying with the bare skin above the provocative edge of her bodice. She stiffened and tried to push back in his arms, but stopped at his muffled laugh.

He raised his head to look at her and gave her a knowing smile. She sensed that he knew both the pleasure and the discomfort she was feeling. His hold on her loosened, but she could not bring herself to pull away.

"Our fathers have planned this marriage." He searched her face in the pale light, but his own was cloaked in shadow. "But I want to hear from your own lips that you will have me."

She had no idea what to say and in the silence he bent his head and claimed her lips again. His mouth left hers to trace the curve of her neck and shoulder. She whimpered as tongues of fire darted through her.

"Tell me, do you want me?"

She was reeling, awakened to a wealth of new sensations, filled with longing and confusion . . . incapable of rational thought. But in the end, reason was not required.

"I do."

He stroked the curve of her cheek and her skin glowed under his touch.

"Your father will be most pleased."

Only during the short walk back to the great house did she fully comprehend all that had transpired. He had kissed and caressed her and, in effect, asked her if she were willing to marry him. With everything already arranged, would he truly have cast it all aside if she had said no? Why hadn't she spoken up? Revealed her early opposition to the marriage, or at least her uncertainty about it?

She stole a glance at his profile as they walked and felt a

guilty trill of pleasure at the way her lips tingled with memory. That was why she hadn't spoken up: that handsome face, those penetrating eyes, the startling discovery of herself as a woman in relation to a man. She wanted to know what it was like to be a bride, a wife, a beloved. She had read too much poetry and too many stories of love and intrigue not to be enticed by the prospect of such things occurring in her own life.

When they reentered the ballroom and sought out her father, he eagerly halted the musicians to announce that his daughter soon would be wedded to Monsieur Trechaud of Paris. And she looked up to find Raoul smiling down at her with what she hoped was genuine pleasure.

Four

THERE WERE ONLY THREE HOURS until dawn when Brien parted from her father and Raoul and climbed the stairs to her rooms. Now that the ordeals of the ball and meeting Raoul were finished, exhaustion weighted her limbs but her mind was still whirring with shape, color, and sound. All she could think about was the storm of interest unleashed by the announcement at the ball of her impending marriage and of the man who stood with her in the center of it.

Raoul. After their tryst in the garden, he had been a perfect gentleman. Escorting her, smiling at her, and respectfully touching her hand as it rested on his arm. He was every inch the attentive groom-to-be.

Ella sprang up from a stool by the fire at the sound of Brien's entrance, and rubbed sleep from her eyes.

"I saw 'im from th' stairs—oooh, 'e's 'andsome as can be!" The little maid took her mistress's wrap and gloves, then pulled Brien to the wardrobe to begin untying her laces. "Got some mighty peculiar servants, though. They ate in th' servants' 'all wi' us. One's big as a 'ouse an' don't say a word. Dumb, they say." She gave a massive shiver. "Not a 'air on 'is 'ead an' eyes shinin' like black glass. Give me th' willies." Another shiver and she was back to her mistress's adventure. "What's 'e like . . . yer Frenchie? What was th' ball like? Was it grand an' thrillin'?"

"Well, Raoul is very handsome. Mannerly and attentive. Very . . . very . . ."

"Good enough t' eat?" Ella prompted with a grin.

"Ella!"

"Naughty an' excitin'? Quick with 'is 'ands in th' dark?"

"No! He's . . . he's . . ." As she struggled to put her impressions into words, she realized that there was something in Raoul's perfect manner that she found unsettling.

"Then, tell me what 'e *said*."

When she tried, Brien could scarcely recall a thing he had said . . . could only remember the low, compelling tones in which he spoke. "His voice is so deep that every word sounds velvety and soothing. When he speaks, you just lose all ability to think straight." The sense of her own thoughts came clear to her. "His voice is like . . . like a cradlesong . . . as if every word is lulling you to . . ."

Ella paused with a wicked laugh in the midst of removing her bodice. "T' open yer thighs, most likely. Not that 'e'd need much 'elp there, what wi' that 'andsome face of 'is. Did 'e kiss ye?"

Brien blushed from her breasts up and the little maid laughed.

"I knew it!" Ella crowed. "I knew when I saw 'im that 'e'd waste no time samplin' th' wares." She shoved her face near Brien's. "And ye loved it."

"I did not," Brien declared with emphatic hauteur. "I found it . . . *interesting.*"

"And?"

"And rather pleasant."

"Come on, my lady, ye loved it!" Ella chided, demanding the truth behind Brien's veiled eyes and furious blushing. "An' ye want more."

"His kisses were enjoyable," she admitted. "I wouldn't be adverse to another."

"I'll bet ye wouldn't." Ella beamed. "Yer *mon-sieur* must be some bloke. One night an' 'e's got ye looking forward t' th' weddin', instead o' dreadin' it."

Ella's words circled again and again in Brien's mind as she climbed into the crisp sheets and watched Ella snuff the candles and withdraw. After one night, a few short hours, he had her not only reconciled to the marriage but anticipating it?

As she lay in the darkness, staring through the dimness at the canopy spread above her, a barrage of impressions and sensations came rushing back: Raoul's handsome face, the feel of his lips moving on hers, and the shivers that went through her every time Raoul trained that penetrating gaze on her or poured his deep, lulling tones into her ear.

He was trying to win her, she realized. That was the reason for the attentive elegance of his manners and the silky persuasion of his voice. But it only made sense, from his perspective. A bit of courtship seemed prudent to get things off on the right foot, considering that they would be living together for the rest of their lives.

But she couldn't help feeling that he was a bit too eager to please, that his charm was a bit too polished . . . even calculated. . . .

Don't be ridiculous, her pragmatic inner self demanded. *Be flattered that he takes the time and trouble to seek your good favor.*

Don't be flattered, another insightful part of her declared, *be cautious. If something seems too good to be true, then it generally is.*

And therein lay the root of her discontent. She was charmed by everything he did, but it was all too clear that he intended everything he did to charm her.

She slipped from the bed, donned her dressing gown, and began to pace.

Everything she had seen of him was what he wanted her to see. What was his true nature? What were his true feelings about the marriage? About *her*? What sort of deal had her father struck with the marquis and his handsome son?

She had asked to see the betrothal documents and learn the terms of her marriage settlement, but her father had dismissed her curiosity as unwomanly and declared that the language of the legal documents was convoluted and would mean nothing to her. Then he had stared at her in a way that shamed and dismissed her once again for displaying unfeminine interests. Now, however, that curiosity had a foothold in reason and an urgency that would not be denied.

Snatching up a candlestick, she stirred the banked coals in the hearth and lighted the wick. The hall outside her door was dark and quiet. She slipped out and tiptoed down the corridor to the top of the great stairs, where she was stopped by a dim glow coming from the salon and the sight of a single candle burning on the center-hall table. It was customary for the butler to leave a candle burning for her father to use to see his way to his chambers after working late in his study. She bent over the railing and scowled, searching the rear of the center hall for light coming down the corridor from her father's study. It seemed dark and she looked back to the light coming from the salon. Perhaps he and Raoul were having a final drink before retiring . . . celebrating the success of the evening. If so, the study would be empty and she would have time to search her father's desk for the marriage documents.

Gathering her courage, she extinguished her candle, clasped her dressing gown a bit tighter around her, and tiptoed down the stairs. Her heart beat faster as she rounded the newel post at the bottom of the steps and hurried toward the rear of the entry hall and the corridor leading to the study. The door was pushed together but not fully closed. Just as she was reaching for the handle, she heard the sound of the terrace door opening and closing inside the study. A gust of wind pushed the door open half an inch and she was horrified to find herself standing in a small slice of light.

She darted to the side and flattened herself against the wall beside the open door. Light and voices—the study wasn't empty! She glanced down the corridor toward the darkened stairs, hoping she could get back to her rooms without being detected. But the sound of male voices kept her from moving . . . one higher but clearly male, the other deep and resonant, instantly familiar. Raoul. With his brother Louis? Surely not; the thin male voice sounded English as it wafted through the opening at the edge of the door.

"Raoul, you dog, I don't know how you do it. You're a cat—always landing on your feet. Give you a disaster and you turn it into a triumph. Great brandy, by the way."

Raoul's baritone was easily understandable. "I do my best." There was arrogance in his tone, unleashed by her father's potent brandy. "What do you think of the place?"

"It suits you."

"Don't be an ass, Cornelius. It's a heap. Refurbishing it would cost a fortune, and in the end all I would have is a refurbished heap. I intend to pull it down and begin again."

The other man gave a low whistle. "That'll cost a pretty penny."

Raoul laughed. "Have you not heard? I am now an extremely wealthy man."

His companion gave a grunt of amusement. "So, the terms were generous."

"The old man is desperate for a grandchild. By the time my dear father was through with him, he'd promised me everything but his wigs and gout-plasters."

"Well, he's chosen the right man for the job. Lord knows you've left offspring in your wake wherever you've gone. Still, I never thought to see the stud of Paris married and settled in the country with a pack of squalling brats."

"Producing offspring only requires that I be present for the planting . . . not the harvest." When Brien put her eye to the slit at the edge of the door, there was a vile grin on Raoul's face. "Speaking of 'harvests,' how fares *la belle Devereaux?*"

"Packed off to relations in Austria, I believe. Your son is now in the care of a gardener's family or some such. Can't say I blame you there—a fair piece of goods, that one. Even used, she'd make a prize bedwarmer." Their laughter grew louder and more humorless.

Shock immobilized Brien. He had already made a child with some young woman? With *several* young women? She clamped her hand over her mouth to contain her gasp.

"A bloody pot of jam, you've got here. Out of the stew and into a pot of jam." A clink of glass betrayed their toast. "Your father . . . how does he take it?"

"He is overjoyed that I have at last realized my responsibilities to the family." Raoul's tone was mocking. "For a paltry investment he rids himself of an infamously fertile son and gains a financial alliance. Southwold is far wealthier than *mon père* supposed, and so deliciously eager to have a grandchild. I have already paid my gaming debts at Madame Fontaine's. And as soon as the first child is born, he will put half of Weston Trading Company into my hands. With the birth of a second child, I will control the rest and he will retire to the country."

"Then you'd best plow your bride well. The sooner she's with child, the sooner you'll control the old man's fortune."

The stranger rose and shuffled across the room to replenish his drink. "And what of this bride of yours?"

Raoul's next words seared into Brien's mind.

"A plump partridge. Docile. I'll have her breeding by Michaelmas. She'll be no trouble."

" 'Plump,' you say? In fact?" The stranger belched. "Always favored them that way myself. Makes for a softer ride. Have bigger tits as well. Has she?" He laughed at Raoul's silent gesture, whatever it was. "If you find yourself detained on your wedding night, I'd be pleased to stand in for you. My"—another belch—"pleas-sure."

Raoul's answer came on an ugly laugh. "Give me time to get my hands on Southwold's fortune, and I may let you have her for a few nights."

"It's a deal." His friend laughed wickedly and there was a pause. "I must get to the inn whi-ilst I can still ride." There was a scraping sound and their voices faded as they moved toward the library doors that led onto the terrace.

"You will arrive a week before the wedding and stay here with me." She heard Raoul clearly. "*Mon Dieu*, it will be good to have your wit to relieve the boredom. Louis is driving me mad with his whining and hand-wringing." Then the terrace door closed.

Brien flattened back against the wall as Raoul doused the candles and the light dimmed in the library. Soon the glow of a single candelabra edged into the darkness of the hall and the door swung back, stopping just short of hitting her. She bit her lip and covered her mouth tighter, panic rising. But the light moved steadily on, ascending the stairs and turning along the balustrade toward the guest rooms.

It was several minutes before she could force herself to move. In the darkness of the hall, she searched for familiar objects to act as guideposts. Her only thought was of the safety of her own chambers. Each step seemed to take an eternity. When the latch of the door clicked softly behind her, she groped for the key and turned it before staggering to the hearth and crumpling into a heap on the rug before the wheezing embers of the fire.

The sun was filtering around the curtains the next morning before she could bring herself to move. She dragged herself to her bed and wrapped her arms around her middle, holding herself together.

No exercise of will or logic could dismiss the horror of what she had heard or its devastating effects on her. She had been sold. To a man who had no regard for her or for marriage. A profligate who had disgraced his family with infamous and immoral behavior. How could her father have struck a marriage bargain with such a man? Did he bother to check anything besides the marquis's balance sheets?

That afternoon a soft tapping came at her chamber door. By the time she roused, rubbed her swollen eyes and slid from the bed, the tapping had become an earnest pounding. When she reached the door and turned the key, Ella burst into the chamber.

"My lady! What's 'appened?" Ella searched Brien's tear-reddened face. "Whatever it was; it stilled yer tongue. Back into bed wi' ye." She tucked Brien back into the covers and wetted a cloth to comfort her swollen eyes. "Now, don't ye move."

Brien lay propped on the pillows with her arm over her eyes. Ella's arrival and bustling concern had given her a much-needed jolt back to reality. And the reality she faced was dire indeed. Her father had sold her to a greedy, conniving rakehell of a man in exchange for a grandchild to carry on the family name. He wanted an heir and she was merely the means, the vessel through which he would realize that abominable ambition.

Every muscle in her body went taut with resistance.

She would never submit to such a barbaric arrangement. Something had to be done, something to rid her of the preening Raoul. She thought of confronting her father with what she'd heard and demanding that he break the marriage agreement.

There would be financial consequences, of course The marquis would demand damages and her father would be furious. Once the conniving Frenchman was paid off and packed off, her father would likely turn his considerable anger on her. And there would be social consequences as well . . . the disgrace of a broken engagement, coming so quickly on the heels of the betrothal announcement. There could be no public explanation, so she would be a social pariah . . . stricken from guest lists and shunned by proper society for decades to come.

Good. She slid from the bed to stand defiantly on her own two feet. She had no desire to experience another night under the quizzing glass of society. She would be quite content to live out her days as the earl of Southwold's plain, spinsterish daughter.

A complication struck her with such force that she swayed and had to steady herself against the bed. No matter how successfully she escaped Raoul Trechaud, her father's motive for matching her with him still remained. He wanted a grandchild, an heir of his own bloodline, and she was the only vessel qualified to produce one. What was to keep him from finding her another husband?

Surely not. She began to wring her hands. Where would he find someone willing to overlook the scandal of a broken engagement? Someone to "plow and plant" a plump social outcast and turn her into one of England's noble brood mares? A sick feeling appeared in her stomach. Turn over any rock between Portsmouth and Edinburgh. The country was full of men to whom piles of coin would be incentive enough to abandon decency and honor and overlook a woman's implacable loathing for matrimony.

Her blood drained, leaving her face pale and her hands icy. She had no intention of jumping out of the frying pan into the fire. Before she spoke to her father, she had to be certain she would not only be rid of Raoul, but would be ineligible for pairing with any other fortune hunter as well.

What did it take to make a woman truly unable to marry? Constitutional weakness? Deformity? Illness? Mental derangement? In the history of England's nobility there were examples of women in just such sad conditions, who had been forced to marry and produce offspring for "dynastic" reasons.

She was certainly of age . . . healthy . . . of sound mind . . . of demonstrated good character. What impediment could she possibly produce that would make her utterly ineligible to marry? She paced intently, going over and over the possibilities, refusing to dismiss any prospective solution, no matter how absurd or extreme. None of them seemed to be free of problems and potential for disaster. When the idea struck she strode faster, her eyes darting furiously over an interior landscape only she could view.

It was dangerous. It was unthinkable. But it was probably her only way out.

The door opened and Ella backed through with a linen-draped tray in her hands. Turning, she stopped dead at the sight of Brien pacing between bed and window seat.

"My lady, what are ye doing? Ye'll catch yer death." She quickly deposited the tray on a bedside table and hurried over to usher her mistress back into bed. "I spoke with 'is lordship a bit ago an' said ye were ailin' an' unable t' go on t' London for yer final fittings."

"On the contrary." Brien resisted Ella's pull and straightened, raising her chin. "My grievous indisposition will disappear in plenty of time for us to set out tomorrow for London, as planned."

"It will?" Ella scowled, puzzled by Brien's emphatic forecast of her recovery.

"It will. I need to get to London as quickly as possible."

"Whatever for?"

"I need to get married."

Ella's scowl deepened. "But ye *will* be married. In yon chapel. In three weeks."

Brien produced a fierce smile that contained equal parts of pain and determination. "I've decided I simply cannot wait that long."

Five

I F YOU WALK OUT NOW, don't bother ever coming back."

Aaron Durham paused with his hand on the polished brass knob. Go or stay. His father's ultimatum had a tempting air of finality about it. Choose now, once and for all.

However inviting that promise of finality might seem, it was in fact an illusion. He had lived long enough to know that if he chose what his father demanded, he would suffer this hollowing pain in his chest again and again ... would revisit this cursed choice every day for the rest of his life. His heart would not let him do otherwise. The sight of ripples on a lake, the smell of the sea riding inland on the wind of a storm ... a toy boat gliding across a garden pond ... any sensation evoking water and movement would be a reminder of what might have been.

His father must have read indecision in his pause by the door. Aaron could feel the old earl approaching, stopping behind him, searching for whatever might tip the balance in favor of rank and duty. What would it take to make his son abandon his absurd notion of *working* like some gritty little tradesman? What would it take to get his son to accept the marriage that had been arranged and redirect his energies into making an heir on the chit?

"It would take more than you have, old man," Aaron said, startling the earl with an answer to those unspoken questions.

"A moment ago it would have taken a few thousand pounds," the old man taunted.

Aaron's hand tightened on the doorknob. "A moment ago, all I wanted was for you to free my accounts so that I could finish my ship. Now I want to finish my ship, *and* do it as far away from you as possible."

"Ungrateful whelp!" The disdain in the old man's voice raked him like claws. "This is a childish fancy . . . playing with boats!"

"*Building ships.* You'll never understand the distinction, will you?" Frustration gripped Aaron's chest so that he had to fight to draw breath enough to speak. "Because you can't imagine what it is like to build something . . . to see your design, your brainchild take flesh and bone . . . to shape it with your own hands and test it against wind and sea. You've never produced anything in your life."

"Except a fool of a son." The earl grabbed his shoulder and pulled, turning him partway. "You've had your last shilling from your mother's legacy. You're cut off and you'll stay cut off. I'm the trustee; I have the legal right. Unless you agree to come back to Wiltshire right now and make plans to wed, you won't see another penny."

"That money is mine." Aaron wrenched free of his father's grip. "My right. My future."

"Not anymore, it isn't." For a moment that declaration crackled on the air between them. "If your brother Edward must take up your title, then he will take up your future as well."

The decision was made. It would take a while for Aaron to appreciate the irony in the fact that it was his father who actually voiced his ultimate and final answer. He was quaking so with anger, that all he could do was storm out the door. Behind him his father spewed impotent fury.

"Worthless . . . ungrateful wretch! You'll regret this!"

The night was cool and the paving stones were wet from a recent rain. Aaron paused in the middle of the square surrounded by fashionable new London town homes and looked back at the doors that had slammed shut behind him. They would not reopen. What had just been done, would never be undone.

Battling the turbulence raging in him, he struck off on the first street leading east, toward the docks. There was only one place for him to go now, only one place he wanted to be.

When he reached the shipyards, he made his way past several dry docks to the berth where his ship was under construction. He stood looking down the long, gently curved keel. The sight of that substantial spine and those long, graceful ribs drained some of the anger and frustration from him. This was what he wanted . . . to flesh out these timber bones with strakes and decking and rigging . . . like Ezekiel of yore, to witness the fleshing of dry bones into something living. Wanted it so badly that he ached.

Climbing the scaffolding, he slipped inside the skeletal structure and walked its length, running his hands up and down the exquisitely curved and planed ribs. In his mind's eye he could see how she would look finished . . . her towering masts, her painted strakes, her polished railings. He could almost smell the oiled teak of the decking and the must of the new canvas sails.

His breath caught as he inhaled, seeking a trace of those half-realized scents.

He would find another way to get the money he needed. Five thousand pounds was a considerable sum, but not exactly a fortune. Perhaps if he went to the courts . . . Most of London's magistrates belonged to his father's damnable club. He might try borrowing. But his father raced horses and went shooting with most of London's bankers. He could sell something—everything. He had a bit of silver, a number of fine garments, a coach and a string of horses. But then, how could he convince others to invest in his new ship design if it appeared to have paupered him?

Anger and loss swelled in him, blocking out all further thought for the moment. He whirled and headed for the nearest tavern.

The Aces & Arms lay just outside the entrance to the shipyards and catered to a seafaring crowd; commercial seamen and navy tars mingled with workers from the lower rungs of the shipwrights' crafts. It was a bright, noisy place filled with a haze of tobacco and fermented sweat and the smell of potent, bitter ale.

He entered, sat down at a small table near the bar, and ordered whiskey and ale . . . and plenty of it. Somewhere in the middle of his second drink, a body slammed into his table, knocking over the pitcher of ale he intended to consume, and causing him to spill whiskey down the front of his shirt and waistcoat.

"Dammit!" He was on his feet in a flash, itching to pound somebody, anybody.

"Ye drunken fool—of all times fer ye to get shite-faced!" A knotty old seaman rolled across the table, hit the floor, and whirled to face his attacker with raised fists. Aaron found himself smack between a crusty old salt and a hard-eyed gent in a frock coat and flashy red satin waistcoat. A roar and a fist came out of nowhere and Aaron reacted instinctively, dodging and reversing to plant a fist square in an anger-bloated face.

The fight was over as quickly as it had begun and the trade resumed as if nothing of consequence had occurred.

Aaron looked down to find the nattily dressed gent sprawled senseless in the sawdust on the rough stone floor. The gent had swung on the old man, but connected with him instead and met his match.

"Now look what ye done—" The old man turned on him with a snarl, but stopped dead. He narrowed one eye, recalculating and correcting course as he looked Aaron over. "Well, now. Ain't you smart. Laid out ol' Jake Stokley straight enough."

Aaron rolled his shoulders in annoyance, straddled his chair, and sat down again to resume his drinking.

"Yer an' officer, ain't ye?" The old man gave a yellowed grin. "Navy, mebee." When Aaron didn't answer, he continued. "Ye been aboard ships. That much I can tell."

"I stood a few watches behind a wheel," Aaron finally answered, mostly because general civility was a damned hard habit to break. He scowled, determined that his breeding and privileged upbringing would not interfere further with the rip-roaring bender he was embarking upon. "Shove off."

"The way I see it, ye owes me . . . seein's 'ow ye cold-cocked my partner an' rendered 'im useless."

"Owe you? Your losses are none of my concern, old man." Aaron looked up with a glint of warning in his eye. "Unless you'd prefer to join your 'partner' on the floor."

The old fellow glanced at the dandified Jake Stokley, who was even now being dragged toward the rear door of the Aces & Arms and the alley beyond. Not the slightest bit intimidated, the old salt began to look him over and then stopped to look him square in the face and stare into his mouth.

"Got most o' yer teeth, 'ave ye?"

"What the devil? Get away from me before I lose what's left of my temper!" Yet, as he poured and drank, the buzzing sea-gnat refused to leave.

"Ye got a wife?"

Aaron blinked, surprised by the old man's nerve, then turned aside with a snort of irritation and poured himself another whiskey.

The old man regarded both him and his response for a moment. "A single man, eh? Then how'd ye like to make a fair bit o' scratch? One night's work. Ye'd make enough silver to keep ye in whiskey for years."

"Go away. Leave me be."

Instead, the old man leaned closer and whispered. "A thousand quid. Mebee more."

A thousand pounds. Sure. And then he'd be invited to tea with the queen. But he found himself staring at the old man. The old salt's gaze was steady and his chin was firm with resolve. Every muscle in Aaron's body began to tighten with attention. He had to be out of his mind—his gaze fell to the amber liquid hovering near his lips—or drunk. He lowered the glass without sipping.

"One night's work, eh?" He searched the old man's face, intrigued by the determined gleam in those age-faded eyes. "Got to be something illegal to net you that kind of blunt. Who are you going to rob?"

The old man leaned still closer, a grin spreading over his wily face. "No thievin', old son. Not for old Billy Rye. That's me. Billy Rye." He jerked a thumb at his chest. "Nothin' dangerous neither."

"Yeah? What would I have to do?"

"Marry up, old son. Ye just git 'itched, sign th' papers, an' then walk away."

THE SOOT-BLACKENED BRICK church was small and looked all but abandoned by the light of the streetlamps. Located on the edge of Whitechapel, the Church of St. Agrippa of the Apostles was considered too gritty and forlorn for the city's middle-class saints, and too grim and unwelcoming for its lower-class sinners. The figure of the church's namesake, Saint Agrippa, which stood in the niche above the weathered door, appeared to be trying to hide his face among the folds of his robes . . . whether from embarrassment at his namesake or horror at the travesty that was about to take place within its walls, it was hard to say. So it seemed to Brien as she stepped from the carriage onto the rough stones of the street before the church.

This was worse than absurd, this was madness, Brien told herself, pulling her cloak tighter about her. She was considering climbing straight back into the carriage, when the church door swung open and a skirted figure stepped into the open doorway.

"Hullo?" The man braced himself against the doorframe. "Are you the ones come to get m-married?"

Brien hesitated and after a moment Ella stepped into the void.

"I'm th' one that come t' see ye earlier, Vicar. My employer . . . she's come t' speak vows an' get proper wedded."

The man edged out into the meager light of the streetlamps to reveal a disheveled split collar and rumpled cassock. It was indeed the vicar of the parish who was leaning against the doorframe, dabbing his forehead and upper lip with a handkerchief. He mumbled something that may have been a welcome, then pushed off and stumbled back through the darkened vestibule. After reorienting himself, he shuffled down the center aisle, going slower as he approached the altar. As he bent a knee before the railing, a coughing fit seized him and for a moment it sounded as if he were turning inside out.

Brien and Ella were halted halfway down the aisle by the vicar's hacking and a thickening slurry of unpleasant smells. The church smelled musty and neglected; the air was sour and carried a taint of mold; and the acrid blend of illness and whiskey on human breath lingered in the vicar's wake.

"What's the matter with him?" Brien whispered, unaware that the acoustics of the church had lost nothing to age.

"Do beg pardon." The vicar straightened and turned to them, dabbing his face and running his handkerchief between his rumpled collar and neck. "S-seems I've come down with a bit of the grippe. Nothing to be alarmed about, I as-s-sure you."

But it was obvious as they approached the brighter light of the chancel, that the reverend's face was overheated and he leaned on the altar for support.

"R-really, Vicar, if you're not well—" Brien began.

"S-sound as a bell," the man declared, his eyes brightened with feverish light. "I just need a bit of t-tonic to ignite these wretched humors." He produced a metal flask from a pocket in his cassock, and tilted it to his lips.

Brien swallowed hard and looked to Ella, whose family and familiarity with the area had helped them locate this needy parish and its accommodating priest. But before she could think of an alternative to this unsavory turn, there was a noise from the rear of the church and they turned to find two figures approaching through the gloom.

Brien's gaze fastened on the taller of the two: a neatly dressed man of more than common height, with broad shoulders and striking eyes . . . which at the moment were tightened into a scowl. His gaze darted over the altar, the vicar and Ella, and then came to rest on her. He paused several pews away and propped his hands on his waist.

"This 'im?" Ella demanded of the old man who accompanied him.

"As agreed," Billy Rye declared, tucking his thumbs into his belt.

Brien's mouth dried. In the scheme that had played over and over in her mind, the part of her bridegroom was always filled by a dark, insubstantial shape that was more vapor than human. Now confronted with this living, reactive embodiment of her plan, she found herself momentarily rattled. Whatever she had imagined, it was not a tall, well-knit man with coppery hair, striking features, and eyes filled with questions.

The man stepped farther into the light and turned toward her, baring a diagonal slash on his other cheek. A dueling scar. Like those that young noblemen brought back from universities on the Continent. She couldn't swallow, much less speak.

Fortunately, Ella was not so affected. She approached the man and boldly appraised him, crossing her arms and walking to and fro to better view him.

"Not bad," she declared, then looked to the grizzled old seaman and tossed him a pouch that jingled as he caught it. "Did ye tell 'im th' conditions, Uncle?"

"I did." Ella's uncle, Billy Rye, folded his arms in a parody of his niece's stance.

"What's this all about?" the bridegroom demanded of Brien, studying her with such intensity that her face reddened. "Who are you?"

"I-I don' understand," the vicar declared, rubbing his face and blinking. "You mean, you don' know 'er name?"

"Just a moment, Vicar," Brien declared, jolted to life by the vicar's alarming question. "I must have a word with my bridegroom." She strode up the center aisle, ordering him to follow with the wave of a hand. When the man settled in front of her, she found herself overwhelmed by the height and heat of him and engulfed by the smell of whiskey coming from him. He'd been drinking. She steeled herself and looked up.

"You've no need to know more than my name." She found her voice. "You need only know that you are being paid a thousand pounds to wed me."

"There"—he raised a finger of exception—"we may have a problem. You see, I require four thousand."

"*Four* thou— Don't be absurd." She lowered her voice and tossed a nervous glance up the aisle toward the feverish vicar, who was swilling from his flask again. If they didn't conclude this business soon, the man might collapse altogether on them!

"In truth, I'm being quite reasonable. Four thousand is my price. You're obviously a lady and in trouble of some sort . . . perhaps in a family way . . ."

"I am *not* pregnant."

"No? Well, *something* has made you seek out a disposable husband. A man willing to speak marriage vows and then just walk away from them. A man willing to sell his matrimonial future for a pittance." All trace of taunting drained from his face and tone. "A man willing to forfeit all chance of ever having legitimate offspring." He studied her for a long moment, seeming sobered by his summary of the requirements of his role here. She caught a flicker of unsettlement in his eyes before he straightened and rolled his shoulders. When he met her gaze again, all hint of misgivings was gone.

"It would seem, my lady, that at this moment and in this place, I'm the best that's available. And I'll cost you four thousand pounds."

He had her. And he knew it.

Brien jerked back and for a moment it was all she could do to resist the urge to slap him. The smug look on his face was bad enough, but there was something else, something alarmingly personal in the insistent, physical curiosity he displayed toward her. She felt exposed . . . as if he might see through not only her cloak and her clothing but her predicament as well.

Four thousand. She called for Ella, whispered frantic instructions, and sent the maid and her uncle back to the town house for the money she had stowed in her trunk. Then while she waited for them to return, she drew her cloak closer about her and took a seat on a front pew. He stared at her; she could feel him visually probing the folds of her cloak, analyzing her features, examining her hands as they lay in her lap.

Aaron sat on the pew opposite the one where his bride sat and wished he were a great deal drunker. Half a quart of fine Irish would have made this whole thing more bearable. As it was, with this interminable delay, he had time to think about what he was doing and consider just how much he might come to regret it. Stop mewling, he told himself. Say whatever you have to say, take the money, and *run*.

Four thousand. It would probably pay for the rest of his materials. It was an unbelievable stroke of fortune. Just when he needed it. A godsend, really. He glanced at the young woman who would soon be his bride. Did that make her an angel? She certainly had the eyes for it. He stared at her slightly rounded shoulders and tried to dismiss his curiosity about what lay beneath that cloak. But every time he pulled his gaze from her, it found its way back.

"Do you mind?" she snapped, turning partway to avoid his scrutiny.

"If I'm to both gain and lose a wife in the next two hours, I intend to make the most of it," he declared, then glanced at the vicar dozing in the chancel chair and lowered his voice. "Take off your cloak."

"I will not."

"I'd at least like to see what color hair you have . . . to see if it goes with those icy gray eyes of yours."

Brien couldn't help turning a bit and since she was turned, she couldn't resist looking across the aisle. He was relaxed, almost sprawled in the wooden pew. *His* eyes were light, she noticed, but far from blue. In the candlelight they had a metallic glint . . . light bronze . . . even gold. Whatever their exact shade, they did indeed compliment his coppery hair. Just as his neatly trimmed hair set off his angular features, his smartly cut coat emphasized the breath of his shoulders, and his expensive boots showed off the elegant strength of his long legs. He was a specimen. No doubt about that.

She started at the realization that she was staring at him and turned so that he could see only her back. The movement dislodged the hood of her cloak and she felt it sliding down her head and coming to rest on her shoulders.

"Ahhh." She could hear his smile in his voice. "Now why would a woman with hair like honey and eyes as clear as a summer brook need to buy herself a husband?"

She hesitated with her answer, trying to decide whether it would make any difference if she told him the truth. "That shouldn't be so difficult to figure out," she finally said. "I'm marrying you so that I won't have to marry another. Ever."

" 'Ever' is a very long time, my lady. What if you decide someday you'd like to marry and have children after all? How will you find me? How will you know if I am alive or dead?"

"I won't know." She met his gaze. "That is precisely the point."

"If you won't know where I am or if I'm alive or dead," he said, the sense of it dawning, "then you'll effectively be wedded to me until the day you die."

"It would take an act of Parliament to declare otherwise," she said, feeling an odd tightness gripping her throat. Another layer of understanding settled over her; this marriage of defiance would change her life irretrievably. Wasn't that exactly what she intended? Yes, but she hadn't understood fully, until now, that even if she never married, she could never go back to the simplicity and innocence of her former life. Assuming that her father allowed her to retire quietly to Byron Place for the rest of her days, she would still have to deal with the memory of kisses and caresses, of stirred desire and crushing betrayal, of possibilities that had died before being fully born.

And what would she do with the rest of those restless and unsettled days?

Ella and her Uncle Billy returned from Harcourt House
with enough gold and folding money to meet the bridegroom's demands. When the funds were duly transferred,
Ella and her uncle roused the vicar. The little cleric was
growing steadily more feverish and disoriented; he could
scarcely stand on his own. Ella and her uncle planted themselves at his sides to keep him upright, and with some
prompting, he recalled that he had left the marriage documents on the desk in his study. They escorted him into the
small vicarage nestled behind the church, and returned
shortly with the documents and a pot of ink and quill.

After watching his hapless attempts, Brien took the quill
from the vicar's clammy hand and wrote her full name,
Brien Elaine Weston, on the proper space. She glimpsed a
worrisome flare of interest in her prospective husband's eyes
as he watched, but at least he made no comment on her
name. It reassured her to think that her father was generally
known by his title, "Southwold." She could only hope her
avaricious bridegroom was not well versed in commerce and
names of trading companies. After a pause, her bridegroom
wrote his name beside hers on the parchment: Aaron
Thomas Durham. It had a solid, dignified sound. Fortunately, too, since from that day forward she would be known
as Mrs. Durham.

Soon the bridal pair were standing before the wilting
vicar, being admonished in rambling terms to observe all
manner of sober respect for the union into which they were
entering. They were advised to honor and cherish and support each other, forsaking all others, through all the "toils
and condi-ssshuns" of life.

With her hands captive in Aaron Durham's, Brien struggled to concentrate on the vows she was asked to repeat. To
love, honor, and obey . . . for richer or for poorer, in sickness
and in health . . . for as long as they both would live . . . She
felt her blood draining from her head as she ended with the
words "I do." The rest of it—the blessing and the declara-

tion of them as man and wife—seemed to take place at a distance and to be happening to someone else.

When it was over, Aaron Durham seized her by the shoulders, lowered his head, and kissed her full on the lips. She was too stunned at first to protest. Warm, soft, a bit spicy . . . she realized with vague surprise that his impulsive action was satisfying her curiosity about what it would be like to kiss those firm, neatly bordered lips. As he raised his head, she swayed and grasped his coat to steady herself. Interpreting that as an invitation to more, he slid both arms around her and kissed her as if both their lives depended on it.

She gasped and then had difficulty expelling that breath. She was engulfed in a tempest of sensation . . . soft lips, demanding kiss, whiskey scent . . . warmth, intimacy . . . wet-velvet tongue teasing her lips, then tracing the inner contours of her mouth . . . a hard body pressed tightly against hers, melting her against it . . . feeling somehow frightened and exhilarated in the same moment.

Air-starved and deluged with startling new sensations and volatile reactions, she broke the kiss and shoved back in his arms. His eyes were dark, his face was red, and his lips looked as swollen as hers felt. It was as if a gate had swung open inside her and she stood on the edge of something deep and unknown and tempting.

"That's quite enough, sir," she declared, giving a second shove that succeeded in separating them.

"Is it?" He propped his hands on his hips, breathing as if he'd just run a distance. He turned a fierce expression on the barely sensible vicar. "Tell me, Vicar. What constitutes a proper marriage in the eyes of church and state? What are the legal standards?"

"L-legal sssstandards?" Sweat was beading all over the ailing vicar's brow, his eyes watered copiously, and his face contorted into what might have been either a grimace or a grin. "Conssent. An' vows," he muttered. "And consum . . . consummmm . . . ation."

The reverend's legs and consciousness gave out at the same moment, and he would have smacked the stone floor if not for the quick action of Ella and her uncle. Aaron Durham jolted to help them, and together they lifted him and carried him out the side door and to the vicarage. Brien snatched up the marriage documents and hurried after them.

The clergyman's residence was little more than a three-room cottage, meagerly furnished but scrupulously maintained. A pair of candles lighted the combined parlor and dining room and allowed them to find a small settee. They dumped him on the threadbare horsehair covering and stood looking down at him until Brien arrived and sent Ella to find the kitchen and some water and cloths.

"He's feverish," Brien declared, placing a hand on his damp forehead. "He needs a doctor." She removed her cloak, knelt beside the settee, and loosened the clergyman's sweat-soaked collar. When Ella returned with a basin of water, she wetted the cloths and bathed the reverend's face, then rose. "We'll find a physician and send him back—"

"Not so fast." Aaron seized her by the wrist and kept her from retrieving her cloak. "We have a bit of unfinished business."

Brien froze at the raw command in his voice, then matched it. "Let me go."

"Did you hear what the good vicar said before he fell? A legal marriage requires three things." He held up fingers as he enumerated them. "Mutual consent. Vows. And consummation." A wry smile bloomed on his face. "I'll give you one guess as to which of the three we are missing."

"Don't be absurd," she hissed, trying to wrest her hand from him. "That was not part of our bargain."

"True." His expression sobered. "Fortunately for you, I'm willing to throw it in for free. In fact, I insist on it. If this is the only marriage I get, then at least I want it to be genuine."

"Absolutely not!" She began to struggle in earnest. "Have you gone mad?"

"Oh, I think you will." Aaron Durham dragged her closer and then caught her to him by the waist. "I may *want* a real marriage, but you *need* one." He pulled her still closer and lowered his head and voice to her ear. "Two hours, sweetness. That's all it requires. Spend two hours alone with me in the vicar's bedchamber and you go on your way a truly married woman. Whatever happens between us, your girl Ella, her uncle, and the good vicar here will be able to swear we were together long enough to make the union legal."

When she hesitated, he added one final, irresistible persuasion. "I won't do anything to you that you don't want me to do."

The warmth and solid strength of him, the taste of his mouth against hers, the galvanic surge of excitement in her as he pulled her into his arms earlier . . . those and a hundred more perceptions came rushing back at once, overwhelming her in a tidal wave of temptation. It was ridiculous to even consider spending two hours alone with him in a bedchamber, much less trusting him not to seduce or ravish her in the process. But there was some part of her, some reckless and long-denied legacy of Eve, that wanted to realize that ridiculous possibility and craved the experience of pleasure, and sensual indulgence at least once in her lifetime.

This was her chance. After all, she was wedded to the man. He was easy on the eyes and probably experienced in fleshly pleasures. Even if the worst should happen and if she were to become pregnant, at least she would be legally married. And there were worse fates than settling in a quiet, secluded cottage somewhere to raise a child. . . . Positives and negatives flew wildly through her mind, propelling her toward what now seemed an increasingly sensible course.

Aaron watched the girl he had taken to wife weighing his words and promises. Her anxiety-softened eyes caused a melting sensation in his gut. She seemed much younger just now, much less in control . . . much more desperate. Warring urges to plunder and to protect her raged inside him until he stanched both impulses and returned resolutely to the strange course that had joined them together in desire and necessity.

He had no doubt of what would happen if they entered that bedchamber together. They would consummate the vows, and she would be truly wedded and fully protected from whatever it was that had driven her to seek that most intimate of alliances with a total stranger. He tried to tell himself that the pleasures of exploring that mouth and those eyes and loosening that primly bound hair and sensible gown were secondary. But deep inside, he knew better. Just looking at her made his damned fingertips itch.

"Two hours," he prompted, his voice husky with needs he didn't fully understand. Two hours ago he had refused a marriage that would have secured his inheritance and paved the way for a life of ease and privilege. Then he had married a total stranger who might or might not have given her real name . . . and was now dead set on claiming her physically. Two hours from now, he would carry the memory of a pair of haunting gray eyes and four thousand pounds away from this fateful encounter. He studied the troubled veil that had fallen over her responses and quietly decided that she would carry more away from this marriage than just his name. He would see to it that each touch, each kiss would be burned into her mind and body forever.

"And then you'll go?" There was a telling quiver in her voice when she finally spoke. "You'll swear not to look for me . . . not to seek me out or demand more money?"

"I'll go." His heart gave a heavy thud. "You'll never see or hear from me again."

He could hardly believe it when she turned to her maid and the old seaman and nodded.

"But, my lady—" The one she called Ella seemed truly alarmed.

Brien Weston Durham, unaware she had just become the wife of the renegade heir to the earl of Wilton, picked up her skirts and shot the maid a tumultuous look.

"Two hours. Find a doctor for the vicar, and wait for me."

Six

THE DARKNESS OF the bedchamber was disorienting at first. Aaron moved toward the center of the room, walking slowly, searching for furnishings with his hands. There was a soft thud as he encountered the edge of a table, then he fumbled for a moment to find a candle and set splint from the hearth to it. A sphere of soft golden light bloomed around them, eliminating the corners of the room and illuminating a simple bed, a table, a pair of sturdy stuffed chairs, and a wardrobe that hung open to reveal a penurious vicar's wardrobe of pious black and splashes of white.

He turned to find her edging out of the shadows near the door, wearing a scowl. She clearly didn't trust him. When he started toward her, she moved quickly to put the table between them.

"I simply meant to help you remove your cloak," he said. She reddened and, after a moment, untied her cloak and laid it over a nearby chair. Then she wrapped her arms around her waist and lifted her chin, as if to counterbalance her own self-consciousness.

"What will you do with your newfound wealth?" she demanded.

"What trouble are you in?" he countered.

Silence fell. Neither intended to answer the other's question. He used the next moment to stroll around the table toward her and saw her brace to defend herself.

"We both have secrets," he said, halting, opening his hands at his sides in a peace-seeking gesture.

"So we do."

"And now we will have one more." He edged closer by fractions of an inch as he openly studied her. "Only the two of us will know for certain what happens between us in this room." He reached for the combs holding her hair and she jerked back, though not entirely out of reach. He nodded, to say he understood, then with exaggerated gentleness plucked the combs from her hair. He paused for a moment, turning the handsome tortoiseshell pieces over in his hand.

"You have beautiful hair. The colors of summer wheat and honey. Is it as soft as it looks?"

Her eyes widened as he leaned closer and, with great deliberation, extended his hand again. The tension in her face almost made him think better of touching her. But his desire to experience her was strong enough to overcome such qualms. He pulled the coil of hair hanging at the nape of her neck onto her shoulder and drew his fingers over it.

"Soft. Like strands of silk." He smiled and began to comb his fingers through that long, honey-colored rope. "You have eyes like a dove's breast. So soft. So gentle. So worried." He stepped closer, so that his boots nudged her skirts. "You needn't be afraid of me. I have never, would never hurt a woman . . . much less one I have just given my name."

She seemed unconvinced as he leaned backward from the waist to better view her, and then used both hands to loosen and spread her hair around her shoulders. That gentle ministration drew some of the tension from her.

"Your eyes, on the other hand," she whispered, looking up into his face, "are the color of a gold coin." She swallowed hard. "Or is that just a reflection of the color you see when you look at me? Gold."

He studied her upturned gaze, searching her even as she was examining him.

"If you truly believe that, why are you here with me?" he said, filling his hand with her hair, luxuriating in the feel of it. "Perhaps because you are curious?"

"About what?" She glanced at the hand holding her hair.

"This." He released that hair and ran his fingertips down the side of her cheek, around her jawline and up her chin to her lips. "You've never been with a man. My guess is: You want to know what it's like before you enter the life of a married woman who lives and sleeps alone. Or is celibacy your aim? You don't seem to be the sort to loathe a man's touch. Perhaps you have a lover who cannot wed you. . . ."

"I have no lover. Nor will I take one after we part." She jerked her head to break that contact with his hand.

"A shame." He gave a wry, quiet laugh. "I hope you do not expect me to make the same promise."

She turned her head sharply.

"What you do after you leave this chamber is no concern of mine."

He absorbed the details of her smooth, unblemished skin, rose-colored lips, and feathery lashes. Her face was heart-shaped and filled with refinement, intelligence, and strain. And the tension of waiting was only making things worse between them.

He slid his arms around her and pulled her stiff form against him. She braced her palms against his chest and stared uncertainly at him. He reeled her closer by degrees, overcoming her resistance but giving her time to adjust to the inevitability of his touch. What or who was there in her life that forced her on to such a radical course?

Finally, they were chest to chest and breath to breath.

"Close your eyes," he ordered softly. "And tell me what you feel."

He watched her lashes flutter in protest, but then close as curiosity triumphed over trepidation. Her lips were tempting, but they had two whole hours and instinct warned him to go slower. He veered instead to her closed eyes and placed a gentle kiss on each of them. She drew a startled breath, but her eyes remained closed. He could feel her fear subsiding, being replaced by surprise.

"Tell me," he prompted. "What did you feel?"

"Soft . . . it was delicate. It felt like a butterfly brushed me."

"Ummm. And this?" He stroked her face with his fingertips, tracing the contours of her cheeks, the rims of her eyes, the faint wrinkle in her brow.

"Touches . . . gentle strokes . . . like a puppy's tongue . . ."

He chuckled. "And this?" He cupped her chin and ran the pad of his thumb slowly over her lips.

"I . . . I don't . . . it tickles." She raked her lips with her teeth and they reddened.

"I take it that's a pleasant thing." Unable to wait any longer, he lowered his head.

Brien's eyes flew open as his lips touched hers, but she quickly clamped them shut and concentrated instead on the sensations that contact produced. Warm, sensuous sliding, massaging, caressing, molding . . . for a time she forgot to breathe. When he ended the kiss, she looked up to see an odd look on his face, which melted into a grin.

"Your turn." When she hesitated, he shook his head. "Don't tell me you haven't wondered what it would be like to be the one doing the kissing. Here is your chance, sweetness." He leaned close enough that his breath bathed her lips. "Kiss away."

How did he know she wanted that? Refusing to over-think it, she surprised herself with how surely she slid her arms up around his neck and pulled him down to meet her lips. A flood of pleasure washed over her, engulfing her in a tide of warmth that buoyed her and sent her on currents of sensation and loosening restraint.

One kiss merged into another and then another. She melted against him, seeking a contact that would assuage the new and strangely pleasurable ache of longing in her. Somewhere in the midst of that stream of sensation, her reserve and mistrust were forgotten. Her awareness narrowed to here and now; to the small circle of candlelight surrounding them, to the circle of his arms. There was nothing but this lush physical closeness, in which discoveries awaited and desire could only deepen. Time seemed to still and each moment, each sensation stretched out with leisurely abandon to claim her.

When his hands began to move over her, she welcomed each gentle, exploratory caress. Instinctively she responded and when he paused, she began to explore him as well. Soon he led her to a large stuffed chair and pulled her down onto his lap. There, he began to loosen her laces and weave a spell in her senses as well as inside her clothes.

Her sighs and responsive movements spoke of her rising passion and directed his touch. Soon she was insensible to all but the feel of his hands on her. Intent, focused on the paths he was tracing on her bare breasts and the burning heat that his kisses stirred in her, she scarcely felt him drawing her skirt upward and parting her petticoats.

All she knew, as those stunning moments carried them along, was that she had never felt such physical delight . . . never guessed that such a thing existed. Her entire body grew sensitive and receptive; every part of her came alive with rapturous possibilities. Modesty and hesitation banished, she covered his hand with hers and guided it so that his touch would linger in some sensitive places and then move on to discover others. When his hands reached the bare skin of her thighs, she shivered and shifted to invite his attentions higher.

She rode a tightening spiral of excitement, feeling a response building in her, feeling herself expanding within her own skin, feeling a divine pressure building in her loins and against the underside of her skin. She pressed against him, instinctively understanding that his hard male body could relieve the burning, tightening sensations building in her. It was need, she realized with helpless wonder. It was *hunger*.

His hands wove a spell of rising excitement and her responses slipped beyond her control. Some primal part of her welcomed that intimate conjuring, actively sought it, then demanded it. She quivered as he caressed her, gasping, clutching his shoulders. She could feel her senses widening, her muscles tightening, her body growing taut and focused with need. Then, as if she couldn't contain another drop of that expanding pleasure, her senses exploded and her body convulsed with response.

She was vaguely aware of transferring to the bed . . . of him removing his coat and waistcoat . . . When he settled his body into the cradle of her thighs, she gave a ragged groan. When he came to her, there was some discomfort at first, but no real pain. His movements were slow and careful as he joined their bodies, allowing her time to adjust to him. Once again she was propelled along a tightening spiral of response that let to a shattering conclusion. This, she realized, was the release sought in the marriage bed, the fulfillment men and women sought in each other.

For a time she floated in a bright, unbounded plane of satisfaction, buoyed by warmth and a fluid sense of completion. Her senses were pleasantly blurred, and exhaustion claimed her for a few blissful moments.

Aaron stood by the bed, righting his garments, watching her face as she slept and seeing in it an alarming youth and vulnerability. The sense of what he'd just done settled like a dead weight on his chest, making it harder to breathe. He'd just wedded and bedded a young woman that he had promised—*sworn*—never to see again. This bizarre arrangement at first seemed a rare bit of luck, then a fleeting and potentially pleasurable bit of diversion, and then a challenge.

But he knew now that this was no game. Nothing that had just passed between them was simple or trivial, and he had a suspicion this encounter would prove anything but transitory in memory.

He had just sold his name, his future, and perhaps his soul for a few thousand pounds. But, sharp trader that he was, he'd wheedled and cozened a bit of a bonus in that unthinkable bargain . . . his benefactor's virtue. She had just given him the single most important thing a woman could bring to her husband in the marriage bed. And all he could think now was that he shouldn't have taken it. He'd had others—more than he cared to count—but no other had filled him with a dread that the pleasure he had taken with her might somehow cause her grief or even harm.

As he slid his arms into his coat, his hand plunged into a pocket that bulged with folded bank notes and gold coins. He had what he wanted, he thought grimly. Now he had to give her what she wanted. As he headed for the door, he spotted those tortoiseshell combs on the table beside the guttering candle. He stood looking down at them for a moment, then swept them into his pocket and strode out.

Brien awakened to the click of a lock, and found herself lying on a strange bed in a half-laced bodice, a swirl of petticoats, and a jumble of hair. As she sat up, her muscles complained in places she didn't want to know she possessed.

Voices just outside, growing louder, made her grab her bodice together and roll up into her knees. The door creaked open and Ella slipped inside.

"My lady!" The maid stumbled to a halt with widened eyes. "Are ye all right?"

"I'm all right." Brien tugged at her bodice and corset, then ran a trembling hand over her tangled hair. "I'm fine. Really. Just help me up and get me laced . . ."

Ella hurried to her and engulfed her in a desperate hug. Instantly Brien lost her battle with surging emotions, doubts, and overwhelming memories, and held onto Ella as if she were a lifeboat on a stormy sea.

"I'm so sorry, my lady." Ella stroked her hair. "I was beside meself wi' worry."

"It wasn't so bad," Brien said, struggling to regain some self-control. "He was quite gentlemanly. I'm afraid it was me who . . ."

"Ohhh, no, ye don't. Ye cannot go blamin' yerself," Ella commanded, releasing her partway and putting on a fierce expression. "Handsome bastard. Right dang'rous one, too. A man like that can make a girl do all manner o' things."

Brien looked up with eyes filled with tears.

"There is no turning back now," she said, gripping handfuls of her skirts as the weight of what she had just done descended on her. "I'm a married woman, it seems . . . in word and in deed."

THE NEXT AFTERNOON, Brien took a deep breath and sent Ella a wince of a smile as she stood outside her father's study, preparing to enter and deliver the news that she would not, could not marry Raoul Trechaud. Ella tucked one stray curl in Brien's upswept coiffure and gave her a brave nod that could not quite mask her own anxiety.

It had been a long, sleepless night and an even longer

day. Brien had awakened at the usual time . . . in her chamber, in her own bed, in her simple nightdress . . . to her usual breakfast of berries, scones, and tea . . . served by a characteristically tart-tongued Ella. She had dressed in her usual garments, endured another of Ella's attempts at creative coiffure, and then spent time conferring with the cook and housekeeper on the day's menus. As she departed for Monsieur Lamont's salon for the final fittings of her trousseau, she glimpsed her father reading *The Times* at the breakfast table, as usual.

Riding through the streets of London's burgeoning Mayfair district, she couldn't help marveling that the sky was filled with a customary early summer haze, well-tended flowers overflowed window boxes on fashionable shopfronts and town houses, and servants bantered eagerly with one another and with pushcart vendors trolling the streets. Everything seemed so unremarkable and ordinary.

How could it be?

The rest of the morning she had reserved a piece of her attention to rehearse what she would say to her father when she delivered the news of her marriage. Now the moment had come. But, in truth, nothing in her mental rehearsals had prepared her for the sight of Raoul sitting casually in a chair by her father's desk, staring at her as if she were a morsel and he were a mongrel.

"I am glad to find you both here. I have something to say to you that will not wait." She tightened her grip on the document she held, and squared her shoulders. "I cannot wed Monsieur Trechaud in ten days' time. Or ever, for that matter."

The earl tossed the ledger he had been studying onto his desk and scowled, clearly having difficulty registering what she had said.

"You cannot marry?" His voice grew more incredulous with each successive word. "And why is that?"

"Because I am already married." Her heart began pounding as she watched Raoul straighten and sit forward in his chair. "I was wedded a day ago in the parish of St. Agrippa of the Apostles, in Cheapside." She held out the marriage document and was relieved that it didn't shake visibly.

"Married? To whom?" The earl snatched the certificate from her and jerked it open to glare at it. What he saw caused some of the color to drain from his face. "Who the devil is *Aaron Durham?* If this is intended as a jest—"

"I assure you, it is not. It is a valid and binding certificate of marriage . . . entered into by myself and Mister Durham in front of the vicar of the Church of St. Agrippa. You are welcome to verify the records and the legality of the vows with the vicar himself."

"You can bet I will!" the earl roared, thrusting to his feet. "How the devil— Why would you— Who could you possibly have—" He glanced at Raoul, who had shoved to his feet and was staring at her as if he could ignite her with his gaze. "Do you have the faintest notion what you're saying? You cannot just walk into my study and break a betrothal agreement . . . ten days before the wedding! There are contracts—legal ramifications—financial obligations. What the hell's gotten into you?"

He rushed around the desk with the document in his hand and seized her by the shoulders. "I don't know what you think you're up to, but I'll not allow you to ruin me and blacken the name of Southwold with some idiocy!" He gave her a fierce squeeze. "I'll find this church and see these records for myself. And if it's true, you'll answer for your treachery!"

He released her with such force that she staggered, and then stormed out of the study, calling for his carriage.

She dragged a much needed breath before looking up to find Raoul blocking her way to the door. His eyes burned like black coals and ominous waves of heat rolled from him, buffeting and unsettling her.

"Is it true?" he demanded, raking her with his gaze.

"It is." She raised her chin. "I am truly and legally married."

He studied her. "Why?" He stepped closer, biting off every word. "I asked for your consent a fortnight ago and you gave it of your own free will." He lowered his gaze suggestively to her breasts. "You were eager enough to have me then."

She suppressed a shiver, remembering that first night in the garden: how beguiled she had been by his kisses and caresses. Then, she'd had no basis for judgment of a man's nature or his attentions to her.

"Then, I did not know what sort of man you are. Now, I do. And I would not marry you if the king himself commanded it."

She lifted her skirts, stepped around him, and sailed out the door.

Raoul turned to watch as she fled up the stairs to her rooms. He peeled his clenched fists open and forced himself to relax. What was done was done. If it were true that she was married, he would still have a small fortune to comfort him. And if it were not true . . .

"I underestimated you, my dear." His handsome features contorted into a smirk as he strolled over to the cabinet containing his host's best brandy. "Rest assured, that will not happen again."

Seven

IT WAS WELL PAST DARK when the earl returned home, blowing through the front doors like a typhoon run aground and roaring her name. Brien heard him from upstairs in her room and went pale. He was even more furious than he'd been when he left to seek out proof of her clandestine marriage. The moment she stepped through the door of her father's study she sensed something was wrong. The anger in his face had a righteously vengeful cast.

"You think me a fool, do you?" he demanded. "Believe I am so far into my dotage that you can pass some preposterous claim of a wedding off on me? Did you honestly think I would be gullible enough to take you at your word?" He pulled his shoulders back and stalked around the desk to wave the marriage certificate at her.

"I went to this church of yours. It was empty and the doors were locked. I tried the vicarage. Padlocked also.

When I asked the local people, they said the vicar left some time ago and no replacement was ever named." He paced away and back, his gaze never leaving her paling face. "But I was not content with that. I finally located an old man who acts as caretaker and persuaded him to open the doors so that I might have a look at the records." He settled bullishly in front of her as he delivered the coup de grâce. "There hasn't been a marriage entered into those parish rolls in over two years."

"B-but that's impossible— I was there— The church was open and—" *Smelled musty and unused, as if it hadn't been opened in months.* She scrambled to think despite the horror seeping through her. "The vows were read by Reverend Stephenson, the vicar at St. Agrippa. Surely if we contacted the bishop—"

"Did you not hear me? Whoever presided over these mythical vows of yours—if indeed there were vows—was most assuredly *not* a clergyman of the Church of England."

"That's absurd. He wore a cassock and clerical collar. He knew the service; he read the vows as if he— He married us, I tell you." *Between consumptive coughs and feverish rambling . . . on his way to becoming insensible.* She was beginning to feel a little hysterical. How could there be no proof of the marriage? "He was ill—afterward we sent for a doctor—and Ella— Ella was there!" Hope surged anew. "She saw it all. It was her Uncle Billy who found—" *Both the church and the bridegroom. For a tidy sum of money.*

"Your maid? Are you daft?" Her father looked astounded. "You expect me to take the word of a servant as proof of my daughter's marriage?"

She reddened furiously. *She had placed her future in a total stranger's hands. Had allowed her maid's crusty old uncle to choose her a husband!* Dear God. She *was* daft! Seen now from the perspective of her father's rank and class, it was madness. Whatever had made her think such a cat-brained scheme would work?

"But the vicar's signature on the certificate— We could show it to the bishop—"

"And have him see my daughter's name on a spurious marriage document? I have no reason to doubt my own two eyes. There is no clergyman at the church. Therefore, there was no legal marriage ceremony!" He stalked closer, crumpled the marriage certificate in his hand, and threw it to the floor at her feet. "Which leads me to the inescapable conclusion that you are not now, nor have you ever been married."

The impact of it blew through her middle like a cannonball. She felt suddenly empty from chest to knees. There was no proof of her marriage. No proof of what had happened to her the previous night . . . except in her very flesh.

He shoved his face down into hers.

"You lied to me and set me running all over London on a fool's errand. Well, you've played out your little game and it's gotten you nowhere. I've spoken with Raoul and he has agreed to go through with the marriage—though it took additional coin to persuade him." He jabbed a stocky index finger at her. "You will wed him as planned, in ten days' time . . . and thank God that word of this has gone no farther than this house."

As the earl pulled down his waistcoat and stalked back to his chair behind the desk, Brien thought of Raoul's brooding eyes and sneering countenance that afternoon and her blood drained from her head. Sick with desperation, she scrambled for a rebuttal.

"Do you not even care that I detest the man?" She rushed to the desk and gripped the edge of the wood. "You might have employed your talent for investigation *before* you sold me to him. If you had been half so thorough then, you would know that he has several bastards. From his own mouth I learned that he has ruined the daughters of some of Paris's best families, and his father was all too happy to send him to England to rid the family of the disgrace. He cares only about your fortune!"

"Enough!" he roared. He paced away and rubbed his hands over his craggy face. "Where on earth did you hear such things?"

"I told you: from his own mouth. I heard him bragging about it to a 'Cornelius' something . . . in the library one night. He was drinking and—"

"Bragging? You heard him drinking and bragging?" He threw his arms wide in outraged disbelief. "Are you so ignorant that you don't know that men in their cups brag about conquests never made and exploits never undertaken? Good God—you'd have me break legal and binding marriage agreements because you heard the man brag a bit?"

"But the other man—Cornelius—believed him. He seemed to know all about it . . . even the name of a girl Raoul had gotten with child."

The earl's hot gaze raked her, assessing her words and sincerity.

"Well, at least he convinced *you*. Why didn't you come to me with these 'foul revelations'?"

"I didn't—" She halted, anguished by the admission she was about to make and by the fact that she had been right in her assessment: He didn't believe her any more now than he would have then. "I didn't think you would believe me."

The depth of the gulf between them was etched in stark relief on his face. Beneath the outrage and incredulity, there were traces of loss and pain . . . which were slowly banished as the earl made his decision.

"Well, you were right. I do not believe the man is the monster you make him out to be . . . any more than I believe you would marry and submit to a total stranger. No matter what the man's faults and flaws, they cannot be worse than your betrayal of him. And of me."

He turned his back on her and braced his arms and fisted hands on the top of his desk.

"You will see this marriage through. You will wed Raoul Trechaud and honor the agreement between our houses. Is that clear?" His voice had the muted, emotionless ring of frozen steel. "He waits outside. You will see him and apologize and begin to mend whatever differences lie between you. And henceforth, you will behave toward him as a proper and devoted bride." He wheeled on her, his eyes blazing. "Because if you don't—"

He bit off the rest, but the threats her own mind conjured had more of an impact than any he could have uttered.

Brien had never seen him like this—quaking with rage. The weight of what she had done settled on her, rounding her shoulders and weakening her knees. She was to be wedded after all to the man she mistrusted and despised. *And had betrayed.* That unpleasant fact was brought home to her when her father stormed out of the study, and she looked up to find Raoul leaning against the doorframe wearing a faintly ominous smile.

"Well, well." He pushed off and strode toward her, his eyes glinting with triumph. "It seems we are to be wedded after all." His smile twisted into a full smirk. "Lucky you."

"If you were any sort of a gentleman, you would release me from a betrothal I so clearly do not want."

"Ah." He chuckled. "But as you seem to have learned . . . I am not a 'gentleman,' I am a nobleman. Personally, I find the notion that you detest me rather stimulating." He reached for her hand and when she tried to withhold it, he seized it forcibly and held it in a punitive grip. "Cooperation in a bride is greatly overrated. A bit of loathing and disdain makes the game so much more interesting. I must say, I wouldn't have expected such spirited resistance from you." He placed a suggestive kiss on the back of her hand before he let her yank it back. The reddened imprints of his fingers were clearly visible on her pale skin. "I promise to show you my full appreciation on our wedding night."

MOMENTS LATER, THE earl stood in the drawing room by the hearth, sipping a brandy he had just poured and watching the main hallway through the arched doors. He saw Brien exit his study with her head high and face flushed, and hurry up the stairs toward her rooms. Shortly afterward, Raoul appeared in the drawing-room doorway looking thoughtful. Then he strolled over to the liquor cabinet to pour himself a brandy.

The earl studied him intently, marking his darkly handsome features and effortless ease of movement. The man was worldly and something of a sensualist; that was clear to anyone with two eyes. It wasn't beyond belief that he'd left a bastard or two in his wake. But to brag about it to his cronies—while drinking his future father-in-law's brandy, under his future father-in-law's roof—betrayed an arrogance the earl wouldn't have believed possible . . . until now . . . until he saw that smug hint of a smile on Raoul's handsome face. What kind of man smirked and swaggered as he came from a meeting with a fiancée who found him so repellent that she faked another marriage to be rid of him?

His heart beat faster.

What had he just done?

"How is she?" he asked.

"Stubborn," Raoul said, studying the amber liquid in his glass.

The earl thought on that for a moment, then turned to his future son-in-law in deadly earnest.

"I fear I must take the blame for that. She was left alone for too long . . . allowed to make her own choices and run her own life. But what is done is done. She is all I have left, Trechaud, and I would not have her hurt in any way." He gave Raoul a meaning-filled stare. "You are not without persuasions. I suggest that you use them in the time that remains before the vows, to see that she is well reconciled to this marriage."

In the silence that followed, each man appraised the other.

Raoul smiled. "But of course."

THEY LEFT LONDON for Byron Place two days later and plunged into a whirl of social engagements that carried them to the eve of the wedding. Raoul was ever present and ever genial. His charming attentions to the ladies—especially his bride—won him the admiration of the county's female contingent, and his shrewd grasp of financial dealings made a strong impression on the male population, many of whom were hard-pressed by losses. Brien watched in growing despair as he entrenched himself with the local gentry and turned charm that she knew to be false and mocking upon her at every opportunity.

But truthfully, her forced proximity to Raoul was only a part of the cause of her deepening mood. Since the day her father returned with evidence that her marriage to Aaron Durham was a sham, she had felt a gulf widening between herself and her one true friend and support, Ella.

The little maid had been unable to believe the news that there was no record of the marriage or even of the clergyman who married Brien . . . that her uncle had played her false. She had rushed down to the docks to find him, but the patrons of his usual haunts declared they hadn't seen him in days, that he was most likely hiding to escape paying some gambling debts. She returned in a haze of disbelief. Then as they packed Brien's new garments and wedding gown to leave for Byron Place, she burst into tears and apologized repeatedly for the harm she had unwittingly caused. Since that day, she had seemed increasingly estranged and tentative in performing her duties.

Brien felt utterly bereft. She now had no one in whom to confide her deepening fears about what would happen after the vows were said, and her father and local society ceased

watching every word and glance that passed between them.
Raoul had promised that she would pay for her dramatic attempt at escaping marriage to him. His recent pleasantries
and graciousness would undoubtedly melt away the moment
the door closed behind them on their wedding night. And
adding to the anxiety that knowledge caused, was the fact
that she still had one more devastating revelation to make.

How likely was he to forgive so grave an insult as wedding and giving her maidenhead to a perfect stranger, just to
avoid giving it to him?

BRIEN'S WEDDING DAY dawned to an unseasonably cool
drizzle from a tired gray sky. Her spirits and physical stamina
were at low ebb; four weeks of constant tension were taking
their toll and she was beginning to suffer increasing periods
of distraction and malaise. To make matters worse, Ella had
been stricken ill the previous day. As Brien spent the night
before her wedding sitting in a chair by Ella's bed, applying
cold clothes and administering medicine, she realized that
Ella's symptoms were alarmingly like those of the man who
claimed to be a vicar. She felt her own heat-reddened
cheeks and prayed the wretch hadn't come off a ship from
some exotic port and given them all the plague.

By the time dawn came and the chambermaids designated to stand in for Ella came to help her bathe and dress,
Brien was afraid she might not make it through the ceremony, much less the horrors she expected to face later. But
it wouldn't matter if she *did* faint from illness; her father was
so determined to see this wedding take place that he would
probably just haul her down the aisle on a stretcher. Her
only support had been the knowledge that Ella would be
with her as she faced Raoul. Now even that was gone.

The picturesque stone church in the local village was
hung with garlands of fresh-cut greenery and decked with
baskets of flowers imported from all over the countryside.

As she stood at the back of the packed church and glimpsed Raoul standing by the altar, waiting, she felt her stomach deflate and slide toward her knees. All she could think was that she had been in the same position and spoken the same words a mere ten days ago, and look where that had gotten her.

There was a collective "ahhh" from the assembly as she and her father started down the aisle, but her attention was riveted on Raoul's duplicitous smile. Each step that brought her closer to him seemed to raise the temperature of the air around them. By the time he took her hand from her father and turned to the vicar, her face was bright red and she was glowing with unwelcome warmth.

Increasingly, as the reverend droned on, she was distracted by physical distress. There were too many people in the church, all staring and breathing out excess heat. She felt a trickle of moisture down the nape of her neck. Why did she have to wear a gown with long sleeves and so many layers of silk and veiling?

She was suddenly aware that the vicar and Raoul were staring expectantly at her. Raoul squeezed her hand sharply and the vicar repeated the first line of the vows she was to speak. She repeated the words without looking at Raoul.

When it was his turn, he reached for her chin and turned her face to his. Caught in his searing gaze, she felt as if the fires of perdition were licking at her feet. Every word, every glimmer in his fathomless black eyes said that he hadn't forgotten and the time of retribution was at hand. She felt hot and dizzy and looked around for an open window.

Then suddenly, she was in Raoul's arms and feeling the press of his lips against hers. It was over. A moment later she was being escorted back down the aisle by her new lord and master, who squeezed her arm tightly and cast her a smile that grew faintly ominous. As they stepped out of the church, she gulped fresh air and used her fan briskly. She had survived. She looked at Raoul, who was busy accepting

the hearty congratulations of their neighbors, and vowed
she would survive him as well.

The rest of the day whirled on about her, the bridal dinner was served immediately upon their arrival at Byron
Place. There were toasts and more toasts, each requiring her
participation. The sips of wine she couldn't avoid consuming made her feel the heat, and Raoul was everywhere with
his hot hands and simmering looks. His behavior was clearly
interpreted by those present as husbandly eagerness; they
made jests and sidelong comments to that effect. She
wished they would all just go home.

But as the afternoon wore on and the guests actually began to leave, she regretted those sentiments and wished her
father had planned for a much longer celebration. Too soon
the sun was lowering, the last guests were departing, and her
father was calling for his own carriage. She was being left
alone with her new husband . . . in their isolated country
house. . . .

STRIPPED OF HER elegant gown, Brien collapsed on the
bench of her dressing table, and cradled her head on her
arms. She was feverish and miserable and beginning to
tremble all over. The chambermaid insisted on bringing her
some cool water and then wetting some toweling to wash
her face and cool her throat.

"There's nothin' to fear, my lady," she declared with a
worried expression. "He's a fine, mannerly fellow, yer husband. He'll do right by ye."

Brien groaned and let her head fall back down on her
arms.

Just after sunset, which came late in the June day, the
house fell silent. With the wedding dinner over and the
clearing away done, the staff and servants had withdrawn to
a celebration of their own by the lake. Only Brien's little
chambermaid and the small retinue of Raoul's personal

servants remained. At Brien's insistence, the long windows of her room had been thrown open and the occasional moan of the breeze passing through made it sound as if the house itself were burdened and anxious.

Raoul had removed his coat and waistcoat and donned a silk dressing gown over his shirt and breeches when he arrived in Brien's rooms. He carried a bottle of wine and two stemmed goblets. His mood was quietly triumphant until he spotted Brien's simple green muslin day dress.

"Still the rebel?" He nodded toward her choice of garments. "You know, of course, what you wear has no bearing on what will happen tonight."

Brien spread her hands on the back of the chair in front of her.

"For once, *monsieur*, we agree."

He studied her ruddy face and upraised chin. "Your wedding night means so little to you, *ma chérie?*" His tone was now challenging.

"I thought it meant a great deal *the first time it happened*. Apparently I was wrong. And I do not intend to suffer such a disappointment a second time."

"The first time?" Raoul placed the wine and glasses on a nearby table.

"When I was wedded—*or thought I was wedded*—almost a fortnight ago. I believed I was legally, morally, and honorably bound. The vows were consummated."

His face hardened with frightening speed and intensity. "You are not serious."

"I've never been more serious," she said. The menace he exuded grew like a dark cloud to engulf her. Her heart raced. Her whole body caught fire.

"I would ask why, but in truth, it does not matter. You are mine now. And it may prove rather amusing tomorrow morning, to have you compare your two wedding nights in detail. In fact, I believe I may insist upon it."

"Perhaps I haven't made myself clear," she said, feeling

an alarming popping sound in her ears and a sudden rush of heat. She was quaking all over now, and had difficulty focusing on what she had to say. "I won't let you take anything more from me than you already have. I will not share a bed with you."

He laughed as he watched her growing distress.

"*Will not?* What makes you think I desire *willingness* in my bed, *chérie?*" He moved closer, savoring the fear that flickered across her face. "How do you plan to resist? Scratch? Kick? Bite? *Stab?*" He paused, his grin curdling into a sneer. "It might prove interesting to add the marks you inflict to my collection of scars."

The shiver of pleasure that depraved possibility sent through him shocked Brien into motion. She staggered backward toward the door that connected to her dressing room.

"Whatever resistance you offer will not only be useless, it will enhance my pleasure in taking you. You see, I've had my fill of sighing and moaning and even shrieking females. I was counting on you proving a bit more inventive." His teeth glinted as he produced a menacing smile. "Don't disappoint me, Brien. I'm not a pleasant man when I've been disappointed."

She tried to dart behind a heavy stuffed wing chair near the hearth, but her legs would scarcely work. She stumbled and just managed to catch and pull herself around the chair, keeping it between them.

"Running? Is this the best you can do, *chérie?*"

"I will never be your wife," she responded, panting, having some difficulty getting her breath. "Seek an annulment, Raoul. You wanted wealth and position—you can have them without the baggage of an unwilling wife."

His fist slashed out with lightning speed, sending the glasses and wine bottle shattering on the floor. Until now she hadn't imagined the depths to which he might sink when confronted and denied. His smile was chilling.

"You think to rid yourself of me so easily? If you think I could be content with a few bags of money, you are sadly mistaken. And you underestimate my fascination with you." He edged closer to the chair and she could see the cords tauten in his neck like bowstrings. He was on the edge of an explosion. "I have never been so thoroughly rejected by a woman before. It makes me want to understand how such a thing could happen. Perhaps if I put you in a jar . . . study you . . . dissect you . . ."

Then he lunged and she scrambled for the dressing room. But her limbs seemed to be weighted with lead. From the corner of her eyes she saw him coming, saw his hand close on her arm. He yanked hard and she snapped back with such force that her vision blurred. Suddenly she was trapped against him and his mouth on hers was hot and devouring. Struggling and bucking against him, she succeeded in biting his lip and ripping her mouth from his as he yelped. Cursing softly, he turned his hunger on that which he could easily reach, her neck and shoulder. He fastened his mouth to her shoulder, then sank his teeth into her, trying to both punish and consume her. Her limbs seemed thick and sluggish as she cried out and beat at his back and tried to reach his face with her nails.

Then just as suddenly as the attack began, it halted, and Raoul's grip on her loosened. Her renewed resistance finally broke his hold and she staggered away, panting, shocked by her abrupt release. She realized that he was looking beyond her and turned to see what had stopped him. Ella stood a few feet away, dressed in a damp nightdress, her eyes bright with fever, holding a cocked pistol that was aimed at Raoul's chest.

Raoul looked from Ella to Brien, his struggle for self-control evident on his face. "So this is your game." He wiped the blood from his bitten lip, looked at it on his fingers, then clenched both hands into fists that fell to his sides. "To have another fight for you. A servant, at that. How common."

Brien saw Ella sway and rushed to her to steady her. The maid seemed to be on the edge of a collapse, and she thrust the pistol into Brien's hand.

"Stay back! Don't come any closer!" She helped Ella to the nearby chair, while holding the pistol on Raoul with a surprisingly steady hand. When Ella was safe, she turned her full attention to Raoul and advanced slowly on him.

"You won't shoot me," Raoul said, trying to engage her eyes.

"Don't bet on that. You should have taken the money, Raoul. Now *I* intend to annul this marriage—and I'll see that you don't get a penny in the bargain. When society hears what sort of husband you make, there won't be a door in England open to you."

"After your lies . . . your father will never believe you," he spat.

She glanced down at her bitten shoulder. "He will after he sees this." She leveled the pistol at his face. "Now get out!"

"This is not finished, *chérie*." Again he produced that chilling smile. "Surely you know that."

As the door slammed behind him, she rushed to it, turned the key in the lock, and braced her back against it. When it became clear that Raoul was gone, she roused and rushed to Ella's side. The maid was slumped to one side, with her head against the chair.

Brien rushed to her, laid the pistol on the table, and seized her hands.

"Ella . . . oh, Ella, you shouldn't have left your sickbed."

The maid's lips were dry and her eyes were glassy with fever. " 'E can be bad if 'e's crossed." She sighed. "I couldn't let ye face 'im alone."

"Oh, Ella." Brien used every bit of strength she possessed to help her maid from the chair to the bed, then perched on the side of the mattress, bathing Ella's face until the maid lost consciousness.

Brien lost track of how much time passed and of how many times she'd cooled the cloth. Then as dawn grayed the room, Brien herself was overtaken by a searing hot cloud of sensation. Her lungs felt hot and crackled with each breath, so that she bent double in a coughing fit. When she managed to straighten, her face, her body, and her limbs were on fire.

A strange, high-pitched whine began in her ears. . . . She felt strangely detached from the world . . . everything started to spin . . . and darken. . . .

Eight

L IGHT SPLIT THE DARKNESS above her and she drifted upward toward it. There had been lights before, and voices, but they hadn't lasted long enough to be meaningful. She was lying down; her whole body felt weighted, but still somehow detached and floating; she was chilled and sweating at the same time. Those incompatible perceptions circled in her head until they righted and she understood them as all part of a general discomfort. She forced her eyes open and struggled to make them focus.

In the dim light provided by two small windows at the top of a high wall, she could make out that she was in a small stone chamber furnished with the bed she lay on, a few barrels stacked along one wall, a table, and what appeared to be a brazier. Her arms, outside the covers of the simple bed, were freezing. It took concentrated effort just to draw them inside the cover where there was warmth. She groaned at both the effort it required and the difference it made.

Opposite the bed was a massive wooden door that was re-inforced with hammered-iron bands. The strangeness of it all finally registered. This looked like a cellar. Where was she? At Byron Place still? She tried to sit up, but it took too much out of her and she wilted back onto the bed.

Her head felt spongy and allowed words and images to leak away before she could link them together into coherent thought. What was the last thing she remembered? It took a while for her to recall the wedding. Then her rooms. Ella. Ella was ill and she had— The gun! Raoul! What had happened after she forced Raoul to leave?

Alarm shot through her and she drew on the strength it provided to sit up and look around. Her hair was loose and lay in damp clumps around her shoulders. She wore a thin nightdress that felt clammy and clung to her. On the nearby table she could make out a pitcher and glass and what appeared to be medicine bottles like those she'd administered to Ella. It began to knit together in her head.

She'd been ill and, from the searing aches in her chest and lungs, she was still recovering. But why here? She slid her feet over the side of the bed and pushed herself up. Steadying herself on the bed, then a chair, then a barrel, she made for the door.

"Hello?" She pounded on the massive oak planks with her fist but was so weak she produced only a few dull thuds. "Is anyone there?" She bent over in a fit of coughing, then tried again. "Can anyone hear me?"

The cold of the stone floor seeped up her legs and her teeth began to chatter. She staggered back to the bed and collapsed, exhausted by that small bit of movement. Her last thoughts as she sank again into unconsciousness were that she wasn't where she was supposed to be and that Raoul was somehow to blame.

When she roused from that troubled sleep, there was

light around her and someone moving nearby. She looked up to find a mountain of a man with no hair and a face full of mismatched features squinting down at her. Raoul's man, Dyso. The one Ella had found so frightening. Brien had seen him occasionally from a distance. He kept mostly to the stables and was assigned to care for Raoul's . . .

"Noooo!" she croaked out, shrinking back as he reached for her.

His coal-black eyes remained fastened on her as she recoiled. She was suddenly seized by a painful round of coughing and he cocked his head as if analyzing the sounds. Moving back to the table, he mixed something from the bottles in a cup and carried it back to her. His movements were slow but far from clumsy. She looked at the delicate china cup in his big, blocky hands and then up at him.

At close range it became clear that the numerous scars on his chin and jaw and around his eyes were what gave him that odd "patchwork" appearance. His head was not just bald, it was shaven, and beneath his frayed clothing, massive muscles bulged. But despite those formidable elements, something about his manner and clear, steady gaze spoke of patience and a nature free of deception.

She finally gathered the courage to reach for the cup.

"What's happened to me?" Her voice was alarmingly weak. "Why am I here?"

He said nothing, but backed toward the door and unhooked a ring of keys from his belt. In one fluid movement he ducked out and closed the heavy door behind him, sealing her in once more.

Her blood rushed to her head. She was a prisoner here. Raoul's prisoner. And that hulk was her jailer.

Looking down at the cup she was gripping, she sniffed and recognized the aroma. Tea. With honey. She sipped and when it proved to be just that, she drank gratefully. She rallied enough strength to place the cup back on the table and then turned back to the bed. That extreme heaviness overtook her again and she sank to her knees by the bed.

When Dyso reentered moments later, he found her on the floor, leaning against the edge of the bed, asleep. With a softening in his battered face, he collected her and tucked her back into the bed, tidying her nightdress around her and braiding her hair loosely to keep it out of the way. He sat with her for a few moments, listening to her breathing, then with a strange little smile of sympathy, padded out.

The next time she awakened, the chamber was entirely dark. How long had she slept? She was certainly more aware of her surroundings and coherent enough to realize she was at Raoul's mercy and thus in real danger.

The key scraped in the lock and the door swung open to admit Dyso, carrying a large candelabra and a tray of food. He placed both on the table, then pulled it to the bed so she could reach it. The light was so welcome that she wasn't aware she had held her breath until he moved back toward the door and she exhaled with relief.

Then she spotted her jailer standing just inside the door, with his arms folded and a shoulder propped against the wall. Raoul spared not a glance for his henchman as he ordered sharply, "Get out." When they were alone, he straightened and walked toward her at a slow prowl.

"My lovely bride. Feeling better?"

Brien said nothing, hoping to hide the fear rising inside her. This was his doing. Ella had warned that he was capable of anything.

"I trust your accommodations are adequate." He stopped near the table, where the candlelight enhanced the glow in his eyes. A chill coursed up her spine. How could he be so beautiful on the outside and yet so degraded inside?

"Where am I?" she asked, feeling as if that one demand took all of her strength.

"Where I want you to be."

"Where is Ella?"

He seemed not to understand, then—"ahhh"—gave a nod of recognition. "The maid. You needn't worry, my dear. She won't be threatening anyone ever again."

"What have you done with her?" Brien threw back the covers and lurched over the side of the bed. A wave of dizziness and nausea hit as she staggered a few steps and she held her head, waiting for it to pass.

"Tsk, tsk. Still you feel the effects of your illness." He made a show of producing a silk handkerchief and holding it near his nose to mask the chamber's smells. "Disagreeable as it is, I owe a debt to whatever illness seized you and rendered you insensible. The housekeeper gave me the keys the next morning when the door was locked and the servants couldn't rouse you. We found you lying on the floor. I was, of course, the perfect bridegroom . . . so anxious for my bride's health that I must tend her myself. For all anyone knows, you are still in my bedchamber, being tended by your devoted new husband."

"What is it you want, Raoul?" she said weakly. "More money?"

"You defame me to imply that mere money is at issue here. I claim only that which is mine by law and right." He abruptly seized a lock of her hair and yanked her closer. "The right to plow you deep and often . . . the right to watch your belly swell with my seed . . . the right to make you to regret your betrayal of me with every breath you take." That flash of frightening intensity faded as quickly as it appeared; he loosened his grip on her with a caustic laugh. "Besides, your *père* has been most generous. There is nothing else you can give me . . . except the pleasure of humbling you."

He pulled her closer, lowering his head to kiss her, and her stomach rebelled. She surrendered to the wave of sickness, retched dryly, and went limp. Revulsed, he released her as if contact with her sullied him. She slid down the side of the bed to the floor and he stood over her, staring, trying to decide whether to vent his anger on her. After a moment he stooped and lifted her head, his fingers digging into her face.

"Look at me," he commanded in coldly compelling tones. When she complied, there was an alarming glitter to his eyes that betokened an unnatural appetite for violence.

"How long do you think you can keep me here?" she whispered.

"As long as it takes, *chérie*."

"For what?"

"For you to be with child." His words fell about her like a steel trap. "My child."

"Never," she breathed, paling even more around the green that circled her mouth.

"*Au contraire, chérie*. As soon as possible." He appraised her crumpled body. "Then you cannot deny our vows, and you will be bound to me in flesh as you are on parchment."

"I'll never bed you," she said, feeling another, stronger wave of nausea rising. She clamped a hand over her mouth and managed to stanch it.

He rose and his nostrils flared in disgust.

"Never is a very long time, *chérie*." He stepped away and flourished his handkerchief to banish the taint of her illness. "I do not believe that you spread your legs for another, but I will take no chance that you bear another's seed. You will stay here until I am certain that you are not pregnant." He gave her weakened body a scathing glance. "And until I can bear to bed you myself." He strolled toward the door. "Until then, Dyso will attend you. He cannot speak, but hears well and has orders to see to your needs." His cold smile made her shudder. "It was he who put you to bed here, so you have no secrets from him." At the door he paused to snarl a final command. "For your own sake, you'd better mend quickly."

The door banged shut and the bolt slid home.

Wrapping her arms around her middle, she sat there on

the cold floor for a time, wishing she could either escape into a faint or, if she was already asleep, to wake up from this nightmare. That was where Dyso found her some minutes later.

He gently lifted her back into bed and tucked the covers around her. Then he wetted a clean bit of toweling to wash her face and came back to the bedside with a small brown bottle. He dabbed some of the liquid inside it on her temples and under her nose. Spirits of camphor. The smell was astringent, but somehow reassuring. It was what her old nurse had always used when she or her sister were ill.

Tears suddenly bloomed and rolled from her eyes back into her hair.

She felt a touch on her hand and looked up to find Dyso staring at her with a look of genuine concern . . . almost . . . compassion. As she dissolved into sobs of misery, she managed to utter two words.

"Thank you."

THE SOUND OF a key in the lock awakened Brien the next morning, and she lurched up, her heart pounding, clutching the covers to her. Dyso entered almost noiselessly, carrying a breakfast tray. Placing it on the table, he removed the basin and chamber pot and was quickly gone.

Stifling a rising despair, she forced herself to think about her dangerous position here. There was no help to be had. Everyone believed them preparing for or already on a wedding trip. With Ella out of the way and Raoul now in charge of the household, she was completely at his mercy. If it weren't for her illness, she would already have been subjected to Raoul's appetite for blending lust and cruelty.

Worse still, she'd caught this vile contagion from the false vicar who married her to Aaron Durham. She swung her legs over the side of the bed and poured a cup of tea from the tray, ignoring the milk-and-bread sops that were meant to help settle her stomach.

The thought of him made her spirits sink unexpectedly. He appeared again in her mind: tall, striking, enigmatic, tender. She had no idea whether or not he was a party to the money-making dodge Ella's uncle had perpetrated on her. But how could he not be? Wasn't he the one who had demanded more money? Four thousand pounds. He'd known they could get more out of her and had held out for it, the wretch.

Again and again in the days between the fraudulent wedding and the forced one, she had refused to think about him. It had been so humiliating to learn how ruthlessly she'd been swindled, that she couldn't bear to remember anything more than that. But now, in her weakened state, she could no longer resist the full memory.

The exhilarating sense of discovery. The tenderness with which he touched her. The bittersweet realization that this would be her one chance to experience passion and pleasure. She thought of Raoul's plans for her. Aaron Durham's loving might indeed be the only pleasure she would experience in life, no matter how manipulative it had been. Desperately, she folded that memory away in a safe chamber of her heart.

She had not heard the key in the lock or the sound of his step, but she sensed that someone was in the room and jerked around. Dyso stood a pace away, his large, dark eyes unreadable as he stared at her. Brien shrank back on the bed, feeling fragile and unable to contain even one more scrap of horror or despair.

He went down on one knee by the bed and she gasped as his fleshy paws reached for and began to gently stroke her hand. She turned her tear-streaked face to him in surprise. He was offering her comfort. His eyes looked sad, and Brien wondered if it was mere pity he felt for her, or a deeper, more complicated kinship. For the first time as she searched that scarred face, she wondered how many of those wounds had been caused by Raoul.

"Thank you for taking care of me," she whispered.

He nodded and made a sweeping hand motion from himself to her. What did he mean? Was he offering her something? She didn't know how to read the signs he made.

"Have you been with Raoul and his family long?"

He nodded and made a cradling motion with his arms.

"Since you were born?" she guessed.

He nodded again.

"Does he beat and mistreat you?"

The big man's face darkened and he drew back, giving such an emphatic shake of his head that Brien knew instantly it was true.

"Please"—she couldn't stop herself—"help me. I beg of you. If there is anything you can do to help me get out of here . . ."

He released her hand abruptly and rose. He seemed agitated, and began to pace back and forth. Then he looked back at her with a fierce glare and exited, slamming the door behind him.

Tears sprang to her eyes. There was no help for her in this place; she was on her own. If she were to survive, she would have to put all of her energies into getting well first. She turned to that tray of food, reached for the milk-and-bread sops, and made herself eat.

That night as she lay in her cellar chamber on her prison bed, a pair of gold eyes escaped forbidden realms in her mind. Together with a reckless smile, they formed the core of a face . . . clean, angular features . . . coppery hair . . . a rakish scar . . . a smile that caused warmth to suffuse her skin. Freed along with that memory, physical need stirred within her . . . a hunger for touch and comfort and sense of safety she had known briefly in his arms. Even if it was an illusion, it was still the deepest contentment she could recall. As she had looked into his eyes, felt his hands on her, and reveled in the warmth and security of his presence, she had known it was more than a legal strategy, more than even curiosity that had made her agree to those two hours together. Now, as she looked again into those eyes, in memory, she understood she would never be able to banish him entirely from her heart. He had taken something precious from her, but had left something of his own in its place.

Even imprisoned and threatened by Raoul, it was the charming rogue Aaron Durham that filled her thoughts.

If that was really his name.

Nine

NEAR DAWN, Brien was awakened abruptly and sat bolt upright. For a long moment she searched the darkness and silence around her, clutching the sheet, her heart racing. Detecting nothing out of the ordinary, she gave a tense sigh and loosened her deadly grip on the coverlet. For an instant she had thought it might be Raoul returning. A second shuddering exhalation expressed her relief that it was not.

Then it came again. Something almost audible, just out of her range of hearing but detected all the same. Fully awake now and at the edge of her nerves, she slipped from the bed and padded across the cold paving stone to the iron-bound door. A faint change—the merest of sensations—raised the hair on the back of her neck. In the deep gloom of the chamber, she could make out the outline of the door clearly and began to search it for some clue to the cause of her rising anxiety. Nerves stretched taut, she ran her hands along the planks and bands until she reached the lock. She snapped upright, drawing in a sharp breath.

"Smoke." As if conjured by its name, the acrid smell seemed to grow stronger. "A fire. There must be a fire!"

Recognition sent a trill of panic through her. She was locked in a cellar with no possibility of escape. She was sealed in a place that would be her tomb!

Desperately, she grabbed the iron handle and pulled with all her might. The door swung open and she stumbled backward over her own feet in surprise. Catching herself, she rushed into the opening and peered into the dim light of a stone passage outside. Her eyes widened on wisps of smoke that could not have come from the torches hung in brackets farther down the passage. She had to find a way out!

Gathering up her gown, she ran down the passage, looking frantically for a means of escape. The hallway led past several half-open doors of storerooms to a long series of steps. If she was in a cellar, the only way out was *up*. She mounted them quickly and encountered thickening smoke that stung her eyes and burned her throat.

At the top of the steps, she spotted an open doorway through the growing haze and groped her way toward it. It was warm to the touch and seemed swollen in its frame. Throwing herself against it, she managed to knock it free and found herself in a wide hallway filled dense with smoke and that was lighted on one wall by hideous tongues of fire. She stopped dead. In front of her hung a familiar painting. This was indeed Byron Place! And this was the core of the house—a warren of servant stairs and passages. Oriented now despite the smoke and darkness, she charted a course for the front doors but found that path—then another and another—blocked by heat and flames.

Weakness in her limbs slowed her, and she panted, dizzy with the effort required to breathe . . . slowing with every step. The carpets and drapes in the dining room were ablaze and the golden light revealed intense fire farther on in the hall and drawing room. Exhaustion and smoke overwhelmed her and she dropped to her knees, feeling as if her very lungs were being seared. She crawled until she could move no more, then collapsed into a heap on a polished floor that burned brilliantly only a few yards away.

Unconscious, she did not feel the strong arms that lifted her up and carried her through the inferno into the cold night air. She didn't hear the shouts of the stablemaster sending his son for the physician and directing the servants to a place of safety. And mercifully, she did not see the roof collapse a short while later, or hear the awesome, thunderous rumble that signaled the end of the glorious old house.

FIRST, THERE WAS darkness and muffled pain, and then an unrelenting thirst. Something heavy was sitting on her chest, making it hard to breathe. She tried to open her eyes, but they stung and kept slamming shut. With effort she forced them open for a few seconds, to behold blurred faces near hers. She couldn't be sure they were real.

She thought she heard someone calling her name, but she was powerless to respond. The sound died away and once more there was blackness.

When next she awakened, she was fully aware of people around her, calling to her.

"Where . . ." she rasped out in a voice that sounded like the smoke had damaged it. "Where am I?"

A woman's voice came through the fog. "You're at Tremaine, my dear. They brought you here after the fire. Squire Hennipen and I have charge of you while you recover."

As she struggled to sit up, gentle but firm hands pushed her back against the soft bed. "No, no, dear, you mustn't. You're far too weak. Just rest." Those same hands lifted her head when she called for water and put a cup to her parched and swollen lips before she lapsed again into darkness.

The third day she awoke with a much clearer head and a howling thirst. She surveyed the darkened room and struggled up, blinking. Her eyes felt full of sand, her face felt swollen, and it seemed she had to fight for every breath.

The door to the cheerful blue-and-yellow room opened and a plump, well-dressed lady entered. Brien recognized Mrs. Hennipen, the wife of a squire whose lands bordered Byron Place.

"Thank Heaven, you're awake." She felt Brien's forehead and cheeks with a cool hand. "You've given us all quite a scare."

"How long"—Brien's voice cracked—"have I been asleep?"

"It has been three days since the fire." Mrs. Hennipen looked away, clearly troubled by the mention of it.

"Fire . . ." Brien started up clumsily. "Where . . . how . . ."

"You've had a narrow escape, dear." Mrs. Hennipen gently pushed her back down. "You must concentrate on getting well." She busied herself tucking the covers around Brien.

"Byron Place burned?" But she supplied her own answer out of memory. "I saw the smoke and flames and ran, but—" She stopped, squeezing the older woman's hand, suddenly remembering more. "Raoul. Where is Raoul?"

"He's gone, dear. The fire . . ." The woman halted with tears filling her eyes.

"Gone?" Brien grasped the woman's arm. "What do you mean?" she demanded. "Dead? Tell me!"

"Yes."

Stunned, Brien released her. "No," she said fervently. "There's been a mistake. He just hasn't been found."

"No, dear. They found him . . . after. Your father identified him. I'm afraid there's no mistaking it."

Mrs. Hennipen admitted the physician who had just

arrived. Brien continued to entreat them for details of the fire and its aftermath until a sleeping draught took effect. Mrs. Hennipen sat with her until the earl came that evening from burying his son-in-law. He confirmed Raoul's death and watched Brien's stunned and emotionless response.

Uneasy at her lack of reaction, the earl insisted on sitting with her that night. She awakened in the wee hours, sitting bolt upright and screaming with everything in her. It was a ragged, unearthly wail, brought forth from intense pain and desolation. The whole household awoke to the screams in the deathly stillness. Her father finally succeeded in calming her by holding her tightly and rocking her as if she were a child. In her thrashing her nightdress slipped to reveal her shoulder—and the fading but unmistakable imprint of a set of teeth.

That bite mark wrapped a cold band of horror around his heart. Who could have done such a thing to her? He could scarcely draw breath as he clasped her to him and faced the fact that it had to have been Raoul. Sickened by that evidence that the man he had forced his daughter to wed was capable of true brutality, he stayed by her all of that night and the next . . . troubled by her wild grief and fearful of his part in the making of it.

The next day Brien began the slow journey back to normalcy. Exhausted, weakened by her illness, and damaged by the smoke and heat, she slept a great deal . . . untroubled by dreams. Soon she was able to manage some solid food and bathe and present a rational mien. She sensed that all visitors to her room eyed her warily, but was unable to remember the unsettling events of recent nights.

When they were alone, Brien asked Mrs. Hennipen for the details of Raoul's death and the good lady recounted that his lifeless body had been retrieved just before the collapse of the main roof. He had not been burned, but had died of smoke and heat. Lord Weston himself had identified the body and had seen to the burial.

The servants had escaped to safety, and each had a different story about how or where the fire started. Some traced it to the grand salon, but the stablemaster identified the kitchen as the starting place. The house was utterly destroyed.

Guarding her words carefully, Brien began to piece together her own story, recounting how she had awakened in the night, just before dawn, to find herself alone. Gripped by the fresh memory of the thick, terrifying smoke, she recalled that she was lost and confused and finally collapsed. Mrs. Hennipen patted her hand and insisted that she rest. The good woman hurried down to the anxious earl and related his daughter's story in full.

Lawrence Weston sat with his daughter that afternoon, not sure how to comfort her, or indeed if she needed comfort from him. She seemed calm enough, despite an occasional tremor in her voice.

"I worried at first when Raoul's message about your illness came," he said, avoiding her searching look. "But he assured me that it would pass quickly and that your wedding voyage was only postponed for a short while."

Brien was distant and preoccupied; the pieces of Raoul's treachery were slowly fitting into place. "How good of him to inform you. What did he say about Ella?"

"He wrote nothing to me personally. But I had luncheon with Magistrate Derringer and he told me the facts of the case. It must have come as quite a shock to you. Still, I suppose she must have stolen quite a bit over the years." He shifted uncomfortably in his chair. "All of these things happening so quickly—it's been trying for you."

"Yes" was all Brien could manage.

Raoul had charged Ella with stealing, to see her disposed of quickly. God only knew where she was and what had befallen her. While Brien was conveniently "ill" during the first few days of their marriage, no one—not even her father—had come to call on the newlyweds. Raoul's plan had been flawless. Except for one thing. The fire.

"Thank you for seeing to the arrangements." She turned her face away from him on the pillow. "Now, if you don't mind, I'd like to rest."

With a few more days of restoring sleep and nourishment, Brien felt much stronger and insisted on being allowed to sit by the window for a bit of sun. The window of her room overlooked the side yard where servants frequently came and went.

A figure in the yard below caught her attention. She could not see him clearly, but there was something familiar in his slow, rolling gait and the broad slope of his shoulders.

Mrs. Hennipen breezed in just then, carrying a vase of flowers from her garden.

"Who is that stacking wood in the yard?" Brien asked.

Peering out the window, the plump little woman smiled. "Oh, my dear, that's your man, the mute one. He's the one who carried you out of the house the night of the fire." She halted, seeing Brien pale. "I'm sorry, I forgot to tell you. He rode with you in the cart and refused to let anyone carry you. He seemed quite fierce and determined, so we let him stay until the doctor arrived. Sat outside the kitchen door for two days. My servants offered him food and shelter, but he would take none. When I told him you were awake and would be all right, he took nourishment and seized an axe. He has cut enough wood for two winters since that time."

Brien's eyes misted. "He was my husband's servant. Dyso is his name. Thank you for your kindness to him."

"He's an odd one. But you draw breath this day because of him."

Two weeks after the fire, Brien dressed and came downstairs for dinner, insisting afterward on walking outside in the midsummer gardens. The air was heavy and still, saturated with moisture. She had been forced to promise that she would not stay long, and after picking a few flowers, started back into the house.

As she rounded the step, she was startled by Dyso looming over her path. She stepped back, staring up into his large, dark eyes. He smiled at her and made some hand motions. Brien knew instinctively that he inquired about her.

"Yes, I'm much stronger now. I have you to thank for that. You saved my life." She straightened, feeling an odd surge of warmth for him. "There will always be a place for you with me, unless you wish to return to France." She was surprised as he went down on one knee in the grassy carpet.

"You will stay?" she guessed.

He nodded and looked up with a smile. There was a certain peacefulness now in his battered face. He rose and pressed something into her hand before lumbering away. It was cold, and she found herself looking down at a large black key. Recognition flowed over her as she watched her rescuer's broad shoulders sway as he returned to his chores.

Ten

THE HENNIPENS INSISTED Brien stay with them in the country while she recovered, and she gratefully accepted. She seemed to flourish in the clean air and sunshine, and the prospect of a summer in London held no appeal. Part of each day was spent helping Margaret Hennipen in her flower garden, and Brien came to cherish those quiet times with her fingers in the soil and the sun on her shoulders. She even began to plan a new garden for Byron Place when it was rebuilt.

Monsieur Lamont himself came from London to arrange suitable mourning clothes and a wardrobe to replace the one she'd lost in the fire. When the little Frenchman saw her, he was speechless. Brien had not seen herself in a looking glass since before the wedding, except to brush her hair. It came as a complete shock when the *monsieur* became so excited during the fittings that he reverted totally to his native tongue. He insisted on taking several of the gowns back to London to be reworked. Brien smiled, remembering their first meeting—his diplomacy and unfailing politeness. She had been dowdy and rustic, but he had done his best to make her presentable for her marriage to—

Raoul. The very thought of him filled her with an almost physical pain.

When dark suspicions arose in the back of her mind, she couldn't suppress them. Raoul was a selfish and violent man. Had he died in a tragic accident or been caught somehow in a scheme of his own making? Had he tried to burn down the house he had once pronounced a "heap" and rid himself of a troublesome and uncooperative bride at the same time? She would probably never know. But if not, then she would see to it that no one else knew the truth of her marriage to the volatile Frenchman, either.

Society dictated that she mourn his loss, and she would do so. But she could not ignore the irony of continuing to live the lie that Raoul himself had created for her . . . after he was dead.

As the days strung together in blissfully restoring weeks, Brien realized that her situation had positive aspects. The few visitors who ventured to Tremaine displayed ill-disguised curiosity toward her, mingled with an exaggerated deference to her slightest wish. She was a widow now, deprived of a virile young husband on the threshold of their life together. No one dared to intrude upon her grief. After a while she would be forgotten and free to do as she wished without interference . . . even from her father.

HARCOURT HOUSE IN London was decorated for the holidays in subdued fashion. The black wreaths that had hung on the front doors were replaced by simple swags of holly tied with black ribbons. The earl himself met her at the door when she arrived, kissed her dutifully on the cheek, and cast an appraising eye over her elegantly attired figure.

"You seem quite recovered. I am glad to have you home where you belong." He didn't notice the way Brien bristled at his words. "I have instructed Mrs. Herriot to take Monique from her household duties and have her see to your needs until you can find a suitable maid. She has already prepared your rooms."

"Thank you, but I have already engaged a new maid." Brien was annoyed by his assumption of authority, fearing it might presage new struggles for control of her life. "She will arrive shortly with my things." Removing her gloves as they entered the drawing room, she decided this was an appropriate time to set matters straight.

"I wish Mrs. Herriot to remain in charge of the house. My future plans are not certain and I wish to disrupt your routine here as little as possible." She had removed her hat and dark veil, using the action to avoid his astonished gaze.

"You speak as though you won't be staying long. What other plans could you possibly have?"

"Some travel, perhaps. I am not sure." She smoothed her severe coiffure in the mirror above the fireplace. "I may purchase a house of my own in London."

Irritated, he rubbed his chin. "What is wrong with Harcourt? It is your home as well as mine. You will live *here* while Byron Place is being rebuilt." She turned on him with her eyes flashing.

"I will decide for myself where and how I will live. My own decisions can hardly end worse than those that have been forced upon me."

"If you refer to your marriage, Brien, you must share the credit for that decision. Your conduct left no other course," he declared defensively. "I trust you will observe a proper period of mourning, out of respect for public opinion if not for the man."

"My marriage and my widowhood are *my* concern, not

yours. I intend to rebuild my life and put the past behind me." She hoped her anger was as plain on her face as it was in her heart. "I have no heir for you from my short marriage, and you may not look for one from me. *Ever.* Of that you can be certain. I will never marry again."

Her words struck him with tremendous force, turning his own anger into insight. A shocked silence spread between them, and Brien opened her fan, plying it briskly to avoid looking at him.

"Was it that bitter for you?"

Something in her stomach settled downward. "I'd rather not discuss it. It is over now." She looked at the gloves she was twisting into strings.

He moved toward her, feeling powerless to stop the hurting inside her. What had befallen her at the hands of Raoul Trechaud, he could only guess, but she had revealed much by her determination to avoid marriage and motherhood. He put out his hand, but withdrew it without touching her.

She had not seen the gesture or the genuine concern in his face. She was tired from the journey. This was neither the time nor the place to air her plans, but she thought it might be good to give him something to think on.

"I've a mind to study commerce and perhaps enter the trading business. I have a quick mind, and it would be good to put my education to practical use."

"Given time, I am sure you will find more suitable pastimes. You have only just arrived and are surely—"

"I shall spend my time as I see fit!" She whirled on him. "I am a woman. That was nature's cruel jest on us both, but I'll not live a life of misery because of it. I have strength and wit aplenty and I've had a stomach full of womanly duty. I am a thinking and feeling person, and I'll not be sold again at any price."

Her glare withered any reply he might have made before it could form in his mind. He shoved his hands into his vest pockets and went to stare out the window. He was a study in bewilderment. His daughter hated her very womanhood, and likely him as well.

"I apologize." A hard-won civility returned to her voice. "I had not meant to say all of this to you now. But perhaps it is best that we set things straight from the start. I don't know what I want." She looked down at the gold band on her left hand. "I only know I don't want what I have had."

The earl turned to look at her. The sorrow and fatigue she felt showed plainly in her young face. Yearning to comfort her and uncertain how she would receive that from him, he gave in to an impulse and crossed the drawing room to take her hands in his.

Compassion filled his face and heart for the first time in years. He knew little of this woman-child of his, but he saw that he had been given a second chance with her. She needed him, and he would not fail her again.

"Rest now, before dinner." His voice was thick with emotion and Brien searched his face as he squeezed her hands. "We will talk about the future later." She nodded and started to leave, but his voice called her back.

"Brien, I only want your happiness."

She studied his face for a long moment without replying, then left him.

THE HOUSEKEEPER AWAKENED Brien the next morning at seven o'clock and handed her a folio of documents with instructions from Lord Weston that he would discuss them with her over luncheon. Brien bounded out of bed, smiling triumphantly.

Each document detailing the architect's plans for resurrecting Byron Place raised more questions than it answered. She hurried to her desk and took quill in hand to make notes to herself. She entered the dining room feeling quite prepared, but for every question she raised, her father had thought of three. When the barely tasted luncheon was cleared away, Brien realized that they had only begun for the day. The rest of the afternoon she spent in close attendance on her father's every word. By dinner, her head ached and she was beyond comprehending more. She excused herself as soon as the last course was finished, and retired.

Lawrence Weston smiled to himself, confident his willful daughter had learned enough "construction" to last her a lifetime. But the next morning she appeared at the breakfast table, fresh and eager to resume her lessons. She had several suggestions for the architect, based on several books she had discovered in her father's library, and had listed their holdings in mines, lands, ships, and commodities, and had questions about them all. The earl rose to the challenge and by evening, Brien retired *before* dinner.

The third morning, the earl was considerably less enthusiastic about this course of education when Brien arrived at breakfast again armed with plans, ledgers, and questions. One thing Weston had already learned about this daughter of his: She was not easily dissuaded.

Brien proved a bright, capable student and by early summer, the earl found himself hard-pressed to best her in knowledge of the design and construction of Byron Place or in the family's assets and financial matters. He took great pains to see that she was consulted on all major decisions regarding Byron Place and, increasingly, on all matters of importance to Weston Trading itself. She possessed a logical mind and was well read and concise in expression. Weston winced to think that his daughter's depth and richness would have gone undiscovered by him, had it not been for a tragic accident.

He had occasional misgivings about allowing his daughter to escape her womanly responsibilities, but had to admit that there were few other options open to her in this year of deep mourning. Her quick mind would be restless and resentful confined to the boundaries of an embroidery hoop. Truthfully, he enjoyed watching her as she plied her unique blend of charm and logic in matters of construction and commerce.

It was only in the matter of marriage that she defied his expectations, and he had not given up hope of steering her back toward more sensible attitudes regarding giving him grandchildren. She could not keep her heart hidden forever, and it was clear that Raoul Trechaud had never captured it.

Unknown to her father, Brien had set their solicitors to work on a private matter, conferring with them about it only in his absence. She hoped to learn the whereabouts of her friend and loyal servant, Ella. They discovered that she had been sentenced without appearing before the magistrate in person and had been packed off to a constabulary to await a prison ship bound for Australia. That was the last anyone had seen or heard of her; the court and shipping records had been destroyed in a fire. Despite repeated warnings that the chances of finding her friend were dim, Brien would not abandon the search. A debt of gratitude kept the search alive when common sense poured doubt on its chance for success.

As the London winter slogged by, the black of mourning and the solitary life began to weigh upon Brien. By the first of April, she decided to end her total isolation and accepted the invitations of a few local ladies for tea.

It was painfully clear to Brien at these modest gatherings that she was the object of intense curiosity. The ladies, a number of whom came from estates neighboring Byron Place, asked thinly veiled questions about her marriage and the tragedy that ended it. Brien was demure and somewhat reticent in answering, unaware that with her studied omissions she gave them a picture of Raoul as a model of manly virtues and desirability. These ladies remembered all too well his dark, probing eyes and sensuous mouth, his broad shoulders, and his charming accent. And when they departed, they were more than eager to relate and even embroider her account.

But their curiosity did not stop with Brien's marriage. They were cloyingly sympathetic, all the while measuring her very body with cool scrutiny. A young and beautiful widow was far more to be feared in the ranks of dowdy matrons than any comely maid. The possibility for temptations, once having tasted the forbidden fruits of marriage, was ever present. Feeling a responsibility to the sanctity of the homes of the community, they investigated all threats, however remote or highly placed. Brien perceived this element early on and let it slip that she was not eager to remarry.

By her elegant appearance and sedate actions, Brien added fuel to the legend springing up about her ill-fated marriage to the French nobleman. Unknowingly, she was becoming the heroine of an idealized love match. Everyone had quite forgotten the quiet, dowdy maid who had sat alone in the family's box at church and was never seen otherwise. By all accounts, she was a beautiful woman tragically bereft of a handsome, virile young husband. Her very desire for a year of mourning seemed all the gossips needed to verify the tales that circulated about her.

But the year passed all too quickly. As the plans were being drawn for the fall social season, she had to excuse herself on the basis of half-mourning in order to avoid the deluge of invitations they received. Her excuse, spurious as it was, merely added fuel to the curiosity raging about her.

It was Monsieur Lamont who provided the spur that sent her out into the world again. He insisted she visit his salon for the final fittings of her new wardrobe, to view his wonderful creations in a wall of mirrors created for such elegant occasions.

Her lady's maid for the past several months, Jeannie, had taken great pains with her hair the morning of the fitting and commented that she had never seen her mistress looking lovelier. Brien put it down to the girl's excitement at attending so elegant an establishment. But when Jeannie finished lacing her into the first of Monsieur Lamont's creations, Brien was dumbfounded. The deep décolletage of the ice-green-and-white silk ball gown barely contained her. The gossamer sleeves were snug on her arms their entire length, revealing while not binding them. The bodice was tight over a demi-corset that felt obscenely free and the high waist and narrow skirt skimmed her body too closely for propriety's sake.

That was an old propriety, Monsieur Lamont insisted. This was the new respectability. One which adhered to more fluid lines and more healthful foundations.

She paced the fitting room in front of the massive mirrors, both scandalized and fascinated. As she whirled, the skirt wrapped voluptuously about her legs.

"You move like a symphony together," the little *couturier* declared.

She tugged on the neckline. "After every dance I shall have to be restuffed into it. And no panniers? How would I dare wear it in public? My father would die."

"The gown was not designed with fathers in mind," Monsieur sniffed.

Brien's face softened with wonder. "It's marvelous. Truly, it is."

By the end of the fittings she was exhausted. Left alone in the room for a few moments, she walked closer to the mirrored glass.

Was that her? Gracefully tapered legs, nicely rounded hips, and a narrow waist. Her breasts rounded pleasantly above the light boning, and her skin was clear and smooth across her bare chest, throat, and cheeks. She stretched her arms above her head, turning slowly to inspect all sides of this new creature. Then she moved closer . . . made faces at herself . . . fluttered her lashes.

She staggered back, unnerved by this new view of herself. Why had she been so unwilling to see the changes that had taken place in her when most girls scrutinized their looking glasses daily for improvements? Was it only that she had always considered herself plump and plain next to her stunning older sister Denise? What else had she been unwilling to face in herself?

Jeannie returned just then to help her dress, but those thoughts persisted well into the evening. She had a great deal of thinking to do.

Eleven

A TRICKLE OF INVITATIONS appeared at Harcourt and on the first of December, Brien beleaguered her father with questions about which to accept. With his advice, she selected a dinner-dance given by Lord Randolph Hazelett, a former Chancellor of the Exchequer.

She was noticeably nervous as Jeannie did her hair and helped her into a gown of midnight-blue velvet, adorned with a tableau of blackwork embroidery that began at the waist and curled up over her bodice and down over her high-waisted gown. Jeannie had created a flow of ringlets and ribbons from the crown of her head down her back, and instead of jewelry she wore a simple black ribbon at her throat.

She held her breath as she descended the stairs into her father's scrutiny, and the earl escorted her to the coach with a beaming smile.

Curiosity about her had spread to London with the story of her ill-fated bridegroom, enhanced by her seclusion and rumors of her beauty. Fairly, it could be said that no one in the room was disappointed by her appearance or manner. She glowed with fresh, vital beauty and possessed a natural grace that immediately put people at ease.

Weston watched his daughter making conquest of the men and confidantes of the ladies and was bemused by her obvious pleasure at the attention. She was no tepid, sighing bride; she was fully, irresistibly woman—perhaps her only legacy from the virile, passionate Raoul Trechaud.

The evening was made all the more memorable for Brien when she retired to one of the rooms on the upper floor where dozens of ladies repaired curls and laces and availed themselves of the facilities behind screens. She was straightening her skirts behind one of those screens when she overheard the excited chatter of some young girls.

". . . never seen anything so elegant. That dress must have cost a fortune."

"I've heard that her husband was deliciously dark and handsome—French, too. They say he was a rake before he met her and gave it all up."

"It's not hard to believe," a third chimed in. "Not a man here has seen anything but her tonight."

The first voice resumed. "They say when she heard he was dead, she howled and wailed like an animal for days—nearly mad with grief."

"I wish I could have a love like that." There was reverence in the second voice.

"I heard she vowed she'd have no other man," the third girl giggled. "He must have spoiled her for all others."

"I wish someone would spoil me like that," the second girl dreamed again.

The voices faded as the girls exited, and Brien stepped out from behind the screen. How many other whispered conversations about her were even now taking place? They believed her marriage had been a blazing love match. The irony of it stunned her; the most painful thing in her life was now the cause of her overwhelming social success.

But there was a brighter, more practical side to this, she thought as she rejoined her father for the dancing. If this gossip was any indication, then she might be spared the matchmaking that plagued young widows in society. Let them talk, she decided, beaming at the curious faces turned her way. She'd not spoil their fun.

When the evening ended and they were again in the coach, Brien sighed and leaned back into the padded seat. "I had no idea it would be so lovely."

"You enjoyed the dinner and dancing?" her father said.

"Of course," she declared, turning to him in surprise, but smiling at the teasing in his eyes. "Do you think they liked me?"

"Liked you?" He pondered it. "Tomorrow we shall have to hire a secretary to manage the flood of invitations we will receive."

Brien laughed contentedly, a melodious sound that the earl had just seen entrap members of Parliament and peers of the realm.

The next morning, news of the beautiful young widow spread like sparks in dry grass. Discreet questions about her to old family friends elicited the tantalizing story of her handsome, lusty, young husband and of a great love dashed by his tragic death. When it was learned that she had accepted the New Year's Ball at the duke of Hargrave's, half of London society made inquiries about attending.

OVER THE NEXT weeks, as Brien worked on rebuilding Byron Place and launching her new life in society, the earl received disturbing news concerning his business dealings in the colonies. The local economy, inflated with nearly worthless paper scrip, was sagging badly. Defying the terms of the treaty that ended the war, several colonial assemblies had declared debts owed to British merchants null and void. Merchants who had speculated heavily by allowing liberal credit in the postwar buying spree, were now driven to the edge of bankruptcy by their inability to collect on the notes they held. Weston Trading, while still solvent, suffered huge losses.

They could look for no relief from the new Congress in the colonies, which was pressed hard by debts of its own and was occupied with the matter of a constitution and consolidating its own power. Complicating matters, communication with the colonies was slow and awkward; documents were often subject to close scrutiny by several pairs of eyes before they reached their destination. Most dealings with British merchants were conducted in an atmosphere of suspicion, despite mutual needs for continued commerce.

Weston's agent in the colonies, Silas Hastings, had forestalled catastrophic losses, but his attempts to collect outstanding debts had been unsuccessful. More worrisome was the news that he was having difficulty insuring the safety of the goods and stores that remained in the warehouses. Vandalism and outright thievery aimed at British-owned enterprises was all too common.

The news came at a singularly awkward time for the carl. He had advanced a sizeable sum to Raoul Trechaud upon the signing of the marriage agreements and after the fire was unable to find any trace of investments his son-in-law might have made with the money. Some of Weston Trading's French properties had been seized and looted in the rioting that had broken out in several French cities, and it looked as if there would be more losses if political and social conditions in Paris didn't improve. Such shortfalls might have been overcome by stringent economies . . . if the cost of the reconstruction of Byron Place hadn't also begun to soar . . . and the cost of Brien's new wardrobe hadn't bloomed . . .

and they hadn't begun to entertain again during the holidays. What had once seemed to be a bottomless dynastic purse suddenly had very finite dimensions.

At first the earl shook off warnings of accumulating losses. Such things came and went, he declared. But as the holidays passed and there was no news to brighten the outlook, he realized he would have to take more direct action.

For the first time in many years holly, candles, ribbon, and pine boughs decked the halls of Harcourt, and new friends were frequent guests. The earl savored the sight of his daughter presiding over a drawing room filled with London's first tier of society and vowed that nothing would interfere with that hard-won pleasure.

Brien was content with her life now and knew she had much to be grateful for . . . new friends, watching Byron Place rise again, the stimulation of studying commerce, and especially her deepening relationship with her father. These past months she had grown very close to the earl and cared deeply for the man who indulged her so shamelessly and tutored her so expertly.

At last she had everything a woman could desire.

THE BALL GIVEN by the duke of Hargrave to welcome the new year was intended to be a fitting climax to a perfect holiday season. When Brien and her father arrived, the great house at the western edge of London was ablaze with lights and awash in the scents of beeswax candles and a richly perfumed society. The entrance hall was as big as a ballroom, and all over the house, double doors separating the rooms had been thrown wide to permit the free flow of music and merriment. Reaction to her presence among them was visible and immediate; heads turned and necks craned.

After they greeted their host and hostess, a series of

Brien's admirers appeared to claim her for dances. Ladies whispered avidly behind fans and men stared in open appreciation as she glided around the ballroom floor with a succession of partners that included Edward MacLeod, member of Parliament, and Reydon Hardwick, heir to the fabulous castle and fortune.

It was with Hardwick that she left the ballroom to seek refreshments. They were stopped along the way by a number of acquaintances and others seeking introductions, so that by the time Brien was handed a cup of punch, she was desperately thirsty and drank it too quickly. Hardwick obligingly refilled it, and she drank the second too fast as well.

Then it happened.

As she gave up following Hardwick's discourse on the latest sensation in the racing world, something in the next room caught her eye. *Someone.* He was tall and broad-shouldered, and as he turned slowly toward her there was something familiar about the line of his jaw and profile. She smiled distractedly, her attention focusing, being drawn taut like a purse string. The man in the dining room talked casually with his companions and made gestures with his broad shoulders that stopped her breath.

As if responding to her intensifying gaze, he looked in her direction and their eyes met. Her knees weakened. She stood transfixed for what seemed an eternity. Her companions sensed her withdrawal from their conversation and expressed concern as they watched her face drain to ghostly white.

Those hot golden eyes scorched her across the distance. She sank slowly beneath the impact of recognition. Reydon Hardwick caught her as she fell, and in the commotion that followed, carried her through the entry hall and up the stairs.

A swooning lady was not uncommon at these affairs, but

Brien Weston Trechaud was not just any lady. Speculation swept through the crowded rooms at the sight of the dashing Hardwick heir carrying the unconscious widow up the steps, followed closely by her father and one of society's prominent doctors.

When she was safely deposited on a bed in the duchess's suite, the physician ordered everyone out of the room except the earl, and proceeded to examine her. He quickly concluded that her condition was not serious and rolled her over onto her side to loosen her corset. He seemed a bit confused to discover that she was hardly wearing lacings at all.

Downstairs in the grand salon, the cause of Brien's discomfort leaned his shoulder casually against a marble mantelpiece and sipped from a crystal goblet. His attention was fixed on the man beside him, absorbing every word Edward MacLeod spoke.

"Breathtaking, that's the word for her. There's not a man here, including the duke, who wouldn't give a year of his life for one night with her."

"You say she's a widow?" Aaron Durham scowled, clearly unsettled by his visual brush with the sensation of the London social season. Brien Weston Trechaud.

"Indeed." MacLeod drew deeply from his glass and continued, "Not a merry one, however. She was only a bride of a month or so before her husband died."

"A *Frenchman?*" Aaron was momentarily confused. But the name was right . . . at least part of it. *Brien Weston.* But *Trechaud?* His friend insisted she was both the earl of Southwold's daughter and the widow of some French nobleman.

"Damned Frenchmen. What is it about those poncy wretches?" MacLeod expelled a huff of disgust. "He must have had quite a month. She's not overeager to replace him."

"Perhaps she developed a distaste for that side of wedded life."

"Cold, you mean?" MacLeod shook his head with a wry grin. "Just one dance with her in your arms and you'd see . . . she's so warm she fairly melts. Her Frenchy was a nobleman with a reputation for getting whatever and whomever he wanted. The ladies say he was devilishly handsome. Gossip says it was a great love. Whatever it was, she hasn't got it out of her system." He caught the intensity in Aaron's face. "Hang on—you're not thinking of having a go at her, are you?"

"Tempting notion, MacLeod, but I won't be staying long enough to give the idea my full attention. I have a ship due to be launched in a fortnight, or have you forgotten? I have a million and one details to attend, and I'll be headed for Bristol soon." Aaron straightened and gestured toward the food tables, heading for them.

"I'll never understand this mad yen of yours to risk your neck at sea," MacLeod said, joining him at the buffet. "You could be sitting safely at home, inheriting a fine title and charming countless females out of their closely-held virtue."

Aaron gave a sardonic laugh. "As for virtue, I've had my share. Overrated, I can tell you. And as to my father's precious title . . ."

"Speaking of your father"—Edward turned to him with a slice of ham dangling from a fork—"have you seen him of late?"

"No." Aaron's flat reply closed the matter.

"What's this?" Edward looked up and came to stand beside Aaron, staring through the doorway into the great hall and beyond. Brien Weston Trechaud, wrapped in a beaver-lined cloak, was being carried down the stairs by a contingent of household servants commanded by her father. They moved through the parting guests on a direct course for the front doors.

"Must be more serious than we thought. Sorry, old man." He thumped Aaron's arm. "You won't meet the beauty of London this night."

Aaron stood in the archway watching the woman he had wedded and bedded more than a year ago disappear through the front doors. His sun-bronzed face was tensed with concentration on a decision he thought he'd never be required to make. He knew who she was. And he knew her secret. The question settling like lead in the pit of his stomach was: What in the devil was he going to do about it?

BRIEN ASSURED HER father she would mend. "No food all day . . . too much dancing and too much punch . . . I'll be fine in the morning." She went straight to her rooms when they arrived at Harcourt, and as she prepared for bed, a servant arrived with a hot milk-and-brandy toddy and orders from her father that she drain the cup.

The warmth of the brandy spread quickly through her, prying the grip of panic from her throat and pouring some warmth into her icy limbs. But when she climbed into bed and Jeannie extinguished the candles and left her, the fear that had felled her earlier came surging back in a cold, breath-stealing wave.

He was there, at the ball. Those eyes— There was no mistaking those golden eyes. And the scar. He had seen her, too; she would swear there had been a jolt of recognition in his face just before she fainted. What on earth would *he* be doing at the duke's ball?

Common sense rebelled. It couldn't have been the same man.

Perception refused to be set aside. Why couldn't it be him?

What did she really know about the man she thought she married? At the time, his name was all that it seemed relevant or prudent to know. She had intended to retire to a modest country house for the rest of her days; encountering him again hadn't seemed even remotely possible. How could she possibly have guessed, when she paid him to wed her down by the docks, that both she and he would show up eighteen months later at the most coveted event of the London season?

It was too horrible to contemplate. Her fatigue and the wine punch conspired to make her see his face, his eyes, instead of those of the stranger. It was just a resemblance.

But as the night dragged on, she couldn't dismiss the possibility that the man who pretended to wed her, the man who swindled her, and the man standing in the duke's dining room were one and the same. Once admitted, that thought begat a litter of ugly, pugnacious threats to her safety and sanity. How could she ever have put herself into such sly, opportunistic hands? What would happen when he learned who she was? What if he threatened to tell what she had paid him to do? What price would he exact for his silence?

The sight of him as he stood in the duke's dining room came flooding back. Aaron Durham, with his strange golden eyes, coppery hair, and rakish smile. Aaron Durham, with his gentle hands and hard-soft lips and tantalizing tongue. She had known he was a gentleman the first moment she set eyes on him. Self-assured. Well-spoken. Entirely too perceptive. Why should it surprise her that he had access to the upper strata of a society in which good looks, fine manners, and quick wits were coveted commodities?

Through the long night, she wrestled with the threat that he posed in her life, and with the memories of a taste of pleasure that had disturbed her dreams too many times in the last year and a half. Beset by unanswerable questions, she finally drifted into a fitful sleep and she was again transported to that room, that bed in East London where Aaron Durham had deflowered, delighted, and ultimately deceived her.

The next morning, she sent her regrets to half a dozen hostesses, pleading indisposition. It was two very long weeks before she convinced herself that he might have every bit as much to lose at the revelation of their fraudulent marriage as she did, and began to venture out into public again. But it would be a great deal longer before she could sleep at night without suffering steamy, Durham-filled dreams that left her edgy and quarrelsome the next morning.

THE EARL NOTED his daughter's distraction, but seeing her glowing good health, assumed she had simply been afflicted by the vagaries of the female condition. The word from the colonies was worse each fortnight, and he resolved to hold it from her no longer. She took the news hard, outraged by the injustice.

"Scoundrels," she fumed. "Biting the hand that feeds them."

"I was afraid you'd take this hard." The earl wagged his head. "You must realize that this is not a vengeful act. Their economy suffers terribly. They simply cannot raise the funds. There are times when the wisest counsel is that which tells us to do nothing." He opened his hands in a stoic gesture. "We must be patient. Our claims will wait."

"Patience is a dear commodity," she declared, lifting ledger sheets that were red with default. "Is there no way we can force them to pay? Attach their property?"

His eyebrows shot up. "This does sting. Who would you take to the courts? Shopkeepers? Farmers? What would you do with wooden cabins and steel plows? And what magistrate would counter a colonial assembly, even for a handsome fee?"

Brien's face colored. "I never meant—"

"I dislike bribes. And if I were a colonial, nothing would enrage me more than the offer of a bit of dirty money from a wealthy English lord. No, no. We will wait."

Brien was deeply disappointed by the news and began to delve deeper into their financial affairs. It wasn't long before the truth of their situation became clear. She had been enthusiastic about their prospects in the colonies and had persuaded her father to risk more investment in American trade than he thought prudent. Her pride smarted at her first business failure, but she heeded her father's advice to allow events to clarify themselves before taking action. It was doubly hard now, waiting for word from the colonies *and* waiting for the reappearance of the treacherous Aaron Durham. . . .

ALL WAS WELL until the first of February. The earl was brought home from his offices feverish and chilling. He had a racking cough and was unable to keep food down. Brien watched him weaken as the fever slowly worsened. Dyso helped her restrain him when the delirium caused him to thrash and rave, and helped her mix and administer the draughts the doctor ordered. The long nights beside his bed blurred into an endless stream of pain and fatigue.

The doctor came daily and stayed several evenings, for Brien would not leave her father's bedside unless the doctor was with him. Then, somewhere in the night during the second week of his illness, the fever finally broke and the relieved doctor assured Brien that her father would recover fully.

The first of March saw improvement in the earl's health and the first bit of hopeful news from America. Silas Hastings sent word that he had collected a percentage of the debts and seized a goodly stock of merchandise for nonpayment. He awaited instructions on how to proceed.

Brien's heart warmed toward the tall, gaunt man whose squinting to improve his eyesight made him appear to wear a continual frown. He had gone to the colonies as a young man and had prospered as Weston Trading's agent, marrying the daughter of a wealthy merchant. Through the years, his first allegiance was to Weston Trading—and his second to his adopted country. The revolution had caused him great personal grief.

She held the news from her father and developed a plan that would take her out of London for a while and solve their colonial crisis at the same time. She would personally travel to America and use every weapon in her arsenal of persuasion to find a cash buyer and liquidate their American holdings.

The earl mended quickly for a man of his age. When Brien presented the news and her plan to him, he was at first adamantly opposed. But she sent orders to their solicitors and began making arrangements for the voyage in spite of his disapproval. The earl finally admitted the soundness of her plan and her ability to carry it out. But it was her own excitement about the venture that tipped the scale in her favor. With no small guilt, he realized the strain of his illness had drained her as well. She desperately needed a change of surroundings and something to engage her restless mind.

Her father arranged for her to be given his power of attorney and sent a letter to Silas Hastings requesting suitable accommodations be arranged. She accepted the invitation of Lord Emery Devon of Bristol, the son of an old business acquaintance of her father's, to be a guest in their home while awaiting her ship. And lastly, they arranged passage on one of Weston Trading's own vessels for late April, sailing from Bristol.

As their departure neared, preparations increased at a frenzied pace—with fittings and shopping, packing and farewells. When they set forth at last for Bristol, she was more tired than excited.

The earl came downstairs to see her off, and she extracted a promise from him that he would take care of himself in her absence. He hugged her and kissed her forehead, saying that he wished he were going with her and envied her this chance to see the colonies firsthand.

Then he glanced at Jeannie and Dyso, who waited near the carriage, and asked dryly if Brien would feel safe traveling with such a small retinue. To be sure, it seemed an odd entourage as they stopped at a country inn for the night: the lady, her maid, and their hulking protector.

Twelve

ON THE TWENTIETH of April, Brien was warmly welcomed to Devon House and escorted to a guest room by Lady Angela Devon, who chatted enthusiastically about the colonial adventure her guest was about to embark upon. It seemed she had spent a summer in Boston as a girl, and had amusing memories of her time there . . . strange foods, rough people, and a general inattention to personal hygiene. At any other time, Brien would have been charmed by her stories, but just now she was tired and hungry and in no mood to contemplate the privations that she might have to endure on her journey. But a warm bath and a light tea restored her equilibrium, and by dinner she was able to once again muster enthusiasm about the adventure that lay ahead . . .

. . . until Lord Emery Devon, who had insisted on going to the docks to see about her passage, announced some disturbing news. The ship *Libertine*, on which they were to sail, had not yet left the Azores. When she put into harbor there to repair damage caused in a storm, a fever felled the captain and crew. Most would live, but it could be months before the *Libertine* would see home port again.

Brien's spirits sagged under the news and Lord Emery promised to personally seek passage for her on another vessel. His broad, earnest face and keen blue eyes made Brien believe he would not only try, but probably succeed.

Proving that her faith in him was well placed, Lord Emery announced two evenings later that he had by the barest of chances secured passage for Brien's party on a new ship making her maiden voyage to America. Brien had just been introduced to the Devons' other dinner guests—Lord and Lady Clermont and Brigadier and Mrs. Wilton—when he made his announcement.

"The ship is called *The Lady's Secret*, a handsome new design," Lord Emery said enthusiastically. "They say she'll cut a full week off the best time. Better yet, she's built with cabins for passengers. Dash it all, Lady Brien, you have phenomenal luck!"

"Perhaps I only borrow yours, Lord Emery," Brien said, flushing with relief, "since it was you who found this solution to my problem."

Lord Emery abandoned his post by the marble mantel to pat his wife's hand. "My dear, I took the liberty of inviting the ship's captain and owner to join us for dinner this evening." He tossed a meaning-filled glance at the Clermonts and Wiltons as he continued. "And I know you will forgive such impertinence when I tell you that the captain is none other than Aaron Durham."

"Oh, Emery," Angela gasped softly. "Are you sure?"

Aaron Durham. Brien sat with the name echoing through her suddenly empty head. Every coherent thought had just been blown from her mind by that verbal cannonball. She felt for her fan and flicked it open. *Captain* Durham. It couldn't be.

"I spoke with him myself this very afternoon," Lord Emery continued. "He was reluctant to take on passengers, this being her maiden voyage. But I explained our guest's predicament and he said he could hardly refuse a lady in need."

"Such gallantry," Lady Angela said dryly, then turned to Brien. "Forgive me, dear Brien, but it seems you will be sailing with Aaron Durham. He's . . . well, he's . . ." She looked to Lord Emery to finish for her.

"Smart. Fiercely independent. And infamous with the ladies," he supplied.

Those were hardly the words *she* would use to describe the wretch she knew as Aaron Durham, Brien thought, taking refuge in a shocked silence that would seem understandable from any point of view.

"Do you think it wise for Brien to sail with him?" Lady Angela asked her husband.

"The man honors his word, my dear. Not a man in Bristol would deny that. And Lady Brien has brought her own ample escort. She will be as safe on board his ship as she is in our own house."

"Captain Durham," the butler announced from the door. A tall, broad-shouldered form swung into the room and paused casually just inside the archway. His gaze flowed over the others and came to rest boldly on Brien.

"Good evening."

Forgetting herself, Brien shot to her feet, causing the men who were seated to thrust to their feet with consternation on their faces. Appalled by her gaffe, she fixed her gaze on the impeccable black broadcloth and gray-blue vest that covered his broad chest, pasted a determined smile on her face, and refused to allow another single hint of her shock to escape.

And shock it was. The man who had pretended to marry

her and swindled her out of thousands of pounds was greeting her host and his guests as old acquaintances. She was slated to sail across the Atlantic with him—thrust into his greedy, unscrupulous clutches for a second time! She fought a rising tide of panic as he worked his way around the room to her; every breath required alarming effort.

At last he stood in front of her, reaching for her hand and brushing it with his lips. Every eye in the room was fixed on them as he straightened, raked her with a thorough glance, and produced a lazy smile.

"Delighted to meet you, Lady Brien." The sound of her name on his lips sent a tingle along her limbs and she jerked her hand back.

"And you, Mister Durham. Or is that *Captain* Durham?" She moved immediately to Angela's chair and leaned against the side of it to steady herself. Her carefully knit composure was coming apart at the seams.

"Whatever you prefer, madame." The warmth of his gaze gave the reply an appalling seductive quality.

"My preference would be to sail for the colonies on one of Weston Trading's own vessels." She saw the flicker of dismay in Angela's face and added shakily: "But I am grateful Lord Emery has managed to secure passage for me on so short a notice."

"When Lord Emery related your predicament, madame"— he nodded with deference to their host—"I could not resist. I am ever accommodating to ladies in need."

A startled giggle escaped Angela and was quickly silenced by a dour look from Lady Evelyn Clermont.

In the silence that fell, Brien made herself look at him and compare him to the man in her memory, determined to find differences. But he looked just as she remembered—the same angular features and tanned skin, the same scar on his cheek, the same mobile and expressive lips. And his eyes— She had convinced herself that such eyes were impossible, that she remembered them wrong, and saw now that she had recalled them with uncanny accuracy. Gold and clear. Like the finest Baltic amber. It had taken months of quelling troubled dreams and purging unwanted flashes of remembrance to undo the impact those eyes had made on her senses, and now a moment in his presence brought it all back with a vengeance.

It was him, all right.

Curse his black heart.

She jerked her gaze away and inserted her fluttering fan between the bare skin of her breast and his focused attention.

"This ship of yours, Aaron," Lord Emery forayed into the silence, "tell us about her. I hear she is quite remarkable." Brien was surprised to hear Emery call him by his given name, according him deference due an equal when he was ... Devil take him, she didn't know what he was. Didn't know the first thing about him. And she had married—*tried to marry*—him and had allowed him to—

"Yes, quite remarkable," Aaron mused, gazing unabashedly at Brien. "She has three main masts and a shallow draft— by British standards. Her hull is V-shaped. I designed her with cabins for passengers as well as cargo holds."

"You think there will be increased travel and trade with the colonies, then?" Brigadier Jeremy Wilton raised an eyebrow.

"Undoubtedly." Durham leaned one shoulder against the mantelpiece and openly appraised the young nobleman. "With common language, heritage, and goals—the two nations stand to gain far more by cooperation than by conflict."

"Nations?" Wilton gave a snort of derision. "I would hardly call that motley consortium of farmers and shopkeepers a nation."

Brien was relieved that this thinly disguised challenge diverted Durham's attention. He seemed in no hurry to embarrass her by recalling their former meeting, but his smug expression said he certainly intended to do so before the night was over.

His smile bordered on the sardonic. "They have promise. They fight well for shopkeepers and ignorant farmers. I was on one of the ships taken down by their elusive John Paul Jones." His hand went up to signal for a truce as Wilton drew breath for a hot reply. "The battles have been amply fought already, Brigadier, and there are far more entertaining pastimes at hand." He flashed a disarming smile at Angela, who blushed. "Is that not so, my lady?"

"Quite right," she agreed, and the subject was closed.

"About your ship, Captain Durham," Lady Evelyn broke in. "I understand she was christened *The Lady's Secret*."

"A provocative name," Angela teased. "Have you many ladies' secrets in your keeping, Captain?"

"Every true lady has some secrets, madame." He glanced at Brien, who coincidentally lowered her head and plied her fan. "And I have met quite a number of ladies over the years."

Brien hoped no one heard her groan.

At dinner, Brien found herself seated opposite Aaron Durham and forced to endure his relentless inspection and increasingly pointed comments . . . each of which threatened a revelation of what had passed between them.

Why couldn't she just faint or come down with a pounding headache?

Because that was the coward's way out and—truth be told—the glint in his eyes said that he would make her life a torment if she didn't deal forcefully with him from the start. If she tried to beg off or even to find another passage, there would be questions she wasn't prepared to answer. Still, if she went through with it, she would have to suffer his presence and perhaps be at his mercy for an entire voyage.

Angela canted a look her way and Brien realized that she revealed too much by her silence and avoidance of the wretch's gaze. She could not shrink from this challenge and survive. Drawing a deep breath, she sat straighter and fired her first volley.

"Since I will be sailing with you, Captain, I believe I am entitled to know your qualifications. After all, there are unscrupulous people about, passing themselves off as things they are not." She smiled emphatically as she read the surprise in his face.

"Really, Lady Brien, I can personally vouch for—" Lord Emery tried to intercede.

"No, no—I insist on answering," Durham declared with a pacifying wave. "It is only fair that the lady know the qualifications of the man with whom she will spend many a starlit night at sea." His smile carried a taunt that made her face flame.

"I left the university at nineteen to join the navy, alas, without a bought commission. I served aboard revenue cutters, frigates, and eventually a man-of-war, winning a commission and rising to the rank of captain. Not long ago, I came unexpectedly into some money and decided to pursue my lifelong dream of building ships. My naval experience gave me insight into what would improve ship design and I was eager to try out my ideas. My ship was launched a month past, sailed from London to Bristol to take on cargo and make final adjustments for her maiden voyage."

"You are too modest, Captain," Lady Angela began. "Your background—"

"Is of no consequence to me now," he interrupted, but so smoothly that his hostess merely smiled and shook her head. "I have no contact with my family and intend to keep it that way." He turned to Brien. "And what of you, my lady? Have you a family? Children?"

"Lady Brien is a widow," Lady Evelyn contributed in subdued tones.

"Indeed?" Durham studied her for a moment before nodding with an enigmatic little smile. "Condolences, my lady."

"It was some time ago, Captain." She felt her skin prickle

under the accusation cloaked by his look. "I am content to live with my father now and care for him."

"But don't think for a moment she is a recluse," Angela said, imbibing more wine. "She stays quite busy."

"Busy evading suitors," Charlotte Wilton said with a giggle. She was apparently sliding into her cups as well.

"I've made it no secret that I harbor no desire for another bout of matrimony," Brien declared firmly, avoiding her nemesis's amusement.

"You speak of it as if it were the ague." Angela laughed.

"Oh, but marriage and the ague are very much alike." Brien narrowed her eyes in defiant emphasis. "Both require a woman to spend a great deal of time in bed."

Lord Emery let out a hoot of surprised laughter and the others joined him a heartbeat later. When she looked his way, Aaron Durham was watching her with reappraisal in his expression. With that riposte she served notice that she was no longer the desperate and vulnerable young woman he had met near the London docks, and he seemed to have gotten the message.

"Surely you will remarry, Lady Brien," Emery said as he sobered. "You are too lovely, too full of life not to embrace all that this mortal coil has to offer. There will surely come a time when you wish to have children. . . ."

"Who can say what desires and wishes time will bring, my lord?" she responded from the depths of her heart. "Fate is fickle and enjoys a jest on us all now and then. I refrain from testing her favor whenever possible."

"A philosopher as well." Aaron Durham studied her with deepening interest. "My lady, there is more to you than meets the eye."

"Be careful, Aaron," Emery warned, "or you may find out how much!"

The others laughed raucously, delighted by this tête-à-tête at her expense. The beauty and the beast paired and evenly matched.

Brien was vastly relieved when Aaron Durham declared he must leave early owing to pressing business the next morning. Her hand was the only one he failed to take before departing. She was torn between irrational disappointment and relief at being spared that test of her composure.

He had no sooner departed than Charlotte scoffed, "Captain Durham certainly lived up to his reputation this evening." She turned to Brien. "I do hope he didn't embarrass you too much, my dear. He is a bit of a rake."

"Charlotte!" Jeremy Wilton scolded. "Lady Brien need not hear such gossip."

"It's more common knowledge than gossip," Angela put in. "Everyone knows his reckless behavior has strained his relations with his family." She turned to Brien and took her by the hands. "You see, Aaron Durham is no ordinary sea captain. He's the eldest son of the earl of Wilton."

"Eldest son? You mean heir to a title?" She looked from Angela to Emery. "But he captains a ship. How can that be?"

"He does so because he loves ships and the sea. Before he ran off to join the navy, he seemed determined to flout his father's rule—and debauch half the maids in Cardiff and Bristol." Angela waved aside her husband's sputter of disapproval. "He seems to truly enjoy women and—in truth—women seem to find him irresistible."

"I hope you will forgive me for putting you in such a delicate position, Lady Brien," Emery declared in a way that made it impossible to resist his apology. "But I honestly believe you will have a safe and comfortable passage to the colonies on Durham's ship. Knowing that his actions will be scrutinized and reported, he will certainly behave in a circumspect manner. I'd stake my life on it."

Brien made her way upstairs later, numb with fatigue and the constant tension of the evening. Aaron Durham had barely behaved within the bounds of convention, even under the scrutiny of a noble audience. Despite Lord Emery's assurances, there would be no check on his behavior at sea. And the glint in his eyes said he would be harder to rebuff with his own deck under his feet.

She rubbed the back of her neck as she opened the door to her room. Jeannie had been ordered not to wait up for her and she faced her evening toilette alone. Eyes downcast, nerves frayed and twitching with unspent tension, she plopped down on the bench in front of the vanity and slipped out of her shoes. With a sigh she closed her eyes, rubbed one foot over the other, and massaged her aching shoulders.

"Would you like me to rub it for you?" A deep voice rumbled behind her.

She whirled about to find Aaron Durham sprawled on his side across her shadow-draped bed.

"You!" she exclaimed, rising. "How did you get—what are you doing here?"

"Is that any way to greet an old *husband*?"

She blanched with indignation. "Get out this minute or—"

"Or what? You'll scream?" The only part of him that moved was his mouth . . . which curled into a fierce little smile. "I have something to say and I'll not leave until I've said it. But if you feel the need to explain me to your friends, by all means." He swept a hand toward the door. "I'd love to watch."

"How dare you come here?"

"How dare *you* declare me a Frenchman and then conveniently kill me off?" He snapped upright, a fierce light ignited in his eyes.

"I did no such thing," she snapped, backing a step. "But what right would you have to complain if I did? You who gulled me out of thousands of pounds—that money you 'unexpectedly came into'—and left me at the mercy of—" Outrage gave way to alarm inside her and she mentally measured the distance to the door. "If you think to extort more money from me—"

"I'm not here for your money, my lady." He rolled from the bed and when he stood up, she felt as if the air had been sucked from the room. She had trouble getting her breath. "I want to know why you've declared me dead."

"I didn't declare *you* dead. My husband—the man I married shortly after you and your cohorts betrayed me—died in a fire almost two years ago."

"Betrayed you?" He planted his hands on his hips and leaned back on one leg, looking bemused. "You married someone else shortly after speaking vows with me, and you accuse *me* of betrayal? Lady, look to the beam in your own eye."

"I married Raoul Trechaud because there was no record of the vows we spoke or of the vicar who presided over them. The Bishop of London himself said that the Church of St. Agrippa of the Apostles had been closed for two years before that night. The whole thing was a fabrication. A fake. A sham." She stalked toward him with her hands curled into fists at her sides. "Don't insult me by pretending that you weren't in on the swindle."

"I wasn't in on anyth—" He halted, searching her anger and finding it all too real. "You're serious. You think the marriage was all a dodge and I was part of the scheme."

"I don't think it, I know it. My father went to the church himself and the place was empty and locked tight. He asked around and no one had ever heard of a 'Reverend Stephenson.' He managed to get inside and search the parish register himself. There was no mention of the vows we spoke that night."

He studied her for a moment, allowing the ramifications of the news to unfold in his mind. That night at the church she had said she married him in order to forestall marriage to another. Curiosity about why she had been so determined to avoid that marriage had deviled him in the wee hours of many a night since. Her plan apparently hadn't worked. After her father brought news that *their* vows were invalid, she was forced to marry the very man that she had tried so desperately to avoid.

"I cannot speak for the others' honesty or intentions, but I assure you, I had no knowledge of, nor would I have participated in, a fraudulent wedding. I believed then—I still believe—that we were legally and morally bound by the words we spoke that night. If that is not so, it is news to me as much as it was to you."

"You expect me to believe you weren't in league with 'Uncle Billy Rye'?"

"I swear to you, I had never met him before that night." His face grew somber. "An hour before we arrived at the church together, I sent his partner—apparently the man he intended for you—sprawling senseless onto a tavern floor. He asked me a number of questions and when he learned I needed money and wasn't married, he made me a proposition. I had no desire for a marriage, but I desperately needed the money. So I agreed to his plan and said I would say vows . . . *if I liked what I saw when we reached the church.*"

Brien searched his angular face, wanting that to be the truth and bewildered by her weakness in wanting it. He was a blackguard and a cad, a seagoing Lothario with a pack of eager females in every port. He would probably say anything to pacify her and keep her from revealing to his respectable acquaintances the source of the money that had made his precious new ship possible.

"And I did like what I saw," he said softly, moving closer.

His unusual eyes filled with light from the flickering candles, and the movements of his big, well-knit body were lithe and assured. A frisson of what could only be called excitement raced through her shoulders. Every line, every motion of him recalled forbidden knowledge of the pleasure that had sealed their faithless marriage bargain.

"Nothing you can say will make me believe you didn't know the vows were false," she said, her throat dry and her voice a whisper.

"Then I won't say that," he responded, edging still closer. "I'll say instead that the vows were anything but false. The promises I spoke were made with true and honorable intent. So unless you plighted your troth with malice of deception in *your* heart—"

"You know I did not."

"Then we both spoke earnest and binding vows before God Almighty. We are married, my lady. Always have been. If anyone has dishonored those vows it was you, with your bigamous second marriage."

She staggered back a step, astonished by his claim and its resulting charge against her. That he might uphold their vows and insist they were truly and still married, was the last thing she would have expected!

"You're mad."

"On the contrary. I am the very pinnacle of logic and reason." He produced a defiantly pleasant smile. "And temperance. What other man, upon learning that his wife had wedded someone else, would be so willing to forgive and forget?"

"I did not— We are not now, nor have we ever been legally married!"

"I beg to differ. If you will recall, that night I inquired as to what constituted a legal marriage."

"The man was a fraud, a charlatan—he might have said anything to—"

"As it happens, I made inquiries of a trusted cleric since then. It seems our questionable vicar was truthful on at least that account. A legal marriage requires three things in British common law: consent, witnessed promises, and consummation. We fulfilled all three requirements. Rather thoroughly, as I recall." His gaze sent a trill of sensual panic through her as it swept her from head to toe. "We are now and have always been legally and morally wedded. What we are lacking, it seems, is documentation."

Alarm shot through her. "You wouldn't." Oh, but he

NOT QUITE MARRIED ∽ 137

would. "You cannot possibly think to press a claim of— I warn you, you'll not have another cent from me!" She was suddenly quaking with fury.

"Money? You think that is what this is about?" He laughed softly. "Ah, my lady. You disparage both the refinement of my tastes and the abundance of your charms, to imply that money is my only motivation." He edged closer and she backed away by the same amount.

"I saw you at New Year's, in London." His tone softened, becoming intimate. He took another step closer, but this time she was too absorbed in what he was saying to counter his movement. "Hearing you were a widow, I decided you must have good reason for killing me off and decided to let the past lie."

It *had* been him!

"But now we have been thrown together again. The fates must find us an entertaining combination. And as a charming lady once advised . . . it is always wise to avoid questioning fate's choices for us. Especially when those choices are so full of pleasurable possibilities."

She fought a treacherous surge of warmth. His presence seemed to envelop her, flooding her senses, causing her to look up into his face. He was so near. So male. So very different from the men she had met in London's powdered and posturing society.

In the last twenty months, she had chided and berated herself for giving in to his callous manipulations after their vows. How could she have surrendered her body, her pride, her virtue to a total stranger? Now she had the answer. He hadn't seemed like a stranger to her.

In the lengthening silence, as she stared at him and he at her, she had that same sense of familiarity that went far beyond what she had actually experienced with him. Their gazes met and she felt a pull of longing deep in her chest. Shocked and suddenly frightened by the need blooming in her, she drew back.

"What's past is past," she declared, burying her hands in the sides of her skirts and seizing handfuls of silk . . . squeezing . . . trying to control the trembling of her hands. "We shall forget it."

"How, sweet lady, do you propose I forget the sight of you tousled and half-naked, bathed in the gold of candlelight? How do I erase the memory of your silky heat against my belly and—"

"Stop!" she cried, wishing she could stop herself from feeling warmer and more susceptible by the moment. "If you have any thought of climbing into my bed because of our regrettable history, you'll do well to rid yourself of it right now."

"A bit late for that, isn't it?" he said, leading her gaze with his to the bed that still bore the imprint of his body. "I have already been there."

"Out! Get out before I call for help." Her eyes burned and her palm itched for contact with his smug face.

"It will be interesting to see how long it takes for you to change your mind." He raked her body visually. "We'll have several long weeks," he continued, drawing an arch overhead with one hand, "with a canopy of stars overhead and the gentle sway of the ship under your"—his hand moved in an arc that suggested her lower contours—"bed."

She stood fighting for control and lost. "Out!"

She stalked toward him, and he retreated to the open window with a wolfish grin.

"Oh, and since you value your honor so highly, I suggest you leave that dress at home." He sat on the sill and paused to give the neckline of her fashionable burgundy silk an appreciative glance before swinging his legs over the ledge. "It has one hell of an effect. Wear it on board, and I'll not be answerable for the conduct of my crew."

"*Get out!*"

She seized pillows from the bed and flung them against the edge of the window, just missing him as he slipped over the edge of the sill. As the sounds of him scrambling across the roof faded, she slammed the window shut and latched it securely. She held up her hands and stared in disbelief at the way they trembled. One night . . . a few fiery words exchanged . . . and she was steaming hot and quaking all over with confusion.

How would she ever survive a whole month at sea?

Thirteen

T HE MORNING THEY SAILED, Lord Emery escorted
Brien's party to their ship and supervised the loading of
their trunks and baggage. *The Lady's Secret* was a hive of activity. Dockhands streamed up the gangplank rolling barrels
and hauling baskets, crates, and boxes of provisions onto
the deck and below; crewmen climbed up into the rigging to
check every line and lashing; and a huge wooden boom was
swinging and lowering pallets and bales into the hold.
Everywhere there were men and cargo in motion. The
sights and sounds of preparing a ship for sea had become familiar to Brien over the last year, but would never be routine to her. Her heart beat faster and her senses sharpened as
they mounted the gangplank and called for permission to
board.

They were met at the ship's railing by a young man in a
crisp blue officer's uniform. He identified himself as Robert

Hicks, *The Lady's Secret's* first officer. His unruly brown hair and lively eyes gave him a youthful and pleasant appearance.

"We are honored, my lady. When the captain related to me that we would have passengers on this maiden voyage, he neglected to mention that they would be so lovely."

"I am sure your captain has more important things on his mind." Brien caught his use of the plural and turned to look at her maid, who was blushing. "May we walk about on deck until we are under sail?"

"Of course. The view will be better from the quarter-deck." Hicks swept a hospitable hand toward the steps to the upper deck at the rear of the vessel.

Lord Emery escorted Brien and Jeannie to the designated deck, safely out of the way of the loading operation, and stayed with them for a time, pointing out interesting details of the ships and harbor. Later, as Lord Emery strode along the dock to his waiting coach, Brien felt a bit abandoned and looked anxiously around her.

It struck her, a moment later, that she was looking for Aaron Durham. Annoyed, she straightened her shoulders and told herself firmly that it was a relief not to find him. But she glimpsed Jeannie's pale and tight-lipped face, and the strain in the little maid's countenance reminded her that she was responsible for more than herself on this trip. And her mission, their safety, and probably their very lives depended on Aaron Durham's competence and integrity. And she had no idea whether she could count on him for either.

She smoothed her soft woolen dress beneath her cloak, as if it might quell the jitters in her stomach. It didn't. Then she spotted Dyso perched on the forecastle railing, watching the loading and studying the crew. His quick, dark eyes didn't miss much, Brien knew, and he was loyal to a fault and deeply protective of her. His solid and dependable presence was all that allowed her to manage the anxiety climbing up her throat. If things with Aaron Durham became intolerable, there would always be Dyso.

While Brien strolled the quarterdeck, Aaron Durham took in her every move from a vantage point atop a dwindling stack of crates on the dock. His eyes narrowed as they flitted over her form, all but hidden beneath the substantial dark wool of traveling garments. His mouth curled into a half-smile. What did it matter how she dressed? The image of her as she was the other night—ripe and luscious, wrapped in an air of hauteur, spilling over a wine-colored silk—was burned into his brain.

For nearly two years she had deviled his every idle thought, growing steadily more lush and tender and sweetly melancholy in his memory. He realized with a scowl that he had allowed her to twine about his imaginings and grow into a virgin temptress who sought out his every need and eagerly fulfilled his desires.

Seeing her in the flesh in London had set him reeling. The focus of his desires had a different form and a decidedly more uncooperative nature than he recalled. Now she had not only a name and a delectable body, but also a formidable wit, an indomitable spirit, and an even more tumultuous history than he had guessed.

No—he rubbed his chin thoughtfully—this was not his private mistress. When he faced her in the Devons' drawing room, he had been stunned by her impact. Every line and curve of her body, every sweep of her lashes, every gesture of her hands reminded him of some half-forgotten element of the pleasure he had experienced with her. His wraithlike "virgin"—the sweet, vulnerable inhabitant of his dreams— was swept away in a heartbeat and replaced by this tantalizing woman of earth and warmth.

Even now his breath was quickening and there was a tightening in his loins. His eagerness for her was unsettling. How much of his fascination with her, he wondered, was caused by the fact that for nearly two years he had believed she was his wife?

That had nothing to do with it. He'd never wanted a wife, had actively avoided all associations and entanglements that might result in such a tie. Hell, he'd thrown the family title in his father's teeth to avoid being saddled with a pedigreed brood mare! Why was he so unwilling to accept her story about the fraudulent vows and nonexistent vicar?

Because he didn't know if it were true or not, he told himself. How could he go about the rest of his life without knowing whether or not he was married? Her story about the missing records and a scheme to swindle her sounded a bit too convenient . . . like something crafted to throw doubt on whatever claims he might press with her. After all, she had wealth, rank, and social position . . . any number of desirable assets.

He was jarred from those thoughts by a cry from the deck to load the last of the cargo—the very crates on which he sat. Climbing down from his perch, he watched Robert Hicks escort Brien and her maid toward their cabins and smiled to himself.

There was only one thing he wanted from Lady Brien Weston Trechaud. And it had nothing to do with her wealth, rank, or social position.

BRIEN'S THOUGHTS WERE still on the whereabouts of the ship's captain as she followed the *Secret's* first officer down the steps to the passengers' quarters. Managing a small jewelry case with one hand and her skirts with the other, she quickly found herself trapped halfway down the steep, narrow steps by her hoops and panniers. The metal bands tilted and scraped along the walls, raising her skirts behind her and binding her legs in front so that every step forward and downward was a battle. Mr. Hicks, who had descended ahead of her, emitted a strangled noise that probably had

begun as a laugh and Jeannie, descending behind her carrying hatboxes and personal items, gasped in horror and tried
to help her mistress.

"Never mind," Brien muttered furiously. "I'll do it."

Halting, she backed up two steps, seized the metal bands,
and squeezed them flat at her sides, causing ripping, popping
sounds and setting her skirts billowing wildly in front and
back. Her face caught fire. Mr. Hicks, standing on the steps
below, was undoubtedly treated to quite a show. She scraped
and bounced her way down to the landing and turned to
proceed down the few remaining steps. Just as she reached
the main floor of the common room, she was yanked back
forcibly by her garments—"Ahhhh!"—flailed, and dropped
her jewel case, which tumbled across the inner deck.

She regained her balance and looked up to find her hoop
caught on the wooden knob at the top of the landing railing. Mortified now, her rear exposed and her movement
hindered by the skirts twisted about her, she heard an
amused chuckle from the top of the stairs, that grew to rich,
deep male laughter. Aaron Durham descended the steps to
relieve Jeannie of her boxes so she could help her mistress.

When Brien reached the common room and allowed her
skirts to billow normally again, she was horrified to find that
they filled almost a quarter of the modest room. She
wheeled on Aaron with her eyes flashing.

"You take strange amusement in others' misfortunes, sir,"
she declared, then turned on Mr. Hicks. "Lead on."

Fighting her way down another narrow passage and
through an even narrower door to her cabin, she was relieved to find the cabin itself large enough to permit her
skirts to billow out once more.

"This will be your cabin, my lady. I hope you will be comfortable here." He turned to Jeannie. "If you will follow me,
miss? Your cabin is at the end of the passage."

"Why is her cabin not by mine?" Brien demanded angrily.

"The captain assigns cabins, my lady. You will have to speak to him about that."

She groaned in frustration, staring at the door where they had disappeared. A moment later, Aaron Durham, clad in a partly open white shirt, dark breeches, and tall black boots, stuck his head through the cabin doorway.

"My lady, if you continue to wear those hoops aboard this vessel, my men will be greatly amused. And I suspect you will be most uncomfortable. I suggest you pack them away until we dock in Boston."

His presence filled the room and she drew her shoulders up sharply to counter it.

"It is clear I've begun to learn lessons of life at sea," she said irritably. "And why can't my maid have the next cabin instead of one at the far end of the passage?"

"Because, my lady, the next cabin is the captain's." He gave her a wicked grin as he ducked back out the door.

He had arranged to have her isolated from her servants, in a cabin beside his? Slamming the door shut, she jerked up her skirts and tore at the ties of her petticoats. Seconds later the doomed hoop lay at her feet and she gave it a kick, wishing it were part of the captain's anatomy.

The gentle rolling of the ship as they got under way calmed Brien's ruffled nerves. But as they met the churning waters of the Atlantic, the swaying increased and she began to learn the true meaning of the term *mal de mer.* She was grateful for the windows that admitted fresh air and light. She lay down briefly on the narrow bunk and found it only made her feel worse.

Then Mr. Hicks knocked on the door to call her to dinner in the common room. Her pale, drawn face and tight lips drew a sympathetic look and a suggestion that she keep something in her stomach and stay upright until she adjusted to the ship's movement. He offered to bring her some crackers and when he returned with them, she thanked him, closed the door, and propped herself upright beside the small window, drinking in fresh air and regretting every prideful and materialistic impulse she had ever harbored—especially those responsible for this trip.

Early the next morning, Brien was awakened by First Officer Hicks, knocking on the door with a tray of food and news that Jeannie was quite ill. She thanked him for his gentlemanly offer to look after the maid, but insisted she would see to the girl herself. At his suggestion, she ate some of the porridge, jam, and tea he had brought her, feeling the stronger for it. As she dressed—cursing the tyranny of fashion and finally dispensing with a corset she couldn't tighten by herself—she realized her head was clear, her stomach was quiet, and she was much steadier on her feet.

Jeannie's small cabin reeked of sickness when Brien entered. She set about opening the window, emptying the chamber pot, and then washing the little maid's ashen face. Jeannie groaned weakly and apologized again and again as Brien helped her change into a clean nightdress and sat down on the edge of the bunk to brush out the girl's hair.

"You concentrate on getting well. I'll manage on my own for a few days." She smiled, but poor Jeannie only groaned and was sick again. Alarmed, she went to the common room, where she found Mr. Hicks drinking coffee before his watch began.

"I need a pint of strong rum, Mr. Hicks, and quickly."

He looked at her in disbelief. "Really, my lady, I-I don't know if . . ."

"It's for Miss Trowbridge. She is quite ill and in need of a strong sedative to help her rest. Now, will you get it for me, or shall I find the captain?"

Hicks soon secured a full tankard of potent, uncut rum for her. She moved carefully back down the passage with it, but just as she opened Jeannie's door, the ship pitched violently, she was thrown against the doorframe, and she spilled it down the front of her dress. Undaunted, she poured some for the girl and helped her to drink it.

This had been Ella's remedy for an upset stomach. A liberal dose of whiskey or strong brandy and sweet sleep. Perhaps it would work on Jeannie.

She sat with Jeannie for a while, then felt her way back down the passage to her own cabin. As she made to enter, the door to the next cabin swung open and Aaron Durham stepped out into the passage.

"My lady," he addressed her and she looked up. "You are a constant surprise. At this hour of the morning, to smell as though you've bathed in rum . . ."

A moment later she was safely inside her cabin, leaning back against the closed door. The wretch. He meant to taunt and torture her with verbal thumbscrews.

The next morning she ventured up on deck for the first time since sailing. Without Jeannie to help, she had managed to put her hair up in a braided loop at the back of her head. Without hoops her skirts were too long, and she had pinned them up under the sides into false panniers. Her petticoats were visible, but that was preferable to tripping constantly over her skirts. It was a great relief to be up in the cool sea air. She felt the breeze pulling the pall of illness from her and freshening her spirits.

Above her, at the wheel, Aaron Durham watched her turn her face to the sun and drink in the cool, crisp sea air. Her hair was a tawny gold in the sunlight, and in her plain, blue dress and large knitted shawl, she might have passed for a country girl on market day. He felt a stab of regret at his earlier taunt. She fared better than most women did at sea. She had gotten her sea legs quickly and had even found a way to stylishly surmount the problem of those bulky skirts.

"Hicks," he called. "Take over." In a minute he was down the steps to the main deck and making straight for her.

She watched the sea, seeming fascinated by the rising and falling of the waves and the endless sky overhead. He stood beside her a full moment before she realized he was there, and glanced over at him.

"How do you like my ocean?" He leaned his elbows on the rail beside her.

"It is magnificent," she said simply, refusing to address his claim.

He was silent for a moment, then turned from the sea to watch her instead. "I'm glad to see that you're feeling better." He glanced up. "It looks like the good weather will hold for a while. We're making good time."

"We can't get there a moment too soon," she muttered.

"I meant to ask . . . what takes you to Boston in such a hurry?"

She thought for a moment, then turned to study him as he leaned against the rail. "I have urgent business there. One of Weston Trading's mercantile ventures has proved unprofitable." She paused, searching his face for mockery or disbelief. When she found none, some of her defensiveness faded. "The colonial assemblies have made it impossible for us to collect on accounts and conduct business with any degree of confidence. I will look for a cash buyer and divest Weston Trading of its American holdings."

"I've heard of the assemblies' cancellation of debts. Unfortunate." He rubbed his chin and tilted his head to study her from another angle. "You take part in your father's company, then?"

"Is that so strange?" Her defenses came up quickly and she crossed her arms.

"Yes, frankly. For a woman of your rank and wealth—"

"To be interested in anything but gowns and parties and gossip is unheard of?"

"For a woman of your station to be interested in commerce, much less traveling across the ocean to conduct business transactions, is highly unusual. As you well know." He studied her. "How did you come to be involved in the trading business?"

"After Raoul—since the death of my husband, my father has taken me under his wing and taught me commerce and finance." She looked out to sea, turning only her eyes back to him. "I've been interested in trade since I was a little girl. He used to take me with him sometimes when one of his ships returned home. I got to see the cargoes being unloaded and hear his discussions with his captains. I never forgot the sights, the smells, and the excitement. My father indulges me."

"But it hasn't always been so," he prompted with a light scowl.

"No, we were not close for several years." She made a rueful smile. "But I am all the family he has left, and since my husband—"

"He forced you to wed the Frenchman," he declared, feeling a turbulence stirring his insides at the thought of anyone forcing her to do anything.

"The details of my marriage are none of your business," she said, straightening, her openness abruptly closing.

"You said that you married me to keep from having to marry another. You married the Frenchman so quickly after . . . it must have been him you tried to avoid."

"Keep your conjectures to yourself, Captain. I owe you no explanations."

"They say he was handsome." He stepped closer, his expression sober and his unusual eyes glowing with intensity. "Was he?"

Brien refused to back away . . . whether from determination to stand up to him or a reckless desire to be close to him, she didn't know. All she could think was that those eyes that were so clear and so readable, were also tinged visibly with *green*. Suddenly she understood. He wanted to know if Raoul had bedded her. Because of what they did that night, he felt he had a claim on her, that part of her somehow belonged to him.

The bastard.

"Yes. He was handsome." She set her jaw and spoke from between clenched teeth. "And determined. And loathsome."

She backed away now . . . in disdain, not retreat. "But he taught me a valuable lesson. It is not what is on the outside of a man that matters, but what is inside. Put another way, handsome is as handsome *does*." She raked him with a searing look. "You know, I hadn't seen it until now . . . You resemble Raoul a great deal." She pulled her shawl tighter around her. "Now, if you'll excuse me, I believe I should check on my patient."

Stung by her declaration, he watched with his ears burning and his fists clenched until she disappeared down the hatch. Until that moment he hadn't given thought to what it must have been like for her when her scheme failed. She'd been forced to marry a man she detested and tried desperately to avoid. "Loathsome," she had said. What would it take for a legendarily handsome man to make himself loathsome to a woman—his own bride, at that? Grasping . . . manipulating . . . taking what she didn't want to give . . .

She had just served notice that she didn't see any difference between him and the man she had been forced to marry. Setting aside his qualms about his own earlier motives toward her, he decided there was a world of difference and he determined to show it to her.

As he turned from the railing he caught sight of Brien's protector, Dyso, sitting on a crate not far away, staring intently at him. He was not used to looking up to other men, and he found it unsettling to be in the presence of a man so much larger and more physically powerful than himself. The hulk's eyes darted toward the hatch where Brien had disappeared and then back to Aaron, narrowing slightly. But when Aaron blinked and focused, that hint of an expression was gone. He felt the big man's gaze following him as he mounted the steps to the quarterdeck and took his post beside the wheel.

The next morning Brien rose early to walk on deck in the chill of early morning. Opening her door, she gasped. Dyso lay on the floor just outside the raised sill, with a blanket as his only comfort.

He started up as the door opened and looked at her, then got up slowly and wrapped the blanket into a ball.

"Dyso, have you been there all night?" He nodded and looked down, whether from anxiety or embarrassment, she could not tell.

"Why don't you sleep in your cabin?" She feared she already knew.

One of his massive hands gestured toward the next door. Aaron Durham's cabin. Then he brought his fists together in a pounding motion and swept them open toward her.

She knew. "It's all right, Dyso. No one here would hurt me." She put one hand on his arm, hoping she spoke the truth. "I lock the cabin door at night. Please sleep in your cabin where you'll be more comfortable."

But he shook his head sharply and moved quickly up the passageway to the steps.

That night after Brien had gone to bed, she heard a quiet thump on the floor outside her door. Dyso had resumed his vigil. Her smile was bittersweet. There could be such a thing as too much protection.

Fourteen

AFTER A FULL WEEK of sitting sedately in her cabin and Jeannie's, tending to her patient and reading over and over the thin volumes of poetry and essays she had brought with her, Brien was slowly going mad from boredom. And by Mr. Hicks's most optimistic assessment, they still had two full weeks to go. Almost as desperate for diversion as she was to avoid Aaron Durham, she approached Mr. Hicks about possible reading matter.

"No shortage of books on board the *Secret*, my lady. Come with me."

He led her straight to Aaron Durham's door and beckoned her inside. The captain's cabin was spacious and elegantly appointed . . . polished teak paneling, mahogany furnishings, silver candlesticks, and soft, well-tended linen. Along one wall was a series of cabinets that included a wardrobe and chart drawers, and on the facing side were two broad sets of shelves from ceiling to floor . . . filled with books.

"Heavens." She ran her fingers over the spines of the books, concentrating on the names and authors to keep herself from greedily drinking in the rest of the cabin. This was the home away from home he had created for himself, the place where he kept his possessions . . . the space where he thought and slept and worked and dreamed. It was a revealing expression of his personal taste and habits. Being there felt to her like stepping into his boots or sleeping in his—

"Quite a collection to find on a ship in the middle of the ocean." She couldn't take her fingers from the tooled and gold-stamped leather of the bindings. "Perhaps I should wait and ask—oooh, Jonathan Swift!" She slid a volume from the shelf and turned it over and over in her hands.

"Oh, the captain won't mind, my lady. He allows anyone in the crew who can read to borrow a book."

"He does?"

"He does. And I can't imagine he would deny you the same privilege."

She looked up at the genial Mr. Hicks's face and hoped her confusion wasn't too evident. Books. He read and owned books and lent them to others. Poetry. Essays. Histories. A rush of memories of days ensconced in the library at Byron Place came over her. She had tended and expanded the wonderful library her father had begun there, and the books had become her intellectual companions. Her throat tightened at the realization that her books were yet another loss in her life, one she had yet to reckon with.

She opened the handsome vellum pages, stared with burning eyes at the rich black print of the opening page. She gave a sigh. It felt as if something parched and dry inside her were being watered. The moisture in her eyes kept her from seeing the way Mr. Hicks slid a chair from the table across the floor to her, but she heard the dragging sound and felt it nudge against her skirts. Sinking into it with a grateful nod, she pored over the prose of the first page and then hurried on to the second. . . .

That was where Aaron found her some time later, in his cabin, curled up on the end of his bunk, leaning against the window with an array of volumes spread on the bed beside her. He stood for a moment in the doorway, appreciating the sight of her on his bed, sun-drenched and slightly tousled, surrounded by his books. His bed. He was surprised by a stir of internal heat.

"Find something you like?" he said, pushing off from the doorway with his shoulder and strolling toward her.

She started and looked up, jolted by her location and reddening.

"I-I . . . Mr. Hicks said I might borrow a book from your . . . and I had difficulty choosing. Then I started reading this one and needed more light . . . and . . ."

"You made yourself quite at home."

"I didn't mean to impose." As she scrambled to the edge of the bed, her skirts slid up to reveal much of her lower legs. The instant she reached the floor, she yanked them down again and snapped upright, clutching his book to her breast.

"Finding a beautiful woman curled on my bed, reading, is never an imposition."

"Nor, I would think, is it a frequent occurrence," she said tartly, eyeing the door.

He chuckled. "You have me there, my lady." He pointed to the book in her arms. "What did you find to interest you?"

"This? A book on the history and prominent families of the colony of Massachusetts. Quite recent. Just what I needed to introduce me to the people and culture of Boston."

" 'Culture' and 'Boston' used in the same sentence. Interesting." He suppressed a smile and glanced at the books on the bed beside her. "What else did you choose?"

"A volume on the development and construction of

ships. It contained a number of helpful drawings. It's no wonder that sailing takes years to learn. . . . I had no idea that each rope and square of canvas has its own name."

"Absolutely."

"And I looked through a well-used book devoted to navigation and shipboard skills, and almost went cross-eyed trying to make sense of the tables and computations."

"So did I, when I was learning navigation. It gets easier the more you work with the calculations. What else?"

"A great collection of poems and essays by Alexander Pope. Some interesting but puzzling things by Jonathan Swift. And Voltaire's *Essay on the General History* . . . shelved right next to John and Charles Wesley's family hymnals."

"I've always felt it prudent to make friends on both sides of an argument."

"Interesting." She studied him openly. "I wouldn't have expected it of you."

He chuckled, seeming more surprised than affronted. "Nor would I of you, frankly. And what degenerate taught you about the precious heretics of the Enlightenment?"

"I had an unconventional tutor for several years. My father paid him too much and asked him too few questions. My sister ignored his wayward rants and discourses, but they found fertile ground in my young mind."

"Your father educated you uncommonly well."

"A fact he was quite appalled to learn. He set out immediately to remedy my independent thinking and ways with a marriage that—" She realized with a start that he had crossed the cabin and now stood barely a foot away, looking down at her.

"That would what? Keep you in line? Make you more docile? Render you witless with domestic bliss?" His words were sardonic, but his gaze was breathtakingly gentle.

"That would make me a *mother*."

He thought for a moment, then smiled in a way that

made her knees weaken. Whatever he said next didn't matter. Her anger and indignation toward him were already melting like snow on a black slate roof, and it was probably only going to get worse.

"Ahhh. Motherhood. A bit drastic, I'll grant you. But a proven mind-duller if ever there was one." One corner of his mouth twitched. "Nasty little buggers, babies. All that crying and spitting and wetting. And talk about the *smell*." He pinched his nose with a pained expression.

She was taken so aback that she laughed out of pure shock. But as her laugh escaped, it dragged a whole string of others behind it. Her face flushed hot and she was instantly aware of every square inch of skin the neckline of her gown exposed. The vivid memory of his mouth pressed to the side of her throat flashed through her, and she sobered instantly and shivered. He noticed.

"You're horrible," she declared without much force, trying to step around him to head for the door.

"No, I'm not." He took a step to the right and cut off her retreat. "I'm curious. And stubborn. And I'm not always able to say the prudent thing rather than the reckless or irreverent thing. That, my lady, is *my* father's great burden. A son who has no reverence for empty tradition and loves to watch well-born idiots learn just how absurd they truly are. And who loves the smell of newly cut wood and freshly stitched canvas, and craves the chance to play with boats until he ripens into pruneful dotage . . . forty or fifty years hence."

Her heart was skipping frantically and her lips felt naked and prominent. He was so close and he was so utterly irresistible to her right now. That coppery hair that was slipping a bit from the cord at the nape of his neck. Those intense golden eyes that could somehow caress her skin across distances. His warm and wicked smiles that could raise gooseflesh on an anvil . . .

She was in trouble. The last thing she needed or wanted

was this sort of attraction undercutting her determination. He was, after all, the man who had extorted thousands of pounds from her while pretending to marry her. A forbidden doubt bloomed defiantly in her mind. Was it possible that he had been duped as well? That perhaps he truly had believed he was marrying her?

Then he touched her.

His hand sliding down the side of her face seemed to draw her attention, her blood, her very will to meet it. Desire erupted from the core of her . . . effervescent with memories that burst against the underside of her skin . . . preparing the way for more and shocking her enough to make her grapple for self-control. A moment later, she managed to regain power over her feet.

"Really, Captain." She stepped shakily around him and headed for the door, praying all the while that he wouldn't try to stop her.

She went straight down the passage to Jeannie's cabin and sat under the little maid's puzzled gaze, pretending to immerse herself in Jonathan Swift's *A Modest Proposal*. Her eyes widened as she forced herself to read *Babies. Again.* Inescapably her thoughts went back to Aaron Durham's sardonic words and realized how much he and Swift had in common. Interesting. Much too interesting. Against her better judgment, she found herself smiling.

THE NEXT DAY Brien was able to take Jeannie up on deck for fresh air and sunshine. Brien hoped the little maid's presence would help her forestall contact with Aaron Durham, but that was not to be. Clever man, he sent First Officer Hicks to distract Jeannie and then sidled up to Brien with a satisfied smile.

"You look happy," she said, making it sound a hanging offense.

"We're making even better time than I had hoped. You

may be on the first ship to make an Atlantic crossing in under three weeks."

She looked up, heartened by that news, and was captured momentarily by the way the wind was tugging at his hair.

"Excellent news."

"It's an excellent ship," he responded archly.

"And I suppose favorable winds have had nothing to do with it," she chided.

"Oh, they help." He smiled. "I'm always willing to give credit where it is due. Especially for good weather. But there has been good weather before, Brien, and the crossing still took a month."

She stiffened at his use of her given name and looked away, scrambling for more neutral ground between them. "So. What improvements does *The Lady's Secret* contain that make this miracle of transportation possible?"

He seemed to have been waiting for just such a question, for he immediately planted himself beside her at the quarterdeck railing and began to point out improvements. Beginning overhead, he pointed to changes in the number, design, and deployment of sails; the rigging tackle, achieving better trim; and a new mechanism for hoisting and lowering the mainsails and moving the mizzens to take advantage of changes in wind. Each improvement had something of a story behind it and, told in Aaron's dry, sardonic manner, those sidelights drew her deeper into his thinking.

Then he went on to explain changes in the ship's proportions . . . longer forward and aft, narrower abeam, with more freeboard and less draft, and a more balanced space for cargo. Refinements to the rudder resulted in more efficient steering, enabling them to employ shifting winds to better advantage. Mr. Hicks was soon drawn into the lecture, prompting him to recall things. Then they took her to the cargo hatch, where he and Hicks climbed down into the hold to point out baffles between bays filled with cargo.

Brien watched and listened, knowing as she did that her resistance to him was eroding like a beach under a storm tide. He was devoted to a very potent dream of developing linkages across the Atlantic that could help shape the fate of both Britain and the former colonies. He was intelligent and inventive, determined and resourceful, competent and—she was loath to admit it—probably dependable.

She tried to rally her resistance by reminding herself that men's behavior in professional and public life often had nothing in common with the way they conducted their private lives. Too often men saw their obligations and promises to women as optional or nonbinding. Even marriage vows—*especially* marriage vows—created a sense of duty that flowed toward men, not from them. She would do well to remember that when tempted to lose herself in Aaron Durham's all-too-appealing maleness.

THE NEXT AFTERNOON Jeannie entered her cabin with news that Mr. Hicks had announced that they would have a special dinner that evening to celebrate approaching the halfway point well ahead of schedule. Apologizing profusely for having neglected her duties, she insisted on putting Brien's hair up in a full coiffure for the evening meal in the commons.

"Shipboard is hardly the place for elegant dining," Brien protested.

"I just thought it might be nice to pin your hair up for a change. You know, you haven't worn jewelry or been out of drab traveling clothes since we started."

If Jeannie had noticed her lack of adornment, Aaron Durham probably had, too. No doubt he thought she did it to escape his notice . . . probably believed she was shrinking, cowering in fear at the thought of his irresistible manliness.

"Very well. Do it up for once." She flourished a hand.

"We won't be at sea forever. And we can't have either of us getting out of practice, can we?"

When she and Jeannie entered the commons that evening, the sun was setting. Mr. Hicks had already gone topside to check the evening watch and Aaron stood by the stern windows, dressed in his customary shirt, breeches, and boots, staring at the gold-kissed waves in the ship's wake. He turned when he heard them enter and his eyes lighted at the sight of her.

She smoothed the long waist of her emerald green cotton and allowed him to help her to the table, which had been draped with cloth and was set with a fine service.

"You are lovely this evening, Lady Brien. I hope you enjoy this special dinner to honor the maiden voyage of *The Lady's Secret*. The food may not be what you are accustomed to, but should provide a welcome change from our usual fare." He smiled broadly at Brien, produced a bottle of wine from a cabinet along the wall, and snatched four pewter cups from nearby pegs before returning to the table to pour.

"To *The Lady's Secret*." He raised his cup. "As fine a lady as I have ever sailed."

Brien scowled at the thought of how many *human* ladies he had probably "sailed." Then he sought her gaze and proposed a still more pointed toast. "To maiden voyages."

She blushed beet-red at the reminder that he had been present for her "maiden voyage" and had launched her into realms of sensation that she would rather not have experienced. She raised her own cup in retaliation.

"May *The Lady's Secret* ply the seas without fear of pirates or privateers," she declared archly, "or others who would constrain or molest her."

"You seem uncommonly preoccupied with freedom, my lady," Aaron said, weighing her words. "Can it be that you hold dangerous Whig views; or is your interest in freedom of a more personal nature?" She shifted in her chair to avoid his probing look.

NOT QUITE MARRIED   161

"Both, I think. If I wish freedom for myself, can I wish less for others?"

"A lot of people do just that," he responded. "It's interesting to hear that you are not among them. *Liberty. Equality*." He wagged his head. "Interesting talk coming from the widow of a French nobleman. You do know that such sentiments could get you arrested and executed in France just now, don't you?"

"Fortunately we are headed *west*, not east."

"Captain," Jeannie broke in. "Would you mind if I took a cup to Mr. Hicks?"

"By all means." Aaron nodded without taking his eyes from Brien.

She felt a sudden panic at being left alone with him, but had no pretext for requiring Jeannie to stay. When the maid was gone, his voice lowered and softened.

"What an interesting woman you are, Brien. You read widely, you harbor dangerous republican tendencies, and you strain your father's patience at every turn. We have a great deal in common, you and I." He pulled out a chair beside hers, but before he could sit she rose and headed for the stern windows.

"Not really, Captain." She clasped her hands tightly and straightened her spine. "We are really quite different."

"Oh? How so?"

"I should think that was obvious. I am a woman and you are a man."

He chuckled and strolled toward her at a leisurely pace. "A state of affairs that shouldn't keep us from coming to some sort of understanding."

"By which you mean: you do what you want and I *understand*."

"Ouch." He paused an arm's length away, lapped his arms over his ribs, and studied her. "You have a rather sad opinion of men, don't you?"

"A sadly realistic one. Experience has taught me that

men insist on morality when it benefits *them*. Men want their marriage vows to be binding, but only on their wives. Men strive for honesty and integrity with one another, but think that a bit of deception in dealing with wives and lovers only proves their cleverness and ingenuity. How can there be understanding between men and women if men don't consider women worth the same basic honesty they give to a stranger who sits down with them for a game of cards?"

"Surely experience has taught you more than that." A spark ignited his eyes. "Be honest yourself, my lady. Haven't you also experienced some of the companionship that men and women can bring to each other? Some of the pleasure?"

"I-If I have . . . I-I cannot recall it." She pressed back against the window seat.

"Well, I can. I remember every moment, every breath, every heartbeat of it." The low, sensual roll of his voice set her fingertips tingling. "Shall I remind you?"

He set hands to her waist and drew her closer. She wanted desperately to push him away, to deny him the opportunity to prove his wretched point at her expense. But every part of her was busy responding to him, growing warm and pliant, opening, remembering. He pulled her against him and his head lowered.

His lips were just as hard, just as gentle, just as compelling as she recalled. It was like sliding into a warm down comforter on a cold winter night and finding comfort, security, and release.

Then he pulled away and she opened her eyes to find him looking at her with a hunger that she was surprised to find echoed what was happening in her. She knew that need because it was so like her own. She understood that desire for intimacy and completion, because it was just what she was feeling.

She knew such things because she had a sense of knowing *him*. Not just his good looks, fluid movement, and arresting eyes. Not just his intelligence, arrogance, determination, or worldly accomplishments. Not just his books and charts and his fascination with the colonies. For she hadn't known those things about him that first night, standing in the gloomy Church of St. Agrippa, and she had felt it even there.

She knew the man inside him . . . the heart, the spirit, the soul of him. It was as if she recognized him without quite realizing it and it was that recognition that caused her to accept when he made his scandalous offer to spend two hours alone with her.

She knew him. Her eyes closed to allow her to concentrate on the pleasure of his kiss and on the response rising in her. Her arms wrapped around him and she opened to his kiss. A barrage of dizzying, exhilarating sensations blocked all thought except that required to appreciate the tendrils of heat curling down her throat and coiling lazily into the tips of her breasts.

She pressed harder against him, feeling almost giddy with relief that what she had dreaded was finally happening. Fear fell away and for a few splendid moments she was free and soaring, unfettered, discovering the dimensions of her own desire. This delicious contact with him opened in her a portal to possibilities. There were so many lush and exotic new sensations to explore—

A sound from the hatchway startled them and they broke apart. She stumbled back and gasped as Dyso thudded down the steps. Stopping at the bottom, he studied them. His scarred face darkened and with two swift hand movements, he asked the questions.

"No, Dyso, I'm fine. The captain and I were just having a discussion," she said firmly, hurrying to intercept him and lay her hands over his clenched fists. With another breath, she reclaimed her shattered composure. "We are about to have dinner."

Both men noticed that her hand trembled as she pointed to the table. A heartbeat later, Jeannie and Mr. Hicks descended the steps, talking cheerily, and the tension dissolved in the serving of a meal.

It was several minutes before Brien could bring herself to look at Aaron. His expression was thoughtful and amicable, showing no trace of the self-assured taunt she might have expected. She blushed guiltily. She wanted to distrust him and resent him. But she couldn't. The outer walls of her defenses had been scaled and breached.

She no longer had to dread giving in to temptation, only where giving in to that temptation would lead. By the end of the meal she realized she would have to see to it that she was never alone with him. The danger of lasting consequences from a night's encounter were too great to risk—even for the pleasure she would find in his arms.

It was dark when she and Jeannie followed Dyso on deck for a breath of air before retiring to their cabins. They had eaten too well and imbibed too much wine. Brien felt overheated and restless and was relieved to find that Aaron had retired earlier to his cabin to study his navigational charts.

The wind had a dampness to it as the clouds darted past the face of the moon. Before long, Brien shivered and suggested they go below to avoid the worsening weather. She needed some sleep to give her perspective on her situation and bolster her determination to avoid the temptation closing on her like an unseen shadow.

She pulled her damp shawl from her shoulders as she stood before her cabin door. She glanced furtively at the next door and thought of—*no!* Safely inside her darkened cabin, she reached for the oil lamp swaying above her and lighted it. Then she removed her shawl and sat down on a stool by her open trunk to remove the combs and pins from her hair. Since Jeannie's illness, she had grown used to doing this for herself and found it strangely comforting.

Shaking out her hair, she lifted her mirror and gasped at the sight of Aaron's face peering back at her from over her shoulder. She whirled on her seat. His long frame was

stretched out on her narrow bed with his arms crossed behind his head. His slow, appreciative smile made her heart
beat faster.

"What are you doing here?" she demanded, jumping up
to put as much distance as possible between them.

"Why, watching you begin your toilette." His innocent
tone was quickly replaced by a huskier quality. "Don't let me
interfere. Now, what would be next?" He rubbed his chin.
"The dress, perhaps?"

"If you don't leave, I'll call Dyso to remove you." She
started for the door.

"Ohhh, no." In a single fluid movement, he bolted from
the bed and planted himself between her and the door. "No
offense, Brien, but your protector has very little humor
about him and I have absolutely no desire for burial at sea."

"Get out of my cabin or I'll scream," she uttered through
clenched teeth.

"Scream, then. And prepare to navigate to Boston safely
on your own."

Silence settled. And lengthened.

After a long, tense moment, Brien crossed her arms with
a determined huff. "If you came here expecting a repeat of
today's lapse of sanity, you've sorely misjudged both your appeal and my mental state."

He gave a start and pulled away from the door, putting a
finger to his mouth in a call for silence. She realized that
Dyso must have taken up his vigil outside her door and
quickly weighed the possibility of calling to him. It annoyed
her to have to admit that Aaron was right; their getting to
the colonies safely probably did depend on his survival.

He pulled her, resisting silently, to a seat on the bunk beside him.

"Keep your voice down and I'll keep my distance." Seeing
her move as far away on the bunk as possible, he grinned.

"What do you want?" she demanded in constricted tones.

"To talk with you."

"You don't need to lurk about in my darkened cabin just to 'talk' with me."

"True." He sank back onto one elbow and swept her with a look. "But would you have me confess in front of my crew that the thought of you in bed, only a few feet away, robs me of sleep? That the sight of you on deck with the sun in your hair sends an ache through me that I can't control? That the scent of you as you brush past me in the passage pours fire into my blood?"

"I am not responsible for your wayward impulses."

"Ah, but you are. Tonight when you kissed me—"

"I did *not* kiss you."

"You kissed me back," he amended, growing more serious. "I realized that I will have no peace until what is between us is settled."

"There is nothing to settle," she said adamantly. "I paid you handsomely to wed me legally and then disappear, and you've kept no part of that bargain. There is no legal record of the marriage and I can't seem to get rid of you."

"We have only your father's word that there were no records. And he was hardly a disinterested party in the search for them."

She was taken aback. "Are you implying that he found the records but just chose to ignore or destroy them? I'll have you know, my father is a decent and honorable man."

"So"—he came up fast from his casual sprawl—"am I. I believed, as you did, that we were being legally and morally bound in wedlock. I believe that we were and are still married. And I believe we should take some time to decide what we want to do about it."

"There is nothing to decide." Alarm sent a cold draft through her. "If we were 'legally' married—*which cannot be proved*—and if we were 'morally' married—*which cannot be enforced*—it changes nothing. There is nothing to be gained by unearthing a marriage that both of us intended to ignore."

"Are you certain about that?" His face and strident posture

softened. "Are you sure that you don't need anything that marriage could provide? Companionship, perhaps? A sense of belonging? Children? Satisfaction? Pleasure?"

Pleasure. A treacherous trickle of anticipation sluiced through her. There it was; the crux of the matter. He wanted her. Physically. That was what all of this was about.

"You forget, I've tasted those marital pleasures and found them not to my liking."

"*You* forget, it was I who introduced you to those pleasures. And your reaction to them was not at all unfavorable." He leaned closer, sweeping her face with a tactile look before sinking his gaze into hers. "You were wonderful, Brien. Sweet and warm. So eager to learn, to experience, to give." He searched her relentlessly, refusing to allow her to retreat from his intimate scrutiny, willing the fear that encased her heart and passions to melt.

Her only recourse was to close her eyes. "I have learned well the ways of men. And I have no need or desire to ever submit to another." Her face took on that trace of sadness that sometimes surfaced when she thought no one was watching.

His irritation melted at once into unexpected tenderness. He reached inside his belt, drew something out, and put it into her hands.

She opened her eyes on two hand-carved combs. Brown-and-amber tortoiseshell. She looked up at him, confused.

"Don't you recognize them?" he said softly. "I took them from your hair that night. It was all I had to prove to me that you were not a sweet delusion."

Warmth flooded her, threatening to inundate her last desperate defenses. She turned her back to him so that he couldn't see the mixture of fear and longing that filled her. She squeezed the combs so that the teeth dug into her hands and reminded her of the pain that lay ahead if she gave in to the temptation he presented.

His hand hovered over her shoulder before settling in a

caress on her half-bare shoulder. She could hardly breathe. Her bones seemed to have turned fluid and she had neither the will nor the power to move away.

His shallow breath moved a wisp of hair near her temple and she closed her eyes, battling fear and reason to remain still.

"Brien, if you want, I'll leave."

Jolted by this offer—just as she had begun to surrender— she summoned enough strength to take one step away. Her heart stopped for a moment as his hands slid around her waist, releasing her.

There would be another time, Aaron thought as he watched her struggling with her conflicting desires, when she would come to him gladly. He knew if he pressed a bit harder, turned her and kissed her, she would respond— But somehow that didn't seem to be enough. He wanted her to choose him . . . wanted her joyful, eager, and free of doubt . . . wanted her to celebrate in his arms. With fresh insight, he knew that was all she asked—the freedom to choose, to give.

And he must give her that freedom now.

Without another word, he stepped up onto the bunk and flung open one of the small windows above it.

"What are you doing?" She whirled and found him standing on her bunk.

"You can hardly expect me to exit over your hulking protector." He gestured toward the door. The sound of the sea drifted in through the small opening, and alarm seized her.

"But you can't go out there—you'll be killed!"

"Ah!"—he brightened—"we do make progress. The lady cares whether I live or die. Don't worry. I designed this ship, remember?" With a twist of his muscular frame, he slid out the window and grasped handholds and footholds.

Brien scrambled up onto the bunk and leaned her head out to see if he was all right. But there was nothing but darkness and a rogue bit of spray that dampened her face. She pulled in and latched the window, mortified by the danger he courted so blithely, and dismayed by her protective reaction.

Moments later, a gentle but unmistakable rap on the wall from the next cabin allowed her to breathe easily once more.

"Wretched man."

Fifteen

THE NEXT DAY DAWNED bright and cool. Brien secured a mug of tea in the commons and used it to warm her hands as she stood on the quarterdeck, looking out over the ship. The view of the long vessel from there was commanding: an acre of oiled and polished decking, thousands of yards of pristine canvas, a maze of new ropes and rows of neatly stowed spars, gaffes, and other tools. She was properly awed as she thought of the overwhelming forces pulling on the vessel and of the courage it took to pilot her safely through an Atlantic crossing.

The breeze ruffled her skirts and made her pull her cloak tightly about her. She watched the way the sailor at the wheel stood erect and held the wheel with both firmness and respect. Suddenly she could see why men loved the challenge and power of the sea and risked life and fortune to test themselves against it. It was exhilarating just to watch.

A pang of envy swept her. She would love to share the communion with the elements and the sense of power and accomplishment the men of the crew must feel as they raced along that sea road. It truly was enough to lure a nobleman to forsake title and comfort. At least, one nobleman . . .

Him again. She gave a long-suffering sigh.

Dyso had followed her up on deck and stood looking out to sea, a strange peacefulness on his fierce features. She left his side to stroll along the railing toward the bow. She did not hear Aaron approach and lean on the rail behind her.

"It won't be long before you'll glimpse America for the first time."

She was glad to have a neutral topic to talk to him about. "Is it very beautiful, this new land?" She searched the horizon that his hand had swept, while fighting the warmth that tingled through her at the sound of his voice.

"Wait until you see it." She could hear his grin and feel the excitement in his tone. "Rich, fertile fields that grow everything imaginable. Thick forests of oak and hickory, maple and walnut . . . millions of acres. Land no man has trod. Views from mountaintops no human has ever seen. And water—beautiful rivers, lakes, and streams. And there are beaver and fox and deer . . . it's a treasure box just waiting to be explored."

When she finally turned to him, there was a new light in his eyes, a passion unlike any she had seen there before.

"Of course, the cities aren't much yet, by continental standards," he continued. "Dirt streets mostly . . . simple houses and shops, open-air markets. But they're growing. Boston, New York, and Philadelphia have fine public buildings and churches, and homes to rival some of the finest in West London. Wealth draws culture to it. With people spreading west, clearing the land and discovering new resources, it can't be long before life in America equals that in England."

"You make it sound like the promised land," she said.

"It is for many people. That's not to say there is no poverty or hardship. Some who come to America see only the potential profit, without realizing how much work is required or how ill-prepared they are to do it."

"And Boston. Tell me about it."

She watched him describing the city, using his hands, chuckling over the characters and the curious local cuisine . . . lobsters, clams, a heavy brown sweet bread, and a mania for beans baked with molasses. She listened with fascination to his colorful descriptions of the newspaper, the local university, the city musical society.

"The place has such vigor," he said, staring off at the horizon. "It throbs with life the way Britain did a century ago. In this country a man is just a man, no more, no less. There is no privileged elite—except that wrought by courage, skill, and cleverness."

"You love it, don't you, this new land." She looked up, feeling drawn to him.

He grew thoughtful. "I suppose I do. In America a man's sons can make their own lives—become whatever they can become, instead of stifling under centuries of tradition."

"And daughters?" she asked. "Are women there still bought and sold with dowries and not taught to read lest they learn how little of the world they may have?"

Aaron was disarmed by her question and looked down at her with a light scowl. Before her, all women were just . . . women. He never considered they might have dreams, ambitions, or curiosity, except in social or domestic ways. Now with a single thought, she turned his neat, "modern" view of the world upside down.

She read the answer in his silence. "No, it will be the same there for women. Men will cast off the bondage of class, privilege, and tradition. Even so, they will press it cruelly on women they claim to love so well." The light dimmed in her countenance and she grew wistful. "Daughters will be forced to wed and bear children . . . to set aside their dreams and aspirations and hand their lives over to fathers and husbands without demur."

He was shaken by her words and how surely they fit her life. How could any fair, honest man fail to see the truth of what she had said? He felt awkward suddenly, and ordinary. He caught her by the arm and turned her to him.

"What is it you truly want, Brien? What dreams did your father trample in driving you to the altar against your will?"

"My dreams were simple. Freedom to see to the welfare of our estate and to learn and use what talents I possess. Most of all, I wanted my father to know that I was more than just a commodity to be dispatched to its proper place. I wanted my wishes and thoughts to matter, to be respected." She drew back and pulled her shawl tighter. "I suppose that sounds laughable to you, coming from a woman."

He stared at her through a confusion of horror and longing. Longing to be with her. Horror at how closely his own attitudes resembled her father's.

She was a woman. She was supposed to marry and bear children and make a home. But what if she didn't want to do that? What if she felt demeaned and suffocated by it . . . like he had when his father demanded he give up his "boat nonsense" and return home to marry an heiress already chosen for him? What if she hated the man she was forced to wed, and couldn't bear for him to touch her, much less bed her?

"Not laughable," he said thickly.

She glanced up from the corner of her eye, as if unsure whether to believe him.

"All of that is past, now." She lifted her chin and turned to go. "Fate intervened to put me on a very different path."

Aaron stood frozen by the gunwale with a sweet misery of desire welling up inside him. His chest swelled so that he had difficulty drawing breath. Nothing in life had prepared him for the avalanche of new ideas and emotions Brien laid bare in him.

He had always avoided entanglements; from youth he had disavowed all claims made on him, even by his family. Now, in a few moments, that pattern was so totally reversed that he reeled from it. He suddenly wanted connection and obligation. He *needed* it. And he understood that it was his growing desire for *her* that caused these unprecedented longings for permanence and possession.

He wanted her . . . wanted to hold her fast and breathe her in, to drink her through her kisses and feel her sighing with contentment beneath him. He wouldn't rest until he did. And just what would it take to make her want him as much as he wanted her?

DYSO, WATCHING FROM the quarterdeck railing, had seen it all. Their words were withheld from him by the distance, but he had read their interaction all the same. A smile crept over his battered visage. He strolled to the bow with his rolling gait, watching the determination on the captain's handsome face.

WHAT DID SHE WANT?

Brien sat on her bunk that evening with her bare feet dangling above the floor and her nightdress bunched up around her knees. Each stroke of the brush through her long hair seemed to whisper that question anew. What did she want? Even in her own ears, the answer she had given him that afternoon had sounded selfish and shallow.

She wanted to do what *she* wanted. To pursue *her* dreams, *her* aspirations, *her* choices. But just what were her choices?

Aaron Durham's face appeared in her mind. Of all of the men Billy Rye might have found wandering around the docks that night . . . Of all of the captains who sailed out of Bristol for the colonies . . .

He wasn't her choice, but he seemed to be *fate's*.

Tall, handsome, clever, tender, irreverent . . . she thought of his ease of movement, his stubborn jaw, and the glint of passion that seemed ever present in his stunning eyes. Her throat tightened each time his lips curled into that roguish smile. Something in him called to her, consuming her thoughts by day and her dreams by night.

Most devastating, he knew her secrets and her passion, and he didn't use them against her for his own selfish ends. Why hadn't he pressed her harder last evening? Surely he knew she needed no more persuasion to make her tumble into bed with him. And even though she was vulnerable and defenseless against him, he hesitated. It was as though he had handed her control as he placed those combs in her hands.

She bounded off the bunk to probe the side pocket of her open trunk. She held the plain tortoiseshell combs up to the lantern light. Amber. Like his eyes.

Desire hit her with gale force and she closed her eyes, concentrating on the tingling in her breasts and the heat collecting in her loins.

She could not know about the future and what was in store for her, but she had to know if her memories of him were real. She had to experience him, be with him one more time. If it were only passion, she would find it out in the cold light of morning and she would be free of him at last.

Her satin robe billowed around her as she stepped out into the passage. Dyso, lying across her doorsill in the narrow passage, sat up quickly, blinking at her with sleep-clouded concern.

She smiled briefly and put forth one hand, motioning him to stay. The hulk watched as she gathered her robe about her and moved to the door of the next cabin. Without knocking, she turned the handle and disappeared inside.

Dyso rubbed his face slowly. A faint smile flickered about

his mouth as he heaved himself up and lumbered down the passage to his own hitherto unused cabin.

Aaron sat at a large table in the center of his spacious cabin. His boots were off and he wore no shirt, as if half-prepared for bed. A stack of charts absorbed his attention until the opening of the door jerked his head up.

The glibness of a lifetime deserted him as Brien floated forward into the soft light of the single lantern swinging overhead. There was a radiance about her that transfixed him. His heart began to pound.

"W-What can I do for you?" he said, finding his throat suddenly tight.

"Would you believe me if I said I wanted another book?"

"No."

"Or a bit of rum to help me sleep."

"I doubt it."

"What would you believe?"

"Are you having trouble sleeping?" He stepped around the table.

"Yes."

"And you think I may be able to help?"

"Yes."

She came to him and stood looking up at him, searching his face. Then she pressed something into his hands.

He looked down at the small tortoiseshell combs in his hands and found it hard to swallow. She pulled her hair back from her face and turned her head, offering it to him. His hands shook as he stroked her flowing hair and then tucked the combs into the locks she held for him.

Then she tilted her face up to his and touched his bare chest. "I . . . I need to know if . . ."

There was no need for her to finish it. He knew exactly what she needed to know.

His hands flew to the ribbons of her robe. It slid down her arms and fell around her on the polished floor. Underneath, she wore a gauze-thin nightdress that clung to her body, revealing her breasts and the enticing curve of her body below. Her roselike scent wafted up to him, sending his thoughts plunging down the front of her.

He ran his hands over her shoulders and down her nightdress to cup her breasts. With a ragged groan, he began to circle her taut nipples with his thumbs.

"Put yourself in my hands, sweetness. I'll have you asleep in no time."

She closed her eyes and gasped as pleasurable sensations cascaded through her. He watched responsiveness stirring in the lower half of her body. Her hips swayed and she pressed harder against his thumbs, wanting more, wanting that same masterful touch on other parts of her. Her throaty sigh sent a lightning bolt of response through him.

He wrapped her in his arms and pulled her hard against him, feeling his blood rising fast against her soft frame. She wrapped her arms tight around him, surging up onto her toes to meet his kisses, hungrily sucking his lips and stroking his tongue with hers.

In a single, swift movement, he scooped her up into his arms and carried her to the wide bunk on the far side of the cabin. Her arms opened to him and he sank down atop her, pressing her down into the feather bed, creating a cocoon around them.

His big hands traced the curves of her body through her thin gown, even as her fingers explored his muscular back. He kissed and nipped her mouth, her throat, and her breasts. She arched against him, wanting more, urging him to more direct contact. He pulled back for a moment, to stare with undiluted lust at the taut, crinkled peaks atop those creamy mounds. He ran his hot face over each cool, velvety nipple and felt as much as heard her moan. He fastened his mouth to each nipple and suckled her until her groans filled the cabin.

When he raised his head to smile down into her eyes, he

found her eyes shimmering like molten silver. With a wanton smile, she pushed him back and sat up to draw her nightdress over her head and toss it on the floor by the bed. Her combs soon joined it and she shook her head so that her hair spread about her shoulders.

He swallowed hard, trying to drink in the details of her beauty: the soft tumbled hair, the full, round breasts; the smooth round hips, and silken thighs. She was far more beautiful than he had remembered. The sight of her flushed with passion and naked in his bed was overwhelming.

She slid down to lie beside him again, pressing her long, tapered legs against his bulging breeches on the way. In a moment, his remaining clothes were discarded and his mouth was fierce upon hers. He slid on top of her, searing her skin with his heat, and she parted her thighs to welcome him. Soon he was sinking inside her, surrounded, enfolded. Claimed. They moved together for what seemed a long time, until they were both trembling, poised on the very edge of climax. Then their passions exploded, fusing them into one soaring, unbounded entity.

Brien gasped for air, shuddering occasionally as the peace of fulfillment spread through her. Aaron moved over to lie beside her, his face mirroring the smoky contentment in her eyes. She snuggled against his big, warm body, exhausted and still under the enchantment of what had just happened between them.

Aaron's mind whirled in lazy, contented circles, marveling at the woman who lay curled against him. She was not the sweet, reluctant maiden of his dreams, nor the troubled, prickly aristocrat who had deigned to sail with him, nor even the self-assured sensation of London society who disdained all claims men made on her. She was a different person altogether, this Brien. Direct and sensual, eager to give as well as to receive pleasure, honest in her confusion, and vulnerable in ways he would never have guessed . . . she was all he remembered and so much more.

"Brien?" Her name rolled sensually on his tongue.

"Ummm?" She rubbed her face against his bare chest and he felt as if she were melting into him, making a niche for herself in his heart.

"Do you think you can sleep now?" he whispered.

"Um-hmm."

He felt her body relax against him by degrees and ran his hand up and down the arm that was lapped over his waist. He refused to think about tomorrow or possible consequences of this pleasurable turn of events. It was enough for now just to have her in bed and in his arms.

Moments later, he too dropped off the edge of the world, into the sweet release of sleep.

BANGING ON THE cabin door awakened Aaron just past dawn. He sat up with a start and looked around the rumpled, empty bed, frowning. The meaty fist at the door grew louder. Mumbling a curse and running a hand through his hair, he bounded off the bunk.

"Save your strength—I'm coming!" he barked as he drew on a pair of breeches.

"Captain," Mr. Hicks called from the other side of the door, "we've hit fog. You're needed on deck, sir."

Aaron jerked open the door. "Did you strike sail?" he growled, pulling on a boot. He returned to the side of the bed for the other boot and his shirt. Mr. Hicks stepped in and peered about the cabin curiously. "Aye, sir."

Aaron caught the man's scrutiny and was annoyed. "When did you take the last sighting?" he demanded, shoving one arm into the shirt.

"Three bells, sir." Hicks pondered the possible reasons for his captain's foul humor. He could readily think of one, but there was no sign of her here. "I was on deck myself when we ran afoul of it. Struck sail and posted watches straightaway."

"Good enough." Aaron finished tucking his shirt into the band at his waist. "Tell the cook to send up some coffee." He caught a glimpse of Hicks's tired face. "Then get some rest; you look like you need it."

With a few long strides, he was up the steps and on deck. The cool, damp mist in the air clung to his face and clothes. The sun was up by now, but the air seemed dark and impenetrable. Hicks had posted experienced hands at the bow and they strained eyes and ears, searching the oppressive cloud that surrounded them. From where he stood on the bridge at the wheel, the bow of the ship was lost in mist.

A fog this dense in midocean meant the strong mix of warm and cold currents, and a danger of icebergs drifting south with the cold, Arctic flow. There was no wind and no way to predict how long the fog would last or how dangerous it might be.

Now in command of his ship and of himself, he allowed his thoughts to flow back to Brien. She had left him in the night. He frowned, not sure why that should trouble him. Then he recalled the pleasure she had brought him . . . by turns coy and playful, then sweet and yielding . . . and he smiled. It was better than his many dreams of her; she brought to his bed the ripened sweetness of her own experience, exciting in ways he couldn't have imagined. With an intense pang of envy, he thought about her marriage and the handsome Frenchman who had called her his wife. How could the bastard have been so stupid as to not recognize the value of such a woman and do everything in his power to make her his own? *He* sure as hell wouldn't make that mistake.

A call rang out from one of the forward lookouts. As his ears strained toward the muffled lapping of the water at the sides of the ship, he scowled. The sea demanded his attention like a jealous mistress.

BRIEN AWAKENED LATE that same morning and sent Jeannie off in search of breakfast while she luxuriated in bed. She thought of the cause of the pleasant languor that possessed her and stretched lazily.

Aaron. She had loved being with him. Every movement was etched into her aching muscles and every emotion of the night just past was stuffed into her full heart. It was everything she had hoped for and everything she had feared. In his kiss and touch she found unexpected strength, skill, tenderness, passion. He was a remarkable man. One who listened when she spoke and didn't instantly dismiss her ideas and ambitions because she was a woman. One who had approached her as an equal in passion, respected her right to choose, and sought her pleasure even as he took his own.

She hadn't expected to feel this way. She had succeeded in convincing herself that she was simply curious, that one night with him would dispel her romanticized memories and free her. But one night in his arms had only validated the dream she had lived with since their first loving. Now this bone-deep feeling of satisfaction refused to let her go, even when she shook her head sharply to clear it and then bounded out of her bunk.

As she drew her nightdress over her head, she recalled removing it in his bed . . . and was brushed by a fleeting chill that whispered there might be consequences from that memorable bout of pleasure. She stilled, feeling that insulating cloak of satisfaction thinning. What kind of consequences?

Pregnancy. She might bear a child even now.

But there had been no babe from their first coupling, she thought frantically. Perhaps she couldn't conceive. Perhaps she couldn't have children at all.

The thought impaled her, bringing her abruptly to her senses. Every last wisp of romantic self-indulgence was blown from her senses. Barren? Her? Her hand went to her belly and she looked down and recognized that protective gesture for what it was.

But wasn't that just what she had said she wanted? A sardonic conscience, hard-pressed and long denied, rose up to taunt her. *Husbandless, childless freedom.*

Frantically seizing clothes from her trunk, she pulled a chemise on over her head and stepped into a full corset, dragging it up over her hips and then yanking the chemise down beneath it. She held her breath, gritted her teeth, and pulled hard on the corset strings. Then harder.

It would serve her right if she were pregnant. Playing with fire. Letting her passions and impulses get the better of her. What was she thinking, going to his bed . . . offering herself up to him like a pure wanton . . . without the slightest thought for what might happen afterward?

THE FOG REMAINED until the next afternoon when the sun burned some of it off and rising winds carried the rest away. The cool white sun seemed distant through the high clouds, but was a welcome sight all the same when Brien emerged onto the main deck for some exercise. A furtive glance told her Aaron wasn't on deck and Mr. Hicks soon confirmed that he was in his cabin getting some much needed rest. Relief and disappointment wrangled for control . . . until she caught herself and muttered what had become a magical charm that never failed to rally her defenses.

"*Consequences.*"

That evening, there was a knot in her stomach as she entered the common room for dinner. Aaron was there, freshly shaved and wearing a dark blue uniform trimmed with gold braid at the shoulders and collar. His eyes glowed as he swept her simple gown with an appreciative gaze and offered his hand to escort her to her seat at the table. She placed her hand in his, briefly, ignoring the extra pressure of it.

Hicks seated Jeannie beside her and Dyso took up his usual place at the end of the table.

"How lovely you are this evening," Aaron said, taking his place at the head of the table. She mumbled a suitable response. "Mr. Hicks no doubt told you why I did not join you for meals yesterday." He was charm itself. She tried not to look. "Fog in this part of the ocean can hold hidden dangers. I was obliged to be on deck."

"So Mr. Hicks explained," she said, nodding to the first mate. "Your devotion to your ship and our safety is commendable, Captain."

"I am devoted to much more than your safety, my lady." When she looked up in surprise, there was a twinkle in his eyes. "I am devoted to your comfort and pleasure . . . as you well know." His brazen reference to what had happened between them astonished her, as did Jeannie's muffled giggle.

"Really, Captain. I am sure you have more pressing concerns."

"None that I can think of, my lady." His smile broadened.

As the steward began to serve, Aaron cleared his throat and asked her where she would be staying in Boston.

"With my father's agent in the colonies."

"And his name is?" he prompted.

"Silas Hastings," she said, only after a significant pause.

"And just where does Mr. Hastings live?"

"I have no idea. I'm to send word to the warehouse when we arrive in port. He will send someone to collect me."

"Oh, but it's Cambridge Road, my lady. Don't you remember . . . that letter . . ."

"Oh, yes." She sent Jeannie a silencing glare and the maid looked chastened.

"Cambridge Road? That's not far from the inn where I sometimes stay. That will be convenient."

No other word in the English language could have struck such terror in her heart just then. *Convenient?*

"I am eager to show you the view of the bay from near there. Oh, and the music society will have its summer musicale shortly after we arrive. And there is a waterfall on the river that is perfect for picnics. . . ."

Each word added to a choking feeling creeping up her neck. He was insinuating himself into her life . . . staking a claim on her time and attention . . . serving notice that she now had to make herself available to him!

"Really, Captain. I doubt I'll have time for such entertainments."

"Nonsense." He swept away her objection with a masterful hand. "It will do you good to get out and see the place and meet the people. It will help you find a buyer for your company that much sooner." He gave her a pointed little smile. "Besides, you can only talk so much commerce in a day. You will have plenty of time for me to show you Boston's charms."

His claims clanked around her like shackles being closed and padlocked. He thought that their loving had somehow given him owner's rights to her!

"How do you know, Captain, how much commerce I can endure in a day?" she demanded, her eyes now crackling with a warning he was bound to ignore.

He put down his knife and fork to look at her with an insultingly personal air.

"I have a fair idea, my lady, what your endurance is like. I'll be certain to see that you get the rest you need."

She gripped the edge of the table, her face now aflame. "My 'endurance'?" She stood abruptly, drawing Aaron and Mr. Hicks up with her. "I can see to that myself, sir! Starting right now!"

She stalked out of the commons, down the passage, and into her cabin, where she slammed the door with such force that every timber in the ship's frame vibrated.

She paced furiously in the dull glow of the lantern, unaware that on deck Aaron paced with equal ferocity. Neither slept well and both awakened in foul humor. When they met briefly in the commons, Brien was seething quietly and Aaron was seething noisily . . . at the cook, the steward, and even poor Hicks. Jeannie and Hicks exchanged bewildered looks as the animosity between the captain and the lady grew. Aaron took his dinner on deck that evening.

In her cabin, dressed for bed but unable to sleep, Brien paced again, trying unsuccessfully to turn her thoughts from Aaron to something—anything—else.

The door handle turned and she looked up to find Aaron filling the doorway, his face set with determination. The soft click of the latch was the only indication of the passage of time for her. Her heart had stopped at the sight of him.

Stop that, she ordered herself.

"Your cabin is next door, Captain," she said irritably when her heart thumped back into rhythm.

"We need to talk."

"I'm really quite tired," she declared emphatically. "It can surely wait until—"

"Why did you come to me two nights ago?" he demanded, folding his arms and widening his stance. He was a colossus. And he'd come for an accounting.

"Is your memory so faulty, Captain? Only three nights ago you visited my cabin to issue an invitation to just such an encounter." She folded her arms, parodying his stance and his determination. "Why should you be concerned with my motives? You got what you wanted."

"I want to know why you came to my cabin."

"Probably out of . . . curiosity."

"You came because you were *curious?*" His face bronzed with heat.

"The truth isn't sufficient, I see. Then tell me what answer you want, Captain, and I will gladly supply it."

"I want the truth, dammit! I wanted you—I'll not deny

it. And I enjoyed it. I thought you woman enough to admit that as well."

"Did you come for a testimonial to your skill, Captain? Surely there are others, of more experience, better qualified to flatter you." The cords in his neck stood out briefly and she edged back a step, wondering if she had pushed him too far.

"What in bloody hell's the matter with you?" he roared.

"*You* are!" she blazed back. "How dare you make such assumptions about me? How dare you begin to plan my time and activities as if they now belonged to you? Dear God, you have an opinion of yourself!" She paced to the side of the cabin and then back. "You believe your loving to be so potent that it rendered me witless and quivering . . . in need of a keeper or a lord and master. And of course, being a man, you assumed that the job would naturally be yours. Well, it bloody well isn't. I'm perfectly capable of directing my own life and conducting my own affairs!"

Her blast left him stunned.

"I never— I don't want to be in charge of— I *never* intended to—" He halted and sank his gaze into hers, searching her. The fury that turned his eyes to molten gold began to drain, and cooler thoughts and emotions prevailed.

"I am not your husband, Brien," he declared, thinking of the Frenchman who had wedded her against her will and ruined forever her trust in men.

"No," she responded, settling into a calmer resolve, "you are not."

It took a moment for him to realize she wasn't speaking of the Frenchman . . . but was instead disputing his previous claims that their marriage was a valid one.

"Having only just regained my freedom and control of my future, I will not surrender them to anyone, no matter how helpful or sincere he might appear to be. However enjoyable or beguiling my time with you was"—she swallowed against the lump forming in her throat—"I will not take such a risk again. When I leave the ship in Boston, I will not expect to see you again." She turned her face away.

He didn't move for what seemed an eternity. Then she heard a jingle as he produced a leather pouch from his belt and held it out to her.

"Then this might be my last opportunity to give you this." When she made no move to take it, he came to put it directly into her hands.

She turned it over and over, feeling the weight of gold coins and a number of bank notes. . . .

"This is the first third. For all of these months, I have considered it a loan and intended to see it returned to you. I'll take no pay for what I did that night."

Her eyes stung with a warning of tears and she turned briskly away.

"Good night, Captain."

Aaron's arms dropped to his sides. Her hair veiled her face from him as he moved to one side. Sensing his movement, she turned her face farther from view. He wanted to seize her by the shoulders and shake her until she came to her senses. Or to take her into his arms and kiss her until she admitted that she wanted him as much as he wanted her.

Not trusting himself to refrain from both, he ducked quickly back out into the passage and slammed the door shut behind him.

Sixteen

*T*HE LADY'S SECRET DOCKED in Boston on a bright spring afternoon. It was not long before Brien's message to Silas Hastings bore fruit in the form of an enclosed carriage dispatched to greet her. As she stood at the midship railing and watched a tall, gangly figure in a dignified frock coat descend from the coach and head toward the gangway, a sense of loss swept over her. The voyage was over and she was leaving behind *The Lady's Secret* and all of its haunting associations.

Resettling the hood of her cloak, she refused to look around the deck for Aaron. She had scarcely seen him for the last three days. As if by unspoken agreement, he had stayed on deck most of the time and she had remained below in the commons and her cabin. Now that the moment of departure was here, she was torn between wanting to see

him one last time and wanting to spare herself that longing
and confusion.

She squared her shoulders and focused on the angular,
graying fellow hurrying up the gangway. He wore a pair of
divided spectacles and Brien was struck by the oddity of
their appearance. Only then did she recognize Silas Hastings—plus fifteen years.

"Lady Brien! I can hardly believe my eyes!" he called,
seizing her hands in eagerness. "I saw you last as a bright and
inquisitive six-year-old. What a beautiful young woman you
have become."

"And you, sir, were a clever-minded and tolerant clerk.
You managed to conduct business and occupy my father's
'shadow' at the same time." Then she realized Silas had
transferred his attention to someone or something behind
her and turned a quarter turn.

"Aaron Durham." Aaron stood behind her, extending his
hand toward Silas.

She bristled. "This is the captain of our ship." She managed to keep most of the irritation out of her voice. "Weston
Trading's agent here in Boston, Silas Hastings."

"Durham? Then you're the one," Silas declared, giving
Aaron's hand a vigorous pumping. Seeing Aaron's frown, he
clarified: "Your ship—she's all that Harold Caswell can talk
about."

"Harold, yes. You know him, then."

"We dine together whenever I am in New York. He
swears you hung the moon." He glanced past Aaron to the
sleek hull behind him. "Do you think I could have a look at
your ship myself . . . see how she's built, firsthand?"

"Only if you promise not to hold me accountable for
Caswell's boasts." Aaron straightened his already officerlike
posture and smiled. "I would be pleased to show you my
ship, sir."

"Shall we say, this Saturday? Saturday afternoon?" Silas's
enthusiasm carried the moment. "Then you can come home

to dinner with me. My wife Helen will be delighted to have something to take her mind from . . ." His eyes widened and he turned back to Brien. "She would have come with me to greet you, my lady, but she will soon come to childbed and I insisted she stay at home and rest."

"Goodness." She flicked a faintly hostile glance at Aaron. "Then I cannot imagine she will be up to entertaining dinner guests on Saturday."

"Oh, no." Silas laughed and looked to Aaron. "Entertaining is Helen's passion. We have one guest already . . . I'm sure she would say it will be no trouble at all to set another place for dinner."

"In that case"—Aaron smiled with a trace of defiance— "I am pleased to accept."

"Excellent!" Silas tugged the brim of his hat. "Until Saturday, then."

As she strode down the gangway, Brien's thoughts were consumed by the fact that she would be stuck across a dinner table from him again . . . having to contend with him in the New World as she had in the old. So much for the fresh start she had intended to make as she set foot on American soil.

Her trunks and Jeannie's and Dyso's bags were soon loaded on the carriage and they were on their way through narrow cobbled streets that hummed with activity. Brien watched the city from the carriage window, leaving her annoyance behind and growing absorbed in the activity and surprised by the familiar scenes and dress of the people. She had expected more exotic sights and now had to admit the wisdom of Aaron's statement that the two countries had too much in common to be separated by petty grievances.

"So much activity." She glimpsed the pride in Silas's face. "It's wonderful."

"I thought you would enjoy it. I was not terribly shocked when your father wrote that you were coming as his partner. Even as a child you had a head for business. We were devastated at the news of your bereavement, Lady Brien." He squeezed her hand gently, heedless of the familiarity of the gesture.

"Life goes on, Silas. Father and I have become much closer of late. I plagued him mercilessly to make me his protégée. Now I must not let him down." She grew serious. "Tell me, do you think we'll be able to find a buyer soon?"

Studying the head of his cane, Silas smiled. "On that issue I do have a bit of good news. The details can wait, but a Dutchman named Van Zandt has recently made inquiries. He is a wealthy man, shrewd in business. I have shown him the warehouse and shops, but have delayed any discussion of price until you arrived. He is interested in the lot, but I'm told he drives a hard bargain, Lady Brien."

" 'Brien' will be fine, Silas." She flashed him a dazzling smile. "I have it on good authority that titles mean little here now."

Silas's three-story brick house was not imposing from the outside, but had a pleasing solidity about it. Inside, it seemed much larger, more comfortable, and was tastefully decorated with fine fabrics and furnishings culled from some of England's finest cabinetmakers.

Helen Hastings hurried into the front hall from the parlor, arriving pink-cheeked and out of breath. Her middle bulged so that Brien marveled that she could walk at all. At first glance of the woman's pretty round face, glowing with welcome, Brien liked her.

"Oh, Silas, is this your Lady Brien?" Helen took her hands and squeezed them. "She's lovely!"

"Brien, this is my Helen," he said proudly, putting an arm around his wife.

"I fear I have come at a most inconvenient time." Her eyes lowered to Helen's middle.

"Heavens, no!" Helen waved her concern aside. "This is our fourth; I'm an old hand now. And I'll be glad of the company. This last bit of waiting is the hardest part." She turned to give the servants orders as to the trunks and rooms and then led Brien in to the parlor.

The room was bright in the filtered late afternoon sun and Brien suddenly felt more at home here than in her own chambers at Harcourt. Helen sat down heavily on the stout sofa and sighed with relief as she propped her feet up on a stool. A stout, older woman entered with a tea tray just then, and Helen gave orders for a bath to be drawn for Brien.

Brien's face grew wistful. "A bath. I'd be so grateful. After so long at sea, I can think of nothing I'd like better than a long, soaking bath."

Helen smiled warmly and nodded.

"But before you go upstairs"—she stretched heroically but ineffectually toward the tray—"would you mind pouring the tea? I'm afraid I won't reach."

At breakfast the next morning, Brien met Helen and Silas's three children. All three had curly brown hair and clear blue eyes. The youngest, Robert, climbed onto Brien's lap as soon as she was seated. Despite his mother's remonstrations, he would not be dislodged, and in the end, took his breakfast on the fairest seat in Boston. Brien chatted with him through breakfast, finding him a talkative and precocious three-year-old, then hugged him affectionately before sending him off to play in the garden with his brother and sister.

"Helen, your children are wonderful."

"Thank you, Brien. But you must not indulge Robert too much. He already thinks rules were made for other people." She smiled wanly. "He is in for a surprise when this babe arrives. He won't be the center of the world anymore."

Silas laid his large, thin hand over his wife's smaller one. "He'll adjust, I'm sure. The others have had to."

Brien thought how lovingly Silas looked at his plump wife. It was clear Helen adored her tall, rail-thin husband, whose graying temples told of a difference in their ages. They were the personification of domestic happiness.

Helen turned to her husband. "Why don't you take a day or two to show her some of the city? Then later, she can return to visit places that interest her on her own." She glanced toward the kitchen and the hulking servant undoubtedly taking breakfast there. "She's brought her own protector."

Brien smiled. "I suppose you must wonder about him. Dyso was my husband's servant. He is mute, but hears well and speaks with his hands." She lowered her eyes and voice instinctively. "The night of the fire that claimed my husband, Dyso carried me from the burning building. He has been with me since. He will be glad to help you in any way he can while we are here."

"Brien, what was your husband like?" Helen's face was wistful as she raised one hand to silence Silas's objection before it was pronounced.

"He was the third son of the French marquis de Saunier. He was dark and quite charming. My father found him a promising student of commerce." She paused to word the next part carefully. "We were barely . . . we were married only a month."

Helen dabbed at her eyes. "And not even a child to comfort you."

Brien squirmed slightly. "Time heals such sorrows. I have decided to devote myself to my father's business and to charity work."

"Ah, but you will surely marry again," Helen declared.

"I fear not, Helen." Brien intended to forestall any attempt at matchmaking. "I will not ever marry again."

"Not marry? Ever?" Helen was incredulous. "Oh, no, Brien. You cannot mourn such a short marriage forever."

"Helen!" Silas cried in exasperation. "Brien has candidly informed us of her reluctance to marry, and we will abide by her wishes." He waggled his finger at her. "No prying and no plotting!" He turned to Brien with an unaccustomed redness in his face. "Helen is loath to let any unmarried person pass under our roof without attempting to remedy what she considers to be God's great oversight."

"Silas!" Helen scowled.

"It's true, Brien. I maintain she could find no one to pair me with and so she married me herself so as not to spoil her record."

BRIEN MARVELED LATER that Silas and Helen were so unlike and yet so well suited to each other. Her early impressions of America were the same; many people, quite unlike in dreams, background, and aims, yet living together as though they belonged here.

The sights and smells of the city were a blend of the familiar and the foreign. Just when she would find a street that she vowed to be the duplicate of a Bristol lane or a Cambridge street, she caught a glimpse of a deerskin shirt or heard a rolling accent that reminded her of the new edge of the civilization here. She was in a different country now, but it was tantalizingly easy to forget.

The next day she talked Silas into stopping by the warehouse and stood in the middle of the main floor staring at a hundred barrels of whale oil, a few hundredweight of raw sugar, several hundred bales of wool, a hundred barrels of crockery and household goods, and dozens of crates of metal tools and implements wrought in Sheffieldshire forges. She had never seen this side of the business; most of the decisions involving a direct inspection of cargoes or warehouses, the earl had undertaken himself. Now she felt a shiver of excitement at discovering, learning yet another aspect of Weston Trading.

The place was a fascinating jumble of smells and sights. Workmen bustled about moving crates and barrels on small-wheeled lorries. She paused to ask questions about the contents of an exotic-looking crate or barrel, or to seek the market price of a given commodity. Her thoughtful gaze and penetrating questions fully engaged Silas, who proved a worthy source for all her inquiries.

In the warehouse offices, Silas presented her with tally sheets and manifests, and pointed out the salient features of their record-keeping system. By the time they were finished, Brien had a fair appreciation of their predicament. Silas had done everything possible to forestall the inevitable, but in such a hostile political climate, there was nothing for them to do but sell. Only two things remained to be settled.

"What will you do when it is sold?" she asked Silas. "Work for Van Zandt?"

"I don't fancy working for another this late in life. Helen's father left her most of his estate and we've made prudent investments. Over the years I have gleaned my share of Weston Trading's profits and have put them to good use. We'll be well fixed, no matter what comes to pass with this business. My only regret is that it must be sold to strangers. If I could have put hands on all my investments, I'd have purchased it myself. I've put so much of myself into it."

"You'll receive a share of the price it brings." She raised a hand to forbid a protest. "That is our wish—father's and mine." Her smile grew a bit pained. "Now, down to the numbers. What price shall we ask for your life's work?"

"The whole lot for thirty thousand sterling—not a whit less. It would be a bargain for any buyer at that price."

"And what will this Van Zandt offer?"

"He is shrewd, by repute. He might begin as low as twenty thousand. I'm told that bargaining is first his sport, then his livelihood."

"And is he trustworthy?"

"I have heard nothing to say he is not. But I know he is not a well-loved man, for all his money."

"Arrange a meeting for us next week if possible. And cross your fingers."

Aaron and Silas had arrived for dinner when Brien swept into the drawing room of Hastings House that Saturday evening. Aaron was leaning a shoulder against the mantelpiece, engrossed in conversation with Silas. Helen had said nothing about other guests and Brien had been reluctant to ask, lest she seem overly anxious.

"I hope I haven't kept you waiting," she said, greeting Helen and Silas warmly.

"No, Brien dear, not at all." Helen patted the settee beside her and Brien sat down.

"For such a delightful vision we would gladly have been kept waiting," Silas said, watching Aaron watching Brien.

"Silas, you are kind. I would not willingly detain anyone—but fashion is a merciless mistress." Looking at Aaron, she said simply, "Good evening, Captain."

"My lady." He bowed from the waist with an irritating air of amusement.

"The way Brien talks," Helen said, "she'd see us all in breeches and boots."

Silas raised an eyebrow. "Surely not, Brien. And deprive us of the unceasing delight of femininity in extravagant array?"

"Delight for you, perhaps, for you do not have to be laced and powdered and weighed down by layers of cumbersome, useless clothing. I assure you, men have the best of it, by far."

Aaron cleared his throat. "I see you have resumed wearing hoops under your skirts, my lady." His impertinence caused Helen and Silas both to stare and Brien to glare hotly at him.

"Yes, Captain, I have," she said, turning to Helen with emphatic poise. "On the ship, the narrow passages would not admit my hoops and I was forced to abandon them while on board, to save my modesty." She fixed a warning look on Aaron, but he simply smiled. "How perceptive. I did not realize you followed ladies' fashion so closely."

"Not ladies' fashion, my lady." He met her annoyance and raised it. "Only a few ladies."

Brien almost strangled on the breath she was drawing. He'd just announced his continuing pursuit of her in front of Helen and Silas . . . who muffled surprised laughs and cleared throats. How dare he?

During dinner, seated across from Aaron, Brien had little appetite even though she had been ravenous only an hour before. She was vastly relieved when Silas plied Aaron with queries about ships and their construction. He said he had heard that Aaron planned a line of fast cargo ships and pried mercilessly into details of the venture. Brien found herself sneaking looks at Aaron, trying to imagine him as a businessman. It seemed she was always having to reassess her opinions about him. . . .

"And your business, madame, have you succeeded in finding a buyer?" Aaron asked, turning to her.

Noting Silas's consternation at the comment, Brien said cautiously, "There is an interested party, but we have yet to fix a price."

"And who is this buyer?"

"That should remain—" Silas started to object.

"There can be no harm in divulging his name, Silas. The captain will no doubt be discreet." Brien gazed at Aaron coolly, making the comment more a command than an observation. "A Dutchman from Philadelphia by the name of Horace Van Zandt is near to making an offer for our entire holdings."

"Van Zandt?" Aaron seemed surprised and not pleasantly so.

"You know of him?" Brien was a heartbeat away from raw fury. Now he had opinions on her business dealings. He was insinuating himself into every blessed aspect of her life!

Whatever had she done to deserve such torture at fate's hand?

"I know him well enough." Aaron frowned.

Brien wanted desperately to ignore his opinion and change the subject altogether. But it was clear that his opinion was counted of some worth by her friends and by others well versed in trading. If she hadn't pursued it, Silas would have.

"You do not make your acquaintance sound like a happy one."

"Van Zandt made his money running the blockade during the war. I ran into him when I served as a ship patrolling the New England coast. It is rumored that even now his ships prowl the Caribbean looking for prey." He scowled, studying the wine in the glass he held. "He played both sides during the war to fatten his own purse. He has no scruples. I can only caution you to see the color of his gold before signing any property over to him." He looked up and met Brien's gaze unexpectedly. She couldn't make herself look away. "I would rather that Weston Trading continue its American trade. This country is growing; the need for goods grows steadily and will make fortunes for merchants with foresight."

"Tell that to the colonial assemblies," Brien said, reddening and looking sharply away. "They are the ones who have forced us to this."

"Give it time." Aaron gazed at her evenly. "They will come to their senses."

Helen turned their attention once again to their meal. "Shall we take coffee in the parlor? The seats there are far more comfortable."

Murmuring agreement, they rose and followed their swaying hostess.

Brien realized that Helen's face was pale and that she had served coffee but had taken none herself. She had noticed that Helen picked at her food and that her hand periodically went to her middle and lingered there. In a flash, the quirks of her behavior fell into place. She was in labor, but was too polite to spoil the evening. Brien was astounded at her friend's self-control . . . and at her own ignorance in such matters.

"Helen, who is your midwife?" She deposited her cup on the table and went to put her arms around Helen's shoulders. "You must come upstairs and we will send for her."

"W-what?" Silas jumped as if he'd been shot. "Has the t-time come?"

"I fear so." Helen smiled apologetically.

"Silly goose!" Silas anxiously wrapped her hand in his. "You should have said something!"

"There is plenty of time." She smiled up into her husband's concern-lined face. Then a sharp contraction caused her to draw breath in surprise. She clutched her stomach instinctively. "Well, things are moving along. I suppose you'd best fetch Mrs. O'Grady."

"But will you be all right until I return?" Silas was ashen as he and Brien helped Helen to her feet and started for the stairs.

Aaron stepped forward. "I can fetch the midwife for you, if you will just tell me where she lives."

Silas shot a grateful look at him. "The little house at the end of Walpole Street. And do hurry."

Brien roused the servants and set them to preparing water and linens. Then she helped Helen undress and get into bed while Silas paced outside the room. When Aaron's knock sounded on the front doors, Silas raced down the stairs to meet him and bustled Mrs. O'Grady straight up to the bedroom. Moments later he entered the drawing room, looking dejected, and asked Aaron to stay and keep him company.

"There doesn't seem to be much a mere man can do in these things." He sank into a chair. "This is our fourth and if we had a dozen, I should never get used to it."

Aaron poured him a brandy and sat down beside him to wait.

BRIEN HAD NEVER felt so inadequate as now when she tried to be useful at this birthing. She had no idea what needed to be done or when help was required. She thanked heaven for Mrs. O'Grady, who issued orders with military precision and calmly explained the signs and stages to her and the other female members of the household.

Two hours of gradually intensifying pain were followed by a sudden release and Helen almost smiled as she brought forth the baby. Mrs. O'Grady did smile, and her countenance and the atmosphere of the room both changed. The worst was past.

Brien held the baby while the cord was tied and cut, and she realized that she was having difficulty seeing. Emotion filled her throat and eyes as she wiped off the wriggling, squalling baby and then wrapped him snugly in a fresh blanket. The glow in Helen's face as Brien placed him in her arms for the first time made her seem the most beautiful woman on earth.

The exhilaration of the moment seized Brien so that she trembled, scarcely able to comprehend the wild mix of feelings whirling in her. As she watched mother and baby discovering each other, she felt privileged to have been a small part of such a life-altering event . . . and sensed that one of the lives that had just been altered was hers.

After they bathed Helen and helped her into a fresh nightdress, Brien hurried downstairs to get Silas. Bleary-eyed and coatless, he jumped up at the sight of her.

"You can go to her now, Silas," Brien told him with a loving smile. "Don't scowl so. Helen and the baby are both fine."

Relief spread through his frame and he squeezed Brien's

hands before bounding out of the room. When she turned back she found Aaron staring at her strangely.

"I didn't know you were still here." She smiled, inexplicably pleased.

"Silas felt the need for companionship." He reached for her hand and led her to the settee. "I was happy to oblige."

She sat down and Aaron brought her a glass of sherry. As she accepted it, their hands touched and a small shock of pleasure raced through her. When he sat down beside her, she felt a rush of warmth and connection to him that she didn't want to have to explain. She looked up at him with all of her joy and reverence for the experience visible in her unguarded eyes.

"It was wonderful." Her voice softened. "I've never attended at a birthing before. It's—" She shrugged with wonderment.

"Miraculous?" he offered.

"A good word for it."

She reached instinctively for his hand and felt him startle at her touch. Before she could withdraw, he had taken her hand between his and raised it to his lips. Moved by her recent encounter with the miracle of birth, she felt drawn to him as never before. She touched his face, tracing the squareness of his jaw as she had done so often in her mind.

"If you could have seen the baby . . . so tiny and helpless. I just wanted to hold and protect him. . . ." She shook her head. "And Helen was so strong and so beautiful. When we put the baby in her arms, I half-expected to hear trumpets sounding from the heavens."

Aaron chuckled and pulled her to him, wrapping his arms around her. She laid her head on his chest, feeling not the slightest inclination to move. He smelled of soap and brandy—a musky, spicy scent that seemed to fit him. She could feel the drumming of his heart against her cheek and felt her own slowing to match its rhythm. She had never felt such closeness, such intimacy with anyone. He seemed to

want to share her very experience and the emotions it
stirred in her. Even more amazingly, she wanted to share
them with him.

It was some time before they heard Silas's footsteps on
the stairs and broke apart. Brien jumped up shakily, smooth-
ing her dress, and turned to greet him.

"I have another son!" Silas said as he strode in, grinning
broadly. "And he is *beautiful*! Let's have a brandy to celebrate."

Brien stole a look at Aaron. He was truly a remarkable
man. She wondered if in a lifetime a husband and wife
would tire of seeing each other. It didn't seem so with Silas
and Helen.

The drift of her thoughts disturbed her. Too much had
happened this night to see it all clearly now. And she was so
very tired.

"No, thank you." She declined the glass Silas offered her.
"I cannot or I will spend the night in a chair. Good night,
Silas." She turned to Aaron and extended her hand. "Good
night, Aaron."

Silas studied his companion as Brien quit the room.
Something had passed between them; he was sure of it. Helen had said as much, but then she always seemed to know
about these things.

He regarded the captain closely as they raised their
glasses. Aaron Durham's rapt attention to Brien had not
been casual desire for a beautiful woman. He was truly smit-
ten. Silas marked that he would give his wise wife her due—
in due time.

Seventeen

T HE NEXT FEW DAYS were difficult for Aaron, knowing Brien was in the city, conducting business with the likes of Horace Van Zandt, and knowing he had no pretext for involving himself in her business. Worse still, he kept recalling the way she had looked that night in Hastings's drawing room . . . with her eyes luminous with earthy pleasure and a poignancy to her half-smile that stirred his heart. She had settled into his arms as if she would be content to never move again.

Now each time he thought of that heart-melting contact his chest felt naked and his arms felt empty. It was longing, pure and simple. And it was nothing short of infuriating.

He fled for a few days to New York, hoping to divert such thoughts by raising capital to expand his shipbuilding venture. But when he met with his friend Harold Caswell and a handpicked cadre of potential investors, he realized that every one of them had served aboard a ship during the war and every one had crossed paths—if not swords—with Horace Van Zandt.

At the end of the war for independence, people had been anxious to put the conflict behind them and were loath to ask questions about the Dutchman's suspiciously lucrative wartime activities. Perhaps, Aaron suggested to Harold and the others, it would be good to have some documentation of Horace Van Zandt's double-dealing activities. They agreed.

Thus as he collected funds for a new ship, he also collected affidavits and ship's logs showing that Van Zandt's much-improved fortunes were the result of the way he had fleeced both England and the colonies at every turn. The question of what Aaron could do with that proof, however, was far from answered. Brien was more likely to be furious than grateful if he produced it . . . would be sure he did it to prove she wasn't capable of conducting her own business.

Successful beyond his expectations, but no closer to achieving what was becoming the core of his desires, he returned to Boston to arrange construction space in a local shipyard, materials, and workmen.

It was at the end of a long day of meeting with shipwrights, strakers, sail makers, and riggers that he stopped at a tavern called The Golden Spar near the waterfront. Seated alone at a small table in the corner, he watched the flow of the trade as he waited for his food and nursed a tankard of good ale.

The service seemed too slow to meet the satisfaction of two burly patrons, backwoodsmen from the look of their rough deerskin shirts and wrapped leggings. They pounded their empty mugs against the planking table and the tavernkeeper disappeared behind a tattered curtain and returned with a serving wench, shoving her ahead of him.

"Get to it 'fore I lay you flat," he growled, brandishing a fist.

The young woman's carriage was erect, her dark hair was

pulled back into a long, thick plait, and she seemed cleaner than most tavern wenches. As she approached, one of the woodsmen laughed drunkenly and grabbed for her with both arms. She pulled back in the nick of time, and he went sprawling on the floor. The trapper's companion howled with laughter, but he came up red-faced and sputtering.

"Uppity bitch! You need learnin'!"

The wench clutched her empty pitcher and backed away . . . toward the corner where Aaron sat. As the woodsman lunged at her again, she swung her pitcher at his head and dealt him a solid blow that sent him tumbling.

For a stunned moment the entire tavern was quiet, then raucous laughter rocked the pump room, mixed with hoots and calls aimed at the remaining trapper. Pride was at stake as the second man bounded up, determined to mete out justice. His bellow froze the wench in her tracks, and as he charged her she stood with shocked eyes, watching her doom descending.

Aaron stepped in front of the wench, and the woodsman—already committed to the action—crashed into his stomach, headfirst. All three slammed back into a nearby table and sent patrons and tankards flying as they struggled to regain their footing on the damp floor. The woodsman went down on one knee, but Aaron's years at sea on rainsoaked decking helped him maintain his footing. He landed a knee up under the trapper's chin and sent him sprawling beside his friend.

Gripping his battered stomach and panting heavily, Aaron turned to the girl, who stood cowering in the corner. As she edged out into the lantern light he was suddenly riveted by the sight of her face. Those features, those same eyes were etched in the recess of his memory. Then it hit him, harder than the woodsman's head . . . *he knew her.*

He tossed a coin to the tavernkeeper, declaring that it was to pay for the romp he'd just had and the one to come.

He hoisted the girl up and over his shoulder, and headed for the narrow stairs that led to the sporting rooms above.

Ducking into the first dingy nook that passed for a room, Aaron straightened and allowed the girl to slide down him, turning her so that her back was to him and he could hold her arms against her sides.

"Slimy, backstabbing cur! Do yer worst while ye can—"

"Not likely." His breath came fast as he fought to maintain his advantage. "I've no taste for the skin of a tavern wench—if indeed that's what you are."

The sense of his words finally penetrated her anger and her struggles slowed.

"You're new to this tavern and to this life, eh?" he continued. "You were of another station not long ago . . . say . . . a lady's maid?" A productively quiet moment passed. "I only want information. If I let you go, do you promise not to flee?"

She nodded slowly, but no sooner had he released her than she flew to the questionable haven of the nearest corner. He reached for a sooty lantern hanging in the passage outside and held it up to look at her.

"You're the one." He nodded. "What's your name?"

"E-Ella."

"You were a lady's maid in England about two years ago, is that not so?"

She nodded, still wary.

"And your lady was Brien Weston Trechaud?"

"Th' same." Her eyes widened as she studied his face. "And now I've a clue who you be. Th' clothes are fancier, but th' scar's th' same. Yer 'im that . . . ." She was instantly hostile. " 'Im that pretended t' marry 'er! Ye'll not get a word outta me—"

"I know who and where Lady Brien is. She's here in the colonies, this moment, in Boston. You need not fear for her safety on my account. I would do nothing to hurt her." Her manner was openly mistrustful, but at least she was listening. He patted a nearby stool. "Tell me about you first. How did you come to such a place?"

"I'm in-den-shured."

"How is that?" No woman of good reputation would choose this life willingly.

"It was that Raoul's doin'. 'Er 'usband. 'E said I stole an' 'ad me carted off while I was too sick t' defend meself." She eyed him, evaluating his face and finally taking a seat on that stool. " 'Ow is she? Is she all right? 'Er and 'er 'usband?"

"She is fine. As to her husband, I cannot say. Nor can any mortal." Seeing her frown, he leaned a bit closer. "He's dead. Nearly two years now. They were wed only a month or so before a fire claimed him."

"No." The girl stared in amazement, then her temper ignited. "No more than 'e deserved, th' bastard. Insisted on marryin' my lady even knowin' she 'ated 'im."

"Go on," Aaron urged when she stopped. "Tell me what happened to you."

"I was sentenced aboard a prison ship bound for some colony. But th' turnkey figured t' make a bit o' coin on me an' a few other women. Sold us onto a ship bound 'ere instead." She looked around the hot, smelly room. "I only been 'ere a few weeks. Before 'im"—she threw a contemptuous look toward the door and her new master—"my papers was 'eld by another innkeeper, out a ways from town. He was a good an' decent man. Not like this limp poker."

"So you were sold illegally as an indenture. What did you steal?"

"*Nothin'*!" She fairly exploded. " 'E 'anded me over t' a pocket justice . . . 'ad me sentenced without a say or a witness . . . just 'is word." She jumped up and glared. "As if I'd take aught from my lady. She tried t' get out of marryin' 'im by marryin' *you*. When they found out th' vows was false, she was forced t' wed 'im anyway."

"Were they false?" He edged forward on his seat. "Was the marriage a sham?"

She lowered her gaze to her work-reddened hands. "Th' bloke who brought ye t' th' church was my uncle. When 'is lordship said there was no record of th' vows, I went lookin' for 'im. Couldn't find 'im nowhere. An' th' church was locked up tight, just as 'is lordship said."

"So, Billy Rye duped you along with the rest of us?" Aaron demanded.

She shook her head. "I can't believe 'e'd do such a thing t' me." Old shame washed over her again. "I tried t' make it up t' my lady. When she told 'im she'd never be a wife t' 'im, th' jackal might have killed 'er if I 'adn'ta been there wi' a pistol."

"You turned a *gun* on him?"

Ella rolled her eyes at his reaction. "She refused t' bed 'im . . . told 'im there'd been another. He left, swearin' revenge. I climbed out o' my sickbed t' go t' 'er side an' after . . . I collapsed. When I woke up later, I was in gaol. Already sentenced." Her eyes and voice lowered. "Lord knows what 'e done t' 'erself, th' brute."

"She told him about me . . . us."

"An' said 'e should 'annul' th' vows." She gave him a fiercely resentful look. "I'd wager 'e made 'er pay well for your time on 'er. An' now ye mean t' wring yer price from 'er as well. More gold, is it? Or is it another toss ye fancy?"

Truth be told, he wasn't sure what he wanted from Brien. But he admitted with chagrin that jealousy had ridden him hard at the thought that she took another husband . . . even unwillingly. Was he relieved to find that she had been forced?

He slapped his thigh and looked up. "Ella, I've had my eye on a house in Boston, but it would take some staff and more time than I wish to spend running it. Loyal as you are to your previous employer, I feel you could be trusted. Have you the education and skills to make a housekeeper?"

Surprise kept her silent for a moment. "I'm sure I could if it was a house of middlin' size. I learn quick."

"If I buy your papers back, will you come to work for me . . . with wages?"

She stared at him warily, then looked around the dirty cove that passed for a sleeping room. Whatever else might be required in the bargain, she seemed to think it could be no worse than the indignities of labor in this wretched hole. She straightened her spine and nodded.

"I will."

HORACE VAN ZANDT strode heavily into the offices of Weston Trading and paused, listing each ledger, desk, and chair on some mental tally sheet. His gaze quickly fixed on Brien, assessing her as if she were part of the acquisition he had come to discuss.

She fought a wave of revulsion to extend her hand to the man. His ponderous weight shifted about his frame as he bent to press bulbous lips to her hand. The thought of being trapped with him in the offices for even a short time was so disagreeable that she insisted they have a thorough, first-hand look at the warehouse and the inventory.

Van Zandt was torn between getting a closer look at the goods he intended to buy and avoiding the exertion it would require. A confident smile from Brien convinced him to make the inspection tour.

More than an hour later, they filed back into the offices. Brien took the chair beside Silas, glad to have Van Zandt across the desk from her. His red face and thick lips had a cruel cast and he breathed in quick snorts, as if fighting his own bulk to draw air. She couldn't wait to be done with this bit of negotiation. If he was unloved, she mused, it was not entirely the result of his business practices.

"Mr. Hastings has supplied you with a listing of property and inventory, I believe." She affected a cordial but official tone.

"He hasss," the fat man hissed, rocking back in his groaning chair.

"You've seen the quality of the goods. Have you any questions?"

"I know all I need," Van Zandt assured her, his beady black eyes narrowing.

"Then all that remains is that we agree upon a price," Brien said firmly, hoping her determination would be taken for confidence.

"I make offer," he growled, "at dinner tonight."

Brien bristled at his arrogance, but bridled her rising anger. Instinctively, she knew that charm would produce results where condescension or indignation would fail.

"I am afraid I have plans for this evening, sir." She smiled politely.

"Tomorrow, den," he demanded.

Her pleasantness thinned. She glanced at Silas, whose eyes widened in warning and she understood the risk she was taking.

"I . . . don't see why not. But if I have an offer, I may think on it today and we may be agreed when we meet tomorrow."

Van Zandt's eyes narrowed to slits as he openly appraised her.

"Den . . . for dis varehouse und goods, I give you twelf t'ousand sterling." His tongue curled around the final "g," drawing it out obscenely.

Brien's heart sank. "I shall need no time to consider that offer, sir. The answer is no." She threw a smoky look at her opponent from beneath a thick fringe of dark lashes. "The warehouse and inventory are worth well more than thirty thousand and you know it. Unless you would care to make another offer . . . closer to the fair worth of these holdings . . ." She studied him as openly as he studied her . . . as one man would assess another.

Van Zandt pursed his thick lips. The game took on new

interest for him and his smile became a fair counterfeit of geniality.

Silas, bewildered by the turn of events, looked from one contender to the other. Brien's steady gaze had the gray chill of winter ice.

Van Zandt slapped an elephantine knee with a hand. "By Gott . . . vat vould you haf me offer?"

"Thirty would be acceptable."

"Den you vill not zell." Van Zandt abandoned all pretense of humor, but Brien marked well that he made no move to leave.

"On the contrary, sir. I shall sell at a fair price." Brien's cool tone now matched her gaze. "Would you care to make another offer at dinner tomorrow evening? By then you may have had time to reevaluate the property."

An ugly smile laid bare Van Zandt's yellowed and decaying teeth. "Ja. I t'ink on it. Who knows? Maybe you soften dis heart of mine." He patted the broadcloth-covered expanse that engulfed what at one time must have been a chest.

"What is good for the purse may not delight the heart, Mister Van Zandt, and vice versa. Silas and I will see you at dinner tomorrow evening. We will arrange for dinner at the Braithwaite Inn. Say, seven o'clock?"

He struggled up, panting with the effort, and brushed the hand she offered with his lips. The floor groaned under his bulk as he swayed out and was joined by two hard-looking toughs just outside the office door.

Brien watched serenely until he was well out into the street, then she grabbed her handkerchief and rubbed her hand viciously where his mouth had made contact with it.

"At least it was short," she gritted out.

"Brien, the man is no fool," Silas warned. "It is not prudent to bait him—or underestimate him."

A gleam entered her eyes as she faced her friend. "I know well the force of cunning, and I don't fear it. I will have twenty-five thousand and not a penny less. Paying a fair price is his cost for having dinner with me."

Silas winced. "You believe he is thinking only of dinner?"

"He will"—she smiled coolly—"when he sees Dyso is my escort."

THE NEXT EVENING, Brien and Silas, accompanied by Dyso, went by carriage to the Braithwaite Inn. The inn's modest name belied an elegance of cuisine that rivaled some of the best restaurants on the Continent. Visiting wealth and dignitaries, lacking their own facilities, often used the Braithwaite's dining rooms to entertain. Thus it was the perfect place for such a meeting.

Brien arranged that Dyso be seated at the table beside theirs and that he be served whatever she herself ordered. Her protector's concern was plain in his face. Brien had told him enough to ask for his alertness, but advised him to show restraint, whatever befell. He indicated clearly that his strong arms were her defense. And she felt relieved.

Van Zandt arrived shortly and drew poorly veiled stares from the other patrons. If Dyso's scarred, fearsome countenance had shocked them, Van Zandt revolted them. The irony of these two associated with the most beautiful woman in the room was made clear by their surreptitious glances.

"Hastings. Madame." Van Zandt stared avidly at her. But whether it was a genuine desire or merely a ploy in the negotiation, she had no way of knowing.

"Mr. Hastings has a new child and may be called home unexpectedly," Brien said, nodding to Silas. "Thus, Monsieur Dyso also accompanied me, to see me safely home." As she indicated her man at the next table, Dyso fixed Van Zandt with a steely glare and the Dutchman caught a glimpse of the chilling potential of the lady's protector.

Van Zandt regarded his lovely companion closely, reassessing her. She had planned well. He would not have expected such canniness and determination in a woman.

"Dis offer . . . I haf t'ought about—" he began.

Brien raised a hand to cut him off, establishing her control of the pace. "Please let us order first. I am famished. Let us eat, then we shall talk."

Brien managed to be polite through the courses of excellent food, even as the revolting Van Zandt mauled huge servings of beef and downed quantities of food and wine. Between courses, he boasted of his adventures, relating some gruesomely detailed accounts of battles during the war. She was soon ruing her tactic of insisting they eat first.

When they were served coffee after the final course, she nodded to Silas, who raised the topic of the sale.

"I trust you have reevaluated the properties," she inserted.

"Ja. I haf done much t'inking." He wiped greasy fingers on his vest and watched her keenly as he delivered his proposal. "Und I offer eighteen t'ousand."

She was careful not to overreact. "Certainly that is fair for the goods and stores. Now on to the warehouse. What will you offer for it?"

"No." His shaking head sent reverberations through his fleshy jowls. "Eighteen for all of it."

"Currently we have merchandise and commodities that are worth twice that figure." She struggled for every ounce of composure she could muster. "As you well know, we cannot collect outstanding debts, due to the vindictive assembly's action. If we will not give the goods to our customers, what makes you think we will give them to you?"

"I t'ink on it. Maybee we meet again—jus' you und me." He gazed evenly at Silas and tossed his head to indicate Dyso. "Sometimes . . . two agree better dan t'ree or four." The implication was clear. Silas had been right; the man would demand more for his money than honest goods and property.

"Really, Van Zandt," Silas sputtered. "To insist on seeing Lady Brien alone—"

She pushed back her chair and rose. "Good evening, sir."

Van Zandt pushed up with surprising speed and grabbed her wrist across the table.

Dyso was instantly at her side, his face murderous. Van Zandt released her and cowered back as Dyso reached for him. Brien managed to restrain him as Silas stepped between the men with his hands extended. "Please"—he struggled to keep his words quiet—"I'm certain Mr. Van Zandt meant no harm."

More than anything else in the world, Brien wanted to let Dyso teach Van Zandt a lesson, but she pulled his arm and motioned to him to do nothing further. Their abrupt movements had created a stir in the room.

"Please sit, madame." Van Zandt seemed unsettled by the reaction his movements had unleashed. "Ve vill discuss more, eh?"

Brien felt the tide of advantage turning in her favor. "We will not. If you should wish to make a suitable offer—say, twenty-eight thousand—then you may transmit it to me through my agent, Mr. Hastings. Good evening."

She turned from the red-faced Van Zandt and walked with great dignity to the door. She didn't see Van Zandt's muttering or the fist he shook at her back. But Dyso, who seemed to have eyes in the back of his head, caught it. He paused to look back into the dining room as Silas opened the door for Brien. His eyes darkened, becoming like chips of black flint.

Eighteen

IN THE FOLLOWING DAYS, Brien settled into a strange, dichotomous existence.

By day she was the perfect guest, dividing her time between the warehouse with Silas and the house with Helen. During her days with Silas she met a wide variety of Boston's tradesmen and shopkeepers and began to see that the troubles that affected Weston Trading were a part of a larger financial morass. The other business owners seemed to believe that once a constitution was in place and the new government began to issue a single coinage, things would improve. On her days with Helen, she enjoyed helping with the children and the new baby, and learned a great deal that had been omitted from her education as a woman. She grew to enjoy reading to the children, giving them their lessons, chaperoning their play in the garden . . . holding the new baby to give Helen a respite.

A week after the birth, Helen was up and about and insisting on inviting a few friends for tea. The women represented a range of ages, stages of life, and political affiliations, but universally they welcomed Brien into their midst . . . chatting, exchanging stories, and making arrangements for entertaining and visiting. She couldn't help contrasting these experiences with those when she had entertained in London, where her class, rank, and marital status had marked her as a prime target for gossip and speculation. With quiet pleasure she authenticated Aaron's view that this place was indeed special—liberating in ways she hadn't expected.

Then there were the nights. She slept with French windows open and the covers thrown back and still had difficulty sleeping. Flashes of heat erupted through her sleep to send her bolt upright in bed, with her hair damp against her neck and her nightdress clinging to her. Again and again an auburn-haired lover came to her in her dreams, teasing, tempting, tantalizing her. Sometimes she awakened furious, other times she awakened tingling with excitement or aching with longing. More alarming, she sometimes awakened feeling a curious weight against her arm and breast . . . as if she had been cradling . . .

The heat and longing of her nighttime struggles began to insert themselves into her daytime existence in the form of incessant thoughts of Aaron Durham. Where was he? Was he standing somewhere at that moment with his legs braced and his arms folded over his broad chest, running his finger over his lip in contemplation? Was some other woman enjoying his irresistible laugh, relishing the twinkle in his unusual eyes, and sighing with contentment in the gentle strength of his embrace? Were those handsome lips burning paths down some other woman's— When would she see him again?

Strangely, the business that had brought her almost halfway around the world seemed less urgent now. A week passed without a word from Van Zandt and she was strangely unaffected. She had adopted an outlook that insisted all would work out for the best. Gratefully, she recalled and heeded her father's advice that time often untangled problems too complex or overwhelming for mere humans to solve.

Then one morning, as Brien sat reading one of Boston's newspapers, Helen's housekeeper appeared at the parlor door with a puzzled look on her face.

"There's a woman come to the back door . . . says she has a word for you, ma'am."

A slender young woman in a simple blue dress stood just inside the kitchen. At the sound of footsteps, she turned and Brien was astonished into speechlessness.

"My lady!" the young woman exclaimed, then clapped a hand over her mouth.

"Ella!" Brien held her arms out to her former servant.

For a long moment the highborn lady and young woman in servant's garb shocked the kitchen staff with their long, tearful embrace. When Brien pulled back to look at her friend, she glimpsed the cook's puzzlement and realized that the kitchen staff had stopped work and was staring at them. She quickly pulled Ella through the house and up the stairs. Once in the privacy of her room, she grasped her friend's hands and held them out from her sides, examining every inch of her.

"You haven't changed a bit!" Brien pulled her to a chair beside the tea table and sat down facing her friend, savoring the moment. "How did you get here? How did you find me?"

"My employer spoke of a lady come from England t' do business, an' when I 'eard yer name I was shocked. Oh, my lady, ye look so beautiful I can scarce believe my eyes." The former maid's eyes shone with moisture. "They say yer a widow now."

"So you've heard that much." Brien sighed under the burden of returning memories. "He died not long after that argument in my room. I fell ill that same night, after I put you to bed. I was feverish for a time and don't recall much except that there was a fire. Oh, Ella, I've pressed our solicitors hard for almost two years for word of you. It seemed you had vanished from the face of the earth. Tell me what happened to you."

Ella poured forth a story of betrayal, greed, hardship, and unexpected benevolence. Her papers had finally been bought by a kindly merchant of Boston who found her working in a waterfront tavern. He had proved to be a fair master and she had been made housekeeper, a position she had always coveted. Brien shook her head in amazement.

"Of course we'll buy back your papers, now that I've found you. And we'll set you up in a shop of your own—or a small inn—or whatever you fancy!"

Her enthusiasm and unbridled generosity made Ella squirm. "Oh, no, my lady." She shook her head. "I owe th' man a great debt. Besides, I'm 'appy now in my new master's 'ouse and I'm not anxious t' leave."

In the time since her rescue from the tavern, Ella had seen firsthand the worth of the man who had bought her freedom. She had witnessed his effect on others and the evenhandedness with which he treated all.

Puzzled by Ella's reluctance to accept compensation for the trials she had suffered, Brien continued, "But you must let me do something for you. You've suffered much on my account and I cannot live with myself knowing you're in bondage when money would set you free. Ella, you must let me!"

Ella smiled sheepishly. "Well, I guess I could allow for a bit o' 'elp. It's just that—I know ye 'ave another maid now an' I feel beholden t' my new master . . ."

Brien, seeing her friend in a noble light, picked it up with a teasing lilt. "So, you're reluctant to leave your new master, eh? And just how good has he been to you, Ella?"

Ella's blush revealed her confusion in a way that validated Brien's assumptions. "So, that's it!"

"Not exactly 'im." Ella squirmed anew. "But there's someone in 'is 'ouse." It wasn't altogether a lie. There was a handsome fellow who came often to do business with Captain Durham. And he had cast a lingering eye on the new housekeeper.

"Then you must take the money for your papers and, by all means, stay on in your new master's house. What is his name?"

Desperate, Ella chose the last one on her thoughts. "George. Anthony George."

Brien went to a chest and threw it open, pulling from beneath a stack of garments a leather pouch that contained folding notes and a goodly sum in gold.

"There." She put the pouch in Ella's hands. "Just more than a thousand."

"Aghhh!" Ella nearly strangled. "More than enough!"

"You will give this to your Mister George and bid him to see you a free woman again?"

"Yes." Ella's eyes were moist as she threw her arms around Brien. "I'll be ever grateful."

A knock came at the door and Helen breezed into the room with the baby in her arms.

"Brien, my dear, I do so hate to ask—" She halted the moment she spotted Ella and realized she had intruded on something private. "I had no idea you had a guest."

"Helen, this is Ella Jenkins, who used to work for me. It happens that she now lives and works in Boston."

"Pleased to meet you." With a distracted smile, Helen turned back to Brien. "I'll find someone else to—"

"Did you want me to take him?" Brien rose and held out her arms for the baby.

"Well"—Helen gave Ella an apologetic glance—"Henry has gotten into another scrape and I've got to see the neighbors and sort it out."

"I'll watch the little one." Brien took the baby and shooed Helen off to see about her eldest son. When she returned to Ella and settled once more, there was a glow about her.

"Well, I never." Ella looked from her to the baby and back.

"Never what?" Brien frowned.

"Expected t' see ye volunteerin' t' mind a babe." She watched the way Brien traced a down cheek with her finger. "Much less cuddlin' one."

Brien's smile contained new and utterly uncontrollable feminine emotions. "There are probably a number of things about me now that would surprise you." She began to tell Ella about her life since Raoul's death, about her shocking reunion with Aaron Durham, about her social life in London, and about her tumultuous trip across the ocean.

"So th' bloke ye married thought th' vows was good, too, then." Ella's spirits drooped noticeably. "I'm so sorry, my lady. I can't think what went wrong. If there was anythin' I could do—"

"You needn't apologize," Brien said, glancing down at the baby that was beginning to stir in her arms. "It has all worked out for the best. If the vows had been valid, I would be a married woman right now. And if Aaron Durham took it into his stubborn head to press his nuptial rights, what recourse would I have?" She gave a somewhat forced shiver. "Can you imagine? Me, married? With a whole houseful of children?"

She looked down, gave the baby an exaggerated smile, and made a cooing sound.

Ella blinked. "Lord knows, ye'd want no part o' that," the former maid said, watching her. "Bein' shackled t' a man's bed . . . havin' t' bear 'is children. It'd be downright intolerable."

JUST PAST DINNER that evening, Ella entered the dining room of the house she now managed for Aaron Durham. He sat alone, savoring a glass of claret and looking over the drawings for his latest ship design. She planted herself before him, and when he raised a questioning gaze, she pulled a leather purse from her apron and placed it in his hands.

"I saw my lady today. She bade me give this t' me new master—t' see me a free woman." The grin on her face matched his as he realized that for things to happen so, his housekeeper must have kept his confidence.

Then he recognized the worn leather pouch in his hand and threw back his head with a resounding laugh. When he sobered, he turned again to Ella's bemused frown.

"Twice paid with the same money. Shall I make the same vow?"

Nineteen

DRESSED FOR BED that evening, Brien paced her room. The sweet night air wafted in through the open windows and set her mind buzzing with the events of the past two weeks. They would soon baptize the babe "Brian" for her and "Lawrence" for her father. Her father would at last have a namesake, even though a friend had been the one to supply it.

Why couldn't she be like other women . . . content to bear children and do stitchery and tend social ties? But she wasn't like other women and in her deepest heart she knew that wishing wouldn't make it so. There was an independence in her and a strong will that wouldn't let her yield control to anyone. There was a curiosity, a yen for learning in her that wouldn't be stifled. And yet, there were times when she felt such longing . . .

Would she ever find a remedy for this restlessness? Had she ever felt at peace?

With a pang of conscience, she realized that she had felt peaceful and fulfilled as she lay in Aaron's arms that night on board *The Lady's Secret*. Something about him and his loving reached inside her to her very soul and calmed her.

Tonight, however, it sent heat and longing welling in her loins. She thought of the way a casual movement of his shoulders or the light pressure of his hand on hers could start a fire in her. She secretly enjoyed the possessive way his eyes flowed over her body whenever they met. Beneath his easygoing manner simmered volatile passions, the combination of calmness and intensity intrigued her. His wit and double-edged conversation challenged her to be at her best—to best him if she could.

She suffered a shiver that warned of another presence in the room. Turning quickly, she spotted a pair of tall black boots in the shadows cast by the curtains. She looked up to find the subject of her thoughts, Aaron Durham, sitting casually on the window seat, watching her.

"What are you doing here?" she whispered.

He rose and stepped out of the shadows into the warm circle of candlelight . . . tall, vital, and intensely male . . . his hair hanging loose and his golden eyes glowing.

"I have come to see to your interests, my lady." His voice had a provocative quality that sent a shiver through her. "I believe you struck a bargain that went sour."

"How could you have heard? *I* haven't even gotten word yet." Her eyes widened. "What have you done? Did you go to see him?" She stalked toward him, thinking only of his audacity and her desire to get her hands around his stubborn neck. "Van Zandt was near to making an offer for our entire holdings and if you've—"

"Van Zandt?" He laughed shortly, put his hands on his

hips, and leaned back. "I'm not here about that business, sweetness. I'm here about another bargain entirely."

"What other bargain?"

"Ours."

She froze for a moment while every bit of composure she possessed deserted her. "We—we don't have a bargain anymore."

"I am surprised at you, Brien." He folded his arms and looked her up and down. "A true businesswoman would have demanded her money back when she found out she wasn't actually married. Why didn't you? Could it be that you secretly wanted the deal to stand? Somewhere in the deepest, darkest recesses of your heart you actually want to be married to me?"

"Fine. I want my money back. Every blessed penny of it."

"Too late. I've decided not to give it back after all." He smiled with infuriating good humor. "I've decided to give you the full value of our original bargain instead."

"Now see here—"

"I am seeing here. And there." His eyes dropped down her frame to the silhouette the candles were casting on her nightdress. "And there. Mmmm, and there . . ."

She looked down at the translucent fabric and wheeled, snatching her dressing gown from the bed and shoving her arms into it. With her face aflame, she turned and found him standing inches away, staring down at her with that mesmerizing gold heat in his eyes. That made it all the harder for her to think . . . which she knew was probably the point of it. Well, part of the point.

"See here . . . the original deal was for you to marry me and then just walk away. Never to ask for more money or to make further demands on me."

"So it was. And I wedded you and walked away. Clearly, I fulfilled my part of the bargain."

"You did not. And here you are making demands . . ."

"I am not demanding. I'm *offering*."

" 'Offering'?" Her heart began to pound as she watched his gaze fasten on her lips.

"My services . . . the execution of my husbandly offices . . . the rights to my assistance and my attention . . . wherever, whenever you say."

"Aaron Durham—" She tried to summon at least a modicum of outrage and back away, but it was hard. Her very bones grew fluid with desire. The warmth of his body engulfed hers. The soap and brandy scent of him filled her head. The memory of his lips on her skin set the tips of her breasts tingling. "It is near midnight, at the least! This is no time and no place to be discussing such things!"

He laughed and spread his arms wide, opening himself to her. "Where would be a better place for me to tell you that my ship is haunted by your memory . . . that I can't walk the quarterdeck or take refuge in my cabin without seeing you and feeling you all around me? When would be a better time to tell you that the feel of you naked in my arms is burned into my flesh? That I see you in my mind the last thing at night and the first thing each morning?"

Finding herself backed against the bed, she swayed, realizing that resistance was probably futile. The misery he was describing was also hers. She watched his tongue appear at the corner of his mouth and sweep slowly, luxuriantly across his lower lip.

Hunger swept through her like a hot wind, trembling her to her very depths. When he reached for her and drew her to him, she slid her hands up his arms, imprinting on her sense of touch the shape and hardness of his muscles.

"Whenever, wherever you say, I will be there. Whatever conditions you impose, I will meet. I'm yours, Brien." The entreaty in his eyes and voice melted the last of her defenses. "All you have to do is take me."

His lips closed over hers and she soared against him, meeting his kiss, reveling in his saltiness and the feel of his big, hard body against hers. Whatever happened, she would not regret being with this exceptional man, loving him. The thought slipped into her deeper regions without a twinge of alarm raised. She loved him.

He traced the curves of her waist and hips through her gown, setting her nerves humming with each stroke. She squirmed with pleasure as he nibbled at her ear and her neck, half-tickling, half-devouring her. Eyes aglow, she pushed back and began to work at his buttons. Soon, his jacket and shirt were a heap beside them on the floor.

He folded her against his bare chest and then sank with her onto the bed. Her hair spread over the pillows like a silken flood and her nightdress twisted tightly over her breasts, exposing the tops of those cool mounds and revealing the outline of erect nipples beneath. He nipped the tip of her breast through the fabric and she closed her eyes, whispering his name again and again, like an incantation.

In a moment, his remaining clothes were on the floor and he came to her, removing her gown and replacing it with kisses and caresses that made her sigh with pleasure and moan with encouragement. Time seemed suspended as they explored each other, memorizing beloved curves and exploring erotic hollows until he finally came to her, joining their bodies degree by luscious degree.

This passion was different from that on the ship. Now they arched and joined without reserve, knowing each other's pleasure and indulging the desire that drew them together. One last soaring rush of pleasure pushed them both into an updraft that sent them hurtling through sensory barriers into sweet release.

They lay joined for a long while. Slowly the room stopped spinning and the thunder in Brien's ears receded. Aaron moved to lie beside her and she felt a sense of loss, as though he took a vital part of her with him when they parted. She was soon comforted by his hand stroking her shoulder and hip.

"You have me under a spell, love," he murmured before dropping a kiss on her swollen lips. "And a night with you every two or three years is all it takes to keep me in your thrall."

She frowned as she ran her fingers through the coppery mass of his hair. "You make me sound cold and heartless, when in truth, you seem to be able to talk your way into my bed anytime you like."

"If it were up to me—" He halted and every part of her focused on what he had been about to say.

"If it were up to you, what? What would you have from me, Aaron Durham?"

"I would have you care for me as much as I care for you."

She made a sound of disbelief and looked away. "Stop right there. Before you say something you may have to live up to."

He seized her chin and turned her face to his, his expression suddenly serious. "You don't understand, do you? I intend to live up to every syllable I uttered before God and the vicar."

Her breath caught in her throat and it was a moment before she could speak. "Why are you doing this?"

"Because I care for you, Brien. Heaven help me, I need you in ways I've never needed anyone."

"But I don't want to be needed. I have a life and a—" She pushed him away from her and sat up, drawing the sheet over her as if drawing a veil between them. But a curious, sweet stab of pain shot through her heart. Before she could censor the thought, she blurted out: "What you said about caring for me . . . is it true?"

As she searched his eyes, her heart all but stopped. He took her hands in his.

"I care for you as none before and none after." He kissed each of her fingertips. "To be in the same colony, the very same city, and still be so far away from you is torture for me, Brien. I don't know how you managed to make your-self so much a part of my heart, of my very being, but you have."

"You do care for me." She closed her eyes sharply so as not to reveal the shock that his admission generated in her. She didn't see the way he lay back, grinning, tucking his arms behind his head.

"That, I think, puts it mildly. And have you no words of comfort for me?"

She sat up on her knees, clutching the sheet to her, but it slipped as she turned to him, revealing a ripe breast to his appreciation. "Tell me what words of comfort you want and I'll supply them."

He paused only a second. "Tell me you love me."

Unprepared for so potent a demand, she tried to slide from the bed, but he grabbed her arm to keep her from fleeing.

"What is it you feel, Brien? I have to know."

"I don't want to feel anything. It's not wise." She averted her face more. "It makes no sense."

"But you do, don't you? Tell me." His gentle command forced the truth from her, but not before she could dilute its strength.

"I care very much for you." It would bind her to him to say she loved him. And what did she know of love? Was this madness she felt continually on his account really love? She had named it such in her thoughts, but now . . .

He turned her face to him and tenderly pressed her lips with his. When she opened her eyes, she saw no disappoint-ment, no reproach in his eyes.

"You can't say it now, but you will. We were meant to be together, Brien. And we will be."

How could he be certain of that, when she couldn't count on her emotions from one moment to the next? Marveling at his confidence in the face of her uncertainty, she circled his neck with her arms and drew his lips to hers.

When Brien awoke, hours later, dawn was graying the

morning sky and Aaron was still there beside her, sleeping peacefully. He stirred at the warmth of her hand on his shoulder and raised his head. Seeing her, he smiled contentedly and reached for her.

Could anything in life compare with the intimacy she now shared with him? After a night of hot, intoxicating loving, to awaken to the cool sweetness of dawn, to a tender closeness of body and spirit. Surely life could offer no deeper pleasure.

She kissed his stubbled chin lightly. "You have to leave. Jeannie will be coming to wake me soon."

"And what if I refuse to move—stay here until she comes?" His eyes twinkled.

"You'll ruin my good name." She was scandalized by the realization that he was tempted to do it. "And destroy my reputation as a heartless widow."

"Or confirm the suspicion that you are not."

She donned her dressing gown, gathered his breeches and stockings, and carried them back to the bed. She felt his eyes on her every movement and reveled in her newfound ability to tantalize him.

While he buttoned his breeches, Brien picked up his boots and hugged them to her. When his shirt was tucked and his belt was in place, he turned to her for his footgear.

She was smiling seductively, and his eyes fell to where her partly bare breast was pressed hard against the top of his sleek black boot. An explosion went off in his blood.

"My boots, my lady . . . I'll have them now." He took a step forward.

"Your boots, sir?" she asked coquettishly, backing away.

"I'll have the boots and you," he threatened, stalking her as she backed away from him.

She ran to the bed and was on and over it before he could grab her. He stalked and chased her about the room until she found herself between corner and wardrobe with no place to run. The game was over and the sweetness of surrender lay ahead.

He took the boots from her and dropped them behind him. His big hands slipped inside her open gown next to her bare skin and he crushed her to him, kissing her to within an inch of her sanity.

She stood against the wall for a moment with her eyes still closed. When she finally opened them, Aaron was standing nearby with his boots on, watching her.

"I should go," he finally admitted.

Finding her will at last, Brien moved toward him. "What am I to do with you?"

He smiled gently. "I am your husband, Brien. By my honor. By my choice. But it is up to you whether or not you will be my wife." He cupped the side of her face with his hand. "Whatever you choose, never ask me to do without you again."

Seeing confusion boiling up in her, he gave her a sympathetic smile. "You will need time; I see that."

With one quick, hard kiss, he was gone.

IN THE LONG shadows of the summer dawn, a lone, coarsely clothed figure at the end of the nearby alley rubbed his eyes and ran a callused hand through a mop of hair. His night's vigil ended with the appearance of a booted figure on a window ledge two houses away. He straightened, watching the figure creep along the rooftops and drop to a lower level before disappearing from sight. Turning his collar up against the morning chill, he shoved his hands into his pockets and slipped away quietly along the fences toward the street.

This was just what Van Zandt wanted. And the Dutchman always paid in silver.

Twenty

THAT SAME AFTERNOON a small box containing a blue Chinese vase arrived, addressed to Brien and bearing the bold signature of Aaron Durham. Brien smiled, gingerly tracing the cool porcelain with her fingers.

"Of course, I can't keep it."

"It's lovely, Brien, and not overly personal." Helen studied her friend. "But to accept it would be to approve the captain's attentions to you. Just what do you think of him?"

Brien's mind flooded with responses, but she finally chose: "He seems to be a man of integrity and strength. His manner, however direct, is disarming."

Seeing Brien pause, Helen picked it up. "And his good looks are enough to warm your blood every time he comes near."

"Really, Helen."

"Oh, Brien, do you think us all blind? He looks at you as

if he were dying of thirst and you are cool water. And when he is near, you stiffen and become proper beyond belief. My dear, *Silas* has commented on it—and Silas is always the last to notice."

At the end of the week a note arrived while Brien was reading in the parlor. Helen delivered it to her and stood by as she read it.

" 'Lady Brien Trechaud is invited for a country outing this afternoon at one o'clock. A carriage will call. A. Durham.' " Brien blinked. "This is no invitation, it's a command. It's unthinkable."

"It would be unseemly to go out with him alone," Helen agreed, studying her reaction. "I suppose Dyso would make a formidable chaperone."

"Helen"—Brien's face lighted with mischief—"how long has it been since your children have had an outing in the country?"

PROMPTLY AT ONE o'clock that afternoon a carriage drew up in front of the Hastings household. Brien hurried out to greet him with the three Hastings children in tow and Dyso lumbered out behind them, carrying a large willow hamper. Aaron's face fell at the growing realization of what would happen that afternoon.

"I should have brought two carriages," he muttered.

"This is so good of you, Captain. It's been quite a while since the children have been on an outing. And I'm burning with curiosity about the countryside." She put on a broad-brimmed hat and serenely ushered the children into the carriage.

After some time, the driver turned onto a tree-covered lane that followed the course of a meandering stream. At Aaron's order, the carriage stopped in an area well carpeted with grass and clear of brush. Venerable old trees lent cool shade and the grass smelled fresh and sweet. It was the perfect place for a picnic.

"This is beautiful," Brien breathed out. She turned to Aaron and found him watching her. "Will the owner mind if we lunch here?"

"Not at all. I know him well. He would be delighted to have you here."

The children crowded about her, begging to remove their shoes and to wade in the water. Seeing Aaron nod approval, she agreed and they bounded off. Dyso placed the hamper on the ground beneath a great oak tree, then at Brien's request, went down to the stream to keep watch on the children until the food was ready.

"Interesting." She watched her big bodyguard remove his shoes and roll up his breeches to wade with the little Hastingses. "The children seem to understand his hand language better than most adults. They're not at all afraid of him."

"He's a puzzle, that one," Aaron said, joining her in looking at them. "He gives me the feeling he sees things the rest of us don't."

She smiled. "If so, I hope he is catching what the rest of us let fall through the cracks."

Brien spread a large felt cloth on the ground, and began to unpack the hamper, unwrapping loaves of fresh bread, slices of cheese and cold ham, raisin tarts and crumb cakes, and two jugs—milk and ale. She turned to Aaron.

"I forgot to ask Dyso to put these in the stream to keep them cold."

"I'll do it." He bounded up and took the jugs from her. When he returned, he removed his coat and sat down in the grass at the edge of the cloth. He reached for a slice of the bread Brien was cutting. The sight of her at so domestic a task was strange to him. He refocused his attention to a damp curl of hair at the nape of her neck. Every time they were together, he found new aspects to her, saw her in a new light.

"Thank you for the invitation, Aaron. But you must have known I couldn't come alone."

"I'll give you that," Aaron conceded. "But did you have to bring a whole regiment for an escort? You have nothing to fear from me, Brien."

"It is not *you* I fear, Aaron, it is *us*. I don't want to embarrass Silas and Helen. Another chance like . . . we just shouldn't be alone together again."

Aaron frowned. "What has brought about this sudden interest in propriety?"

"I have a great deal to think about and you complicate things."

"Good. Then at least you think about me." He grinned. "And I think you are the most charming when you're the most improper. Like you were the other night."

"And what if another such night saw me with a child?" She colored hotly. "It wouldn't be *your* life that was ruined."

His grin faded as he realized she was right to think of consequences. "Surely you know that I would be responsible in such a matter."

"I don't want you to be 'responsible.' " The remark was more cutting than she intended, and she closed her eyes to regain her bearings.

"If you were with child, Brien, I would happily declare myself your husband. The question is, would you declare yourself to be my wife?"

"I don't want to be a wife," she said, feeling cornered by the idea. "Not yours, not anyone's." She got up and brushed the leaves and grass from her skirt as she went to call the children for lunch.

Aaron tried to be angry with her, but it was no use. Pushing was a poor way to lead. He must be patient; she would come about.

During lunch, Brien teased the children and promised to wade in the stream with them later. Aaron agreed it would be safe to explore farther up the lane and their afternoon was set. After finishing off the delicious food and packing away the remains, Aaron and Brien led the children up the lane toward a scenic spot. As the young ones explored and ran on ahead, Brien and Aaron walked slower, putting distance between them and their charges.

It was so peaceful here, strolling under the old trees. Brien found herself wishing fervently that they were her trees, that this was her place. When they crested a rise in the road, Brien spotted the drop-off ahead and called the children back to her. Together, she and Aaron carried them to the edge of the cliff and she was surprised to find a whole valley spread out below them. The children took in the view for a moment, then begged to be allowed to explore a nearby tree with low branches perfect for climbing. Dyso motioned that he would watch over them and she relented.

Turning back to the view, she felt a calm descend on her. The hills in the distance bore a bluish haze that gave her the strange sense that she was standing at the top of the world itself. They could see for miles along that valley, and there was hardly a human-made structure in sight. It was a small glimpse, she realized, of the vastness of this new land.

"What do you think?" Aaron asked, watching her reaction.

"It's wonderful. It's so . . . big."

"And just think, this is just one small valley in a colony filled with valleys and rivers and harbors and meadows and fields and woods. And there are thirteen colonies, most of which are a lot bigger than Massachusetts. And there is a lot more unexplored, uncharted land to the west. Room for new colonies and new people . . . new riches to explore. This is the future, Brien. This place. Breathe it in." He drew the sweet air deep into his lungs. "Let it into your blood."

She did just that . . . breathed deeply . . . once, twice . . . It was exhilarating. Intoxicating. She wanted to throw open her arms and twirl around and around . . . to wrap her arms around the place . . . and for a brief, unfettered moment she did. When she staggered to a stop, the rest of the universe kept spinning. She had difficulty regaining her balance. Planting her feet firmly, she refused to sway anymore, and the world gradually settled back into a dependable motion.

She was in deep trouble, she realized. The cursed place was wreaking havoc on her common sense and equilibrium . . . not to mention her priorities. A moment before she was hanging on every word, soaring on every image of the grand vision he unveiled for her. She was becoming too blessed attached to this land and to the man standing beside her.

"It's time we went back." She headed for the children and was soon helping Dyso pull them out of the tree and herd them along. When Aaron caught up with her, he slipped his hand around hers and squeezed. She quickly pulled it free.

"Tell me about your family," he said as if searching for a more neutral topic.

"My father is Lawrence Weston, Earl of Southwold, and my mother was Alice Garrett of the House of Leighton," she said, relieved to be able to impart the structure of her life without having to plumb the substance. "My mother died when I was twelve. I had an older sister named Denise, who died when I was thirteen. My father and I are all that's left. We have few relations—not even a male cousin for the title, after my father."

"Go on," Aaron prompted and she grew a bit more cautious. Why did he ask?

"My sister Denise was the beauty of the family. Sweet-natured and delicate."

"Like you."

"*Not* like me." She shrugged a bit self-consciously. "I was plain and plump and bookish. My father engaged a tutor for us when I was nine years old. Monsieur Duvall introduced me to the world . . . spread it before me like a banquet . . . but never bothered to warn me that I wouldn't be allowed to sample it. I heard my father once say that I should have been a boy."

"Then he is a fool." Aaron stopped abruptly, his face suddenly sharp and serious.

"Well, I am curious and stubborn, and interested in things unseemly for a woman—like commerce and finance." Memories uncoiled in her mind and suddenly she was telling him more. "When I was little, I despised dolls and tea parties and drawing lessons. Father called me his 'little shadow' because he took me with him everywhere . . . to his offices, the warehouses, and to meet his ships when they arrived in port. Poor Silas was just a clerk, but he bore my harassment splendidly." Some of the light in that memory faded, in her heart and in her face, as she thought of the estrangement that had come later.

"Perhaps he was right. I would have made a better man than woman."

He stepped in front of her and she stopped abruptly to keep from bumping him.

"And what makes you think that interest in the world and persistence and stubbornness are the measure of men and not of women?" he demanded.

Brien was stunned by both his words and the fact that he had been the one to say them instead of her. Such sentiment coming from a man—even a very special man— Her heart began to drum in her chest. She stepped around him and walked faster, feeling pushed toward a decision she didn't want to make.

When they reached their picnic spot, the little Hastingses begged to go wading again and Brien granted permission. Dyso went with them while she sat down on the blanket with her back against a tree trunk. Aaron lay down on the blanket beside her and gradually worked his way closer. When his hand slid over her knee toward her lap, she gave it a censuring rap. He sighed.

"Well, if you won't favor me with your charms, then

favor me with your business news. How comes the sale of your assets?"

"Not well." She could have bitten her tongue a heartbeat later. What was it about him that made her want to surrender up every little detail of her life? Including the most private, inane, and humiliating.

"Van Zandt is proving a hard man to win, is he?"

"He had made two offers, both insulting. And I told him so." She shuddered. "I'm not sure I should sell to him, even if he meets my price."

Aaron frowned and pushed up on one elbow, facing her. "Brien, I warned you . . . Van Zandt is not to be toyed with. I ran across him during the war. He has no scruples, no principles, no higher nature you could appeal to. He seems to desire a modicum of respectability now, and perhaps thinks that the purchase of Weston Trading will afford him that. But just as easily, he could turn his considerable resources against you." His seriousness shook her to the core. "Don't underestimate him. Your air of nobility may charm others . . . even me. But to Van Zandt, it will be like a spur in the side. Be careful you don't use that spur too hard or too often."

Brien's huge eyes told him his message had struck home, but there was not a trace of fear in them. Aaron's lips tilted in a wry smile.

"Thank you for the advice. But if Van Zandt makes another offer, it will be in Silas's office in the presence of a raft of solicitors."

"That's good. Hearing you dined with him, I began to wonder at your taste in men."

"And just how did you hear about that?" she demanded.

"I make it a practice to keep abreast of all sorts of news." He had the grace to look a bit sheepish. "All right, I asked around."

"Stay out of it, Aaron," she declared shortly. Scrambling to her feet, she fixed her gaze on the Hastings children splashing about in the stream and impulsively kicked off her shoes. "It's too beautiful an afternoon to waste on business. How long has it been, Captain Durham, since you went wading?"

WHEN THEY RETURNED to Hastings House that evening, Silas met them in the front hall with a letter in his hand. But he was swarmed by his children, who deluged him with details of their adventures, all talking at once. He listened, hugged them distractedly, and sent them off with the housemaid to tell their mother all about their day. When he turned back to Brien, she knew something was wrong. He beckoned her into the drawing room and Aaron followed them.

"What is it? What's happened?" she asked, reaching for the paper he offered.

"A fire. The Cambridge shop burned last night," he said, just as she read those very words in the note penned by the shopkeeper.

"Burned." Brien was jolted by the news.

"The cause of the fire is unknown," Silas continued, looking at Aaron. "The stock was destroyed, but the building is repairable." His hands dropped helplessly to his sides. "Thank God no one was hurt. Terrence Harvey, the shopkeeper, was unharmed. He's a good man—and honest."

"What could have caused it?"

"I suppose there could be a thousand reasons for a fire in a store with such varied inventory," Silas answered.

"Well, it's a bad time to have a fire." Her lips drew into a thin line as she stared at the paper in her hand, and rose. "That shop was one of our smaller ones, but it will still mean a loss. If another of our shops should suffer a similar fate, it might frighten away potential buyers."

"Which means it would be prudent to take steps to

protect your investment," Aaron said, inserting himself into their lines of sight.

" 'Steps'?" she said, struggling with competing urges to tell him to mind his own business and to give thanks that he was both present and qualified to offer an opinion.

"If it were me"—he watched her reaction to his suggestion closely—"I would want to post a night watch at each of my other shops."

"But surely you can't think . . ." Brien halted herself. It was ridiculous to dismiss the idea that the fire might have been intentionally set just because Aaron was the one to suggest it. She glanced at Silas and even he was nodding agreement.

"Accident or not," she said, facing the unpleasant possibility head-on, "we must see that it doesn't happen again. Will you see to the watches, Silas?"

"Of course, Brien," Silas said, showing relief at her decisiveness.

Aaron watched her coolness and resolve with admiration. A metamorphosis from stubborn young woman to pragmatic business owner had occurred before his eyes. Hope spread over his face in the form of a grin. If she could change her mind about business, then she might yet change her mind about him.

As if reading his thoughts, she straightened. "I have allowed this business to languish of late, but no more. I want you to make up a list of prominent business owners in the Boston area, Silas. We'll find a buyer, if we have to go door to door." Then she turned to Aaron. "Thank you for the lovely picnic, Captain. Let me see you out."

The minute they were in the hall and out of Silas's hearing, she tossed him a glare.

"Don't you dare say it," she ordered irritably.

"Say what?" He gave her a look of supreme innocence.

"I told you so."

"But I did *caution* you to be careful in your dealings with—"

"There's no proof that Van Zandt had anything to do with this fire."

"True. But it's hard to overlook the fact that he *burned* nearly every ship he intercepted and plundered during the war. Fire is the man's trademark."

That alarming little tidbit caused a hitch in her stride and a moment later she halted in the middle of the hall, lifted her chin, and extended her hand to him. "Thank you for the warning. Now be so good as to keep your nose out of my business."

She lifted her skirts, wheeled, and hurried up the stairs.

Aaron watched her go with a mixture of admiration and frustration. The good news was, she wasn't easily intimidated. And the bad news was, she wasn't easily intimidated. She was unholy stubborn and she had no idea how ruthless a man like Van Zandt could be. It could prove to be a deadly combination.

THE NEXT AFTERNOON a message arrived by courier for Brien. Thinking it was from Aaron, she tore into it. The coarse scrawl and improper English left no doubt as to the authenticity of the signature—"Horace Van Zandt." Her throat tightened as she read his proposal that they meet the following day to negotiate the final sale of Weston Trading's colonial holdings.

The timing of this new offer, so soon after the fire, was suspicious, but thus far, Van Zandt was the only buyer who had shown both serious interest and ready coin.

"When can we meet?" she asked Silas, who worriedly began to clean his spectacles with a handkerchief. "Will Friday be too soon for you to arrange a meeting with the solicitors in your offices?"

So it was that on a sultry, early July morning Brien sat

once more in the offices of Weston Trading, awaiting the final bargaining for property she was increasingly reluctant to sell. Silas and two of their local solicitors were present to witness the agreement and bind it with appropriate written documents.

The groan of boards and the scrape of chairs in the outer office announced the buyer's arrival.

"Welcome, Mr. Van Zandt," Brien said tersely, waving him toward the stout chair in front of Silas's desk and then seating herself in Silas's chair. "May we offer you some tea?"

His nod set his jowls quivering, and she focused on serving.

"Perhaps you have heard of the recent loss of our Cambridge shop," she continued.

Van Zandt showed no surprise. Her hand was steady as she offered him a steaming cup of tea, but she noted a tremor in his as he accepted it.

"Of course, we shall adjust the price accordingly," she said reasonably. "We have reconstructed an inventory of the goods destroyed in the fire and calculated it to have been worth two thousand."

"*Ja, ja.*" He waved his hand disinterestedly.

Brien's composure was strained by his arrogance. "Then, have you an offer, Mr. Van Zandt?"

"I gif you offer." His bilious eyes became fat-framed slits. "Privately."

Brien was relieved to be able to show incredulity.

"These men are my advisors." She gestured to Silas and the solicitors. "They are privy to all my affairs, sir. You may speak freely and in confidence before them."

"Vhat I say, I say to you alone."

He was so adamant that Brien's resolve to keep Silas beside her wavered. She asked him and the lawyers to leave them. They quitted the room reluctantly, with Silas commenting pointedly that he would be just outside.

Cynical amusement played at Van Zandt's mouth as the door closed on them.

"Now ve talk." He rolled forward on the creaking chair.

Brien folded her hands on her lap, mostly to control their trembling. She could see now that everything Aaron had said about him was true; he was a man without moral or social restraints. His next words sent a chill through her.

"You vill sell to me for nine t'ousand pounds."

Stunned by the absurd figure, Brien stared at him. "If you mean nineteen, sir, you are still well below my minimum price." Brien knew she had heard him correctly, but bought time in which to react more carefully.

"No," he declared. "Nine t'ousand. Und you vill sell to me for dat."

"Never." Brien's coolness surprised them both. "Your last offer of eighteen thousand was unacceptable. What makes you think I should agree to half that?" Her eyes burned with the volatile combination of anger's flint on will's steel.

"You agree because your noble name cannot stand a scandal." Seeing her frown, he raked her with an insultingly personal stare. "You haf visitors at night in your rooms—all night. What vill Boston think of a highborn English tart who parades around—high-and-mighty—but spends nights rutting vit men?"

"Men?" Brien was incredulous. He had somehow learned about Aaron's visit . . . and enlarged upon it. Her mind raced to match and anticipate his moves. His intention was clear: blackmail. She shoved to her feet, her face taut with outrage.

"How dare you call me foul names and try to bully and coerce me into giving you my property?"

"For all I know, you haf many men," Van Zandt said with a snarl.

He meant to disgrace her by bringing forth a throng of "lovers" to attest to her debauchery and ruin her reputation. The panic that gripped her throat kept her from a hasty response. What of Silas and Helen? They would know it for a lie, but there were others in these colonies all too willing to believe the worst about any well-born English. Dear God—what should she do? Then she realized that her lengthening silence was fueling Van Zandt's sneer.

Her eyes narrowed. She thought of Aaron's warning and of what he would do in such a circumstance. There was only one course.

"Immorality, like beauty, is in the eye of the beholder, sir. You see sin and degradation in others' actions because you can only imagine that they will behave as you would." She stepped partway around the desk, her head high and her eyes flashing. "I would not sell my American holdings to you now at any price." She flung a finger toward the door. "Get out of this office and never again foul Weston property with your revolting bulk!"

In a flash, his hamlike hand grabbed her outstretched arm and pulled her partly across the desk toward him. As she struggled, she felt the pot of tea beneath her and instinctively grabbed it up and flung the hot liquid in his face.

Bellowing, he released her to grab at his scalded skin.

Dyso burst in through the side door and, seeing Brien unharmed, flew at Van Zandt. The Dutchman was knocked back against the shelves with a cry, and the office was suddenly filled with Silas and solicitors and shouts and confusion. Furiously, Dyso shoved the panting, cursing Van Zandt through the side door that led to the alley. Still reeling from the assault, Brien caught only snatches of the wretch's ravings.

One word stood out from the rest.

Burn.

Twenty-One

A LARGE, MUSCULAR FIGURE moved stealthily toward *The Lady's Secret* as she lay berthed in Boston's docks, emerging from the shadows to challenge the watch on the gangway. Before the watchman could call for help, he was knocked unconscious and dragged back up the gangway to the deck. Depositing the seaman carefully on the deck, the intruder silently made his way to the hatchway and entered without hesitation.

Aaron sat poring over manifests in his cabin when the door slammed open. Instinctively he reached for a nearby sword, baring its cold blue edge.

"Dyso?" He blinked, still coiled for action. "How did you get past the watch?"

The big bodyguard stopped just at the naked point of the blade, pointed to Aaron, then swept his hands toward the door. Seeing the puzzlement on Aaron's face, he repeated the sequence more slowly.

"You want me to come with you?"

A quick nod was the only confirmation.

"Did Lady Brien send you?"

Dyso shook his head and one massive hand pointed to Aaron, then closed in a fist that tapped his chest above his heart. Dyso came because he knew Aaron cared for her.

"Is she in trouble?"

Some of the tension in the big man's face drained as he nodded.

"Take me to her, my friend." He clasped Dyso's mighty arm and started for the door, but the servant grabbed his arm and held it. Aaron scowled. "If she is in trouble, I want to help. But I must know what has happened."

Dyso's glare softened and his eyes darted as he tried to think how to portray it. His free hand flew in a series of gestures that indicated a belly grown large.

"Is she with child?" he asked, feeling his throat tighten at the prospect.

The enigmatic hulk smiled, then shook his head slowly. He repeated the gestures, adding an almost comical puffing of the cheeks to the routine. It was crystal clear.

"Van Zandt!"

A terse, relieved nod told Aaron much.

"Damn," he muttered. "I warned her! Have they quarreled?"

Another nod. The large black eyes burned now as the two massive fists pounded together. Aaron stared at them, marveling at their potential.

"Has he tried to hurt her?" Anger was rising inside him. When Dyso shook his head, Aaron went on. "He's threatened her?"

"I feared as much." Aaron paced the cabin anxiously under the protector's gaze. "I tried to warn her." Turning to the puzzled Dyso, he mused, "I'll wager the confrontation was most interesting. I'm surprised we didn't see the fireworks two days out of port!" Grabbing a long dagger that lay on the desk, he tucked it into his boot.

"Perhaps we should pay a late call on Mr. Van Zandt."

The streets were quiet now that it was well on toward one o'clock. After a short distance, Dyso gestured suddenly to an alleyway and was moving quickly down it before Aaron could utter a word. Dyso led him through a maze of streets until at last he slipped through a partly opened gate. Dyso pushed him back against the fence and Aaron saw that the rear door of the large brick house before them was guarded by a burly seaman armed with a brace of pistols. Van Zandt's residence. How the hulk had known where it was and that it was guarded, mystified Aaron.

They waited as the watchman yawned and began to doze before creeping in through a side door. The house was not difficult to navigate in the dimness. Up the stairs, they tried only one empty bedchamber before finding the one where Van Zandt slept, propped up on pillows in a huge bed, snoring loudly.

Aaron lit a candle as Dyso drew the drapes at the window. Then he approached the sleeping figure, pulling the dagger from his boot and motioning for Dyso to keep watch at the door.

"Wake up, Van Zandt." Aaron touched the point of his dagger to the wattle of red flesh overlying the Dutchman's neck. "We have business, you and I!"

Van Zandt came up with a start but, encountering the point of the blade, blinked and sank back under its pressure.

"*Vas meinst du?*" he rasped.

"Remember me?" Aaron's exaggerated politeness gave evidence that this task was not altogether unpleasant for him. "I was first officer on a brigantine you ran afoul of during the war—the *Challenger*. Aaron Durham is my name."

Recognition crossed Van Zandt's face. "I remember."

"I haven't come to discuss old times." He pressed the

sharp point harder against Van Zandt's neck. "You have dealt dishonorably with a friend of mine. That ends now, before real harm is done."

Van Zandt's bilious eyes flickered with recognition. "Dat English whore."

"Lady Brien," Aaron corrected him coolly. "You will not press her to sell to you, nor will you make good your threats." Aaron gambled that he would soon draw out the nature of those threats from this miserly mass, and he was soon rewarded.

"Soon, everyone knows vhat a whore she is."

"So it's her reputation you've threatened." Cold determination set Aaron's face with predatory sharpness, turning his pleasant features into a stony mask. "You propose to embarrass the lady. Well, I'm afraid I cannot let that happen."

"You t'ink you scare me?" the fat man challenged. "Go tell your whore I am not afraid."

The anger rising inside Aaron was more dangerous than any of Van Zandt's baiting. It would be so easy; it was so tempting to let his hand apply a bit more pressure and rid the world of this wretch's evil.

"You underestimate her, Van Zandt. She didn't send me. She is a true lady. Proud and stubborn to a fault, but not a whore or a coward." He sniffed the fetid air of the room. "What is that smell? This place stinks like a skunk's lair." He leaned toward the fat man and sniffed again. "Damn, Van Zandt, that's *you*. Come to think of it, all of Boston would smell sweeter with you gone."

"You don't scare me, Durham," he said, growling like a trapped animal.

"Well, I should. I have friends who remember your activities during the war, Van Zandt." Aaron's voice suddenly matched his blade: cold and sharp. "I visited New York recently and called on a few mutual acquaintances. They have placed their testimony at my disposal and would gladly bear witness to your wartime deceptions. Get out of that bed and start packing. If you are not gone with tomorrow's first tide, I will lead soldiers to your door and arrest you myself."

Long-held rage and suppressed memories flooded back to tighten Aaron's throat and shiver his taut muscles with tension. The burning powder's smoke once more burned his eyes and seared his lungs, while a quivering heap of flesh pleaded with the captain of the *Challenger*, begging and bargaining for his life . . . offering to turn coat.

In the end, Van Zandt had won a stay, bought with treachery and blood. He'd agreed to furnish information on colonial movements, even other smugglers, for the right to ply his trade unhindered and free of competition. Playing friend to the colonial cause, Van Zandt lined his pockets while betraying the rebels at every turn. And ironically, Van Zandt was proclaimed heroic by the colonials for his successful breach of the British blockade. They never suspected that his "luck" was provided by the British navy itself.

"Your treason will hang you in any of these thirteen colonies," Aaron said. "Which will it be? The gallows of Boston or a plantation in the Indies?"

VAN ZANDT PUSHED his bulk about his lavishly furnished bedchamber, snatching up costly items, gathering them into leather bags. A small, gray-faced serving woman moved similarly about the adjoining sitting room, hurriedly packing what she could into two large wooden barrels in the middle of the room. The scene was being repeated in other rooms of the house, but much would be left behind. He had always known this day might come. He gave the chest on the bedroom floor a possessive stroke as he passed. That was why he kept most of his wealth in portable gold and precious jewels.

He thought of the cause of his hasty flight and his mood darkened.

"Dat whore." His yellow smirk appeared. "Her and

Durham . . . I leave dem somet'ing to remember. Hulda!" His voice rumbled through the house over and over until the worn little woman appeared at his bedchamber door.

"*Ja, mein herr?*" She dipped nervously before him, gauging his mood and the safety of her proximity to him.

"Forget vhat you do. Fetch Steiger and Moran. I haf one last job for dem to do."

THE NEXT MORNING Van Zandt was in a cabin on the ship *Marguerite*. The captain had orders to sail with the tide for Jamaica and an armed guard from the *Secret* had watched the ship until late afternoon when she sailed.

As Aaron watched the ship clearing the harbor, he felt little satisfaction and no relief. Van Zandt's simmering but subdued manner, as Aaron escorted him to the ship, had made him uneasy. The Dutchman had surrendered too quickly. And where were the toughs that always accompanied him?

As the ship disappeared on the horizon, he sought out the chief constable of Boston and deposited with him a packet of documents that proved beyond doubt Van Zandt's treason during the war. Warrants would be drawn and if he ever set foot again on American soil, he would be arrested and likely hanged.

Once more on board *The Lady's Secret*, Aaron puzzled over his lingering anxiety. Van Zandt had left too quietly. The *Marguerite*'s captain was trustworthy; he would certainly deliver the Dutchman to the islands. His hatred for Van Zandt rivaled Aaron's.

What, then? A plan for revenge? It would be weeks before they reached Jamaica and triple that time before Van Zandt could mount an expedition. Did he plan to strike at *The Lady's Secret*? She would sail within two weeks for England—too soon to feel the Dutchman's wrath. Unless . . . unless a plan for revenge was already set in motion.

Aaron prevailed upon Hicks to pay a call on Jeannie Trowbridge and to carry a message to Dyso. It was just before sunset when the hulk appeared on the gangway.

"Something isn't right," Aaron told him. "I believe our lady, her property—or both—are in danger." He watched the big man carefully. "You must not leave her, even for the shortest time, until we find out what he has planned. Can you manage that?"

A quick, determined nod was the reply. Then, before Aaron could continue, one huge hand knotted into a fist and was soon wrapped carefully, tenderly in the other one.

Fascinated by the simple eloquence of the gesture, Aaron stared at him. Then he shook his head to clear it and once more focus his mind.

"I'll take my men to watch the warehouse and send Hicks around to check with you every few hours. I think it best that Brien not know of our concern or our efforts."

Dyso, already halfway to the door, turned back from the door with a glimmer of what Aaron fancied as amusement in his eyes. Then he was gone.

THE WARMTH OF the July night droned onward, making the vigil a battle between boredom and fatigue. Sweat trickled down his neck and the occasional buzz of an insect near his ear increased his annoyance. Then, toward dawn, his determination was rewarded.

A faint light appeared in the alley near the rear door of the warehouse. He rose stiffly to his knees and waved to a crouched figure on the warehouse roof, who repeated the signal to another in the chain of men stationed around the warehouse.

Aaron coolly calculated their steps as he climbed over the rooftops to join two dark figures near the gable of the roof. A handful of shadows in the alley below moved swiftly to cover the doors and the lower windows, to cut off any escape attempt.

The weathered gable window yielded easily to the pressure of Aaron's shoulder. His heart drummed as their rope uncoiled into the darkened void below. Their descent seemed to take forever as the rope ate into his hands and his eyes raked the darkness.

Once at the bottom he tugged the rope as a signal and silently moved away, pulling a pistol from his belt. Feeling for the wall he knew must be near, he touched the cool, rough brick and suddenly had his bearings. Hicks joined him moments later and together they edged forward through the darkened warehouse.

Muffled voices and dim light came from the area where cotton bales were stored. Aaron motioned Hicks to circle around the other side and they separated, keeping to the shelter of stacked crates and barrels. Suddenly Aaron spotted them. Two men. Van Zandt hadn't cared to pay too handsomely for his revenge.

Small, bright tongues of flame licked at the oil-soaked rags they had tucked at the bottom of some cotton bales.

"It's caught." The shorter, scrawny figure rubbed his sweaty palms on his thighs.

"Aye," the other one growled. " 'At's good enough. Let's git now. Our part's done." In a hurry to see the job done, they turned to leave the growing circle of light. But they stopped short, eyes widening.

The cold black barrel of Aaron's pistol hovered inches away from the short one's face.

"No sudden moves, gents," Aaron said with icy calm. "Get your arms up and turn around slowly."

Hicks stepped out of the shadows and searched the pair for weapons.

"Just knives, Captain. They're half-drunk, to boot."

The flames licked hungrily at the bales and showed an eagerness to spread. A quick glance told Aaron there was no time to lose. He snatched up shovels and blankets and tossed them to the thugs, yelling at them to start beating out the flames.

"Get the others," he ordered Hicks, who took off for the street door to summon the rest of the *Secret*'s crew.

Soon the warehouse was filled with the smoke of extinguished flames and the arsonists were trussed and being trundled out to Boston's central gaol.

Brien awakened the next morning to the sound of knocking and of Helen's strained voice calling to her through the door. When she slid from the bed, she spotted Dyso lying across the threshold, blocking the door from opening.

"Dyso!" She knelt beside him and touched his shoulder to make him look at her. "What are you doing here?"

Before he could answer, the door banged open and Helen squeezed in and stared at the bodyguard and the blanket on the floor.

"He's been in there, lying across your door all night?" Helen asked. "Why?"

Dyso wasn't forthcoming, but within minutes they had the answer anyway. Silas came rushing up the stairs with news of an arson attempt at the warehouse and of its timely discovery. Brien realized Dyso had slipped into her room to protect her.

It seemed some sailors, rousted from their night's amusement for lack of funds, had spotted smoke billowing out a window, and they sounded the alarm. The arsonists were trapped inside by the commotion and were unable to flee the building. When the fire was extinguished, they were hauled out gasping, and confessed to a plot to burn all of Weston Trading's properties one by one. Fortunately, they had chosen to begin with the main warehouse and the damage there had been confined to a few cotton bales.

Brien gasped as Silas revealed the name of their employer— Horace Van Zandt. A cursory search of the Dutchman's residence showed he had fled, taking little with him. The search would continue, but the constables believed he was well away from Boston.

Brien insisted on going down to the docks to see the damage for herself. They arrived just after dawn, and in the street outside the warehouse she spotted familiar faces.

"But they're from *The Lady's Secret*," she said, hurrying toward them just as Aaron stepped out of the warehouse with the fire warden. Suddenly it began to fall into place. Aaron's warnings about Van Zandt . . . the sailors "happening" by in the dead of night . . . Aaron striding from the warehouse with an air of authority . . .

"What the devil are you doing here?" she demanded, planting herself in his path.

He halted, looking down at her with glowing eyes.

"The men who first reported the fire were—"

"From your ship." It sounded like the accusation it was. "And the first person I see upon arriving at the scene is you. Not exactly a coincidence, is it?" She stalked closer. "What did you do—plant them here to watch the place?"

He opened his mouth to protest her ingratitude, but closed it.

"Yes, I did."

She blanched. "But we had already posted a watch."

"One old man who was bashed over the head before he could make a noise. Not very effective protection." He folded his arms and stared down at her. "If you like, I can take it all back . . . go in and set everything on fire again . . . let you and your senseless watchman discover it on your own. How does that sound?"

"Don't be ridiculous."

"Then don't be ridiculous yourself," he said shortly.

"I've told you to stay out of my business."

"And I've told you that I intend to honor a commitment I made. That includes helping you when I know you need it." He lowered his voice and his gaze. "Isn't that what friends do for each other? Help in whatever way possible?"

"So now I'm your *friend?*"

"Unless you'd rather be known by something more binding and personal."

" 'Friend' will do," she declared, feeling her hostility taking a last sickly gasp. "Why didn't you just tell me you suspected a threat?"

"It wasn't anything more than just that, a suspicion. You'd have dismissed my hunch as just more interference in your life and your business. Wouldn't you?" He nodded to induce an affirmative answer, and when she bit her lip to remain silent, he edged closer and lowered his voice even more. "Look, I would have done the same for any friend. It was the right thing to do, and I'm not going to quit following my conscience and common sense just because it might annoy you." She opened her mouth to speak, but he added one last thing. "Needing help now and then doesn't mean you're weak or incompetent, you know. Even kings and queens need allies."

She stared at him, feeling a strange empty sensation in her stomach. He was right; he had done exactly what any good and rational man would have. She had needed help, and she was foolish to disdain it just because it came from him.

"I'm sorry, Aaron." She suddenly felt a little woozy. "I appreciate what you've done here . . . how you helped to save the inventory and warehouse." She prayed it was the dizziness talking. "I don't know how to thank you."

He laughed.

"Well, I do. Invite me to dinner on Sunday."

ALL THROUGH SUNDAY dinner, Aaron could hardly take his eyes from Brien. They took coffee in the small parlor after dinner. After a bit of conversation, Helen excused herself and asked Silas to come and help her in the garden. After a puzzled silence, the reason for her sudden interest in their weedy rear garden struck and he followed enthusiastically. Helen drew the parlor doors discreetly together behind her.

Brien groaned in frustration. "Now see what you've done."

Aaron smiled lazily, leaning back in his chair to better appreciate the sight of her. "Our hostess is a perceptive woman. I doubt her leave-taking was all my doing. It was you who invited me to dinner."

"In a moment of weakness, I assure you."

"Let us not disappoint our hostess. Come sit, and let me woo you properly." He patted his lap, grinning. Brien did sit down, but on the far end of the couch.

"What is your father like, Aaron? You've made reference to hard feelings between you. Surely, it has not always been so."

He was silent a moment, analyzing both the question and the motivation behind it. "My father is a man of keen mind and great ability . . . much of which he has buried under the burdens and duties of his title. I respect his loyalty to his duty, but I know I could never live the kind of life he has. From the time my mother died, when I was seven years old, until this day, I cannot say I have seen him smile. He's as hard as the walls of Coleraine."

In the pause, Brien watched his serious expression and wished she could reach into his darkened thoughts and draw him back to her. She squeezed his hand instead.

"When I left to make my home in Bristol," he continued, glancing up at her briefly, "he swore to disown me entirely if I did not return to beg his forgiveness. I told him my brother Edward would make a much better subject for his ambitions."

"Will you go home now, Aaron? Now that you have your ship?" She was thinking of her own father and how narrowly she had missed knowing and loving him. His reply startled her.

"No. He has nothing I want and I have nothing for him."

"You can't mean that."

"I do mean it. I will never be an earl. I have left that all behind me now."

"But your duty—"

"Is to conduct my life according to my values and principles. And foremost among those is the conviction that freedom is more precious than wealth or fame or privilege or a hide-bound tradition that places greater value on some men than others. Freedom to speak and learn and change . . . freedom to pursue a dream . . . freedom to use whatever talent and effort and resources you can muster to achieve a dream . . . that is the promise that America holds for the world. And I want to be part of it.

"I am not proud of some aspects of my life, Brien. But I have tried to be honest in my dealing with men and women alike. I don't ask favors or privileges, don't expect special treatment because of the circumstances of my birth. I only want to have the chance to live my own life as I see fit . . . to build something of value in this world."

Brien felt for the first time the real impact of his rejection of the class to which they belonged. Her heart skipped. Until now she had harbored a suspicion . . . *a hope* . . . that fate had somehow destined her for a life with him. He was a true match for her in every sense, even to the fact that his father's rank matched her father's exactly. In the quiet of her bed at night, she was coming to think of her life and his, side by side, someday linked by more than just fate.

"Brien, I must tell you. The coming trip back to England—*The Lady's Secret* will bear American colors."

"What does that mean?" she asked, realizing as she did that he was declaring his intention to leave England permanently. Registering his ship as an American vessel would mean declaring himself a citizen of the rebel provinces.

"No," she breathed as the sense of it overwhelmed her.

"Brien, I intend to make Boston my home." His golden

eyes probed hers deeply for her response, even as she searched her own heart.

Both found only confusion.

She had felt that she understood his rebellion against tradition and his father—but to give up his citizenship as a final stab at his father's position and authority—to cast away every tie to his land, his people, his home—

She stood up, feeling compelled to action but at a loss for how to halt the widening of the rift between her convictions and her emotions. She turned to the window and stared, unseeing, out into the balmy afternoon.

"I thought you should know." His voice was steady behind her.

"When did you decide this?" Brien fought the despair overtaking her.

"It has been my plan for some time."

For how long? While he poured out his heart to her in their talks aboard ship? During that sweet, steamy night in her chamber? On that hilltop overlooking America's bountiful promise? And what did he think she would do when she heard the news? Wish him well in his new life on the far side of an ocean? Surrender and sink into his arms?

Suddenly it was all too clear. He expected her to choose. *Him.*

But to have a life with him she must abandon her father, her position, her country—everything she had known and loved.

A sardonic voice rose inside her. And if she chose him, what would she have? The lot of a sea captain's wife? Lonely months in a strange country while he was at sea, plying his carefree trade? Years of resentment at having handed her life over to him just when she had found it? An inner door crashed shut, sealing away newly awakened feelings and trust.

The silence grew strained. He joined her by the window

and tried to put his arms around her. She pushed away, shaking with emotion, and turned to him.

"You've already made the decision . . . by yourself, for yourself. Do you not see what this does to us? You're throwing away the very things that bind us together."

"What? The fact that we were both born into noble houses in a society that—" He searched her as he followed that trail of thought. "I see. Now, without the promise of a title, I've lost my appeal."

"It's not like that. I never thought of you as having a title." But his accusation echoed strongly in her. If he went back to his father, assumed the life of a proper English earl-to-be, would her objections to a life with him just fade away?

"All I have is yours, Brien. But all I have is in America now."

There it was. The ultimatum she dreaded, delivered with staggering effect. By his choice, he had put an ocean between them. Now she must choose . . . between everything she knew and loved and this extraordinary man who had claimed her desires, her body, and finally her heart.

Her internal battle finished quickly and vanquished hope crept back into the recesses of her heart. She turned pointedly away from him and felt a pricking in her eyes. A deathly calm descended over her. There was no trembling or weakness now, only a cold, sobering wave of self-reproach.

Aaron stood behind her, trembling, feeling furious and foolish, hurting in places he hadn't known he possessed.

He had just lost the battle. His chest tightened so that it was difficult to breathe. For a long, excruciating moment, he wavered. If he took it all back and undid his decision . . . if he returned to England . . . to Wiltshire . . . to his lordly father . . .

After a painful silence, he turned on his heel and strode out of the room.

Two days after the fire, an offer came for the purchase of Weston Trading. A man named Harrison, from New York, made a firm offer of twenty-four thousand sterling. Brien received the news with overwhelming relief and set about making plans to return home. By week's end she had signed the papers, taken possession of the bank drafts, and secured passage on a ship called the *Morning Star* bound for London. And she said good-bye to Boston and the colonies with an aching heart.

Twenty-Two

THE PASSAGE HOME was long and miserable. The *Morning Star* was not designed with passengers in mind and rolled and pitched on her square bottom like a warped bucket. Brien fell sick on the first day out of port and spent her mornings hovering over the chamber pot. As the day wore on, her health improved and she was sure this odd bit of seasickness would pass. But the next morning she would be seized again by violent spasms, and blamed the miserable craft for her inability to keep food in her stomach.

To make matters worse, Jeannie was once again deathly ill. Being confined with her in the small cabin they were forced to share was almost intolerable at first. Unable to exercise on deck and bundled like a mummy to withstand the cool air from the open windows, she had a great deal of time to think.

Inescapably her thoughts returned to Aaron and the

details of his beautiful ship. If the *Star* was typical, it was small wonder the *Secret* aroused such interest. Inexperience had kept her from understanding just how remarkable an achievement his ship truly was. And if she hadn't appreciated the ship, how much more had she undervalued the talents and abilities of the man who had designed it?

Being so far away, she felt it safe to let down her guard and remember the pleasure of his presence . . . his tart wit, his exhilarating kisses, and his warm, comforting touch. Then she recalled the pain and frustration in his face as he turned from her that afternoon in Silas's parlor. It was harder now to stay angry with him for a decision that he was probably destined to make.

Desperate to escape the sadness and sense of loss that accompanied thoughts of him and the colonies, she tried instead to conjure images of the life to which she was intent on returning. She needed to anticipate something, someone . . . anything, anyone.

She concentrated on Harcourt but the vision paled and it was impossible to bring specific colors and room arrangements to mind. She thought of her new friends, and discovered that Charles Medford merged into Reydon Hardwick, and Celia Evans was virtually indistinguishable from Sophie Etheridge. Closing her eyes, she thought of *home*, and what came to mind was an image of Byron Place before the fire. That Byron Place didn't exist anymore. In its place were stone piles and scaffolding and wooden beams that resembled nothing quite yet and held no memories or allure. The only thing of substance that she managed to conjure in her mind and heart was her father.

She thought of the earl's face as he watched her carriage drive away from Harcourt. He'd looked so gray and drawn and sad to see her go. She could only pray that he'd continued to recuperate and she would find him in better health and spirits. He was her family. All she had.

By the end of her third week at sea, the weather calmed

and her seasickness seemed to ease. She spent some time tidying the cabin and taking care of Jeannie, who seemed to do better the closer they came to London. When Brien roused herself and insisted that Jeannie join her on deck for a bit of fresh air and exercise, Jeannie groaned and sank back onto her bed, holding her middle and complaining that as if the ravages of the sea weren't enough . . . her courses had just come upon her. Brien winced with sympathy, pulled a thick shawl around her shoulders, and left the cabin.

Halfway up the steps to the deck, she stopped dead.

Courses.

How long had it been since she had experienced a similar complaint?

Her blood drained from her head as she realized that she had not suffered her usual course since . . . since she was aboard *The Lady's Secret*. Six weeks? More like two months. Her eyes widened and she looked down at the front of her heavy blue woolen gown. Surely not.

But as she stood there, holding the railing, she went back over the events of the last two months, searching for evidence that she was wrong and finding none. Her knees weakened. Not a day's indisposition. Not a single ache or bit of discomfort. Until she stepped aboard the *Morning Star* and began losing her breakfast every blessed morning.

Not seasickness. *Morning sickness*.

She sat down on the steps with a plop.

Helen had spoken of it . . . had told her that it was a bit different with each woman during pregnancy. Some were deathly ill; others didn't lose so much as a single step to discomfort. It was just one of many lessons in womanhood she had learned from her American friend. And now she found herself forced to apply that alarming lesson!

No courses. Morning sickness. She looked down at her breasts, which suddenly felt full and tender in a way that alarmed her.

She was pregnant.

Putting her face in her hands, she tried to will it and then wish it away. But several minutes later, when the captain of the *Morning Star* started down the steps and found her there, the reality of it was still the same. She was with child. And Aaron Durham was the father. Assuring the captain that she hadn't fallen and wasn't grievously ill, she allowed him to help her up onto the deck and stood looking off the stern of the ship . . . toward America and Aaron and all she had left behind.

Pregnant.

What on earth was she going to do?

AS THE SHIP sailed up the Thames, Brien and Jeannie emerged from their cabin to watch the English countryside glide by. It was late summer and the grasses were tired and yellow and the fields were full of harvested stubble. All along the river were shacks and clutches of small boats . . . dead fish, refuse, and butchers' offal floated by on oily slicks of waste from tanneries and whale-rendering vessels. As they slowed and waited for the tide, she watched some fishermen on the nearest shore begin a brawl over the rights to a net that contained just a few bottom-feeding fish. It was hardly the homecoming she had hoped for. Everything looked so tired and old and worn.

Alarmed by the comparison she was making in her mind, she banished that thought and forced herself to focus on the comfort of Harcourt's snug, warm rooms, plentiful hot water, and soft down coverlets. But foremost in her mind was her desire to see her father, to reassure herself that he had recovered fully from his brush with death, and to share with him the news of her successful trip.

When she saw the earl of Southwold waiting on the dock, her heart surged with joy. He looked ruddy with health and stood straight and tall beside the carriage on the dock. The tears that formed in her eyes told how much she had missed him. She waved excitedly to him and as soon as the gangway was in place, hurried down it into his outstretched arms. It was a full minute before either could speak.

"Oh, Father, it's so good to see you!" she cried, locked securely in his embrace.

"My darling Brien! How I have missed you." Weston's face was red and his eyes watered with unspoken emotion. "So much has happened these last two months—the rumors of war and all—I was afraid you would have trouble securing passage." He pushed her back to look at her. "Great Heavens, but you look wonderful. The very picture of health."

"So do you." She blushed, wondering if he could in some way sense the secret she now carried inside her. "You're more handsome than—what war?"

"With France." His brow crinkled in surprise. "Haven't you heard?"

"I have been at sea for almost a month; I've heard nothing."

"There's been a revolt in France," he declared, waving his footmen up the gangway to help Dyso with the trunks stacked on the deck. "They've toppled the king and now there are rumors that the new regime will wage war on England. Our French relations barely escaped in time."

"But we don't have French relations." Her smile disappeared.

"Not we. You." Weston watched her face carefully. "The marquis de Saunier and his family have escaped to London and are even now searching for a suitable residence. It seems the marquis invested with London banks and brokerages whatever he could smuggle out of the country."

A chill went through Brien at the news that Raoul's family was in England.

"On the way home," her father continued, "you must tell us about your trip."

She put her arm through her father's and then stopped, realized he had spoken in the plural, and was looking ahead to where a tall, dark figure was descending from their carriage. She slowed. Her heart stopped as the man nodded.

"The marquis insisted on coming with me to greet you," her father said tersely, nodding to the man standing beside the carriage steps.

There stood Raoul Trechaud . . . plus thirty years. Her blood ran cold as she watched him stride to greet her . . . with Raoul's movement, Raoul's bearing, Raoul's fathomless eyes. She suddenly had difficulty getting her breath.

"Ahhh, so this is our dear Brien," the marquis de Saunier declared, doffing his hat to reveal black hair with handsome silver temples and time-etched lines around his eyes. "You are every bit as beautiful as your father and my son said." He reached for her gloved hand and brushed the back of it with his lips . . . broad, sensuous lips scored by years of pursing with disdain.

"How gallant of you, my lord," she managed through her constricted throat. Swallowing hard, she continued. "Forgive me. Your appearance was startling. Your resemblance to Raoul . . . how strange that he never mentioned it."

"My son was not one to bide time on unimportant matters. No doubt he was too busy praising your beauty." His dark eyes slid over her in a tactile way that made her feel assessed like a commodity and claimed. When he brushed her hand with his lips a second time, she drew it back and clamped it around her father's arm. "Or perhaps he was too busy enjoying your beauty . . . eh, daughter?"

Brien retreated half a step, repelled by his familiarity. *Daughter?*

"The marquis called on me shortly after arriving in London and I offered our assistance in helping him and his family find suitable lodgings," the earl declared, watching Brien's reaction to her father-in-law. "A pity, Marquis, that you and Brien couldn't have met under more favorable circumstances."

"Yes." The marquis still stared intently at her. "The whims of fortune. But for them, our houses might now be joined in the person of *le bel enfant. Quel dommage.*" He forced a smile that sent a shiver down Brien's spine. "But it was not to be."

She was frantic as her father handed her up into the carriage and climbed in behind her. Her breath caught in her throat as Dyso appeared beside the carriage, carrying the small jewelry case she had forgotten in her hurry to greet her father. She slipped to the side of the carriage to look out and saw her beloved Dyso standing face-to-face with the marquis. The hatred that simmered in the gentle giant's eyes caused her to gasp.

The sound caused Dyso to look her way and he held out the case to her, then rolled on toward the back of the carriage. The marquis turned to the carriage steps with a smirk of amusement.

"I see you kept the dumb brute," the marquis said genially as he settled back into the seat across from them. "How *sentimental* of you."

Brien looked at her father, who had caught the volatile exchange between the Frenchman and Dyso. Weston quickly hid his startled reaction beneath a bland, aristocratic smile.

"Dyso is a most loyal and capable servant," Brien said, wishing she could stop the carriage and toss the Frenchman out in the street. "He saved my life the night of the fire."

"Yes." The marquis's aristocratic mask slipped briefly to reveal a glimpse of simmering contempt. "A pity he could not have saved my son's as well."

For a few moments, no one spoke.

"*La marquise* did not come?" Brien said, trying to find a neutral topic.

"*Non,*" the marquis responded. "Her health suffers in

this tribulation. She seldom ventures out. You must call on us. Soon. Come for dinner." He relaxed back, watching Brien closely. "And there is another who longs to see you. Louis is away looking at property. He will be devastated that he missed the chance to welcome you home."

"So Louis is in London, too." She found his exaggeration suffocating.

"Perhaps you will find time to receive him at your home, yes?"

"Perhaps. I've been away for more than two months. I've a great deal of catching up to do. I will be quite busy."

"My dear, surely you will not deny us the chance to get to know you better," the marquis said with a bit too much force, then smiled. "You are a most beautiful and eligible young woman. We, like the rest of London society, appreciate both qualities."

"As to my beauty—or lack of it—others must judge. But I can say with certainty that I am not the least bit *eligible*. I shall never marry again." She met the Frenchman's penetrating stare head-on and refused to blink.

"So firm a stand for one so young," the marquis remarked, turning to her father.

"Those were once my sentiments." Feeling the strong undercurrents of meaning, the earl measured his words carefully. "But as you come to know my daughter better, you will find she has a fine head on her shoulders. I have come to trust her judgment . . . especially in these matters."

"How very English of you," the marquis said with a hint of a smirk.

A sense of foreboding hung over his subsequent words, weighting them with layers of meaning. There was a magnetism about the man, an animalism that Brien had experienced full force in Raoul. His presence overwhelmed and absorbed those around him, even her. And it wasn't a pleasant surrender, as with Aaron, but one that whispered warnings to her every nerve to be on guard.

By the time they delivered the marquis to a gentleman's club, Brien was gray with distress and her hands were splayed protectively over her waist. As the carriage continued toward Harcourt, her father reached over to pat her arm reassuringly.

"Brien, I realize that the Trechauds' presence here may recall painful memories for you. But they have been through a great deal in these past few months. It behooves us to behave with civility toward them."

Brien was relieved to be able to speak her mind. "I owe them nothing. You should know . . . I won't be accepting their invitations to dine and if we chance to meet otherwise, I will be civil and no more."

Meeting her father's troubled expression, she made it clearer still. "All legal claims they might have held over me were voided by Raoul's death. If they try to press for money from the marriage settlement they will have my full and unequivocal opposition. And they will find me a worthy adversary."

"I suspect they will." The earl smiled. "I leave the matter entirely in your hands." But as they neared Harcourt, the earl rubbed his chin and sighed quietly, wondering if his daughter were not further from a settled and happy life than ever.

BRIEN SLEPT BADLY on her first night home and, despite the comfort of familiar surroundings, awakened with a sense of dread that she laid squarely at the feet of the dark marquis. Climbing from the bed the next morning, she fought a wave of nausea to pad across the floor to look at herself in the pier glass. Her waist was still narrow and even under close scrutiny, her belly gave no indication of what was happening inside her. Perhaps, she told herself, she should have a physician's opinion and advice.

She smoothed her nightdress down over her belly and

imagined it growing. Her chest tightened at the realization that the child she carried was the proof of her time with Aaron Durham. As such, it was precious to her. And if worse came to worst—

What was she thinking? Worse *had* come to worst, and it was about time she faced it! The consequences she had feared and dreaded were now realities. She was going to have a child. A baby. A beautiful little child. With that simple statement her own wishes, her desire for independence, and her own freedom became moot. She would soon bring a new life into the world, and from this moment on, her needs would come second to those of her child.

It amazed her that she felt no hesitation and not the slightest reservation or resentment. How could her feelings have changed so totally in so short a span of time? She thought of the whirlwind of emotions Helen's baby had stirred in her and wondered how much more powerful they would be for her own child. Already she felt a curious sense of connection . . . of pride . . .

As she ran her hand over the small mound of her belly, her entire body warmed and softened with longing for the little life cradled inside her.

Aaron's child.

There would be questions and speculation and a flurry of gossip to contend with. For a moment she anticipated how that avalanche of outrage and disapproval would feel. Vicious. Overwhelming. But her stubborn common sense returned to steady her plummeting spirits. She always found the strength to cope, to stand up for herself and those she loved. She could deal with it all and survive. But not alone.

Her father wanted a baby, an heir so badly . . . and she had been so adamant about not producing one . . . Would he now condemn her for what he would surely see as a scandalous moral failure? Or might he be persuaded to accept the child into his heart and his household . . . to embrace his grandchild the way he had finally embraced his head-strong daughter?

Tenderness swept over her and she knelt, wrapping her arms protectively around her belly. For one moment she had a fierce and overpowering impulse to share the joy of that new life with someone. Someone specific.

Aaron.

It was his baby as well as hers. And she had left him half a world away.

TEN DAYS LATER, on the eve of the Opera Ball, the earl was summoned to Bristol by an urgent communiqué from his solicitor in the city. A ship of Weston Trading's fleet had been lost at sea; its valuable cargo would mean a terrible loss to the trading company. Nervous investors had already gotten word of the loss and had begun clamoring for payment. The earl's calm, controlled manner was needed to help restore order to the chaotic situation.

He arranged for the duke and duchess of Hargrave to escort Brien, and left her with strict instructions to carry on as though nothing were amiss. She must attend the Opera Ball as planned, for Weston Trading, if for no other reason. Her most urgent pleas could not move him to relent and allow her to accompany him instead.

Candlelight, bent and scattered by crystal prisms into thousands of tiny rainbows, flooded the main hall of the duke of Stafford's palatial home. That elegant light shimmered in the sea-green watered silk of Brien's dress and cast a golden glow about her honey curls and creamy skin. Her excitement mingled with trepidation as she floated into the ballroom on the duke's arm. Would society remember her? Would they accept her as before?

Her question was answered as the countess of Albermarle, one of society's great doyennes, greeted them warmly as they entered the grand salon. Soon, admiring looks and murmurs washed over her from all directions. She responded graciously to old friends and new, while battling butterflies in her stomach and lightness in her head.

To Brien's perception, the lights were brighter and the mood gayer than ever before. Talk of war with France had heightened the pleasures of the here and now. There was a feeling that "now" was all that could be grasped, and with that feeling came a freedom to take pleasures as they came. This was the last fling before the rigors of war settled over London. The gowns were more daring, the music louder, and the wine flowed more freely.

Charles Medford and Reydon Hardwick were there to claim dances and offer her glasses of wine punch . . . which she sipped sparingly. Then she heard an announcement of guests that sobered her instantly: *the marquis and marquise de Saunier and Lord Louis Trechaud.* As victims of the revolutionary muddle across the channel, they were welcomed roundly—even applauded—by their fellow aristocrats. Brien felt her capricious stomach revolt at the prospect of facing them, but had no reasonable excuse to avoid them, especially when they set a course straight for her with half of London watching.

"My dear Brien." The marquis seized her hands and kissed them. "I don't believe you've met my marquise." The delicate dark-eyed woman kissed both of her cheeks with an air of sadness. "And of course you know our Louis."

"Brien," Louis said with a courtly bow. "How wonderful to see you again. You are beautiful, as always."

"You flatter me, *monsieur*. And your English is so improved that I can understand it now." She managed a stiff smile. Pale, gentle Louis had always been different from the cunning, mercurial Raoul. She felt relieved to be able to show acceptance of one member of the family in front of so many inquisitive eyes.

"I—along with the rest of my family—have been eager for your return," Louis said, offering her his arm. She was forced to accept in order to escape the marquis's acquisitive stare, and allowed Louis to escort her into the drawing room.

"I have only just returned from America . . . a business matter. And you? I understand you have been traveling as well."

"One step ahead of the revolution. Not an especially comfortable way to travel."

She looked up, sensing pain behind his words. "Has it been horrible for you?"

"Horrible. And worse." He glanced down. "And now I am forced to impose upon your good graces to help me find some acceptance in my new home."

She winced, feeling a reluctant tug of sympathy for him. Spying a group of young men gathered in the dining room, she decided to solve the problem of what to do with him and satisfy her guilty desire to help him with the same course of action. "Then come . . . let me introduce you to some new friends."

As the night progressed, the merriment took on an increasingly frantic quality. The laughter was too raucous, the lights were too garish, and everything seemed to be happening too fast. Suddenly everyone seemed to be half-drunk but Brien.

When Louis appeared at her side at the end of a set in the ballroom, she was grateful to escape the increasingly crass and clumsy attentions of her dancing partners. She accepted three dances in a row with him. The third time, as she and Louis swept gracefully around the dance floor, it cleared. The buzzing in her head, caused by fatigue and the incessant noise, blotted out all but the simple and reassuring movement of the dance. She didn't see the marquis mount the small stage where the orchestra sat. The volume of the music lowered, but the strains continued—as did their dancing.

Then, suddenly, they were swept up in a rush of well-wishers. Bewildered, she was sure they had mistaken her for someone else . . . until . . . she caught the word "engaged" being tossed about. What were they saying? Who was engaged?

Dread punctured her isolating barrier and began to peel away the fog of her exhaustion. Grabbing Louis's arm, she yelled to make herself heard above the noise. "What's happening?"

His wine-reddened face leered back at her. "I think I may be drunk."

"Well, I'm not, and I don't want to stay here any longer." People were pointing at them, at her, at the way she clung to him. Without knowing quite why, she pushed away from him. "I have to find the duke and duchess. I need to go home." With a frisson of panic, she struggled on alone through the increasingly raucous crowd toward the great hall. "Have you see the Hargraves? The duke and duchess?" she asked individual faces in the press of the crowd. "Have you seen them?"

"Have you seen the leather in my new coach?" one drunken lout responded, leering. "Come on, girlie, I'll show you!"

"I saw 'em out in th' rear of the garden," another declared, shoving a flask in her face. " 'Ave a nip an' we'll join 'em!"

Maniacs! If she couldn't find the duke and duchess, she would find somebody else to escort her home!

Louis caught up with her as she reached the doors, seeming suddenly more sober and insisting on escorting her home. He called for the marquis's carriage and she was in no condition to object. Once she was outside in the cool air, a pounding headache had set in and she felt like she was going to be sick. Something had just happened. Something bad.

Now both sick and frantic, she turned on Louis and clutched the front of his coat.

"They were staring and leering at us. Why?" Her stomach began to roil in earnest.

"My dear Brien," Louis said thickly, "I believe my father had just announced our engagement."

That news sluiced through her overheated body like icy water. "Engagement?" The full meaning refused to settle and sink into her mind. A wave of nausea struck and she clenched her fists, willing it away. "Are you sure?"

Louis nodded miserably and Brien realized he knew—he had known all along!

Louis's "rescue" from her disagreeable partners in the dancing, the loud comments that prevented her from hearing what was said . . . then the ribald comments from their fellow revelers as they left the ballroom.

"This can't be happening." Anger magnified the quaking of her body. "How dare he? And you—you were a party to it? You knew he was going to do it, didn't you?" When he didn't respond, she cried, "You did, didn't you?"

"Yes," he blurted out. "I knew." His hands came up to cover his drink-reddened eyes and he drew a long, shuddering breath. "I'm sorry, Brien. I knew what he intended."

She drew back in revulsion, seeing him in an entirely different light.

"I told myself you were different from Raoul . . ."

"Don't you see, we have to go along with it. The marquis will have us married. It is inevitable."

"Is it? We'll see about that. Engagements easily made can be just as easily broken. Rest assured, this one will be broken first thing tomorrow."

"Brien, you do not understand. My father is a powerful man. He gets what he wants. And he wants this marriage. We have no choice."

"*You* may have no choice. But *I* have one. Tomorrow, all London will know of the loathsome tactics he employs to acquire good English land and wealth." She glared at Louis, who was pressed miserably back into the seat, and felt only contempt for him. She had thought him soulful and gentle, when in fact he was just weak.

"You disgust me." A wave of familiar nausea surged in her, reminding her that she now carried the fate of two souls in her hands . . . making it all the more important for her to repudiate the marquis's claims on her. She spoke not another word until she climbed down from the carriage in front of Harcourt. Her voice was low, but distinct, as she gave the driver orders.

"Dispose of this baggage as you will."

Twenty-Three

*T*HE LADY'S SECRET SAILED up the Thames, completing the final leg of her maiden voyage, and docked to an eager crowd of seafarers and shore ravens. Aaron left the registration of the manifest with the harbor master to Hicks's capable hands and escaped as quickly as possible through the throng meeting his ship.

He stalked through the streets of the waterfront district, stopping shopkeepers and passersby, asking the whereabouts of a little brick church. Soon he stood in front of the Church of St. Agrippa of the Apostles, comparing the dingy brick structure with the one in his memory and feeling tension wrenching its way up his spine. It was the place, all right, and it looked deserted.

He almost walked away, but something made him try the door. When it swung open unexpectedly, he nearly fell over the doorsill and caught himself. Stepping inside, he paused to let his eyes adjust and was drawn into a stream of time-faded memories.

He called out. There was no answer, but he noticed a few penny candles burning at a side altar and took that as confirmation that the church was at least in occasional use. He strode down the center aisle and paused for a moment at the spot where he and Brien had exchanged vows, feeling his heart begin to pound. Growing more determined, he exited through a chancel door that he knew to lead to the little vicarage.

Hearing a noise behind a door, he burst through it into a kitchen and startled a short, paunchy fellow in a half-assembled cassock, so that he almost dropped an earthen dish he was holding.

"Hullo . . ." The fellow stared at him in dismay, then set the pot of oniony bubble-and-squeak down on the small brazier, and frantically yanked his cassock back up his arms and tucked it beneath a rumpled split collar. "The civil thing is to knock, you know."

"Sorry, Vicar. I didn't think anyone was here."

"Thus the urgency to invade. I see." The vicar quickly buttoned his garment. "If you're here to steal, I'm afraid you're a bit late. The church and residence were picked clean some time ago. Still, if you're in dire need of a well-thumbed missal or a dog-eared bit of hymnody . . ."

"I only want information, Vicar. You're new here, I take it."

"New enough to still have some hope for this sad little island of ecclesiastica," the vicar said, coming to stand before Aaron with his hands planted high on his sides.

"Did you know the vicar who was here before you? A fellow named Stephenson?"

The vicar scratched his head. "Doesn't ring a bell. There was a fellow here for a while a year or two ago. Just back from some mission post. Took ill for a while."

"Yes, yes! He was ill. Wretched sick. Burning up with

fever!" Aaron grabbed the bewildered cleric by the shoulders. "Where is he now? I've got to find him."

"I have no idea. I should imagine the bishop would have a record of him. Bishops do that. Keep records. What is it you need? Perhaps I could assist you instead."

"Sorry, Father, I have to find this Stephenson fellow. He presided at my nuptials two years ago and apparently forgot to record the vows. I'm having a devil of a time proving to my bride that we're legally bound."

"Oooh. That is a bit of a muddle." The vicar thought for a moment. "You know, when I took over here, things were a disaster. Thieves had gone through the desk and scattered papers everywhere. Never been one for the clerk work myself, so I didn't pay it much notice. But perhaps . . ." Scowling, he pushed past Aaron into the threadbare parlor and went to a wooden box filled with paper sitting beside the cold hearth . . . beneath bundles of kindling and several hunks of coal. He cleared away the coal and carried the box to the table near the window.

"You're using the parish records to light kindling?" Aaron shook his head.

"Well, it *seemed* like refuse." The new vicar looked suitably chagrined. "Fortunately, I arrived in summer and haven't yet needed a fire."

They went through the papers one by one, and found a list of potential contributors, which the vicar pocketed, and drafts of several moribund sermons, which the vicar also pocketed. There were due bills and notes regarding parishioners. Near the bottom of the box, they discovered two crumpled papers that turned out to be baptismal records, a bit of correspondence regarding funeral services, and a fully executed marriage certificate . . . bearing the names Brien Elaine Weston and Aaron Thomas Durham.

"This is it!" Aaron engulfed the vicar in a ferocious hug and danced around, rattling the teeth in the poor man's head. "We *were* truly married—I knew it! It was legal. It *is*

legal. And binding." Then he halted, looked down, and released the horrified cleric. "Where's the parish register? I
want to see this marriage recorded with my own two eyes."

"Register?" The cleric winced. "That, I haven't been able
to locate as yet."

"Well, there's no better time to look than now."

BRIEN SLEPT POORLY and rose early the morning after the
Opera Ball, taking tea and scones in her room to steady her
capricious stomach. She declined her usual toilette and
asked Jeannie instead to prepare to take a letter to the over-
land courier's office. Struggling to focus beyond her rebellious anatomy, she sat down at her writing table intending
to pen an urgent message to her father and then compose a
terse, carefully worded denial for the *Times*. Her hands grew
icy and trembled as she explained to her father the devastating fraud perpetrated under the cloak of the night's fes-
tivites: The marquis had announced her engagement at the
ball in order to coerce her into a marriage he knew she
would never willingly accept. She begged her father to return to London straightaway—

Jeannie burst into the bedroom at a run.

"A nobleman . . . down in the parlor . . . demanding to
see you." The maid gripped her side and leaned on the vanity for support.

"The marquis." Brien stood up too quickly and swayed.
"Tell him I'm not—"

"Phillips already told him you weren't receivin' callers,
but he shoved his way right past Phillips and demands that
you come down straightaway." She groaned. "If only Dyso
were here. He took two of the horses to the smithy this
morn—"

"No, it's better that Dyso isn't here." Brien recalled the
hatred in the big servant's face when he encountered his
former master. She cradled her forehead in one hand,

steadying herself and forcing herself to think. "I have to deal with the wretch myself."

"What's happened, my lady?" Jeannie paled and struggled to understand. "What's going on?"

"The marquis has— He's spread a rumor about me that is ugly and untrue. Here." She sealed the letter to her father and handed it to the little maid. "Send young Harold with this to his lordship in Bristol. And tell him to hurry! Go. Now!"

Jeannie nodded and rushed immediately for the back stairs.

Brien's head throbbed and her stomach churned again as it had on the *Morning Star*. She made herself breathe deeply and smoothed her simple skirts with her hands. Gathering all of her courage, she proceeded down the stairs to the parlor where her adversary waited.

The marquis was accompanied by a man Brien had never seen before, and as she entered, they both turned on her like hawks ready to strike.

"My daughter," the marquis greeted her, "how lovely you—"

"How dare you push past my servants into this house!" Brien's strategy was to get straight to the point and toss them out as quickly as possible. She saw the other man move to draw the parlor doors together and tried to intercept him. But he shook her off his arm and planted himself between her and the door handles.

"I must ask you both to leave." She turned on the marquis. "Immediately."

"My dear—" the marquis began with a thinning veneer of geniality.

"I am not now, nor will I ever be, your 'dear.' Your appearance here this morning is an affront to decency. I will never marry that sniveling wretch you call a son. Furthermore, by week's end all of London will know of your loathsome attempt to trap me into a marriage." What had begun as sparks in her eyes now flared to full flame. From the surprise on his face, it was clear the marquis had not expected such resistance. But the hope his expression gave her was short-lived.

"I shall not leave until you have heard me out," he declared, recovering quickly.

"You have nothing to say to me, except in apology. To insult my father's hospitality and to plot against me, who was once married to your son—"

"And will be again." He folded his arms across his chest and the gesture made him seem to swell before her eyes. "Despite your protests, you will marry Louis and once again ally the great houses of Southwold and Saunier."

Standing in her own parlor, he ordered her to obey! With her face and temper both ablaze, she rushed for the bellpull.

The marquis lunged after her and hauled her back with an ironlike grip. She tried to free herself, but as they struggled, the fierceness of his black eyes bit deep into her determination. He was ready to use violence, if necessary, to have his way. The realization broke through her resistance, slowing her struggles.

"That's better. From now on, you will listen and do exactly what I tell you." He loomed over her, his chest heaving from the exertion. "First, you will send a letter to the *Times*, announcing your upcoming nuptials." He turned to the man standing guard at the door. "I've taken the liberty of drafting the letter myself. All you need do is sign it."

"I'll do nothing of the kind," she said furiously.

"Oh, but you will, *chérie*." The marquis grabbed her by both arms and dragged her to the writing table near the window, where he pushed her down onto a chair in front of the paper, quill, and ink his accomplice laid out on the desk.

"Sign it," he commanded.

"I will not." She tried to wrest her arm from him, but his hand clamped tighter.

"You will acknowledge your engagement to Louis or all of

London will turn out to watch you hang." His coal-black eyes seared the words into her mind so that she was hardly aware that he released her. "*For murder.*"

" 'Murder'?" Her heart convulsed. "Just whom am I supposed to have killed?"

"My son Raoul." The look in his eyes was chilling. He held her now by a force of will as powerful as any physical contact.

"That is madness." She tried to swallow, but found her throat paralyzed. "Raoul died in the fire. Everyone saw . . . my father identified his body."

"I have a witness who claims otherwise." He cast a glance over his shoulder at his accomplice, who had casually draped his frame over one of the stuffed chairs. Physically the man was nondescript, of foppish bent, and not as young as she had first supposed.

"I've never seen this man before." She gripped the edge of the table. "How could he possibly know anything about my marriage?"

"I wouldn't expect you to remember me," the man said, swinging a leg suggestively over the arm of the chair. "I was merely one of the many guests at your wedding." His accent was not French, but a flat, East-London English. His pallid complexion and watery eyes made him appear as unhealthy as his speech was common.

"But I was your husband's companion during your 'illness' after your marriage. He confided to me the nature of your particular malady and of his proposed cure."

The voice finally teased out a wisp of recollection. It was him! The man Raoul had conspired with that night in the library at Byron Place—the night she learned the truth about him. He had been at Byron Place while she was imprisoned there— Had he been Raoul's accomplice?

"This is absurd! If there was a murder attempt, it was on *my* life, not Raoul's!"

"Not so, my lady," the stranger intoned. "Before his

death, your husband confided to me that you had taken a lover before your marriage. He said you only married him to provide a name for the child you bore. As soon as the child was born, you intended to leave him—a plan he resisted. Finding no other solution to your passions, you schemed to lose him in a fire."

"That's a lie! Raoul held me at Byron Place against my will. I barely escaped the fire with my life! Who would believe this disreputable cur?"

The marquis's mouth curled into a sneer. "This 'cur' is my nephew, Cornelius Pitt. His father was English, and his story would be given full consideration by any English magistrate. Think, my dear. If you were being held prisoner, how is it you escaped and my son is dead? Could it be your lover helped you escape and set fire to the house to do away with Raoul?"

"No!" She reeled, horrified by the plausibility of his fabrication. "You were there." She turned on Pitt. "You know what happened."

"Yes, I know." Pitt smiled. "And so will everyone else in London when I tell them how Raoul pleaded with you to be a proper wife and not use him so cruelly."

"The spite was his, the pleading mine. If anyone was meant to die, it was me. He plotted to kill me in order to inherit Weston Trading and my father's wealth." Even as frantic as she was, Brien recognized that he did not deny her charge. If he didn't know it for a fact, he at least suspected it was true. Steadied by the resurgence of her own reason, she grasped desperately for a defense. "Raoul set the fire himself. Or had it set. I have a witness, too. Dyso."

"Who would believe that dumb brute?" The marquis gave a snort of contempt. "Especially when we find your 'accomplice' and persuade him to come forward in the interest of justice."

"I had no accomplice," she declared, her face flaming.

"I am certain it won't be difficult to find one," the marquis sneered. "Perhaps *more* than one."

The full horror of her predicament was now clear. There would be as many witnesses and accomplices as the marquis's gold would allow.

Sensing her softening, the marquis pressed on. "You said yourself . . . I am more cunning than Raoul. I will not allow passion or pride to interfere with my plans as he did. You will marry Louis. And you will do it as soon as possible." The marquis reached for the quill, inked its tip again, and held it out to her.

After a long, acrid moment, she accepted the quill and lowered it to the paper.

As she signed, the marquis moved closer. "You see, this isn't so difficult. I believe you and I will come to get along quite well, *chérie*." His hand slid possessively over her breast and she knocked his hand away. With a coarse laugh he reached for the letter. Perusing her signature, he gave a grunt of approval and motioned his nephew to the door.

"The announcement says you will hold the ceremony within the month," he declared. "I have taken the liberty of sending a letter to your father in Bristol, informing him of the betrothal and of your delight in the match." He paused before the door, looking pleased. "I am most eager to have you as my . . . *daughter* . . . once more."

Brien sat feeling boneless as they left the parlor. Every ounce of will and fortitude was drained from her. She listened to their retreating footsteps and the close of the front doors but, strangely, didn't hear Jeannie creep into the parlor. The feel of the little maid's arms around her shoulders startled her. She began to tremble violently and wrapped an arm across her belly.

"They will stop at nothing to force me to marry him. Ohhh, Jeannie, I can't let them do this to me. I have to protect us. I have to find a way . . ."

JEANNIE WAS WAITING in the stable when Dyso returned that afternoon.

"Thank God you're here." She touched his arm so that he would look at her. "My lady is in trouble. The marquis . . . the one whose son she married . . . he was here. He wants to force Lady Brien to marry someone." Seeing anger welling inside of him, she hurried on. "Harold took a letter to his lordship in Bristol. But who knows how long it will be before he gets it and comes back to London? She's frightened, I can tell."

He brought his massive fists crashing together.

"No! You can't! If you try to harm him, they will say she sent you and blame her. Please, Dyso," she pleaded, "we have to find another way."

Anger filled the big man as he led the horses back to their stalls and methodically set about feeding and watering them. His emotion ran so powerfully and his manner was so controlled that Jeannie feared it had been a mistake to tell him.

"Dyso," she pleaded, "we must wait for the earl. He may be able to help my lady." She caught up with him and clutched his sleeve, hindering him little. "Until then, we have to keep her safe. Promise you won't go near the marquis." She shook his arm. "Promise!"

There was no agreement in his fierce face as he wrenched his arm free.

Watching him lumber away toward his quarters, she called after him, "Dyso, wait!" But he neither looked back nor slowed his determined pace.

That evening, after dinner, Brien called Jeannie to her rooms.

"I cannot stay in London. I have to put some distance between myself and that jackal. But where can I go? Byron Place still isn't habitable and we have no relations that—"

She looked up with fresh hope. "Squire Hennipen! The marquis would never think of looking for me there." She squeezed Jeannie's hands, taking a much-needed deep breath. "Tell Dyso to prepare the carriage."

Jeannie's stricken look jolted Brien.

"What is it? What has happened?"

"I-I told Dyso about the marquis." Jeannie looked grieved. "He was furious. I tried to calm him but he wouldn't listen. This evening when Cook went to call him for dinner, he was gone. He didn't take anything with him—just left." Her chin quivered as if she might cry. "I'm so sorry. I'll never forgive myself if—"

"Dyso is gone." Brien felt dangerously weakened. She swayed and caught herself against the bedpost. She had no protection now. Her hand went to her waist and then slid below it. "He would have learned about it sooner or later." Brien put an arm around the maid. "We must get away from London as quickly as possible. Find Phillips and have him bring my trunk out of storage."

Alone once more, Brien was filled with mixed emotions. She hated the marquis, and part of her wished to see him beaten and destroyed. But not by her Dyso. The gentle giant would be hunted down like an animal and punished. Ridding the world of the marquis's foul presence wasn't worth losing her beloved Dyso. She could only pray that he had gone to fetch her father.

What would the marquis do when he found her gone? Would he fulfill his threats?

She straightened and made herself think of the child growing inside her.

Not if he couldn't find her.

A COLD AUTUMN rain had settled over the countryside, making their flight through the darkness all the more difficult and depressing. They arrived at the Hennipens' comfortable house well past midnight and Squire and Mrs. Hennipen hurried downstairs in slippers and nightcaps to take her into their arms and hearts. She explained her need for refuge and they declared that she and her maid were more than welcome. They showed her to the very room where she had stayed while recuperating from the fire, and they swore to keep her presence there a secret to all but a small circle of trusted servants.

As Brien settled, exhausted, into the thick down comforters and snowy linen of a familiar bed, her last waking thought was of Aaron. And for the hundredth time, she regretted the foolish pride and the impossible distance that separated her from his strength and the comfort of his embrace.

WHO DID YOU say?" the Bishop of London demanded testily, looking up with a scowl and lowering his newspaper to the breakfast table in front of him.

"The Reverend Henry Powell, your worship," the secretary said with a shrug that said he hadn't recalled the fellow either. "I checked. He's the one you sent to St. Agrippa's . . . that wretched little parish at the edge of Whitechapel, near the docks."

The bishop rubbed his forehead and dragged his hand down over his eyes. "The place that missionary lout left in such a mess. What was his name?"

"Stephenson, your worship. This 'Powell' fellow is accompanied by the earl of Wilton's son."

"What the devil do they want?"

"Parish records, I believe."

"Good God."

Moments later, the bishop greeted Aaron Durham and the new vicar of St. Agrippa's, offering them coffee and then listening to their request. He assessed the pair before him and decided on a surprising course of action: the truth.

"Vicar Stephenson, alas, made a muddle of every post and task he was given from the day he left university. Bucolic country chapels, teeming tropical missions, dockside relief parishes . . . nothing too large or too small for him to mugger up." He lowered his voice. "When he got back from Africa, I sent him down to a little church at the edge of Whitechapel and the blighter promptly fell ill and almost died. When I found out he'd been taken to a hospital and left the place unattended, I went down there myself and closed the church. Brought the register back here with me." He sent his secretary down to the library to look for the book, then turned back to them. "Can't imagine there would be anything of interest in it. The wretch wasn't there long enough to do any business."

"I wouldn't be so sure about that, your worship," Aaron said with a smile, glancing at Reverend Powell and drawing a folded piece of rumpled paper from his pocket.

THE BUSTLE OF activity that accompanied the arrival of a trading ship in port had died by evening and *The Lady's Secret* now lay quiet and serene in her quayside berth. Aaron paused for a moment to admire her lines and reflect on the worth of her maiden voyage. They had brought back raw materials that would fetch a high price now that there was talk of war again in England. But the excitement, the feeling of satisfaction and of completion that he wanted, would not come.

He propped a booted leg on one of the dock pilings, braced his arms across it, and thought of the other aspects of the journey he had just completed. As always, *she* bloomed in his mind. With only a moment's thought he could feel her in his arms and smell the faint scent of roses in her hair. Just closing his eyes he could see her as she was that day on the hilltop overlooking his land, outside of Boston . . . her eyes sparkling with discovery and her cheeks glowing with health and womanly vitality.

He slid his hand into his pocket and over the rumpled paper that was both his torment and his salvation. Would it have been better to have left it alone? To let both Brien and the powers of officialdom go on thinking no marriage existed? What did he hope to gain by proving what he already knew in his very core . . . that she was his and that he was unalterably hers? Here, in the same city, they might as well be an ocean apart. Her life, her world was here. She wanted no part of a marriage to a noble scapegrace who had just abandoned all ties and claims to a respected title—

"There 'e is!" came a shout from the quarterdeck of the *Secret*. Shortly Hicks was rushing down the gangway toward him. The first officer's face was red and Aaron could have sworn his lip was smashed on one corner.

"Captain!" Hicks grabbed him by the arm and pulled him into motion. "Thank God you've come. He just showed up—fighting furious—and nearly took the ship apart looking for you. He'll be waking up any minute now . . ."

Moments later Aaron found half a dozen of his crewmen standing around a large form lying inert on the floor of the commons. They were nursing battered jaws and noses and watching for any sign of movement from the big man.

"Dyso?" He knelt by Brien's servant. From the looks of things, he'd dealt out more punishment than he'd taken. He shook Dyso's arm and braced for a reaction.

Dyso roused, shook his head, and began to thrash and strain against the ropes that bound him. Aaron grabbed him by the shoulders and called to him. Recognizing the voice and face he sought, Dyso stilled and looked up at him with darkness that Aaron found impossible to read.

"All right, I'm going to free you," Aaron declared, glancing up at his men and seeing his uncertainty reflected in their faces. Then he looked back at Brien's protector. "And you're not going to knock any more heads together. Right?"

Dyso nodded and when he was freed, sat up and rubbed his wrists. Now drained of hostility, the big man rose and rubbed his face wearily. Aaron noted that his boots and his usually neat clothes were flecked with dried mud . . . a sign that he'd ridden hard from somewhere. The signs of strain around his eyes said he'd recently gone without sleep. Aaron sent to the galley for coffee.

"Why have you come?" Aaron eased into a chair across from him, recalling the last time Dyso had sought him out. When the bodyguard traced an hourglass curve with one hand, Aaron knew instantly: Brien was in some kind of trouble.

"Did she send you?" Getting a shake of the head, Aaron continued. "You came to get me to help her?" Affirmative, this time. "What's happened?"

Dyso's face suddenly showed more animation than Aaron had ever seen in it. Casting about for a way to explain, he spotted a thin brass rod attached to a candle snuffer and bent it forcefully around the third finger of his left hand. Caught up in the symbolism of the bending, Aaron missed his main point.

"Someone bends her? Forces her?"

Dyso shook his head in frustration and pointed to the ring of brass on his hand. It was a moment before the meaning got through to Aaron.

"She's getting married?" Aaron felt as if he'd just taken a cannonball in the gut. "*To whom?*"

Dyso shook his head, grabbed Aaron's arm, and forced the ring of the metal onto one of *his* fingers instead. Then he repeated the action more emphatically. Hicks was the first to glimpse the truth behind his pantomime.

"She's being forced to marry?" the first officer guessed.

With a relieved nod, the big man turned to Aaron and seized him by the arm, pulling him toward the steps. Aaron resisted briefly, telling Dyso to wait. Laying down orders for his crew to stay aboard ship and keep alert, and for Hicks to grab a weapon and prepare to ride with him, he ducked into his cabin and returned a moment later with a sword in his hands and a brace of pistols tucked into his belt.

"Let's go, my friend." He clapped Dyso on the shoulder. "Show us the way."

Twenty-Four

BEING ONCE AGAIN under Squire Hennipen's roof immersed Brien in a sea of memories, not the least of which was an unwelcome visitation of her time as Raoul's prisoner. He had declared that he would keep her locked away until she bore proof of his seed, when in fact he was plotting to do away with her. She thought of all of her regrets and recriminations in those early days following the fire. She had nearly been suffocated by a fog of guilt over what had happened between them, thinking that if she had only tried harder or had sought a genuine reconciliation with him . . .

Looking back now, it was clear that nothing she could have done would have changed the outcome. No woman—no matter how wise or saintly—could have truly shared a life with Raoul Trechaud. His cunning and avarice would have consumed whatever, whomever he touched. Then, with age and experience, he would have gradually become the marquis. She shuddered to think of what it would have been like to have such powerful greed, ruthlessness, and lust for control turned on her.

A chill ran through her at the realization that she was confronting those very things. In the person of the marquis himself.

Was there no way out? What of her father? Would he stand by her in this? In the carriage that day, she had made plain her thoughts about renewing ties with the house of Saunier. Surely, he wouldn't be fooled into thinking that she had changed her mind so quickly.

But in her deepest heart she knew that he still believed she should someday marry, and he hoped to someday persuade her to reconsider giving him grandchildren. Would he see this as the perfect opportunity to force her to do what he believed to be the right thing? How strong was the bond that had grown between them in the last two years?

Guilt settled over her, weighting her spirits further. How strong could it be if she had withheld the most important thing that had happened to her on her colonial journey . . . her experiences with and deepening feelings for Aaron Durham? How could she tell her father that she'd fallen in love with a decamped nobleman with a yen for ships and sea? Or that he happened to be the same man she believed she had married in an attempt to escape the marriage he had arranged for her? Worse still, how could she explain her confusion about Aaron's decision to make his life in Boston? And worst of all . . . how could she tell him that she was having a baby . . . his longed-for grandchild . . . but that the child would have no father, no name but hers, and could never be his heir.

It was a mess, and each passing day seemed to bring some new catastrophe.

All the next day she watched the road from her upstairs room in the Hennipens' comfortable house, hoping against hope that her father had already gotten the second message she sent, telling him of her plan to seek refuge with their old friends. The day dragged by and though the Hennipens tried to bolster her spirits, she grew steadily more apprehensive. If only Dyso were there with her . . .

Mrs. Hennipen insisted Brien have some dinner to keep her strength up and as they took coffee in the parlor later, a commotion arose in the hallway. The front doors banged open, feet shuffled, and voices rose. Brien bounded up and rushed out into the entry.

"Father—" She stopped short, with the rest of the greeting dying in her throat.

"How warmly you greet your once and future father-in-law." The marquis bowed with mocking gallantry.

"What are you doing—" She halted, seeing in the fact that he was accompanied by the loathsome Pitt and the limp-willed Louis and another sinewy henchman that pretending either surprise or pleasure would be a waste of time. "How did you find me?"

The marquis produced a letter from the pocket of his elegant frock coat. A letter bearing a familiar wax seal. A *broken* seal.

"How accommodating of you to write out your plans in a letter so that we could track you here." As he tossed the letter packet on the hall table, her heart skipped wildly.

"Is it his lordship?" Mrs. Hennipen called as she hurried out into the hall after her. At the sight of the four strange men, she rushed to Brien's side and put a protective arm around her, demanding, "Who are you?"

"What in blazes is this?" The squire rushed out into the entry hall behind his wife.

"Why don't you introduce us to your host and hostess, my dear?" the marquis demanded with his eyes glittering.

"The marquis de Saunier." Brien complied more to share her anxiety with the Hennipens than to alleviate theirs. "My late husband's father."

"What brings you to my door at this hour?" the squire asked in a tone that teetered on the edge of incivility.

"I wish to have a word with my lovely daughter-in-law in private," the marquis declared, glancing back and forth to choose a room with doors. He extended a hand to Brien and when she refused to take it, he swept along into the drawing room ahead of her. She reluctantly followed. When the Squire and Mrs. Hennipen moved to accompany her, Cornelius Pitt stepped forward to prevent it.

"I believe the marquis said it was *private*."

Seeing him and the other man closing in with their hands inside their coats, Brien turned back to reassure her friends.

"No, it will be all right. I'll speak with them alone." Mind racing and stomach churning, she joined the marquis and Louis inside, and she flinched when the great doors slammed shut behind her.

"What is the meaning of this?" she demanded.

"You thought to hide in the country while you tried to find a way to prevent the marriage from taking place." He made a *tsk*ing sound. "So very predictable." He strolled closer, looking her over. "But it wouldn't have mattered if you *had* realized your house was being watched and your communiques were being intercepted. Your wedding, *chéri*, was never meant to wait upon anything as insipid as banns. The announcement to the *Times* was merely for appearances."

Her mind raced and her mouth went dry. He had planned this all along.

"You know little of me if you think I will submit to this without a fight."

"I expected no less." The marquis sauntered casually about the large room, touching the furnishings appraisingly. "So we have come to see you properly wedded this night, before some foolish action might mar your chance for marital bliss."

"*This night?*" Brien fought to control her panic.

The marquis casually brushed his sleeves. "You will come with us to the church and marry Louis this evening. Another of my men has gone ahead to alert the priest. He will have made ready by the time we arrive." He leveled a possessive look on her. "Beautiful as you are, even a simple dinner frock will suffice as a bridal gown."

"I won't go," she said, raising her chin and scrambling for a larger show of defiance. "You cannot force me. The marriage will not stand if I am forced."

A sharp sigh and nod from the marquis signaled Louis to throw open the doors to the hall . . . where the Squire and Mrs. Hennipen stood gasping in the choking grip of the marquis's men. Pistols were aimed at their heads.

"No, my lady, don't—" The hand at the squire's throat tightened to cut off the rest, and his face reddened dangerously.

"No!" Brien rushed toward them but stopped when the henchmen tightened their hold on the hostages and began to drag them out the front doors. "Let them go." She turned on the marquis with her eyes blazing. "They have nothing to do with this."

"I beg to differ. Your presence here has brought them into the game . . . as pawns. So the good squire and his wife will accompany us to the church. If you fail to do exactly as I say, they will suffer for your obstinance . . . in most eloquent ways."

She was bested. She would hazard her own safety and fortune, but she would not barter the very lives of those who had sheltered her. The fires in her eyes dimmed, banked with the rest of her resistance.

"I will go with you." She glanced contemptuously at her clammy-faced bridegroom. "But if you harm the squire or Mrs. Hennipen, I'll not be married long, whatever the price."

Satisfaction oozed from the marquis. He had won.

Numbness settled over Brien as Louis led her outside to a
coach, where two more men waited. The Hennipens were
bound and gagged and tossed into the footwell between the
seats. Time seemed to stand still as they traveled to the
church. It might have been a moment, an hour, or an age
before the carriage slowed and stopped. Louis and the marquis bolted out and Brien—feeling like a spectator of her
own fate—stepped out of the carriage and into the clutches
of the marquis's men.

The familiar details of the courtyard of St. Anne's became clear in the light of the carriage lanterns. Her hopes
rose briefly when she recognized it, only to fall when a
gaunt, dour-faced man in cleric's garb admitted them to the
rectory.

"Where is Vicar Stonegate?" she asked.

The new priest turned on her with a scowl. "Stonegate
was transferred nearly six months ago to a parish in
Cornwall."

"Do you know who I am?" She prayed that her name
might give the vicar pause.

"A spoiled and defiant young woman who refuses to wed
a man who has offered honorably for her," the vicar
snapped, leading the bridal party back into the sanctuary,
where he'd lighted candles in preparation. Even caught
hard between Cornelius Pitt and the marquis's hired henchman, Brien refused to surrender.

"I'm Brien Weston—"

"Trechaud," the marquis intervened. "My son's widow.
And . . . I have learned to my dismay . . . my other son's
mistress."

"Don't listen to him," Brien cried as the vicar turned
away to light a few more candles. "The marquis's henchmen
are holding Squire and Mrs. Hennipen at gunpoint to
force me to do this. Look in the coach outside—see for
yourself—"

"Lies and accusations." The vicar nodded in confirmation to the marquis, then looked back at her. "I was warned you would spout all manner of nonsense."

"Then call the archdeacon, Mr. Samson . . . or the warden, old Willie Beverly . . . they know me."

That gave the vicar unexpected pause for a moment, then he brushed it aside.

"The archdeacon has been off visiting his daughter in Plymouth for two months and your other witness, Willie Beverly, died six months back. Both of your references, it seems, are unavailable." The small-eyed vicar scowled in final judgment. "Just what I would expect from a woman so insolent and unrepentant that she refuses to wed the father of the child she carries."

Her shock and silence were all the clergyman needed to confirm his vengeful charge. He strode off to the sacristy to don his vestments and get his prayer book.

She looked around her in the dim light. This was the little church she had attended as a child . . . where she was confirmed . . . where she had done charity work . . .

How could he have learned about the baby? Tears welled in her eyes. She hadn't said a word to anyone, not even Jeannie . . . who probably suspected something by now, but would never have said anything about it. Or was the story of a baby just a ploy to gain the sanctimonious vicar's cooperation . . . to make him believe he was setting a brazen and unrepentant sinner right?

Did it matter? She and her baby—Aaron's baby—were prisoners of Raoul's greedy and depraved father. Her last bit of hope flickered out, carrying her spirits with it.

When Louis took her by the arm and led her to the railing before the altar, she didn't resist. But as she stood there, avoiding the marquis's purposeful stare and waiting for the vicar to return, a horrifying new thought occurred to her. When it was over and she was married to Louis, it still wouldn't be over.

What would the marquis do to the Hennipens when he

no longer needed them to ensure her cooperation, and they became merely witnesses to the fact that she was forced to the altar against her will?

A SMALL KNOT of servants sat huddled by the fireplace in the kitchen of the Hennipens' home, warming themselves and wondering at the events that were taking place in the house. Their master and mistress and their lady guest had received some visitors and then left abruptly with them, without saying a word to any of the staff . . . even to Lady Brien's maid, who was beside herself with worry.

The sound was faint enough at first, but the butler, whose ears were sensitive from years of close attendance on sound and gesture, detected it. He grabbed the globed candlestick from the kitchen table and jerked open the door that led to the carriage turn at the front of the house. Three riders on horseback came up fast out of the darkness. As they bore down on him, he scurried to the front steps and stood squinting past the limits of his light, trying to make out who they were. He could see only that they were big men, equipped for the foul weather and a hard ride.

"Dyso!" Lady Brien's maid rushed out the door behind him and waved frantically to the three men. The butler sagged with relief as the three approached and he recognized the scarred giant who had spent time at the Hennipens' some time ago.

"Come in out of the weather," he beckoned, leading them inside.

"Robert! Captain . . . Dyso . . . thank God you've come!" Jeannie cried, touching the others only briefly before throwing her arms boldly around Hicks's neck.

"They said at Harcourt that she had come here." Aaron asked Jeannie, looking around, "Where is she?"

"I don't know. I was upstairs after dinner and they were in

the drawing room . . ." Jeannie halted, shaking her head, and the Hennipens' butler took it up.

"There were four men . . . one called himself a marquis. They arrived in a carriage with horses tied behind. I admitted them and then went out to call the grooms to see to their horses. When I got back inside, they were all gone . . . Lady Brien, the master and mistress."

"Dammit! Where would they have gone?" Aaron asked of himself as much as the butler. "A marriage—he has to have taken her someplace to say vows. Where would be the closest place to get married?"

"St. Anne's is the closest church. There is a new vicar there . . . something of a narrow wicket . . ." The butler snapped to attention to give them directions. "Half a mile back down the road, then left at the fork . . . and another three miles or so straight on . . . to the edge of the village. You can usually see the cross by night."

"Hurry," Jeannie said, giving Hicks a squeeze before releasing him. "They've been gone the better part of an hour!"

LIGHT FROM THE rectory windows glowed a dull yellow as they reined up a safe distance outside the churchyard. Above the stone wall, Aaron glimpsed a coach and four and a single man pacing back and forth with what appeared to be a gun in his hands. There was a flash of red just inside the open gate, at the side of the bushes. A second guard was lighting and drawing on a pipe. The scent of the tobacco began wafting toward them in the light breeze. Clearly, the marquis and his men weren't expecting any trouble.

Aaron smiled, as he put a finger to his lips to signal for quiet and then swung down from his horse. The others dismounted and leaned close to listen while removing their raincloaks and stretching aching shoulders and legs.

"Dyso, you take the one by the gate," he said, motioning.

"Make it quiet. Then spread out to cross the courtyard. I'll get the one by the coach. The rest are inside."

There was only a small grunting sound as Dyso eliminated the first guard. Keeping to the shadows, the three crept forward in the grassy courtyard, giving no hint of their presence until Aaron was close enough to lunge for the guard and whack him soundly on the head with the butt of his pistol. The man fell like a log, but Aaron and Hicks caught him just before he hit the ground with a thud. A moment later, a thumping came from the carriage and Aaron opened the door. Squire and Mrs. Hennipen lay in the footwell, trussed hand and foot, their mouths stuffed with rags. As Aaron and Hicks freed them, Mrs. Hennipen was frantic.

"Albert—is he all right?" she cried softly, pulling him into her arms as they worked to free his hands and feet. "Albert, look at me—" The squire seemed barely conscious at first. "His heart—Albert!"

"I'm all right," the squire said in dry, forced tones as he struggled up.

Frantically, she looked up at Aaron. "We must get the doctor—from the village—"

"No." The squire gamely began to haul himself up and out of the carriage floor. "I'll be all right." He looked at Aaron and Dyso and recognized the big servant. "Thank God you're here. That bastard has your lady." He looked at his worried wife. "I'm not going anywhere until I see that cursed Frenchman get what's coming to him."

Aaron grinned and clapped the squire on the shoulder. "Stay here." He pulled a pistol from his belt and thrust it into the older man's hands. "Don't use it unless you have to. How many of them are there?"

"F-four, I think," Hennipen answered. "All well armed."

Aaron turned to Dyso as he surveyed the outline of the building in the gloom. "Do you know this place? Can we reach the chapel through there?" He gestured to the nearest door. Dyso nodded.

"Is there another way in?"

Another nod.

"We'll have to separate . . . hit them on two fronts. I'll go this way. Hicks, you and Dyso go around the other side. Don't make a move until you hear my voice."

They turned to go, but Aaron caught Dyso back by the arm and scowled at the cold, violent set of the big man's scarred face.

"We're here for your lady. We don't have time for old grudges."

Aaron fancied there was a ghost of a smile on the big man's face as he nodded.

Suddenly Aaron was alone at the church door. He pushed it back and entered a dimly lighted stone passage, walking in a crouch. His scabbard scraped the doorway and he quickly flattened against the stone wall to listen for signs of his detection. There were voices in the distance, but it seemed his entry had gone unnoticed. Ahead of him the hallway opened on one side into a niche filled with pegs full of cloaks and vestments and shelves . . . a sacristy.

The voices dwindled to a single nasal drone that grew more irritating as he approached the sanctuary. A tapestry-weight curtain was all that separated him from them now, and he peeled back the edge of it to determine their positions and potential for opposition. It was just as the squire had said. Four of them inside. An elegantly dressed older man, a young fop, a fellow who looked fit enough to give an accounting of himself, and a disinterested waterfront tough holding a musket.

Brien stood at the front of the church, before the steps that led up to the altar. Above her, waxing righteous about the wages of fornication, was a lean and vituperative vicar. Behind her stood a richly attired older man with lace at his wrists and a smile that contained about as much warmth as an Atlantic iceberg. Beside her stood a whey-faced dandy who looked every bit as miserable as she did. And she *was* miserable. Her face was pale and strained, her eyes seemed huge and oddly vacant, and she was clutching a rough carriage blanket around her as if it contained the promise of salvation.

BRIEN FELT AS cold as the stone walls of the chapel itself. For the second time she stood in that beloved chapel . . . trembling . . . being swallowed up by another's ambition. All she could think was that a month ago she'd had everything a woman could want in life and she'd thrown it all away.

"Do you, Louis Armand Phillipe Trechaud, take this woman to wife?" With some prodding from the marquis, the vicar had finally gotten down to the real business at hand. "To love, honor, and protect her as long as you both shall live?"

"Of course he would." A clear, deep voice rang out. "If he were a man to take a woman at all."

Shock registered through the whole wedding party at the sight of a man with drawn sword bursting through the sacristy curtain.

Before anyone could react, Aaron vaulted up the altar steps and planted himself beside the stunned vicar, his sword tip leveled at Louis Trechaud's throat. Brien stared at him in disbelief, unable to respond at first.

"Who are you?" the vicar demanded.

"What do you think you are doing?" The marquis lurched forward.

"Make no sudden moves, gentlemen," Aaron warned him back, pushing the tip of his blade harder against Louis's neck. "Or this farce of a wedding will become an earnest funeral." He glanced at Brien. "Are you all right, my lady?"

"Yes," she managed numbly, clearly in shock. "All right."

"How dare you desecrate a House of God," the vicar sputtered.

"The same might be said of you, vicar," Aaron snapped, sweeping the gathering visually, noting a sword that he hadn't seen earlier, hanging at the marquis's side. The odds were four to one. Where the hell were Hicks and Dyso? "This wedding is not one of mutual consent. It couldn't be."

"Forced or not," the vicar protested, "she is with child and must be put to rights."

Aaron glanced at Brien, who was rubbing her face frantically, fighting to regain control of her faculties. She could lend no support to his next pronouncement.

"If she is with child, my good vicar, the fault is *mine*, not his."

"And who the devil are you?" the marquis sneered, edging closer, his hand inching toward the hilt of his blade.

"Her husband. Her freely taken, duly pronounced, fully documented *husband*. And unless you are eager to lose this sad excuse for a son, you'd better spread your arms out at your sides and keep them away from that blade."

"H-husband?" The vicar looked from Aaron to the marquis, whose eyes were darting over the scene with recalculation. He pointed to Louis. "But you said he was the father."

"It's a lie, of course," the marquis declared, raising his arms as ordered, but also edging back slowly toward the two men standing in front of the first pews. "Get on with the vows, vicar. He cannot prevent you from performing your anointed office."

While Aaron's attention was focused on the marquis's movements, the better dressed of the other two men slid silently closer to the chancel railing . . . out of Aaron's line of sight. Then he made his move, lunging up the steps past Louis—only to be intercepted in midair by an explosion of human muscle from the nearby pulpit. Hicks collided with Cornelius Pitt and together they hit the slate floor with bone-cracking force.

The fourth man jolted forward to help, and Aaron plunged down the steps, pushing Brien's bridegroom into him and sending both men crashing back against the front of the family boxes. The groom tried to crawl away, but the marquis grabbed him and shoved him back at Aaron, who was now struggling furiously with the other henchman for control of the musket. They traded several blows before Aaron managed to double him over with a kick to the groin . . . then wrenched the musket free and brought it down full-force on his head.

In a rage, Aaron turned on Louis, who produced a pistol but hesitated too long before using it. He slashed at it with his sword just as Louis fired—the deflected ball splintered part of the altar railing. Abandoning his blade, he wrestled with Louis and delivered several blows that ended with a ferocious uppercut. Louis flew back across the front pew with a shriek and rolled along it, trying to keep his feet.

The marquis de Saunier backed down the center aisle, cursing his son's weakness and reading in the shifting fight the collapse of his desperate plan to reclaim all Raoul's death had lost him. He shot a look at the doors behind him, calculating the odds of help from the men still outside . . . recalculating them as he realized that for Brien's rescuers to have made it inside, the men out there had to be either down or fled.

With a furious string of curses, he turned to flee down the aisle and out the main doors. Before he reached halfway, Dyso sprang out into the aisle, blocking the way.

"You," the marquis said, drawing his sword. "Out of my way."

Dyso's eyes burned and his chest swelled as he faced his one-time tormentor.

"I once had your tongue for your insolence," the marquis said with a growl. "I'll have your head this time." He lunged at his former servant with his blade raised.

Dyso swayed, avoiding that fierce downward cut, then

reversing sharply to grab at the marquis with his bare hands. Brushing only the edge of the nobleman's coat, he drew back and crouched, waiting for the next attack. The marquis came at him again and again, slashing viciously . . . each movement a killing blow that narrowly missed its target. Dyso moved quickly, feinting, dodging, and rolling across the tops of pews to avoid the blade. Each near miss made the blood roar that much louder in the Frenchman's head and drew him farther down the center aisle toward the altar . . . and the rest of the fighting.

Saunier's slashes grew wilder and more desperate as Dyso repeatedly lunged at his old enemy then sharply retreated, wearing him down. It was a deadly cat-and-mouse game, in which the cat was slowly losing his patience and his edge.

Then, as Saunier slashed furiously and his blade cut into the top of a pew and caught, the tide changed. Dyso straightened, his eyes glittering and his face set with cold vengeance. He caught the marquis's gaze and held it before lunging inside the ineffective arc of the blade and lashing his arms around the marquis's body. Carried by the momentum, they toppled onto the floor and the marquis's blade was dislodged and sent clattering between the pews.

Stripped of the insulation of wealth, status, and the fiction of superiority . . . reduced to muscle and sinew and emotion and reflex . . . they rolled and grappled savagely before Dyso's huge fists began to deal out the punishment they had absorbed and stored over a lifetime. Rising on his knees astride the tiring Saunier, Dyso saw the Frenchman's contempt turning to fear and the fear turning to pain. Each blow the big man landed transferred a part of justice's debt back to a man who had lived most of his life in a world where he was exempt from consequences.

As the rest of the fighting ended, Aaron and Hicks hurried to Brien.

"Aaron?" She recovered her voice and she came out of

her sensory fog as he threw his arms around her and scooped her against him. "Oh, thank God."

"Are you all right?" he demanded, pushing her back to look at her.

"Yes. I'm—you got here just in time." She touched his face and neck and shoulders, unable to believe he was real. "How did you know where to— Aaron, the Hennipens, they're—"

"Free," he told her. Then he spotted Hicks rushing to the center aisle where there were still sounds of grappling and flesh smacking flesh, and followed, pulling Brien along with him. Once there, he thrust her partway behind him, to shield her from the sight of Dyso pounding the now helpless marquis.

"Dyso, stop!" Brien called as the marquis's eyes closed and his head snapped from side to side. She gave Aaron a frantic shake. "Stop him—he'll kill the marquis and they'll hang him for it!"

Hicks and Aaron sprang to drag the big man from Saunier's body and it took all of their combined strength to pull him off and then restrain him. When Dyso finally quit struggling, Hicks knelt to check the marquis and declared he was still breathing.

"Good," the squire's voice came from behind them. "We need him alive."

They turned to find Squire and Mrs. Hennipen hurrying in from the sacristy.

"Why? So he can stand trial and publish all manner of lies about us?" Aaron said, still holding Dyso back.

"S-squire! You're really here?" The vicar crept out from behind the altar, looking horrified as he realized the ramifications of what had just taken place. Then in an instant he turned the blame outward—on Brien. "If you were already married, young woman, why didn't you say something?"

"I— I—" She leaned back against Aaron, unwilling to

dispute the story he'd told, but unable to quickly think of a way to explain her silence. "Would you have believed me?"

"No more than he believed the Hennipens were in danger," Aaron answered her.

"If I were you, Father," the squire said, drawing himself up to his full height as he addressed the vicar, "I would find some rope to bind these 'sinners' as they wait for the constables." He patted his wife's hand before setting it from his arm and striding over to look down at the unconscious marquis. "But this one . . ." His usually genial face was suddenly like red granite. "He deserves something more appropriate."

"He deserves nothing," Brien declared hotly. "The man is a brute and a monster."

The squire smiled coolly. "Did I ever tell you, dear Brien, that the name 'Hennipen' comes from the Norman? French, don't you know. I still have some relations and a goodly number of acquaintances in France." He gave a sardonic little sigh. "Some of the poor wretches are infected with that pernicious revolutionary fervor. . . ."

As Brien and Aaron contemplated that, the squire went to Dyso and pulled the big man down by the arm to whisper in his ear. Whatever he said brought an easing of tension and after a moment Dyso nodded. The squire pressed a length of cord into his hand and then turned to give Hicks a thump on the arm.

"If you would be so good as to help out our big friend here with the marquis. . . ."

As they bound the unconscious Frenchman and carried him out to the coach, the squire paused by Brien and gave her a pat on the arm. "You needn't worry about him, dear girl. Ever again."

Aaron and Brien watched the little squire escort his wife outside through the sacristy, and followed. They watched Dyso and Hicks drop the marquis in the footwell of the coach and hand the squire and Mrs. Hennipen up into the seats. After a private word with Aaron, Hicks volunteered to drive at least as far as the Hennipens' house, where Jeannie Trowbridge anxiously awaited word of her mistress. As the coach pulled away, Brien looked up at Aaron.

"Is it over?" she asked, shivering suddenly in the cool, damp air, feeling like she was awakening from a horrible dream.

"There may be a few questions. We have to find some-place safe . . . someplace where no one will look for us right away." He thought for a moment and then nodded firmly. "I know just the place." He looked around and spotted the horses tied nearby. Three. Just enough. He looked down at Brien. "Can you ride?"

"It's really you." She looked up and threw her arms around him. "I was so afraid I'd never see you again. . . ." He slid his arms around her and held her for a moment.

When they looked up, Dyso had collected the horses and stood waiting with the felt cloaks the three men had dis-carded earlier.

Aaron held her back at arm's length and studied her with a worried expression. "We have to go, sweetness. Can you ride?"

She smiled, feeling as if the weight of the world had just been lifted from her shoulders.

"Just watch me."

Twenty-Five

THEY RODE HARD for a while, heading west-northwest. The rain had stopped, the clouds had thinned, and the roads were drier. As they picked their way across the landscape by the light of an emerging moon, they were able to shed their raincloaks and slow the pace to spare the horses. Brien caught her breath and had a chance to ask some of the questions whirling inside her.

"How did you know where to find me?"

"Dyso came to get me," Aaron said, nodding across her mount to where the big servant was riding. "Where else would he go when you're in trouble?"

She looked at him in amazement. "How did he know where to find you? How did he even know you were in England?" She straightened in the saddle. "Jeannie! She'll be worried sick."

Aaron chuckled. "Hicks went home with the Hennipens to tell her."

"You know where she is, too?"

"We went first to your house in London." He smiled wryly. "Fortunately, your servants talk. We persuaded your housekeeper to tell us where you'd gone, and Dyso apparently knew where to find the Hennipens. We got there not long after you'd left with the marquis . . . Jeannie and the other servants told us he'd been there. From there, we simply tracked you to the nearest church. Not really very inventive of the marquis."

He searched the moonlit contours of her face. "Are you all right? They didn't hurt you? . . ."

"I'm fine. But I still don't understand how Dyso knew where to find you." She looked at her big protector. "How did you know where he was?"

Dyso gave her an enigmatic smile and kicked his mount into a faster gait that left her staring in puzzlement at his back.

"I think he likes being something of a mystery." Aaron chuckled. "The truth is, I mentioned in front of him that we'd be sailing for London shortly after . . . after the fire in Boston. He just took a chance and came to search the docks for *The Lady's Secret*."

"Thank Heaven he found you." She focused on Aaron's profile, giving thanks for every stubborn and assuming and persistent bone in his body. "The marquis announced an engagement between Louis and myself, and then tried to coerce me into going through with it." Anxiety threatened to rise as she spoke. "He produced a witness—that other man, Cornelius Pitt—to say that I had intentionally started the fire that killed Raoul. He swore he'd see me prosecuted and hanged for the murder of his son if I didn't marry Louis."

"That's absurd. Who would believe such a thing?"

"Anyone might, if he produced witnesses claiming to have seen and heard things." Her voice thickened with

rising emotion. "Pitt had learned from Raoul that I demanded an annulment. He knew about you. Not who you
were, exactly, but he knew there had been someone else."
She took a shuddering breath, recalling the marquis's
threats and the sick feeling she'd had in the pit of her stomach. "I was frantic. My father had been called to Bristol and
then Dyso disappeared." Her voice shrank as she recalled
those awful, desperate hours. "I've never felt so alone in my
life."

He studied her for a moment, then reached out to put his
hand over hers. "You're not alone now, Brien."

The gentleness beneath the strength and certainty in his
voice freed the emotions she had held in check for the last
three days. Anger and relief welled in equal proportions in
her and began to overflow in big, salty tears that she was
glad the darkness hid. She threw herself into the task of riding . . . urging her mount faster, reveling in the movement
and the freedom that she had come so close to losing.

They rode through the rest of the night, stopping only for
a bit of food and a change of horses the next morning. It was
midafternoon before they reached the stone pillars and
wrought-iron gates that marked the carriage lane leading to
their destination.

A friend's house was where they were bound, Aaron had
said. A place where they could stay until they sorted everything out. But it was, in fact, a sprawling manor house made
in the Elizabethan style, with a sweeping entry drive, huge
windows, and a facade of hand-cut marble that glowed in
the afternoon sun.

Brien looked at her elegant refuge with uncharacteristic
indifference. All she wanted, she had told Aaron for the last
ten miles, was a bug-free bed and twenty-four hours of unin-
terrupted sleep. Now that the journey was over and they
were dismounting, the reserves that had sustained her for
the last four days finally ran out. She was suddenly too

fatigued to move a muscle, much less make a proper dismount. When Aaron sensed her difficulty and came to help her down, she had difficulty prying her stiff fingers from around the reins. Her legs turned to rubber when her feet touched the ground; she had to lean on Aaron to steady herself.

Any other time it would have been humiliating to have to depend on someone so thoroughly. But just now she was too exhausted to be stubborn, independent, or even embarrassed by her weakness. She managed to walk stiffly across the gravel drive and up the approach to the house, but when she tried to lift a foot onto the first of several steps leading to the front doors, it refused to leave the ground.

She yanked her skirts aside with numbed fingers and looked down at her unresponsive feet in horror. Her entire body seemed to be rebelling. She was too overwhelmed to protest when Aaron pulled her against him and scooped her up in his arms. The way he panted up the steps with her made her feel guilty. But not so guilty that she insist he put her down and let her walk.

A pair of impressive lacquered doors swung open and slack-jawed servants in full livery stared in dismay as he carried her across inlaid mable floors and thick Persian rugs and up a sweeping staircase.

"Master Aaron." The butler bowed awkwardly as he passed.

"Peters. The master suite"—Aaron threw over his shoulder—"is *he* here?"

"No, sir. Cambridge, sir," Peters answered.

"Good!"

A heavy blow from his boot opened the door to a sumptuously furnished suite of rooms, the first of which was dominated by a massive rosewood bed draped in gold silk damascene and piled with pillows that looked so soft that she groaned with pure longing. When Aaron set her on the side of the bed, she fell back, rolled over onto her stomach, and crawled clumsily toward those sumptuous pillows. The feel of a goosefeather pillow and soft linen beneath her face was the last thing she remembered.

Aaron stood by the bed watching her collapse into the pillows and felt a curious trickle of pleasure that had no basis in the physical. He had quit listening to his body several hours ago. If he hadn't, he would be swamped with complaints of "aching back, swollen feet, overextended shoulder, saddle-sore buttocks, cramped hands, strained arms, pounding head . . ."

Sweet Heaven Almighty. He couldn't remember ever being this tired.

And yet . . . one look at his sleeping bride on the bed and a primal surge of pleasure transformed his exhaustion into a spongy, enveloping sense of exhilaration.

She stirred after a moment, punching the pillows and burrowing into them. Her eyelashes were a dark, thick fringe against her fair skin and her lips were parted. He imagined them moist and luscious against his own.

Later.

Much later.

He trudged around the bed, feeling his limbs turning leaden, and glanced at Peters, who stood watching in astonishment from the doorway.

"The big fellow downstairs is Dyso. He's my wife's servant and he'll need a good bed and plenty of food when he awakens." He staggered over to the bed and fell onto it beside her.

"Draw the curtains and take her shoes off," he muttered into the pillow. "And if you want my advice, you'll let her sleep until she wakes up on her own."

JUST PAST NOON the next day, Brien raised her head to look about. She was in a lavishly furnished bedchamber, lying on a bed the size of the *Secret*'s quarterdeck. Aaron sat in a stuffed chair nearby, with his feet propped up on a Chinese-print silk ottoman. He was freshly bathed and dressed in clean clothes, and his auburn hair was damp and looked slightly tousled from toweling. He seemed newly wakened himself and was watching her with a very pleased expression.

She sat up quickly and a coverlet slid from her shoulders. She was relieved to find her clothing still intact and reddened at the thoughts that prompted the inspection.

"Where are we?" she asked, thinking it might help to begin with the basics.

"My father's house. Coleraine. I doubt that anyone will look for us here. We're more than halfway to Bristol."

"How long did I sleep?" she said, feeling as if her eyes were full of sand and her mouth were lined with cotton.

"The better part of a day."

"I feel as if I could sleep another whole day and barely be even." She slid to the edge of the bed, wincing at the stretch and groan of her muscles. Her bottom felt as if it had been pounded for tenderness. As she reached the side of the bed, she thought suddenly of the child she carried and her hands went instantly to her abdomen. No cramps, no pain. After a moment's assessment, she concluded that the grueling ride hadn't done any damage. Sagging with relief, she looked up to find him watching her intently and realized her motions and expression were probably much too revealing. She jerked her hands away from her middle.

"I'm starved," she said abruptly and then reached up to inspect her hair. "And I need a brush. Badly."

"I think I can do something about both." He boosted himself out of the chair and headed for the door. Stepping just outside in the hall, he called to Peters that they were ready for food and plenty of it. Then he strode back inside and to a small vanity table in the adjoining dressing room, to retrieve a brush and a hand mirror. She melted at the sight of them and sat down in the sunlight streaming onto a window seat to take down what was left of her coiffure.

"How long do you think we have?" She dragged her fingers through her tangles.

"As long as we like," he said with a relaxed sigh.

She paused, thinking of what he'd said about his relations with his father. He was being optimistic. "I need to send a message to my father and explain—" She looked up in surprise. "How far did you say Bristol is from here?"

"Not far. If it helps . . . Dyso left before I awoke this morning. I think he may have gone to Bristol to look for your father."

"I'm not looking forward to facing him, but the sooner we have this muddle cleared up the better. He has undoubtedly gotten the marquis's letter about my engagement to Louis and is confused and outraged. Oh, and I have to send a retraction to the *Times* as quickly as possible. . . ." She halted and rubbed her face briskly, trying to wake up her lumbering wits. It all seemed so overwhelming.

His chuckle caught her by surprise. He was seated by the table with his feet on the seat of another chair, wearing that reckless smile she found so irritating and endearing.

"This isn't funny, Aaron. Do you know what will happen if we are found together like this?"

"Your father will welcome me into the family?"

"Don't try to pretend that you've gone mad—no one would notice the difference," she said, brushing her hair with furious strokes.

"It's madness that a husband and wife share bed and board? I always thought it was the custom." He folded his muscular arms across his broad chest and watched as his words found their mark.

" 'Husband and wife'?" Images that had been clamoring for attention in the back of her mind began to push their way forward. At the church, he'd declared to the marquis and vicar that they were married. Quite convincingly.

"Don't think I don't appreciate what you did in rescuing me. But this is not the time or the place to air your convictions about—"

"But it may be just the time and the place to give you the good news," he interrupted. "Or the bad news . . . depending on how you see it.

"*We are indeed married, you and I.* Duly and legally so." He went to the chair beside the bed where he had tossed his coat the night before, and pulled a rolled document from his pocket. For some reason her attention fixed on the scarlet ribbon around it as he placed it in her hands. "It appears we have been married all along."

"Wh-what?" She tore off the ribbon and unrolled the parchment to find a smaller, more rumpled document inside. The color drained from her face as she recognized it. Her own signature. And his. And the mythical Reverend Stephenson's. She turned quickly to the larger document to which the certificate was attached. It was a "By-this-all-men-should-know" declaration that attested to and verified the registration of a marriage . . . their marriage. And it was signed and sealed by the Bishop of London.

"We're *married*," she said as though the idea had only now occurred to her.

"Most definitely. By the authority of the Church of England and dotty old George himself." He bowed grandly. "Your husband, madame."

Was she taking the news well or not? He couldn't say. He hadn't expected her to fall into his arms straightaway, but he hadn't expected her to be quite so shocked either.

Brien's mind began to function. "Where did you get this?"

"That's an interesting story, actually. I had to know, one way or the other, so when we reached London a few days ago, I went to the church where we were married and tracked down the truth about our reportedly fraudulent vows."

"And you went to the bishop?" She stared in horror between his smug expression and the documents in her hands.

"I did. And learned that a fully ordained man of the cloth named Stephenson was indeed assigned to the parish at the time we were there. He was carted off to a hospital shortly after we left and it seems he never returned. The church was closed and padlocked against vandals and sat empty for some time. That must have been when your father searched for the records. The bishop looked over the papers we found in the vicarage and checked the register, then agreed to furnish this certification of our vows."

"And you had him declare our marriage binding by decree."

"The bishop was quite clear on that point. He couldn't declare us anything we weren't already. But we *were* already. And so he did."

"So, I've been rescued from the marquis's marriage trap, only to be snared in yours," she said, looking a little dazed. "Lucky me—I've traded bondage for bondage, without even knowing it!"

"I don't believe the term 'bondage' applies here," he said testily, "since *you're* the one who asked *me* to marry you, and you signed the documents of your own free will."

"Two bloody long years ago! Where was all this when I *needed* a husband?"

"Right under your nose, and your father's. And . . . if there was ever a time you *needed* a husband, sweetness, it was standing in front of the vicar of St. Anne's the other night. Think of it this way: Our marriage wasn't able to save you from the first Trechaud, but it did yeoman's duty in preventing you from having to marry a second one."

She opened her mouth to protest, but closed it again when she realized that she had nothing to say in rebuttal that made the least bit of sense. He was right. She had needed the protection and help of a husband *again*, and he had fulfilled those tasks admirably. More than admirably.

He'd ridden all night through rain and mud, and braved guns and swords to see her free of the marquis's plot. He'd gone beyond the call of duty and decency and even friendship. She couldn't have asked for a more conscientious or devoted or unselfish—

Then, just as he was winning the battle with silence, he had to open his mouth. "Someone had to make an honest woman of you"—he produced a knowing smile that galvanized every defense she possessed—"and own up to the child you carry."

He knew.

"Ch-child? Don't be ridiculous." She tossed her head.

"The vicar was quite clear as to why he intended to knit you and lily-livered Louis together over your objections. He said you were with child. Are you?"

That point-blank question set off a brushfire of a reaction in her. She flushed crimson hot from her toes to the roots of her hair. She was having enough difficulty dealing with the fact of being truly and irrevocably married. She sure as the devil wasn't going to throw in the complications of having a baby as well!

"Did it not occur to you that the marquis might have *lied* in order to get the vicar to marry us?" she demanded, summoning all of the righteous indignation she could muster.

Aaron didn't answer, but noted that she hadn't actually denied the accusation. Was that a slip on her part, or had she just felt it beneath her to deny it?

"I won't discuss this with you when you're not rational," she declared, tossing the brush aside and standing up. "I'm starving and I don't intend to say another word until I've had some food," she said curtly. "Hunger makes me irritable."

With a chuckle, Aaron shot to his feet and threw open the door. "Dammit, Peters!" he shouted. "Where is that food?"

Sweet, smoky ham. Potato savory made with onions and peppers. Boiled eggs sliced and peppered and layered with pungent cheese from Cheddar. Heaps of golden butter melting into every nook and cranny of featherlight scones. Strawberry jam dripping through her fingers . . . fresh, sweet milk . . . it was heavenly.

She sat in the sumptuous dining room of Coleraine with Aaron, eating as if she hadn't seen food in weeks. For the moment she didn't even care that Aaron's eyes widened a bit more each time she refilled her plate or groaned with pure animal satisfaction . . . behaviors that would have horrified her only weeks ago. It was wonderful, all of it, and nothing was going to interfere with her gustatory pleasure. Nothing. Not even Aaron's incredulous, you-certainly-seem-to-be-*eating*-for-two expression.

She finally sat back with a sigh and dabbed the corners of her mouth a good bit more daintily than she'd dirtied them. "That was wonderful." She looked around the dining room, taking note of the coffered ceiling, the silk wall hangings, the substantial but graceful furnishings. "This is such a beautiful house. Did you live here as a child or were you sent away to school?"

"A bit of both. Want to see my schoolroom?"

On the third floor they came to a nursery suite in the middle of the house, overlooking the gardens and reflecting pool. The heavy curtains in the main schoolroom were faded, but as she pushed them back to admit light, they discovered that the rest of the walls and furnishings were still as bright and inviting as when Aaron was a child.

"It's beautiful," she said, making a circuit of the room, touching books and slates and the huge wooden globe. She paused at a rocking horse carved and painted to look like a dragoon's valiant steed. She drew her hand along it and looked at her fingertips.

"You know, there isn't a speck of dust in this entire room. Yet it's been how long since you or anyone else used it?"

"At least twenty years," Aaron said, looking around the room, growing steadily more somber. "My father has always insisted on a spotless house . . . keeps twice the usual number of maids and keeps them all busy."

"He's kept it in perfect order," she mused, picking up a toy drum and running her fingers over the painted tin rim, "as if just waiting for the next generation of young lords and ladies to appear."

Looking up, she caught the unguarded emotion in his face and her heart melted. "Why did you bring me here, Aaron? To your home."

"It's not my home anymore," he said quietly.

"But you were proud enough of it to show me your schoolroom and the place where you grew and learned. There must be some part of you that is still proud of your heritage, of your birth and upbringing."

He scowled, but to his credit, didn't deny it. "I brought you here because I figured no one would expect me to do so." When she continued to look at him with expectation, he added: "And . . . I needed to get the one thing I intended to have, come hell or high water, from my hostage inheritance."

"What is that?" she asked, wanting to put her arms around him.

"This." He fished inside his belt for a moment. Then he came to her, took her left hand in his, and slipped a gold ring set with a facet-cut diamond onto her third finger. "It was my mother's. And it was always intended for my bride." He smiled broadly. "Now my bride has it."

She stared at the sparkling gem through a prism of moisture.

"We're married." She said it with a reverence that made it sound as if she were embracing the possibility of it for the first time.

"So we are." The tenderness in his face made her heart skip a beat.

"I'm not sure what that means," she said quietly.

He cleared something from his throat. "For most people it means living under the same roof . . . sharing bed and table . . . sitting by the fire and at social gatherings and on a church pew together . . . having and raising children."

"I don't think we're 'most people,' " she said quietly.

"True." He sat down on the edge of the heavy schoolroom table and studied her. "For us, it's been never knowing if or when the other would show up . . . sharing a few stolen moments of paradise . . . sitting on opposite sides of the table, the city, and the damned Atlantic, pretending not to know each other . . . while suffering near-continuous bouts of frustrated desire."

"A pretty dismal picture," she said, picking up a string of painted wooden ducks.

"Thus far." He thought for a moment. "But it doesn't have to be."

"No, it doesn't."

There it was. The first visible sign of a thaw in her opposition to their marriage. To his credit, he didn't pounce on it. Or even acknowledge it. Showing the wisdom he had failed to demonstrate so many times before, he clamped his mouth shut. As the seconds ticked by, he learned the truth of a very important male dictum.

Women despise silence . . . give them enough of it and they begin to fill it.

"But even if we wanted to be more like 'most people' . . . and I'm not suggesting that we do, necessarily . . . but if we did, we would have quite a few problems to overcome." She paused, but when the conversational void grew too large, she sallied forth again. "I mean, there is the problem of how we met and why we married. We could hardly go around telling people I paid you to wed and bed me."

There, he had to speak up. "Strictly speaking, the money was for the wedding alone. I threw the 'bedding' in for free."

"A distinction 'most people' won't appreciate," she said with an arch look. "Thus, I suggest we keep the details of our 'courtship' to ourselves. Then there is the problem of how to convince my father that I haven't taken complete leave of my senses . . . showing up with a two-year-old marriage, when I've been ranting and raving about hating wedlock and motherhood and everything in between, for those very same two years."

"Hmmm." He nodded. "He was married himself at one time, wasn't he? He should be used to women saying one thing and doing another."

She sent him an exceedingly narrow look. "Then there is the more immediate problem of 'one bed or two?' "

"One. Most definitely," he answered, sitting straighter.

"One house or two?"

"One."

"One country or two?"

He was a bit slower in answering. "One."

Then she asked the question that had no easy answer.

"Which one?" She moved closer, her light tone gone, her eyes filled with questions that had burdened her heart for weeks. "Which country will we live in and call our own? You once said to me, Aaron, that I only had to name the conditions. Is that offer still good?"

She held her breath as he studied her.

And he learned the truth of a second important male precept.

If for some reason the woman doesn't fill the silence . . . the man had better.

To fill that silence with the right answer would be to fill the rest of his life with joy and belonging. But in giving that answer, he would put his life, his destiny in her hands.

Designing ships, making his own mark in the world, helping to carve a new country out of a vast sea of wilderness and possibility . . . all of those things paled to nothing if she weren't there to support him and share the struggles and the successes. Life with her was what gave striving and accomplishment meaning. It was what he needed above all else, and it was time he faced that truth.

"After we left Boston, I sat in the cabin of the *Secret* for three and a half weeks, remembering the way you looked when you opened my door that night . . . how your touch warmed my skin like the Caribbean sun . . . how I absorbed your kisses like April rain . . . and feeling like a part of me would just wither up and die without those touches and kisses. Suddenly I couldn't imagine living the rest of my life without you.

"I'd rather argue with you than agree totally with someone else. You turn my attitudes and ideas upside down and inside out, and make me take a different look at things I've always taken for granted. You make the right of things seem more urgent and the wrong of things seem completely unthinkable. Around you, the decisions of life seem a whole lot clearer and easier to make. Including this decision." He stood up.

"Hell, yes, that offer is still good."

When he opened his arms, she walked straight into them and released the breath she'd been holding. She buried her face in his chest and held him fiercely . . . letting his warm, vibrant presence search out the cold, empty pockets of her heart and fill them with love and acceptance and new possibilities. From that moment on, there would be nothing closed off, nothing held back. She would live the rest of her life with him on the new path spreading out beneath them and ahead of them.

The right path. Destiny's choice.

"Then I accept."

They made love right there in the middle of the schoolroom, on the rug where he used to build ships of wooden blocks and pretend to sail them into a dashing future. It was quick and hot and explosive and when it was over they lay breathless and entwined and giggled like naughty children.

"I love you, Aaron Durham," she said, exulting in the moment.

"I believe we just established that." He grinned and she gave him a playful shove.

"But there is one thing I must have and have soon, or the deal is off."

"More food I suppose. Another gallon of milk . . . a second bushel of bread . . . a fresh side of beef . . ."

She glared at him and he laughed. A bit nervously. It was reassuring to see that he wasn't entirely without sensitivity.

"No, dear husband. Hot water. And plenty of it."

He threw back his head and laughed. "A bath it is. And maybe *then* another side of beef." He collected her gaze in his and refused to release it until she yielded up the truth. "You are with child, aren't you?"

She quickly slid her hands across her waist and abdomen. It was almost a relief to admit it for the first time outside her own head.

"Yes, I am."

"I knew it!" His face nearly split with a grin as he hugged her to him and rolled with her to put her beneath him. "A baby. I'm going to be a father!" A moment later, as the impact of it sank in, he sobered. "And just when were you going to tell me about our offspring? Presumably sometime before he or she made me a *grandfather*. . . ."

"I-I was coming around to that," she said, reddening. "I just wasn't sure you would be happy about having a child who would be raised in England."

"How could I possibly not want . . ." He scowled as the ramifications of it struck, and she could see it would take some adjusting.

"There are worse fates, you know," she prompted. "I mean, *you* were raised in England and look how intelligent and wise and sensible and upstanding and forward-thinking you turned out to be."

"You make a very persuasive argument," he said dryly, his frown easing.

"You learned to design ships and sail them, to fight for what you believe in, and to stand on your own two feet."

"That's fighting dirty."

"You charted your own course, lived your own way, found your own love and your own destiny. What makes you think our child—with all the love and support and guidance we will give him—won't be able to do the same?"

After a moment he drew a deep breath and sighed heavily. "Remind me never to get into a real battle with you."

She laughed and pushed him back, scrambling to her feet.

"Now, about that bath . . ." She lowered her lashes and gave him a look through them that made the skin of his belly heat. "Do you suppose dear old Peters has a tub big enough for two?"

Twenty-Six

GOLDEN LIGHT FILTERED past the edges of the heavy brocades at the windows the next morning. A footman had come earlier to stir and rebuild the fire and, upon a meaningful scowl from Aaron, had withdrawn and warned the other servants not to disturb them.

Now, almost an hour later, Aaron heard something that sounded like distant voices . . . raised voices. Peters wasn't the sort to roar and bully. The earl wasn't likely to be home this soon, even if he'd left Cambridge the instant he'd gotten the message Peters had undoubtedly sent. Aaron slid from the bed and hurriedly donned his breeches and boots. The voices grew louder as he grabbed his blade and bolted out the door. They had been found. And from the sound of things, not by friendly forces.

The entry hall was clogged with redcoats pushing their way past Peters and several of the footmen.

"What's going on here?" he demanded, bracing halfway down the stairs, his blade poised for action and his heart sinking at the sight of a dozen muskets . . . swinging around to aim at him. "How dare you charge into a nobleman's home uninvited?"

"Where the devil is she?" A tall, well-dressed man of fifty pushed to the front of the soldiers. "What have you done with her?" Before Aaron could answer, he turned to the officer and ordered, "Search the place! She must be here somewhere!"

"What have I done with whom?" Aaron demanded, descending two more steps and coiling to resist the soldiers coming toward him. "Who are you—" Just as it came out of his mouth . . . just as they launched up the steps toward him . . . just as he spotted Dyso through the open door— dragging four soldiers who were trying to hold him, up the steps with him . . . he realized who that hot-eyed man in the elegant gray frock coat was.

"Wait!" he cried as they grabbed him and dragged him down the steps. "You've got to listen to me—Brien—she's all right—"

But Dyso chose that moment to throw off his captors and try to grab Brien's father. The soldiers, thinking he was attacking the earl, reacted swiftly, and shortly Dyso was lying facedown on the floor of the great hall, with a lump the size of a goose's egg on the back of his bald head.

"What the hell did you do that for?" Aaron cried. "He was only trying to tell you—"

"Father!" Brien's voice cut through the noise and caused every muscle in the hall to still. Every eye looked up to find her standing near the top of the stairs in a filmy silk dressing gown she was holding together. "What are you doing here? With soldiers?"

The earl blinked at the sight of her, his jaw dropped, and he drew in his chin. "Well, I . . . Dyso came to get me . . . and after that letter from the marquis, I expected . . ." He stiffened with outrage. "Dammit, Brien, I came racing out here, expecting to do battle to free you from . . . and now I find you . . ." He swept her exposed form with a furious hand, then ran out of words to express the depths of his outrage, and stalked to where the soldiers were beginning to loosen their hold on Aaron.

"Where is Saunier?" He pushed his face into Aaron's. "And you—who the devil are you?"

Aaron swallowed hard and looked up at Brien.

"He is my husband, Father." She answered for both of them.

There was a moment's shocked silence. "Damn and blast!" the earl roared, his arms exploding out from his sides and his face catching fire. Aaron was close enough to see the veins standing out in his temples and feared he might have an attack of some kind.

"Please, your lordship—we can explain," he called, trying in vain to wrest his arms free. "The marquis kidnapped Brien—two nights ago—"

"I had gone to the Hennipens and he found me there," Brien clarified. "He forced me to go with him to St. Anne's, and the new vicar tried to make me marry Louis, and Aaron got there just in time . . . but then it turned out it wouldn't have mattered, except that they might have started another fire to try to get rid of me . . ."

"And Dyso, your lordship. He was with me and my first officer, Hicks . . ."

"He rescued you from a forced marriage"—Weston pointed at Aaron—"and you wedded *him* instead?"

"Not exactly," Brien said, hurrying down several steps and halting as her father stiffened in horror and backed up several steps. "It turns out . . . Father, my dear, dear father . . . that we've been married for nearly two years."

Another of those pregnant, suddenly-the-world-makes-no-blessed-sense silences fell over the hall.

"That does it!" the earl bellowed, turning on the young

redcoat officer. "It seems I've led you on a fool's errand, sir. I deeply regret the inconvenience to yourself, your commander, and your men. Now if you would be so good as to withdraw."

"Father, wait!" She ran down the steps as the soldiers released Aaron and began to file reluctantly out the door, bumping into one another as they craned their necks to catch what would happen next.

Aaron hurried to check on Dyso and, deciding his injury wasn't serious, called the visibly unsettled Peters and the footmen over to carry him to his room.

"You have to give me a chance to explain," she cried, grabbing his arm to keep him from striding out the front doors. "Please, hear us out. I beg you."

"There is nothing to explain," Weston declared, turning, looking from her to Aaron and back. "I have two good eyes. I can see for myself that you had no need of rescuing." His mouth twitched with humiliation. "You've succeeded in making a mockery of me more than once on this very point. One would think that after a while I would learn—"

"But I did need help. It's just that . . . Aaron rescued me first. I knew the marquis had sent you a letter and I was afraid you would be frantic . . . then Dyso took it upon himself to go and look for you . . ."

Weston watched the footmen struggling to hoist and carry Dyso's limp form from the hall, recalling how frantic the big servant had gotten when he went to the garrison and insisted the commander give him a squad of soldiers to help him free his daughter.

"He made all of those damned signs of his." Weston made a flurry of wild hand motions. "But he nodded 'yes' when I asked if the marquis had you."

"It was all a misunderstanding, Father," she said, entreating him with every weapon in a daughter's emotional arsenal.

A moment passed in which Weston searched his daughter's anxious face and saw tears forming. He closed his eyes and mustered every scrap of his much-abused patience.

"All right. One hour. I'll give you one hour to explain."
He jerked his head and gaze to the side. "But only if you
make yourself presentable."

Her face flamed. Dearest heaven! He must think she'd
gone completely mad, running around a strange nobleman's
house clad only in a thin wrapper.

"Yes, Papa." It was a term she had not used for him since
she was a small girl. It caught Weston by surprise and inserted a wedge in the closing door of his pride.

He stumbled over to a boot bench at the side of the front
doors and sat down with a thud, watching his daughter grab
the arm of the brigand she defended so passionately and
haul him up the stairs with her. Now that the pair was side
by side, Weston could see he was a formidable man . . . tall,
broad-shouldered, and striking. And he could see in his
daughter's behavior that she was quite familiar with him.

He looked up moments later to find the butler approaching. "My lord. Perhaps you would care to wait for Master
Aaron in the salon."

Shoving to his feet, Weston clasped his hands behind his
back and followed the butler into a grandly appointed salon
more suited to a London great house than a country estate.
He chose a couch upholstered with feather-stuffed cushions
and sat down.

"Anything else I can do, my lord?"

"Brandy," Weston said with a bit of a wilt. "A big one."

A few minutes later, Brien's "husband" strode into the
salon, wearing breeches, boots, shirt, and coat . . . looking
freshly shaved. Weston looked him over, took another drink
of the coffee that damned officious butler had brought
him instead of brandy, and had to admit that this "Durham"
fellow looked fairly respectable when fully clothed. Better
than he had expected. And the fellow's speech and manners
were refined enough, a reasonable counterfeit of culture. But
just as he was tempted to let down his guard, he remembered

his daughter in dishabille, in this blackguard's bed, and his defenses were back at full alert.

Young people these days . . . a bit of paper with a vicar's name on it and they believed they were married. Well, he happened to know that a real marriage was a great deal more than just a romp in the hay with a few words dusted over it. There were all manner of things to consider . . . lineages and incomes and prospects and suitability . . .

But in fairness, as he cast the fellow alongside his willful progeny, he had to admit it was a fair-looking match. *If* they were really married, *if* they stayed married, and *if* they had children—*he deemed all those possibilities remote*—then they would make beautiful children.

Straining for civility he little felt, Weston launched his investigation. "Tell me, Durham, how do you come to be in this nobleman's house? Are you related?"

Aaron poured himself a cup from the tray Peters had provided and sat down opposite the earl to answer. "The earl is my father."

Weston nearly choked on a mouthful of coffee.

"You find that hard to believe," Aaron stated, still gazing at Weston directly. "I can't say I blame you. If it will help, feel free to check the family Bible in the library and to interrogate the servants. Some of them have been here since before my birth."

"I . . . well, I . . ." Weston stammered. The man was disarmingly direct and Weston found himself drawn to the man in spite of everything that had occurred. "I will."

Aaron smiled. Weston was shrewd. His willingness to hear them out lent credence to his reputation for fairness, but Aaron knew that the battle was far from over.

"And where did you meet my daughter?" He searched his memory and found no recollection of Aaron Durham's name.

Aaron rose from his chair and stood near the fireplace, a smile playing at the corners of his mouth. "I captained the vessel that carried Brien to the colonies this last spring. My ship, *The Lady's Secret,* is berthed even now in London."

"How is it you, the son of a nobleman, captain a vessel?"

"I designed my ship and she turns a tidy profit for me. I press no claims against my father's title or wealth. All I have is what I have made in this world."

The earl was both intrigued and deflated. He had hoped, if the man were truly of noble birth and had access to reasonable resources, the situation might be saved.

"And just what have you made?" Weston demanded.

"I own one ship and am building two more. With two fellow investors, I just purchased a mercantile concern in the colonies, I own a large parcel of land on a river near Boston, and I have recently leased a house in Boston proper."

"In other words . . . you don't have much," Weston said sharply.

"It's a fair and reasonable start, your lordship," Aaron declared, setting his cup down with a clatter and rising. "And it's all been earned or made with my own two hands."

Weston jumped up to meet his glare. "Then it's a pity you weren't born with four!"

"Father! Aaron!" Brien stood in the doorway looking shocked and alarmed at the exchange she had just witnessed. "How could you?" She planted herself between them and shoved a rolled bit of parchment at her father. "Perhaps this will provide a basis for you to trust what we say."

"You're not helping matters," she said to Aaron in a loud whisper as she joined him by the settee. "He, like me, needs time to adjust to such drastic changes. Can't you show him a little consideration?" She slid her hand into his and her clear gray eyes were an arousing mixture of indignation and pleading that Aaron found irresistible. He relaxed.

"The bishop?" the earl said irritably. "He knows about this now—I shall never live it down." Then he looked back at the papers as if he half-expected the wording to have changed. It hadn't. "You're married. Truly, legally married."

His shoulders rounded slightly. "You must admit I have ample cause to doubt you . . . not the least of which is that until this day, I have never heard the name of Aaron Durham. I come to rescue my daughter and find her ensconced in a man's bed, claiming to be his wife . . . when only days before I heard her with my own ears declare that the institution of marriage was little more than sanctioned slavery."

Brien took his hand and held it tightly in her own. "Please, Father, I know this is hard for you. But it's not easy for me either." She went to his side and drew him down on the settee beside her. "And you're wrong. You have at least seen the name 'Aaron Durham' before."

"Oh? Where?"

"On the document I presented to you when I told you I couldn't marry Raoul."

It took a moment for that news to sink in, and Weston's jaw dropped. "No. That can't be. I checked. I went to the church. I saw the register. . . ."

They explained to him the events that prevented their marriage from being registered, and how the proof of it sat in a half-burgled church rectory for the better part of two years. When Weston insisted on knowing how they had met in the first place, Brien could only say that they met through a mutual acquaintance and Aaron quickly shifted attention to when they remet, on the ship bound for the colonies.

"I saw him several times at Silas and Helen's house in Boston, while I was there," Brien said, looking at her husband with unabashed affection. "He was charming and helpful. When that fire started at the warehouse, it was his crewmen who helped catch the men who set it. One thing led to another . . ."

"When my ship docked in London a few days back, I went to search out the truth about our vows. I"—he gave Brien a stubborn look—"couldn't believe that we'd both been hoodwinked. When the new vicar and I located the certificate, we had to go to the bishop to see it registered. And the bishop himself offered to issue the second certificate."

"So . . . you're really married." Weston looked at his daughter, reading in her glowing face her contentment with the bargain she had made. "Must have been a nasty shock to the marquis when you showed up, Durham."

The earl related how he had refused to believe the marquis's announcement of her engagement to Louis. The marquis's letter described Brien's delight in the match and begged the earl's forgiveness for the unorthodox manner in which it took place. He had blamed it on the impetuosity of the young. But Weston, knowing Brien's feelings about the marquis and the Trechaud family, knew something was amiss. He made plans and was just setting out from Bristol when Dyso arrived, behaving as if Brien were in imminent danger.

Brien felt burdened by her father's grave concern. "I was in trouble. When I fled London, the marquis guessed that I planned to resist the marriage further. He followed me to the Hennipens' to force me to marry Louis right away." This next part was even more difficult. "He claimed I started the fire that killed Raoul . . . that I meant for Raoul to die. And he produced a witness to swear to it. I was all alone and when Dyso left to find Aaron . . . I didn't know what to do. I was afraid you might think it could be true."

Weston had fidgeted uncomfortably beside her and suddenly pulled her into his arms, cutting off the flow of words. She was his child, his lovely Brien. He knew her honesty and now her truth. There was a long quiet moment as he held her against him, trying to quell the emotions that clouded his voice. Aaron sat uncomfortably by, knowing that this must be their time of reconciliation, but somehow envious of it.

"When I got to Bristol," Weston continued, "I found the ships late, but not unreasonably so. One docked a mere three days after my arrival and my head clerk disavowed all knowledge of an urgent summons." He released Brien from his tight embrace and stared down into her sweet face. "Probably more of the marquis's work." The muscles of his jaw worked as he struggled to contain his emotions. "If I could get my hands on that man, I'd see he was finished in London, I swear it. I'd see him ruined."

"I don't think you need worry about that," Aaron said. "When we last saw him he was senseless and tied hand and foot, and headed to the coast for a visit with some of Squire Hennipen's hardheaded French relations." Weston's frown prompted Aaron to be a bit more explicit: "He's headed back to France. And a marquis, especially a greedy, brutal one, has a fairly short life expectancy in Paris these days."

During the hearty breakfast that followed, Lawrence Weston watched his daughter and her rescuer-husband. Why was he always the last to know things where his daughter was concerned? He remembered the womanly glow about her when she returned from the colonies. He had marked well that the rigors of the voyage hadn't dissipated her vitality one bit. So it was Aaron Durham that had put that womanly glow in her cheeks and that twinkle in her eyes.

He watched those eyes now as they flitted over Aaron's face. And he saw the color that flooded her cheeks when Aaron returned her gaze. The captain was strong and, from the scar on his face, no stranger to conflict. But his unusual eyes glowed adoringly when they turned on Brien, casting a gentler light over his angular features.

They were in love. The thought caused an ache in the middle of Weston's chest. What more could he have wanted for his daughter than that?

IN THE END, the earl agreed to stay on another day. All that Aaron had told him was confirmed that very afternoon as he pored over books and documents in the library. The earl found himself liking the man's boldness and honesty, admitting rather proudly that he couldn't have imagined, much less conjured, a man whose stature, quickness of mind, and temperament would have mated so well with those of his offspring. Before dinner that evening, the earl was more than resigned to the match; he was pleased by it.

Only one thing disturbed him. Each time he delved into the man's future or inquired about his prospects, Brien carefully, even slyly, steered them away from it. Weston watched her, troubled by her possible motives, even while admiring her skill.

"And what of this trading company of yours, Durham, what is it called?" Weston tried once more to broach the subject as they sat down to dinner.

Aaron threw a guarded glance at Brien before answering. "The Harrison Company, thus far. Most of the property is a recent acquisition and I've had little time to plan for its future. But I'm sure it will need a strong, understanding hand on the helm."

Brien looked at him in surprise. She had no idea he had assets other than his ship. What trading company? Then the name "Harrison" lodged in her mind. "Harrison" was the name of the company that bought—

"You?" She sputtered. "You're Harrison? You bought Weston Trading?"

Aaron faced her with a coolness that fascinated Weston. He hoped the man could deal with the full fury of his daughter's wounded pride. He would hate to lose this son-in-law just as he was getting used to the idea of having one.

Aaron leaned forward and spoke in quietly determined tones. "I told you I would hate to see so promising a venture fall into the wrong hands. It was an excellent investment, with a real future in the colonies." Aaron leaned forward with a dazzling grin. "Now don't be prickly about this, Brien. I won't deny I had some personal interest in the holdings because of you, but I would never have risked my partners' money in any venture, based solely on sentiment."

"Your partners' money?" Brien's irritation was rising.

"I used some of the money I raised in New York to buy your holdings. My mother's name was Harrison before she married and I felt it only proper that her name should be used." He smiled with bone-melting charm into Brien's narrowing eyes. "She had a good head for business, you see, and invested wisely. Unusual for a woman."

Weston looked on, amazed by the man's courage in the face of his stubborn and independent-minded daughter's stinging pride.

"I thought if . . . if Brien Weston Durham wanted a hand in running the business, she could have it," he said. "But the business is in Boston. And, of course, I don't know how much time she would have anyway . . . what with working on the house and all."

"House?" She was gripping the edge of the table. Her eyes were white-hot.

"The one that sits half-begun on my land just outside of Boston. You remember the meadow and lane near the stream? It sits there, awaiting your word on its completion. I felt certain that, with your experience here, you would do a better job at it than I would." He watched her struggle inwardly with her pleasure at his revelation and her decision that they would stay in England. "But, of course, that house would be in Boston."

Then he played the final card in his desperate hand. "I took a house . . . until the new one is finished. I even engaged a housekeeper. She's quite capable, but—I swear—she has the tongue of a fishwife when crossed. Knowing how you love a challenge, I thought I would leave it to you to deal with Ella."

"You— You're her mysterious Mr. George?" She looked as if she might stab him with her fork. "Oh, that's low, Aaron Durham. You employed Ella as your housekeeper and you think you can use it to lure me to Boston. You think I'm so in love with you that I'll follow you halfway around the world to your precious colonies . . . and build ships and trading companies . . . and have babies and have adventures . . . and stare into western sunsets with you until I'm old and gray. . . ."

Aaron smiled. "I can't say what you'll choose to do. I can only say that's how much I love you."

Brien's eyes started to prickle with tears and she produced a handkerchief and dabbed frantically at her eyes.

"Wretched man. I hate it when you say things so beautiful that they make me cry."

Weston sat with his fork poised halfway to his mouth, watching between his daughter and her husband as revelation after revelation unfolded. Astounded, he put down his fork and picked up his wine glass and drained it.

There really was a God in heaven, and He really did answer prayers.

Twenty-Seven

AFTER DINNER, Brien left her father and Aaron in the salon, sharing a brandy, while she went up to their rooms to freshen up. Aaron cast more than one look toward the door as he listened patiently to Weston's latest news of the East India Company and the commodity trade. Weston pretended not to notice his son-in-law's restiveness. He was, for all intents and purposes, newly wedded and no doubt eager to sample the delights of the marriage bed. Weston smiled to himself. Let the young buck wait.

The sound of the doors opening and raised voices in the hall caught them both by surprise, and they rose like one man. As Aaron gained the door first and stepped into the entry hall, the familiarity of the action dawned upon him. He suddenly felt as though he had responded just so a thousand times before.

He stopped short in the hallway as the driving force

behind that well-remembered action loomed up before him. For a moment there was no sound or motion in the hallway as father and son faced each other.

"So." The earl eyed his prodigal son appraisingly. "You're home."

"How did you know?" Aaron asked, tilting his chin upward to parry his father's intense gaze.

"Peters."

"I expected as much. Did he also tell you why I'm here?" Aaron's voice was lower, tighter than usual.

"Some nonsense about a marriage."

Aaron's voice and stubborn mood mirrored perfectly those of the man he confronted, even to the impatient twitch of the corner of his mouth. "I *am* married," he said. "She is here with me."

The earl handed his hat and gloves to Peters and headed into the salon, brushing by Aaron and totally ignoring Weston, standing in the doorway.

Weston considered making a discreet exit, but the drama was too high, too tempting. In the end, he followed Aaron back into the salon and sat down in an out-of-the-way chair. This didn't seem an auspicious start to an introduction, but at least he would see what manner of family his daughter had married into.

"Why have you come back?" The rail-straight earl of Wilton sounded less hospitable by the moment. Weston winced as he thought of his outrage upon learning of their marriage and imagined what a howl this acerbic old aristocrat would raise.

"We needed a place to stay," Aaron replied.

"Why not a public house?" The earl tossed his words like javelins. "Or has your waywardness wasted all of your resources?"

"We came for other reasons," Aaron answered tightly. Then a reckless urge to honesty goaded him. "To avoid disgrace and possible arrest."

Weston's eyes widened at the audacious way it was phrased. The boldness of an experienced captain became pure, thoughtless rebellion when faced with his father's hostility. Weston's mind raced to gather facts and nuances and to trace them to their melancholy conclusion. The man, however worthy, would never fulfill the ambitions of his lordly father, however courageous he was, whatever he became or built, it would not matter. He would be an ungrateful, rebellious wastrel in his father's house . . . unless . . .

Weston was jolted back to the present by the earl's heated charge. "Caught cuckolding some fat merchant or bedding his wayward daughter?"

"No, only assaulting a peer of France and spiriting away my lawful wife."

"If you were married legally, then it could not have been honorably, to send you skulking back to the shelter of my house."

"You have no right to judge my honor . . . or my wife's." Aaron's voice was too low, too controlled for the heat contained in those words, and Weston sprang to his feet.

"I'll judge who I want to judge in my own house—including you and your illegal strumpet."

Only Weston's physical intervention prevented Aaron from striking the older man. The elder Durham stood his ground regally. Only then did Thomas Durham take notice of the well-dressed observer who had intervened on his behalf.

"Think, man—" Weston strained against Aaron's youth and strength, summoning his every reserve. "Would you bring such disgrace upon your head, upon your wife?"

At Weston's reference to Brien, Aaron eased and straightened. Weston sensed the younger Durham was again in control, but with passion full-blown and all the more dangerous for it. What a turn. He now feared for his daughter's husband, when only hours before he had practically sought the man's head! He stepped slowly aside, to keep both father and son in sight.

"Who are you?" Thomas Durham demanded, confronting him.

"I, sir, am the *strumpet's* father . . . who yesterday led an attack on your son for abducting my daughter." Weston's dress and cultured bearing were all that prevented Wilton from ordering the insolent wretch thrown out. "I shall excuse your distasteful reference, for it is clear you have no knowledge to speak from. But it is clear you know even less about your son than you do about my daughter. A deplorable fault in a father, sir, however it is justified."

"The effrontery!" Wilton exclaimed. The redness that flushed his prominent cheekbones let Weston know his words had found a mark. "Just who do you think you are to lecture me in my own house?"

"I am your son's father-in-law. Otherwise known as Lawrence Weston, seventh Earl of Southwold."

At the name, Thomas Durham's eyes widened; he had heard of the wealthy Southwold, but had never met the reclusive nobleman. Then his eyes narrowed. It would take more than a fine suit of clothes and a bit of cultured speech to convince him of the authenticity of the claim.

"Clever you are to bring so accomplished a liar as an accomplice," Durham declared, searing Aaron with a look. "But it will do you no good. Whatever you seek, you will go away empty-handed."

"What makes you think I want anything of yours?" Aaron declared angrily. "Had I known you would return so soon, I would never have stayed."

"I see." An ugly curl crept into the elder Durham's lip. "You thought to rob me blind in my absence . . . you and your trollop."

Weston had had enough. He grabbed Durham's arm and yanked him around to give him the tongue-lashing of his life. "You arrogant, insufferable, foul-minded—"

NOT QUITE MARRIED ❧

The senior Durham drew back in outrage and before he was even aware of making the decision to do so, reversed and planted Weston a facer.

Weston staggered back, shocked from his toes to the roots of his hair. And then, igniting with equal outrage, he lowered his head and charged at Durham, sending him sprawling back onto the settee and gasping for breath.

Aaron stifled the urge to join the melee, but could not bring himself to stop it. They were healthy and reasonably well matched in age and size. In a few energetic exchanges they both were panting and swinging furiously, but without much effect. At least once each man was brought to his knees—an even bout to Aaron's incredulous scrutiny. Somewhere in the midst of watching his rigid old iconoclast of a father engage in a full-out knuckle-banger of a fight with another peer of the realm, his own anger was spent.

By the time Brien's voice split the air, they were more than willing to halt.

"Merciful God! What do you think you are doing?"

Weston got up heavily from his knee and Thomas Durham leaned over the back of a chair, panting. Their clearing gazes turned to her at the same time. All of them stared—each for a different reason.

She was a vision in a borrowed dressing gown that highlighted her smooth skin and womanly curves. Her hair had been brushed and was pinned loosely atop her head. Her cheeks were flushed and her eyes flashed indignation.

"What is going on here?" she demanded, steadying herself on a nearby chair.

Aaron cleared his throat as the others looked to their clothing and bruised faces.

"It seems our fathers had a difference of opinion." Amusement played at the corner of Aaron's mouth.

"Father?" She turned on the earl in disbelief. "Whatever possessed you?" Without waiting for a response, she moved on to Thomas Durham. "And you, sir, to brawl with a guest in your own home . . ." Then she turned on Aaron. "And you let them? You're as daft as they are! What possible provocation could they have had?"

There was an uncomfortable silence in which not one of them would meet her eye.

"My father doubts our marriage and your father's word on his identity, and thinks I am here to steal him blind." Aaron's brutally simple summary told Brien all she needed to know.

She approached the earl with a display of determined grace that made her father hold his breath and made her husband bite his lip in anticipation. Her effect on Thomas Durham was harder to read, but his sidelong glance at Weston hinted that he was reconsidering his earlier stance. She clearly was not what he expected.

He took Brien's proffered hand awkwardly.

"Since no one seems to have the manners to introduce us, I am Brien Weston Durham. Your son and I were married some time ago. The circumstances, while unusual, cast no doubt on the honor or legality of our union. Tomorrow morning you may inspect the marriage documents yourself, if you wish."

"I . . . I shall." Durham's jaw slammed shut.

Brien withdrew her hand. "I do not know what you have been told, but I shall tell you the truth as I know it. Aaron and I were lost to each other for some time before being reunited on the maiden voyage of his new ship to the American colonies."

"So," Durham cast a caustic look at Aaron, "you managed to complete your little boat without your inheritance."

"I learned a great deal about him during that voyage. I learned how smart and talented and creative he is. I learned how honorable and capable and dependable he is. And I learned that, unlike many men, he doesn't have to prove his manhood by controlling and manipulating others."

"Well." Durham seemed a bit less acerbic when he said,

"Congratulations. You finally managed to convince some-one that your daydreams are grand and noble visions."

"Unfortunately, when he told me that he was going to stay in the colonies, to make his life there . . . to register his ships under and sail under the colonial colors, I couldn't imagine how anyone could abandon a life of privilege and opportunity in England for the hopes and promise of some-thing not yet built. It took a voyage back to England and a lot of thinking for me to realize that to look at a sprawling land filled with raw, untamed beauty and see it built into a fine, strong, prosperous new country takes a very special vi-sion . . . something given to very few men, whatever their birth. Aaron is one of them."

Durham stared at her with his lips drawn into a tight, im-pregnable line.

"You should know the rest." Her calm, determined voice had the ring of a steel blade on stone. "Aaron rescued me from an abduction and very nearly a forced marriage. He risked life and limb, fought bravely and honorably to save me. I owe him my life as well as my happiness. But with all of that, he would still have let me go if I wanted to leave. He knows, in a way few will ever know, that to love someone is to free them. To want them to grow and live and use their talents as they see fit.

"I wasn't certain I had done the right thing in marrying him. But I find now that being Mrs. Durham—*Brien Durham*—living with and loving your son has become the very foundation of my life." Her coolness in the face of an obviously hostile father-in-law surprised even her a bit. But if the earl rejected them totally, at least she would have the satisfaction of setting the pompous old curmudgeon straight. "I intend to live with him until my dying day."

"Surely you cannot expect me to welcome you with open arms," Durham said, pulling his chin back and reddening. "For all I know, this is a ruse—and a diabolically clever one at that. I warn you, you'll not get a shilling!"

Brien's gaze grew withering as she drew herself straighter. "If you weren't so blind and stubborn, you would already know that Aaron wants none of your money. And he desires your title even less." She looked to Aaron, then back to his father. "Having seen how nobly you wear the honor, I make it a condition of my marriage to him that he never even consider it." She edged closer to him, eyes now blazing. "It doesn't matter what you think of me or my family, your lordship. But you must be the world's greatest fool to disparage the honor and courage of a man as exceptional as Aaron Durham, solely on account of his being your son."

The earl looked as if he'd just been doused with cold water.

She stepped back slowly, her mind racing and her heart filled with a jumble of indignation, pride, and sadness. This was the scorn Aaron had lived with until he could bear it no longer and had fled to the open and hungry arms of the sea. She looked at him with all the love in her heart visible in her eyes, vowing silently to love him all the more dearly for the hurt he had suffered here.

"You needn't worry about being bothered with us." She turned on Thomas Durham with fresh fire in her eyes. "We plan to make our home in Boston in the colonies. There, at least, a man is judged by his own skill and cleverness and courage—not by the confines of a lifeless tradition."

She stepped back, raking him with narrowed eyes. "This I will take from you, your lordship: I shall spend what is left of this night in *your* bed. Tomorrow, I shall take nourishment at *your* table, and I will leave shortly thereafter with *your* son, to make my life with him."

In the silence that followed, she crossed to Aaron and took the hands he extended to her. She turned to fire the finishing salvo. "In return, sir, I will give you beautiful grandchildren that will honor their father, their grandfather, and the name of Durham. Only you must come to Boston to claim them."

"Boston?" Aaron grinned. "Are you sure, sweetness? I don't want you to ever regret—"

She put her fingers to his lips. "Whatever conditions I choose, you said. That was our deal, right?"

"Right."

"Well, I choose *Boston*."

Aaron picked her up and whirled her around in his arms before putting her down and pulling her toward the stairs and the bed waiting at the top.

Weston's eyes misted as he stared after them. As he reached for the decanter that stood on the tray nearby, his fatherly pride bubbled over in an rush.

"Isn't she something?" Then he glanced at Thomas Durham, who looked like he could use a stout drink, and held up a goblet. "Brandy?"

Epilogue

THE GREAT SAILS FLAPPED lazily in the breeze, their job done for now. The gentle lapping of the water about the piers and the sides of the good ship were mingled with the cries of seabirds soaring and calling, and with the scraping of wood on wood as the docking vessel nudged against the quay.

Lawrence Weston gazed up at the sky and mused on the appearance of the sun as they made landfall. His spirits began to lift. A movement on the wharf caught his eye. A handsome black coach, drawn by matched horses, turned onto the dock and halted near the ship's mooring. There would be no need to send a message after all.

He paced impatiently until the gangway was in place, then he was down it in several strides and making for the coach. The door swung open and a tall figure bent through the opening and landed on the ground.

"There you are!" Weston cried, shaking his son-in-law's hand while wrapping him in a burly half-hug. He spotted Dyso standing beside the coach and nodded, smiling. Dyso grinned back.

"By God, man, it's good to see you again." Weston's voice was husky and he cleared his throat to vent the emotion welling up inside him.

"And you, sir, you look splendid. Brien will be so pleased to have you with us." Seeing the earl peering into the coach, Aaron shrugged apologetically. "She was to have come with me, but at the last minute Garrett began to cry and rather than delay collecting you, she sent us on without her."

"Ah." Weston was not seriously disappointed. "It will be a sight indeed to see Brien mothering a baby. I never thought to see that, or to hear that my headstrong daughter was constrained to marriage and motherhood she swore were not for her."

"There is quite enough left you will recognize." Aaron laughed. "She's planned quite a time for you here; I hope you've come well rested."

Weston smiled. "I am eager to get my hands on that grandson of mine. For that privilege, I'll endure her worst." He glanced over his shoulder, his face sobering as a thought occurred to him. "Uh . . . Aaron, there is something . . . I've brought a friend with me and need to know whether you will provide lodging for us both, or if I must seek accommodations elsewhere."

Aaron frowned at the tension in Weston's face. "Any friend of yours is welcome in our home, sir, you must know that."

Clasping his son-in-law's arm, Weston sighed happily. "I thought as much."

Before Aaron could inquire further, Weston was moving back up the gangway. A friend? A *lady* friend? Was the old boy bringing a new bride, to obtain his daughter's blessing?

Weston acted as though he fully expected his son-in-law to refuse to accept his friend as a guest. Lifting a brass-bound trunk with Dyso, Aaron failed to see Weston's friend approach the carriage.

Hearing Weston's polite cough, Aaron wheeled about, leather satchel in hand, to flash a welcoming smile at Weston's lady. And he nearly dropped the bag as his eyes met the cold gray of ones he knew too well.

"Aaron," Weston's friend addressed him, proudly, but with a softer edge than the younger man could ever remember.

"Father." The pronouncement took great effort and left Aaron otherwise speechless. For a long moment, father and son reached beyond old memories of each other for clues to the present state of their relations.

Weston expelled a long breath, only now realizing that he had held it for a while.

"This is my friend, Aaron," Weston said. "You have offered us both the hospitality of your home, have you not?"

Aaron surfaced from that intense exchange. His father-in-law's quiet smile undercut his indignation. It was a time for closing old wounds and setting things right.

"I have offered such." He looked at his father. "You are welcome as our guest."

In the coach, as they moved along the streets of Boston with the drapes drawn back to afford a view of the city, Weston relaxed back into the seat and chatted easily about the latest news and the events that had occupied him over the past year.

"I have induced Thomas to buy a house in London near Harcourt and have introduced him to several widows of my acquaintance. He seems to have the Durham touch with women. I swear he is all they see when he is about. I find myself ignored, mostly."

Aaron studied his father, who shifted uncomfortably under his son's scrutiny. This was a new view of the man, one which unsettled Aaron even as he welcomed it. He knew the price of pride his father had paid to undertake so long and costly a journey, risking rejection at the destination.

"And he is the only man in London who can give me a real game of chess. But he fears I shall make a soft-living idler of him and insists upon returning to Coleraine frequently to oversee its doings. I've told him the servants manage better without his interference." Weston chuckled as Thomas Durham snorted disagreement.

"Someone has to see to it that things are done," Durham said shortly.

"He chafes because his younger son has just announced he yearns for the cleric's collar," Weston said, "and will stay in Cambridge to train further."

"Edward? A vicar?" Aaron sat up straighter, eyeing his father.

"It seems my mantle has been twice rejected." The nobleman looked uncomfortable with the topic, but seized the opportunity for one more observation. "It has been a bitter winter. I see now there are things in my life I would change, if I were given the chance."

It was the closest to an apology Aaron had ever heard from his father. A catch in his throat prevented him from replying, but the expression he gave his father was warm.

Weston noted all that transpired and smiled with satisfaction. Things were moving better than he'd expected. It had been a difficult task, getting Thomas Durham to end his moping and self-indulgent pessimism and move to London. More work had been required to constrain his new friend in the matter of his second son's choice of vocation. And this last, the voyage, was nothing short of miraculous. What the man needed was the chubby little fist of a grandchild to grab his rusty heartstrings and shake them free of the rust of loneliness and frustration. Brien's child.

IN THE SPACIOUS parlor, the sun streamed through the leaded panes, warming and cheering the comfortable greens and golds of the furnishings. Garrett Durham sat on the floor beside his mother, who held up brightly colored beads on a string and named the colors to him in a low, melodious voice.

Voices in the hall alerted Brien to the arrival of her husband and father. She got to her feet and ran for the hall, where Ella was taking the men's hats and greeting the earl as an old friend.

With a cry, Brien ran to her father's outstretched arms, not seeing anyone else in the hall just then. They embraced for a long moment before Weston, his eyes moist, thrust her back to arm's length to study her. "Let me look at you." If anything, her new life lent her greater beauty, in the form of a warm and openly contented charm.

Seeing past her father now, Brien's eyes widened as they came to rest on the third member of the party. She sought Aaron's face with a questioning look. Puzzled at his acceptance of his father's presence, Brien looked back to her own father.

"Brien, I must see this grandson of mine—I can wait no longer!" he roared.

"Oh, yes!" She caught Weston's hand and drew him into the parlor. Aaron followed, beckoning to his father.

By the time they reached the door, Weston already had Garrett up in his arms and was staring at the child's alert eyes and interest in him. He touched the little hands that grabbed fearlessly at his nose, and suddenly his eyes were wet.

Aaron went to his wife and drew her against him. Resting his chin atop her head, he watched in silence as love between grandfather and grandson was born.

Past her husband's arm, Brien glimpsed Thomas Durham standing just inside the doorway, his face a heartbreaking mixture of memory and longing. Whatever brought him so far, Brien could not imagine. But she read clearly and compassionately the state of his melting heart just then.

Wordlessly, she left Aaron's side and took the babe from her father's arms, to carry him to the proud old aristocrat who had come halfway around the world at her invitation to claim his grandchild. Softening visibly, he accepted and cradled the baby. When he raised his eyes to Brien's, they were wet and shining with pride and gratitude.

He carried Garrett to the settee and sat down beside his wise and generous friend, Lawrence Weston. Together they made all kinds of noises earls of the realm seldom make . . . but grandfathers often do.

Brien again sought the warmth of Aaron's arms. Together, they watched as the flow of destiny bound their two families together in the love that surrounded one auburn-haired child.

ABOUT THE AUTHOR

BETINA KRAHN—having successfully launched two sons into lives of their own and still working on launching her two pesky schnauzers *anywhere*—has traded the snowscapes of her beloved Minnesota for soaking up both sun and ideas in fertile Florida. Her undergraduate degree in biology and graduate degree in counseling, along with a lifetime of learning and observation, provide a broad background for her character-centered novels. She has worked in teaching, personnel management, and mental health . . . in spite of which she remains incurably optimistic about the human race. She believes the world needs a bit more truth, a lot more justice, and a whole lot more love and laughter. And she does what she can to help provide them.